The
Man
of
Her
Dreams

Sarra Manning has been a voracious reader for over forty years and a prolific author and journalist for twenty-five.

Her novels, which have been translated into fifteen languages include *Unsticky, You Don't Have to Say You Love Me, Rescue Me* and *London, With Love*, published in 2021. Sarra has also written a number of YA novels, and several light-hearted romantic comedies under a pseudonym.

She started her writing career on *Melody Maker* and *Just Seventeen*, has been editor of *ElleGirl* and *What to Wear* and has also contributed to the *Guardian, ELLE, Grazia, Stylist, Fabulous, Stella, You Magazine, Harper's Bazaar*, and is currently the Literary Editor of *Red* magazine.

Sarra has also been a Costa Book Awards judge and has been nominated for various writing awards herself.

She lives in London surrounded by piles and piles of books.

The
Man
of
Her
Dreams

SARRA MANNING

HODDER &
STOUGHTON

First published in Great Britain in 2023 by Hodder & Stoughton
An Hachette UK company

1

Copyright © Sarra Manning 2023

A CIP catalogue record for this title is available from the British Library

Hardback ISBN 978 1 399 70783 1
Trade Paperback ISBN 978 1 399 70784 8
ebook ISBN 978 1 399 70785 5

Typeset in Sabon MT by Manipal Technologies Limited

Printed and bound in Great Britain by Clays Ltd, Elcograf S.p.A.

Hodder & Stoughton policy is to use papers that are natural, renewable
and recyclable products and made from wood grown in sustainable forests.
The logging and manufacturing processes are expected to
conform to the environmental regulations of the country of origin.

Hodder & Stoughton Ltd
Carmelite House
50 Victoria Embankment
London EC4Y 0DZ

www.hodder.co.uk

Dedicated to anyone who prefers a rich
inner life to reality.

Le temps sont durs pour les rêveurs . . .

I

The last Saturday in February, 2022

Esme Strange hated getting up early. She especially hated getting up early on a Saturday morning.

Sunday mornings were reserved for a legendary lie-in. Esme would set her phone to 'do not disturb' and refuse to surface much before noon.

Whereas on Saturdays, she had things to do and places to be: a yoga class at the local church hall or walking her elderly neighbours' equally elderly pug. Meeting friends for a stroll on Hampstead Heath, then lingering over a long brunch and the papers at one of the many cafes in NW3 and NW5 that did a decent shakshuka. A trip to the local farmers' market, where Esme would have every intention of buying in-season organic vegetables and cold-pressed sunflower oil but would always end up with quite a lot of cake and cheese. None of those wholesome activities meant she had to stir much before nine.

But this Saturday was different. When Esme had got up for her usual four in the morning wee, knowing that she had only another two and a half hours in bed had made it impossible to get back to sleep. Even though she'd set her old-fashioned alarm clock and a series of alarms on her phone she was lying in the dark, listening as the seconds ticked by, occasionally sitting up so she could grab her pillow, turn it over, thump it and rest her head on the newly cool surface.

Esme tried a little trick she'd learned from a sleep therapist whom she'd interviewed back in her days as a magazine journalist. She worked her way through the alphabet, naming vegetables as she went. She started strong with artichokes, asparagus and arugula but by the time she reached l for lettuce, Esme got sidetracked as she pondered whether lima beans were vegetables or legumes. Though in French, of course, legume was the collective word for vegetables and oh my goodness, she was never going to get back to sleep.

There was nothing else for it but to start rifling through what she thought of as her rich inner life Rolodex to come up with an agreeable little fantasy to take her mind off things and lull her back to sleep.

Her current top three fantasies, the ones she had in daily rotation, were, in no particular order:

Esme and Harry Styles on a yacht moored off the coast of Southern Tuscany. Harry looking lean and foxy despite his shit tattoos, with a devilish glint in his eyes when Esme approached him. She was svelte and lightly but attractively tanned in high-waisted navy bikini bottoms and a matching bikini top, her hair cascading down her back in artfully tousled beach curls. Esme dismissed this one before she and Harry could even embrace because thinking about being on the open water would make her want to get up for another wee.

Then there was the one where she was a high-ranking witch on the run from dark forces within MI5, ably assisted by her really good-looking bagman, who resembled vintage Tom Hiddleston before Taylor Swift ruined him. It was a fantasy that had persisted through various permutations for decades and a rewatch of *Buffy the Vampire Slayer* over Christmas had brought it back to the fore. But Esme was trying for a sleepy vibe, which wouldn't be achieved if she were having to wreak complicated magic on a troop of black ops SAS types.

There was only one option. Her favourite fantasy. Number one with a bullet. She settled back under the covers with a happy little sigh and conjured up the imaginary boyfriend who was never that far away from her thoughts.

'Christ, woman, stop wriggling,' rumbled a voice in her ear. 'Go back to sleep.'

'Easy enough for you to say,' Esme pointed out.

'Not that easy when you're doing a good impersonation of a whirling dervish.' He kissed the side of her neck, gently scraping her skin with his teeth, and now Esme wanted to squirm in a way that had absolutely nothing to do with her insomnia. That was the thing with having an overactive imagination. It often overruled the sensible bit of her brain. She'd wanted to go back to sleep and yet now she was wanting something else entirely.

'It's far too early for *that*,' she murmured as one of his hands snaked into her pyjama bottoms and began to trace figures of eight against her belly.

'Are you sure?'

'I haven't got time.'

Esme opened one eye to confirm that it was five minutes since she last opened one eye. Yet, somehow it was now only ten minutes before her alarms were due to go off. How could that be? She was sure she had at least another hour of staying in her warm, cosy bed.

'I don't need long to get you off,' he drawled in her ear, then bit down on the plumpness of her earlobe. When he used his teeth, God, it made Esme shudder. In a good way. In a very good way.

'You'll get me all messy,' she said, even as she arched against him.

3

'But you're going to have a shower anyway so I might as well make a mess of you first, sweet girl.'

Esme sighed, shut her eyes again. Just for a moment. His touch was causing havoc. Maybe if she was really quick . . .

'Fuck me!'

Her alarm clock clanged into life, the first of her phone alarms following close behind, and Esme jerked fully awake, her heart pounding. She groped for the clock on the bedside table, then for her mobile phone.

Her dozy, dreamy, not-quite-in-the-land-of-the-living fugue state was gone. She was at one with reality. Which meant that she was alone. His arm was her own arm curled round her stomach. It had been her hand loosely tucked into the waistband of her pyjama bottoms, not his. The rumbly voice in her ear provided by her own fevered imaginings.

Then the second alarm on her phone beeped urgently and with a groan Esme forced herself upright and, with an anticipatory shudder, pulled back her duvet.

Twenty minutes later, Esme was racing down the stairs from her little attic sanctuary with its sloping ceilings. It was on the fourth floor of a mansion block a stone's throw from Parliament Hill Fields. Literally. If Esme stood at the southern end of her road with a large pebble in her hand, and if she could actually throw with any degree of accuracy, it would land with a triumphant splash in the middle of the Lido.

She reached the ground floor, wrenched open the door that led to the basement and tore down the steps to retrieve her bike from her tiny storage space.

There wasn't another soul in sight on her street full of imposing Victorian edifices, described by the late, legendary poet, Sir John Betjeman as 'red brick gloom' because he'd been born in one of them. A shameless snob, he'd famously declared himself 'glad that I did not live in Gospel Oak' even though Gospel Oak Station was another thing that Esme could hit with a stone, if she felt so inclined.

It was a chilly five-minute cycle down Highgate Road to her dentist in Kentish Town. Esme's body bowed against the bitter February winds, hanks of hair blowing in her face. The only good thing about cockcrow on a Saturday morning was Esme being spared the usual heavy traffic and exhaust fumes. All too soon, she was chaining up her bike and only five minutes late for her dental appointment.

'You are an absolute piss-taker,' said Sunil, as Esme arranged herself in his chair. She'd been coming to the same dentist surgery since Sunny's father had been in charge and Sunny was a nervous dental school graduate only allowed to operate the suction machine. 'I opened early to fit you in and you're not even on time.'

'I'm sorry. Not sure how that happened,' Esme said as Sunny handed her a very attractive pair of orange-tinted glasses to shield her eyes. 'I think maybe subconsciously I didn't want to be on time for my own torture.'

'You'll be fine,' Sunny assured her. 'Do you want numbing gel before I give you the anaesthetic?'

'Yes please, very much so,' Esme said. She was here at such an ungodly hour to have a wisdom tooth out. It was of no use to anyone and shunted right up against her back molar, where it kept causing gum infection and intense jaw ache. 'I'm not going to be brave. I have a *really* low pain threshold.'

'Look, Esme, maybe you should go to hospital and have a general anaesthetic . . .'

'No, let's get it over and done with. Just yank it out!' Esme gave Sunny a tremulous smile, which was the last thing she'd do with her mouth that didn't cause her untold agony for the next forty-eight hours. 'How bad can it be?'

Fifteen minutes later, even after numbing gel and Novocaine, Esme wished like she'd never wished for anything before for a lovely general anaesthetic, which would render her unconscious.

That was right about the time that Sunny had one hand braced on the countertop to get purchase, the other hand gripping some fucking medieval instrument of torture that was wedged deep in her mouth.

He had to *break* the tooth to get it out – the roots were embedded – and it was very traumatic. Very, very bloody. Esme could hardly get out of the chair because her muscles had been locked rigid for the last half hour.

Finally, she was standing on her own two feet as Sunny gave her a long lecture about not eating or drinking for the next couple of hours, and not getting something called dry socket, which sounded absolutely horrific.

'Go to the chemist, don't fanny about with paracetamol or ibuprofen, get co-codamol; it's got codeine in it. Take it, go back to bed.'

'Won't I be all right now that the bleeding has stopped?' Esme asked thickly as the hurty part of her mouth was still thankfully numb.

Sunil shook his head pityingly. 'Oh sweet summer child.'

'It's just that I'm going out tonight,' Esme said as she followed Sunny out to the reception area.

'It's good to have goals,' Sunil agreed as his receptionist handed Esme an invoice that made her want to cry all over again. 'When you take your tablets, remember no rinsing. No spitting. You really do not want dry socket. In fact, just try and avoid doing anything with that side of your mouth for the rest of the weekend and, it should go without saying but I'm going to say it anyway, absolutely no alcohol.'

'I can see that I'm in for a brilliant evening,' Esme said forlornly as she tapped her PIN into the card reader.

At least her legs weren't wobbling anymore by the time she found a chemist that was open at such a godforsaken hour. As instructed, she bought a box of co-codamol, though the pharmacist wouldn't relinquish them without an interrogation and a dire warning that if Esme took them for more than three days in a row, she'd end up constipated. Fun times!

'I doubt I'll even need them,' Esme declared, because now she was over the initial trauma she felt surprisingly fine.

So fine that, after cycling back up Highgate Road, instead of going straight to bed as planned Esme made an unscheduled stop at the farmers' market, which was slowly coming to life.

It was impossible to go more than a few metres without bumping into someone she knew. Esme had lived in and around the area for over half her life so, within the space of ten minutes, she said hello to her old art teacher from school, cooed over the newly hatched twins of a woman from her yoga class, waved at assorted neighbours and hugged her friends Marion and Jacinta, who lived on the ground floor of her block with their elderly pug, Buster, who also wheezed a greeting.

'I feel like my mouth is twice its normal size,' she said to Marion as they stood in a shaft of weak winter sunlight while Jacinta queued for sausages. 'Do I sound weird? Am I dribbling?'

'You sound perfectly all right to me, but I would get home before the anaesthetic wears off,' Marion advised. 'And I'd steer clear of sourdough bread. I lost a crown from a piece of sourdough toast.'

'Good advice. Though I feel much better than I thought I would. I might even go to yoga later,' Esme said, which made Marion snort like a little dragon.

'Ah, the optimism of youth!' she said, though Esme was thirty-three and didn't feel very youthful. In fact, she'd started making a strange huffing sound when she got up if she'd been sitting down for too long. Which was one of the reasons why she was making such a determined effort to go to yoga after booking a block of lessons.

After she said goodbye to Marion, Esme didn't even bother with the pretence of sizing up a few organic courgettes but made a beeline for her favourite stall, where she bought two slices of their carrot cake with lemon mascarpone icing. She deserved cake, even if she wasn't allowed to eat it for at least another two hours.

Before a mug of tea and cake, she was definitely going to her yoga class, Esme decided as she threaded her bike through the crowds of people.

But by the time Esme got home, put her bike away then climbed the stairs up to her flat, the anaesthetic was wearing off.

She'd been so worried about the bleeding, then potentially missing yoga, that she'd forgotten about the pain. The fucking excruciating pain, like someone had punched her violently and repeatedly in the face.

What an idiot she was!

Esme pulled off her jeans and jumper and got back into bed. Then she had to dry swallow two co-codamol because she was terrified of taking even one sip of water in case she washed away the scabs forming in her mouth wound.

Could this day get any worse? Esme doubted it.

It was decidedly one of the worst Saturdays that Esme could remember. A monotonous cycle of: try to get some sleep. Wake up in pain. Dry swallow more pills. Try to get some sleep. Repeat to fade.

At 5 p.m. she gave it up as a bad job. After staggering to the bathroom to pee, she steeled herself to look in the mirror.

Sunny had warned her that she might end up with a black eye from all the tugging and yanking. Esme had been spared that, but her face was swollen and bruised, and all she wanted to do was stay home. Make a cave of cushions and blankets and throws on her sofa. A nice true crime documentary about a serial killer on Netflix. Maybe choke down some soup.

She headed back to her bedroom to retrieve her phone. There was a message from her best friend Lyndsey checking to see that Esme hadn't bled out on the dentist's chair. But mostly, while she'd fitfully slept, the Seren Hen WhatsApp group had been busy. Very busy indeed.

> **Seren Dipity**
> Don't forget to bring your crystals tonight, goddesses! Hope you all remembered to recharge them during last night's full moon.

Kemi Udo
Crystals fully loaded. Can't wait!

Allegra Dickenson
Might have to forgo the clubbing. We're having lunch with Oliver's godfather tomorrow and I'd rather not do that with a hangover.

Seren Dipity
Completely understand, Ally. But this is meant to be good vibes only. Don't harsh the mellow.

Muffin Spencer
Coming in hot with an attitude of gratitude. Tonight is going to be lit.

Seren Dipity
Esme, why are you not replying?

Seren Dipity
Esme, where are you?

Seren Dipity
Esme, stop being such a Leo!

> **Esme Strange**
>
> Sorry, guys! Had my wisdom tooth out but I'm back in action and raring to go! Wouldn't miss it for the world! Really looking forward to it! Can't wait to see you all! X

'Fuck my actual life,' Esme muttered, which made her mouth hurt even more.

She was under no illusions – if she didn't attend this hen do, then Seren would hunt her down like a dog. They'd actually had a hen party back in November 2019, a weekend at the Soho Farmhouse, which had nearly bankrupted Esme. Then the April wedding had been postponed because of Covid. There'd been a hen Zoom the night before the wedding that never was, where they'd all helplessly watched Seren cry while offering platitudes.

Since that unhappy unoccasion, Seren and Isaac had got married twice ahead of their rescheduled 'official' wedding this coming Saturday. There'd been a legally binding civil service at Marylebone Registry Office between lockdowns with very few guests. Then a second, three-day wedding celebration in Lagos with all of Isaac's extended family last summer. Now third time was the charm, though, as far as Esme was concerned, one wedding was bad enough, two was foolish and three was absolutely batshit insane.

As was having a second full hen party, especially one which involved the crystals Seren always gifted for Christmas and birthday parties; Esme would have much preferred Liberty vouchers.

Esme wasted valuable time searching for said crystals, which were scattered around her tiny flat. Seren had an elephantine memory and would know at once if Esme was missing any crystals, such as the hunk of black obsidian she'd received last Christmas with a note that read, 'This will hopefully balance some of your negative energy.'

Eventually Esme assembled a respectable pile of crystals, which she dumped into a sink of hot water and Fairy Liquid so they could soak while she had a wardrobe panic.

The dress code was 'granola glam', though Esme didn't really know what that meant. She opted for comfy over stylish: black velvet corduroy jumpsuit with a black and red polka dot long-sleeved tee underneath. No heels because, since the pandemic, her feet refused to be squashed into shoes that caused them pain. It had been hard enough to transition back into clothes that didn't come with an elasticated waistband as standard. Even bending down to put on socks and trainers put pressure on Esme's battered face.

She then attempted to hide the horrors of her wisdom tooth extraction with a lot of make-up but with very little success. Lipstick, even the lightest lip gloss, wasn't going to happen. Her pasty face was red and swollen, and now it looked as if her left eye was starting to bruise. Her body didn't feel much better. Like Allegra, Esme decided that she'd try and bow out early from the evening's festivities. Then, as if she'd summoned up an evil spirit, there was a buzz on the intercom.

'Why aren't you down here waiting for me? You're not even ready, are you?' enquired the querulous tones of Esme's older sister Allegra, who preferred to forgo the social niceties and just get right down to business.

'Almost ready. Come up.' Talking was definitely going to be a problem this evening.

There was a hiss of annoyance. 'I'm not climbing all those stairs in heels. Come down. And be quick, it's bloody freezing.'

Esme stuffed her still damp crystals into her handbag and, with heavy tread and heavy heart, mentally prepared herself for what was going to be a night for the ages.

Her heart grew even heavier when she opened the street door. Allegra had interpreted 'granola glam' to mean a gorgeously soft and expensive-looking camel coat, little black dress and ridiculously high black suede heels, which had to be responsible for the petulant expression on her face. An expression that Esme knew only too well and which meant that Allegra was absolutely determined not to have a good time tonight.

There were eleven years and an ocean between them. The last thing Allegra had wanted just as she'd started secondary school was a baby sister. No longer was she an only child, plus here was undeniable proof that her constantly warring parents had actually stopped arguing long enough to have sex.

When they were growing up, Esme had imagined that, one day, they might become friends. She'd idolised Allegra, who seemed infinitely glamorous because she had lovely joined-up handwriting, was allowed to stay up very, very late, wore make-up and had boyfriends. Allegra was a far more inspirational role model than their mother Debbie, who lived in paint-splattered dungarees and was forever trying to teach Esme how to change a plug or unscrew a U-bend. Skills which would come in pretty handy in later life but not when Esme was eight and far more interested in writing elaborate stories where she was the sixth and most talented member of the Spice Girls.

Esme had always hoped that Allegra might realise that there was more to her little sister than a constant thorn in her side. Sadly, that had never come to pass and, in the end, Esme had stopped trying to make Allegra love her.

'You all right?' Esme asked, brushing past Allegra. They'd never been a family of huggers or kissers and besides, Esme's mouth was too sore to even think about air kissing.

'Why can you never be on time?' Allegra asked as she fell into step with Esme. 'It's so arrogant. You assume that your life is more important than mine and that I have nothing better to do than wait for you.'

Esme made a big show of pulling her phone out of the pocket of her squashy faux fur. 'Oh my God, I'm a whole two minutes late. Call the police!'

She waited for Allegra to ask her how the dentist had gone. Was she in a lot of pain? And actually, it was very brave of Esme to soldier on. But . . . tumbleweed.

Allegra sniffed. 'Anyway, now that you're *finally* here, I'll order an Addison Lee.'

'I'm not going halves on a car when the bus will literally take us door to door,' Esme said, gesturing at the bus stop, which had come into view as they stepped out onto Highgate Road.

'But hardly anyone wears a mask on the bus and it's Saturday night, it'll be really crowded . . .'

'We'll be wearing masks and we'll crack open a window,' Esme countered, though she doubted that Allegra would expect her to chip in for the car. Even so, it would be just one more thing that Allegra would hold over her. Yet more proof that Esme was an agent of chaos who couldn't look after herself properly. 'I'm not getting a car. End of.'

'Fine!'

'Fine!'

They crossed over the road, then waited at the bus stop in a silence that grew more tense until Allegra couldn't bear it any longer.

'You might have made more of an effort, Esme. A jumpsuit and trainers!'

'These trainers were very expensive.' It was Esme's turn to cast a carefully cultivated dismissive glance at her sister. 'Anyway, how is what you're wearing granola glam?'

Allegra put a beautifully manicured hand to her heart, her nails a perfectly understated shade that was somewhere between pink and beige, the diamonds on her engagement and wedding rings glinting from the glow of the streetlights. 'I've worn everything several times before so technically all my clothes are recycled.'

'Whatever.' The cold was making Esme's mouth hurt even more or maybe it was the way she was clenching everything because Allegra was being even more annoying than usual.

'Have you even combed your hair?' Allegra asked as the bus came into view. Instead of answering her, Esme pulled her Air-Pods from her coat pocket and stuck them in her ears, but still managed to hear the indignant huffing noise that Allegra made.

It was a short trip into town. Ordinarily, Esme liked the route, which took them along the outer edge of Regent's Park and the white stucco Nash terraces, but it was too dark to really see anything and every time someone moved past them to get on or off the bus, Allegra drew herself in and turned her head away like they were all riddled with Covid.

Allegra had had Covid before Christmas, and not even a bad case of it, so Esme didn't know what the theatrics were for.

They still weren't speaking when they got off the bus at Oxford Circus and crossed over Oxford Street.

'Are you OK to walk to Soho?' Esme asked in a vaguely conciliatory tone as she looked down at Allegra's shoes, which had to be killing her by now.

'I suppose.' Allegra pulled a face but then she leaned in towards Esme and nudged her with an elbow. 'Tonight is going to be awful. You're the creative one; can't you think of some excuse to get us out of this? Preferably in the next five minutes?'

Esme shrugged helplessly. 'I got nothing. Sorry.'

Allegra straightened her shoulders. She was half a head taller than Esme but they still looked unmistakably like sisters. They had the same delicate features: arched brows and prominent cheekbones softened by wide-spaced blue eyes. But Allegra had their father's aquiline nose before it had grown red and bulbous from all the booze and Esme had a small pouty mouth while Allegra had full generous lips, though they were looking pretty tight right now.

They even had the same fine neither-here-nor-there hair that wasn't straight or curly, but wavy with a tendency to frizz. It wasn't blond or brown either but some indeterminate in-between shade, darker in winter then lighter in summer. Of course now Allegra could afford expensive straightening treatments and every six weeks she got her highlights and her roots done, whereas Esme would get a half head of highlights sometime before Christmas and by now, in late February, they'd mostly grown out and faded.

Allegra pushed back a strand of her glossy hair with an impatient hand. 'It's just ridiculous. A second hen night before the *third* wedding. Who does Seren think she is? Meghan bloody Markle?'

'She's your sister-in-law. You married into the Dickenson family,' Esme helpfully pointed out. 'I'm just Dickenson adjacent, but I'm here, I've made an effort . . .'

'It doesn't look like you've made an effort,' Allegra sniped.

'I had my wisdom tooth out this morning and I feel like death warmed over but I'm going to this hen and I'm going

16

to pretend that I'm happy to be there because that will make Seren happy and you're going to do the same.' It was Esme's turn to nudge her sister. 'What did Gran always say when we had to do something we really didn't want to?'

Allegra smiled reluctantly. 'Tits and teeth, girls. Tits and teeth.'

Esme stuck out her chest and bared her poor aching teeth in a vague approximation of a smile. 'It's one evening out of our entire lives. We can do one evening, Ally.'

'I suppose so,' Allegra agreed as they began to walk down Carnaby Street. 'And in an hour or so, your mouth will be hurting . . .'

'My mouth really is hurting . . .'

'Imagine how much more painful it will be in an hour or so,' Allegra said cheerfully. 'So you'll have to go and I'll come with you just to make sure you're all right. Deal?'

Esme was tempted to point out that Allegra hadn't cared how much pain she was in until she'd realised that she could use her little sister's agony to her own advantage. Then again, she and Allegra were always at their best when they had a mutual enemy. 'All right, deal. But you owe me one.'

'I'm sure if you counted up all the favours I've done you over the years you'd find that actually you owe me, but fine, OK, I owe you one,' Allegra said, as they arrived at their destination.

3

Skál was a low-key minimalist wine bar, its logo in a sparse Helvetica font, which only served organic wine to a subdued clientele wearing a muted colour palette.

The barman, who was clearly between jobs as a model for Scandi-inspired leisurewear, actually winced when Allegra asked where the hen party was. They were directed down a studded metal staircase to a private room, all open brickwork with a roaring fire, where the other hens were already assembled around a circular rustic wooden table covered in foliage and tea lights.

'Hello, ladies! Sorry we're late,' Esme called out jovially as she and Allegra approached. Seren was very sensitive to bad vibes and people who brought said bad vibes anywhere near her. 'Who'd have thought last time round at Soho Farmhouse we'd be having a second hen?'

'And that you and Isaac would be married twice already and now gearing up for a third go.' Allegra clearly still wasn't on board with the good vibes only theme.

'But who could have predicted Covvy 19 and anyway, three weddings is romantic,' said Muffin, Seren's best friend, and the other hens rushed to agree with her. Only Seren was silent and still. Her long brown hair was arranged in the most perfectly tousled yet uniform ringlets, her pretty face completely expressionless. Then she blinked big brown eyes.

'Actually, according to our charts this Saturday is a much more auspicious day to get married than the original date we had in 2020.' She allowed herself a small triumphant smile. 'It's almost as if the universe wanted us to get married now and not then.'

Behind her, Esme heard Allegra scoff at the implication that the universe had arranged a global pandemic which had killed hundreds of thousands of people and sent the world economy into freefall, just so that Seren and her investment banker betrothed could get married on a date that better suited their astrological charts.

'So, it's all worked out then,' Esme said. She found it very hard being good vibes when she was experiencing physical pain.

'Now that you two are here, we're going to break off into smaller groups to have our tarot and charts done, then gather here to vision board before we eat,' said Ngaire, Seren's friend from New Zealand whom she'd met on a meditation retreat in Goa.

All of Seren's friends were cut from the same kind of bespoke cloth. They might be in touch with their spiritual side, but they were still all long-limbed, glossy-haired posh girls with a sense of entitlement. Manifesting wealth simply meant that their trust funds were performing well. Esme was under no illusions – she was very much a third-tier member of the bridal party, there because Allegra had married into the Dickenson family and Esme had been an add-on. An inferior gift with purchase, like a free make-up pouch when you forked out a couple of hundred quid on premium cosmetics. As far as Seren was concerned, Esme was the human equivalent of a sample size foundation in slightly the wrong shade, some hair mist (who even used hair mist?) and a glycolic acid facemask guaranteed to give the user a breakout.

Yet Seren was still easily the most welcoming member of the Dickenson clan and, bless her, she did try to kick against her parents' expectations. She was more Glastonbury than Glyndebourne. More reiki healing than Royal Enclosure. More kombucha than Cristal.

Speaking of which, a server appeared with a tray full of glasses of murky pink liquid. 'It's a cranberry-infused, small batch kefir from a local micro-brewery,' she said.

'Yum!' Esme accepted a glass though she was still worried about potential dry socket and sat down next to Seren, who'd been a Sarah until that meditation retreat in Goa, when she'd decided that she was more of a Seren. 'Because everyone who knows me, knows that I'm a very serene person.'

Despite all the inner consciousness and mindfulness, Seren in bride mode was the absolute opposite of a serene person. She'd even banned Virgos from her bridal party. 'What would you have done if Muffin was a Virgo?' Esme had asked when Seren had first dropped this bombshell.

Seren had thought about it for a good minute. 'I would never be best friends with a Virgo anyway, so it's not really an issue.'

Now Seren was looking at Esme's outfit in faint disbelief. 'You could have made more of an effort, Esme. Is that jumpsuit from a sustainable brand? Did you remember your crystals?'

Before Esme could reply or get out her crystals, which were squeaky clean thanks to the Fairy Liquid but probably drained of all their crystal goodness, she was frogmarched off to have her cards read by a woman about her age who had a calm, comforting air about her, flowing white garments, all with asymmetric hemlines, and the overpowering whiff of patchouli oil.

Despite the woman's kindly face, soft voice and the deft way she handled the pack of cards, Esme's tarot reading was not a huge success.

'You're currently stuck,' she was told, 'but soon you'll be at a major crossroads. I advise caution. Extreme caution. Danger lurks at every turn.' The woman sucked in a breath and, despite the roaring fire and the many expensive Diptyque candles merrily burning away, Esme felt a chill wrap round her.

She shivered.

'Maybe I should get the brakes on my bike checked.' Where were the good vibes only that Esme had been promised?

'Why don't you draw a card,' the woman suggested as she fanned out a tarot pack, face down, in front of Esme. 'Close your eyes and focus on the card you feel most drawn to. There should be an energy coming from it, like a faint tingle in your fingertips.'

Esme screwed her eyes tight shut and hovered her hand over the cards. Try as she might, she couldn't feel a tingle coming from her fingertips. She had no option but to place a finger on a card, any card, and hope for the best.

Her best turned out to be the Death card, featuring a skeleton carrying a sickle and riding a white horse through a field of the dead and dying. Another icy wave of foreboding made Esme shudder. The woman stared down at the card. Esme waited to be told that it didn't actually mean death but rebirth, new roots, new beginnings and all that jazz. Instead, the woman looked like she was going to throw up. 'You know what? I can't do this. You're giving off some serious toxicity; it's really messing with my biorhythms.'

Esme didn't set much store by tarot cards or astrological charts or recharging her crystals by the light of a full moon, but neither did she want to have such toxicity that people shrank away from her.

'I've just had my wisdom tooth taken out, it's probably that,' Esme said in a hurt voice, because she really had been trying to be a positive party person.

She glanced across the room to where Allegra was having her astrological chart done. For all her sister's whingeing *en route*, she now looked pretty engrossed and didn't notice when Esme signalled that she wanted to go home. There was nothing for it but to head back to the main table where everyone had a white A3 piece of card and, with the aid of a pile of magazines, scissors, glue and glitter pens, were vision boarding.

Vision boarding seemed fairly harmless, though Esme had no idea what vision she actually wanted to board.

'There must be some goal you want to attain,' Muffin said, gesturing down at her own board, which was looking quite sparse. So far, she'd only managed to write 'Manifest Your Dreams' in a pretty cursive with a pink glitter pen on the board. 'Now that we've finished the house renovations, I might vision board world peace or reversing climate change. Give something back to the universe.'

Muffin worked in art, though mostly she was married to a hedge fund manager because her art jobs never seemed to last. The first time they'd met, she'd told Esme a very funny story about getting sacked from her first gallery job for sending a painting to Burkina Faso instead of Buenos Aires. That in-attention to detail seemed to be a general theme of her career.

'Yes, there must be something you want, Esme. If you're not growing, you're dying,' Ngaire said as she returned from having her hands henna tattooed.

All this talk of death . . . Esme took a big but careful sip of her kefir, which tasted absolutely rank.

'I don't think I want to grow much more, Ngaire. My needs are quite simple. I have a nice place to live, I like my job, I love my friends . . .'

'A life partner?' Muffin suggested.

Esme would much rather talk about death than where this conversation was headed. 'No thank you. Had one of them. Never again,' she said with what she hoped was a crushing finality and was relieved to see Kemi, Seren's soon-to-be-other-sister-in-law, descending the stairs.

Kemi caught Esme's eye and waved, a gritted teeth grin on her face, as she hadn't been particularly keen on coming tonight either. 'A second hen is just rude,' she'd WhatsApped Esme earlier in the week. They'd met at Seren and Isaac's engagement party four years ago and hit it off. But it wasn't until the first Soho Farmhouse hen party a year later that they'd become ride or dies.

'Ladies,' Kemi said as she approached the table in three long strides. She was wearing a jumpsuit made of a shimmery white silk jersey, accessorised with gold jewellery and a killer pair of gold heels. Her weave featured a dramatic flicky blond fringe and she'd dusted her cheekbones with glitter. The whole effect was mesmerising and sadly wasted on a dull, minimalistic, organic wine bar. Kemi wouldn't have looked out of place pictured in between Andy Warhol and Bianca Jagger at Studio 54. 'Have you finished summoning up malevolent spirits, because you know how I feel about that? As it is, I'll be getting up early to pray for your poor blighted souls.'

'We're not summoning evil spirits,' Seren said heatedly because she rose to this particular bait every time. Then she smiled slyly. 'Unless by evil spirits, you mean talking about Esme's love life.'

'I don't have a love life,' Esme said, rolling her eyes at Kemi, who was pulling out the chair next to hers.

'But you date,' Seren pointed out.

'Yeah, I also go to supermarkets, it doesn't mean I want to live in my nearest branch of Sainsbury's.' Her phone pinged and, relieved for another distraction, Esme withdrew it from her pocket. 'Proof! A voice note from Mo, even though I told him that I was busy tonight.'

Seren rubbed her hands together. 'You didn't tell me about Mo. Is he nice?'

'We've only been on a couple of dates.' Esme shrugged. 'He's all right, I suppose. Teaches history. Likes travel and working out. Hates chutney.' She held her phone up to her ear so she could listen to what turned out to be a very whiny voice note about how much Mo was missing her and that maybe they could get together later.

'We all know what happens on a third date,' he finished with a high-pitched, hopeful intonation, not realising that he'd just marked his card for the final time.

'Have you got a picture, Es?' asked Muffin but Esme held up a hand to pause the conversation as she voice-noted him back.

'Mo, I told you I wasn't seeing you tonight. I was very clear,' Esme said sharply. 'I think it's best that we stop seeing each other. Please don't contact me again.'

'That's kind of harsh,' Kemi said with a theatrical wince. 'Why don't you give him another chance?'

'I have a three-strike rule. Being unable to follow even the most simple instructions was Mo's third strike,' Esme explained.

'What were the other two strikes?' Ngaire asked. 'What could he have done that was so bad?'

'First strike, he wore loafers without socks.'

'That doesn't seem so bad,' Muffin said, because her hedge fund husband was exactly the sort of man who went for loafers without socks when he was doing weekend casual.

Esme grinned through the pain. 'Second strike, he referred to women's breasts as titties.'

'No! Ewwwww!'

'I wouldn't even have let him stick around for a third strike!'

'Hanging's too good for him!'

'Talk about getting the ick.' Kemi pretended to dry heave.

'So you see, there's no point in being vague about my intentions,' Esme said as she blocked Mo from all her socials. 'You have to be blunt with men. They don't understand nuance.'

'Do you hate all men? You don't hate Isaac, do you? Why do you hate him? He's a very kind, very spiritual person,' Seren asked fretfully.

'I don't hate Isaac,' Esme insisted, though he was an investment banker, a bespoke suited symbol of neoliberalism and late stage capitalism, and therefore part of the problem and not the solution. But it was impossible to hate Isaac. Without Isaac falling in love with Seren, Esme wouldn't have met Kemi and also, Isaac was so chilled that if he got any more laid-back, he'd be permanently horizontal. 'It's not like I hate all men.'

'Well, then . . .' Seren settled back in her chair.

'But that's only because I haven't met *all* the men in the world and generally most of the men in the world are liars and fuckboys until proven otherwise . . .' Esme said, all her good intentions about bringing the party spirit suddenly abandoned.

'You're all coupled up,' Kemi added in solidarity. 'You don't know what it's like out there. It's brutal.'

'I think that's a really limiting belief,' Ngaire said. 'You just haven't fallen in love yet.'

'I did fall in love with someone and they trampled all over my heart. I have the decree absolute to prove it,' Esme said, then wished she hadn't as Seren sucked in an angry breath at Esme daring to raise the spectre of divorce at her good-vibes-only hen night. 'Look, I'm happy. I really enjoy my own company and being alone is very different from being lonely. So, Seren, what are you vision boarding?'

Judging by the board in front of her, Seren was vision boarding her future children (who exclusively frolicked on beaches and flower-sprigged fields in boho baby gear).

None of the other hens had really got started on their vision boards, though what did you vision board when you were a woman with everything you could possibly want?

'I think you should vision board a sexy, empathetic man who isn't a liar or a fuckboy,' Seren said with a steely tone that she got sometimes when she forgot that she was meant to be serene. 'We'll help you.'

'That's very kind but I don't want to hog all the vision boarding . . .'

'A great idea!' Muffin pushed away her board, as if world peace wasn't that important compared to making a visual interpretation of Esme's ideal man.

'Honestly, I wouldn't know where to start . . .'

'Absolute rubbish,' Kemi said, with a glint in her eye that Esme knew very well and it never led to anything good. 'We all know that Es has got an overactive imagination. Remember what happened at the Soho Farmhouse hen?'

One of Seren's cousins, Esme could never remember her name, gasped in outrage. 'I still have nightmares about that!'

During a lull in proceedings at the first hen when they'd been gathered around a firepit drinking champagne, Esme had improvised a ghost story, full of all the obvious clichés. A nearby monastery that had been sacked during the Reformation, the monks hacked down as they tried to flee. The vengeful spirits of innocent women accused of being witches and burnt at the stake. The local legend of a vagrant called One-Eyed Jake who'd been set upon and thrown in a nearby river, and how all their ghosts tramped about the otherwise bucolic surroundings, moaning and moping, and when one of the logs in the firepit had cracked loudly, the cousin whose name Esme could never remember had actually wet herself in terror.

'I might have a fantasy boyfriend,' Esme conceded. 'But really, haven't we all?'

Judging by the blank, almost pitying looks, Esme was an outlier when it came to having a fantasy boyfriend.

Seren grabbed a copy of *Vogue* from the pile of magazines on the table. 'Let's vision board him,' she said with the same missionary-like zeal she got when she was extolling the virtues of hemp juice smoothies. 'Fantasies are just wishes that you haven't manifested yet.'

'Oh, come on, Esme! It will be fun.'

Esme was sure that it wouldn't be, and she didn't relish her deepest, darkest desires being exposed for a bit of roundtable, hen party entertainment.

But then again, she didn't want to be the sulky, single girl at a hen. She'd keep it light, not give away too many of her secrets.

4

'Sometimes I just want something quick and easy with Harry Styles,' Esme said carefully, even as Muffin started frantically leafing through magazines for a picture of Esme's Plan B fantasy boyfriend. 'But other times, I want something, somebody, more layered. With a subplot. Supporting characters.'

Much like the time when she'd scared them senseless with her tales of ghosts terrorising the Oxfordshire countryside, she had the other women looking at her expectantly, hanging on her every word.

Esme could never resist an audience.

'Well, he's about five years older than me, so late thirties. He's been around the block a bit and he's kind of cynical, but not jaded. You want someone with some history, a past, a bit of baggage but not so much baggage that they're completely fucked up.'

'Um, Esme, can you give us something to work with here?' Kemi brandished her scissors. 'Things that we can cut out and stick on your vision board.'

'He's from the North. Manchester. What? I like a Mancunian accent and a no-nonsense manner,' she said a little defensively as Kemi raised her eyebrows. Meanwhile Ngaire had managed to find a picture of the Manchester Ship Canal.

'What does he do for a living?' Muffin asked.

'Something creative. But creative adjacent,' Esme said, because her ill-fated first and last marriage had been to an actor, which had been enough to shatter all her young dreams about falling in love with a musician/artist/anyone who could behave appallingly and blame it on their artistic sensibilities. 'Like a chef or an architect.'

'An architect would earn a lot more . . .'

'But a chef is sexier,' Kemi said as she cut out a black and white picture of a scruffy but foxy-looking man in chef's whites, his arms covered in full sleeve tattoos. 'You like the messy-looking ones, don't you?'

'I do,' Esme agreed.

'Oooh, what does he look like?' Seren wanted to know.

'Tall, lanky but with a little bit of heft to him. Dark hair, dark eyes.' Alex, her ex-husband, had been fair and only a couple of inches taller than Esme and she was a very average five foot four. Not that she held his height against him. No, there were plenty more worthwhile things to hold against him. 'Tans easily. When it comes to clothes, he usually goes for jeans and a band T-shirt but he actually has their records. He's not the kind of poser who wears a band T-shirt to look cool.'

'You've really thought about this,' Seren's cousin said, her tone a little too accusatory for Esme's liking.

But Esme was determined to keep things light, and anyway, vision boarding the man who'd lived rent-free in her head for a considerable amount of time, at least five years, was kind of *fun*.

So she shrugged. 'What can I say? I have a very rich, very fulfilling inner life.'

Esme had always been a daydreamer. As a child, she'd had a whole posse of imaginary friends, much to her parents' annoyance. They had no time for idle flights of fancy when there were run-down houses to flip and screaming arguments to be had.

So Esme had learned to be quiet about the people who lived in her head. Though by the time she started secondary school, of course she didn't have imaginary friends anymore. It would have been like still believing in Father Christmas or the Tooth Fairy. Instead she had a complex multiverse where, at any one time, she might be an Olympic showjumper with a pop star side hustle or a seemingly ordinary girl with magical powers who might be called upon to save the world at any moment. Sometimes she was the princess of a minor but very rich European principality. However, in all her many other lives, Esme had ruthlessly killed off her parents and Allegra, so she could be a plucky orphan who always managed to triumph over adversity.

Inevitably, by the time she was a teenager, Esme's fantasies had evolved into writing self-insert Harry Potter fan fiction on her LiveJournal. Thankfully under a pseudonym because she couldn't remember her LJ password to delete all the evidence and if anyone she knew ever discovered them... Esme often blushed just thinking of what she'd made Severus Snape do with his wand.

Esme had long given up writing fanfic but she hadn't given up the alternative lives that ran concurrently with her external day-to-day life. Back in her magazine days, she'd once interviewed a psychologist for an article on daydreaming. The eminent doctor had taken a very dim view of the fact that anyone could spend hours in their own head in a reality where they always got the job, the dress was always in their size and on sale, and they had an amazing boyfriend who never treated them badly.

'It sounds like you have maladaptive daydreaming disorder,' the man had said condescendingly, though Esme had claimed she was talking about a friend. 'It's a coping mechanism in response to trauma and abuse. Instead of confronting and processing difficult experiences from their past, sufferers escape to a complex, self-created world and often lose their ability to function in daily life.'

'But I, I mean my friend, she's always had quite intense daydreams, even when she was a kid,' Esme protested because yes, her divorce had been traumatic and abusive but she'd had her head firmly wedged in the clouds ever since she was old enough to think coherently.

'Then maybe your "friend",' he'd had the nerve to make air quotes around the word, 'is actually suffering from dissociative identity disorder. Though, of course, I'm loath to diagnose someone on hearsay.'

Esme had tried really hard not to daydream after that. For a good three or four days. But life was so boring without a delicious little fantasy to while away the time as she waited for a bus or wandered around the big Sainsbury's or was in the midst of an insomnia jag.

Then she'd interviewed another psychologist who was much more simpatico and insisted that daydreaming was a great creative tool and a way of processing past experiences in a safe environment. 'As long as it's not replacing human interaction or making it difficult to function in social or work environments,' she'd said cheerfully.

It wasn't, so Esme decided that there was nothing wrong with having an overactive imagination. It was a gift.

Now the hens were happily cutting out pictures to create a collage of imaginary boyfriendliness. Manchester, where he came from, as per Esme's instructions. The Belstaff coat he wore, unbuttoned, but with collar up to keep out the chill. The gastropub that they'd decided he owned after a successful but self-destructive career as a chef, culminating in two

Michelin stars and a cocaine habit; that had been Ngaire's contribution. Kemi and Esme had always suspected that there was some darkness in *her* past too. A picture of David Bowie because both Esme and her imaginary boyfriend had a theory that when the Thin White Duke had died, it ripped a hole right in the universe and explained the chaos that had ensued around the world.

'Also, he's really funny. A very dry sort of funny but also the sort of funny where he can make you laugh so hard that if you've just taken a drink, you're going to spray it everywhere.' Esme came to a halt so she could point a rigid finger at Muffin. 'That picture of Jimmy Carr isn't going anywhere near my vision board, thank you very much.'

Esme was also busy cutting out lots of pictures of men: models, a young George Clooney, but none of them really captured *his* image until she came across a picture of a young James Stewart in a feature on Alfred Hitchcock in an old *Sunday Times* supplement.

There was something a little anarchic, a little wild, about James Stewart and also he was long and lanky, and Esme liked long and lanky very much.

This vision boarding, or rather thinking about a man who didn't exist even though Esme had spent years in his company, was actually quite a pleasant way to spend time. 'And he's very kind,' Esme said, as she stuck James Stewart down with a Pritt Stick and watched approvingly as Kemi cut out a picture of a male model cuddling a Labrador puppy. 'Very kind but also when it comes to sex . . .' She paused to make sure she had everyone's attention. Which she did. Of course she did.

'The sex?' Muffin prompted, practically quivering where she sat.

'Absolutely *filthy*,' Esme said with relish as Kemi hooted next to her. 'He's done things to me which I'm pretty sure are illegal in at least half the states of America.'

'Don't lower the tone,' Seren said, but she was smiling too as Muffin wrote 'absolutely filthy' in glitter pen on the board. She gave Esme a thoughtful, considered look.

'You know Es, you could have this man if you wanted him enough. You just have to ask the universe.' Seren tapped a finger on the board. 'Where are your crystals?'

Seren was sure to know that Esme had bathed them in Fairy Liquid rather than the light of a full moon. But when Esme handed over the repurposed make-up bag, Seren rifled through them without saying a word. Then she placed several of them on the board.

'You are deserving of a man like this, Esme, you know that, don't you?'

For some reason that she couldn't quite fathom, Seren's question made Esme's eyes prickle like she was about to start crying, which was just . . . ridiculous.

'I know I'm deserving of him, but the perfect man doesn't exist.' Esme stared down at the vision board, which was now a pretty good visual representation of her fantasy boyfriend.

'You say he doesn't exist but maybe you don't have enough faith in yourself to make your dreams a reality,' Ngaire said earnestly. 'All the tools you need to make him real are here, you just need to believe.'

Esme took another sip of kefir. Her mouth throbbed.

'There's no harm in sending some positive affirmations out into the ether,' Seren said, her eyes fixed on Esme so it was quite hard not to squirm under the bride-to-be's limpid gaze. 'Come on, Es, you might as well do this properly.'

What harm could it do to toss a lot of woo woo word salad? It would make Seren and her friends happy, and it made no difference to Esme either way. Though if her perfect man suddenly became a real live boy, which he wasn't going to because that would be impossible, then it would be win-win.

'OK,' she conceded graciously. 'What do I do?'

'Let's all hold hands so we can add our womanly power to Esme's affirmations,' Ngaire suggested, which made Kemi snort faintly, but she still took hold of Esme's left hand as Muffin grabbed her right.

Esme looked around for Allegra, who was now having her tarot cards read and chuckling away quietly with the woman who was doing it like they were old friends, which was infuriating.

'First, you need to rid yourself of all your limiting beliefs,' Seren said. 'I want you to imagine that you're packing them in a bag and sending them on their way.'

Esme didn't think that she had any limiting beliefs. She was pragmatic, realistic, stoic. Lots of things ending in -ic – apart from when she was living in a world of her own creation.

But now she visualised her decree absolute and Alex's stupid sneering face. She saw all the men who'd ghosted her, breadcrumbed her, gaslit her. She pictured the faces of all the men she'd met for lacklustre dates. Thought about all the dick pics she'd been sent from men she'd matched with on dating sites. Then the dick pics from randoms sliding into her DMs.

Esme saw them all and she shoved them, with great force, off the edge of a cliff. 'Goodbye and good riddance!'

She hadn't even realised that she'd said it out loud, but Kemi snorted again while Seren and Ngaire gave Esme approving smiles.

'You're being so open to this, I love it!' Ngaire exclaimed.

35

'I'm actually a very open person,' Esme said, and now that she'd pushed a lot of her emotional baggage off a cliff, she did feel lighter. Though that could have been because she'd had nothing to eat since last night's jacket potato with beans and cheese. She ignored the sudden rumble of her stomach. 'So, let's affirm this bad boy. What do I do?'

What Esme did was repeat after Seren, with as much sincerity as she could muster:

'I am deserving and worthy of love.'

'I savour all the positive and loving relationships in my life.'

'I attract love very easily.'

'I am open and ready for love to pour in and make me whole.'

'I know that my soulmate is waiting for me.'

'Our hearts and our souls are meant to be together.'

'I trust the universe to find me my perfect, absolutely filthy match.'

'OK, Esme, now you need to let go of all your expectations and believe that true love will find you. Let it go. Let everything go but the belief that the universe has your back and will send you your soulmate,' Seren ordered.

Esme was so caught up in the moment that she didn't even break into a rousing chorus of 'Let It Go' but imagined herself freed from all her usual bullshit that she brought to dating: the preconceived notions, the suspicion and the absolute belief that it was never, ever going to work every time she swiped right.

It felt so good to be free.

Esme wasn't a crier, not anymore, but suddenly tears were splashing down onto her vision board and her crystals, which were sparkling in the candlelight in a way that they'd never done before. Not even on the rare occasions when she had remembered to recharge them by the light of a fucking full moon.

'Oh, Es, don't worry. That's the negative energy leaving,' Seren cooed. 'You're washing it all away with your tears. Good on you!'

'Are you all right?' Kemi asked quietly, releasing Esme's hand so she could gently pat her on the shoulder.

Esme shrugged and shook her head. She was also crying because she knew that even if this man that she spent so much time dreaming about were suddenly made flesh, she wouldn't be *his* soulmate.

On paper, Esme was an excellent catch. She was funny, kind, a devoted friend and on good days, but definitely not days twenty-three to twenty-seven of her menstrual cycle, she thought she was okay on the eyes.

But even on her very best days, she'd built a fortress around her heart and thrown away the key. Even though she'd been divorced for eight years now, Esme worried that she was still as bitter and as angry as she was the day that she'd sold her wedding ring and donated the money to Women's Aid. She knew that she should be over all the hurt and heartbreak by now, but for some reason she was unable to move towards the light.

Maybe if she'd met one good egg in the meantime. But so far, Esme had only met very, very bad eggs.

And so she cried, as the hens looked away and talked among themselves in low whispers. It was very hard to cry silently and not give full voice to the sobs that were threatening to unleash themselves. Esme tried to wipe her tears off the crystals but had to snatch her hand away when she felt a painful charge zap her fingertips. What had she ever done to offend that hunk of rhodonite, apart from callously dunking it in Fairy Liquid? She stared down at her hand, which looked as unremarkably hand-like as ever, even though the tips of her fingers were stinging.

She reached out again, to tentatively prod a jagged lump of rose quartz, but as Esme felt another wave of static nip at her fingertip, all the candles on the table suddenly spluttered and snuffed themselves out. Esme couldn't help but shiver, a sensation rippling down her spine, as if a whole gaggle of geese had just walked over her grave. 'Must be a draught from upstairs,' Ngaire said, scraping her chair back. 'I'll get someone to close the door and bring us some matches.'

'A firelighter would be more environmentally friendly than single-use matches,' someone said officiously and ordinarily Esme would have rolled her eyes at that remark, saving it up to tell people later, but she was a little bit preoccupied . . .

'Oh my God, Esme, are you *still* crying?' Muffin asked in scandalised tones, as if Esme's display of raw emotion was now verging on unseemly. 'You shouldn't keep crying on the crystals. It can't be good for them.'

'I'm sorry that my energy is so toxic and negative,' Esme snapped, because she was once again back in the familiar embrace of her limiting beliefs, where she felt most at home. 'It's a wonder anyone wants to spend time with me.'

'We like spending time with you,' Seren insisted. 'But people who give out love get love back in return. Allegra says that it's impossible to get close to you . . .'

Esme's head shot up as Allegra, who was approaching the table, came to an abrupt stop. 'Allegra said that, did she?'

'I was talking generally, not specifically,' Allegra said vaguely and quickly, to dismiss the notion that she'd been discussing her sister's post-divorce failings with the sister-in-law that she

professed to dislike. 'Is the food coming? I'm starving. Anyone else starving?'

Seren patted Esme on the arm gingerly. 'I only say these
things because I care deeply about your spiritual wellbeing.
Now, have another kefir and vodka.'

Esme turned to her in disbelief. 'Wait, there's vodka in
the kefir? I thought it tasted funny. I'm not meant to drink
alcohol!'

Another agonising hour slowly ticked by. There were
platters of vegan comfort food for dinner: miniature seitan
burgers, falafel wraps, dairy-free mac 'n' cheese and tofu
'halloumi' fries. Then a salted caramel and chocolate praline
tart with peanut butter ice cream that everyone agreed was so
creamy it was hard to believe that it didn't contain any dairy.

Esme could barely eat anything except the ice cream, because
of her mouth. Instead, she stared down at her tear-dampened
vision board and wished she'd spent the night at home. Maybe
watching Netflix; maybe walking through a detailed scenario
featuring her fantasy boyfriend.

It was Saturday night so he'd be at his critically acclaimed,
beloved of the locals restaurant in Exmouth Market, called
Picky Bits, which served what could best be described as
modern British tapas. A series of delicious things, like Welsh
rarebit or devilled eggs, Scotch quail's eggs, mini Yorkshire
puddings with a gravy dipping sauce, all designed for sharing. The site had originally been a butcher's shop and still
had all the original Edwardian tiles and wood panelling. Esme
had picked out the enamel plates and found the cutlery and
glasses, which had a whole *fin de siècle*, Art Nouveau vibe,
from a French wholesaler (in Esme's fantasies, Brexit had
never happened). Esme always had the best seat in the house,
at the bar, so she could chat to the bar staff when they weren't

busy, though when they were busy she'd been known to pull the odd pint herself.

But mostly she'd watch him, because Saturday night in his little restaurant was when he was at his best. At ease, in control, amusing, whether he was greeting customers as they came through the door, taking drinks orders but also not taking any shit from the chef. Occasionally, he'd drop a kiss on top of Esme's head as he passed or shoot her that slow, lazy smile of his from across the room, then later they'd walk home with all sorts of goodies that were left over from the day's pass. God, she wouldn't even be able to kiss him on account of dry socket . . .

'Seren, this is ridiculous. Just look at her! Esme needs to go home,' she heard Allegra snap, though it wasn't like Allegra to be so solicitous of her younger sister's emotional and physical state. 'I'll go with her, make sure she's all right.'

'No, I'm happy to stay,' Esme said sweetly, because there was no way that she was letting Allegra wriggle out of her social commitments by using Esme as a human shield. Besides, this whole unpleasant evening was Allegra's fault; Seren was her sodding sister-in-law. 'I want to stay and celebrate you, Seren. Be, er, abundant, in my good wishes.'

Another half hour passed at the same rate that it took glaciers to shift across tectonic plates until, finally, it was time to leave. But only to prolong the agony by going on to a club where they'd meet up with Isaac and his rah-rah mates from Charterhouse and Cambridge and Deloitte, who, sadly, weren't as laid-back as he was.

It was a rainy night in Soho, the pavement and road glistening in the persistent drizzle, softening the neon lights from the bars and restaurants and frizzing up Esme's hair as the collective hens huddled together while Seren read Ngaire the riot act for not remembering to order two cars to take them to some bougie club in Chelsea.

'Maybe this is God's way of telling me to call it a night . . .' Esme started to say, but her words were drowned by delighted squeals as not one but two black cabs slowly came towards them, both with their lights on. Which had to be God's way of telling Esme there was no way she was getting out of this, not when she was being bundled into a cab, still clutching her vision board, like she was twenty-five years younger and taking it home for her mother to stick on the fridge.

Not that Debbie had ever been one for cooing over home-made Mother's Day cards and other art class-mandated displays of affection. She nudged Allegra who was sitting opposite; Esme, having lost the seating battle, was perched uncomfortably on one of the tip-up seats. 'Do you remember the time I made an Easter card at school and when I brought it home Debbie made me redo it, because she said it was rubbish and I just hadn't tried hard enough?'

Allegra frowned. 'What? No! Sounds like Mum though.' Then she recalled that she and Esme were kind of in a fight. 'You're like an elephant, the way you hold on to grudges. You never forget anything.'

Esme certainly wouldn't be forgetting this night and the many wrongs that Allegra had done her. She stared fixedly out of the window, not joining in as Allegra, Muffin and was it Flora (or Fiona?) chatted about how hard it was to get a decent nanny since the pandemic and Brexit because a lot of people had left Britain for more welcoming places and the ones that were left didn't want to work fourteen hours a day, five days a week anymore. 'So you have to pay them more to work less,' Allegra lamented, even though she had a younger sister who happily provided free childcare every

Friday afternoon so that their nanny could work a four and a half day week.

They passed Hyde Park, speeding Esme further and further away from her own bed, until the cab reached Sloane Square (the Uber home was going to be ruinously expensive) and at last they were on the King's Road. Another couple of minutes, another couple of pounds on the meter, and they were at their destination.

'If you could just put it on your card, Esme, plus tip because you still haven't paid me the money for tonight,' Muffin said, as she clambered out of the cab. 'We'll settle the rest later.'

Esme paid the fare. The cab had already been corralled by a group of braying teenagers, so she had no choice but to get out roadside.

She opened the door a sliver and squinted into the rain-soaked night to make sure that no cars were coming, got out, turned round to shut the door behind her and then . . .

The cyclist seemed to come out of nowhere, hard and fast. The brutal collision tangled Esme up in metal. The wheels, the chain, scraping at her legs. Then there was a hand pushing her so violently in the chest that it knocked the air out of her lungs . . .

'You stupid bitch! Get the fuck out of my way!'

It all happened so quickly but the moment seemed to last for ever as Esme was slammed off her feet by the force of the blow. She fell backwards, hands clutching at air, the night sky rushing up to meet her, and the last thing she saw before her head connected with the wet bitumen was the exasperated look on Allegra's face.

'Oh, Esme, typical . . .'

Then, nothing.

5

When Esme opened her eyes, she was lying in the road. Apparently, she wasn't dead. So that was a good thing.

'I'm fine,' she heard herself say in a rusty voice. 'I'm fine.'

There were a lot of faces peering down at her, all of them indistinguishable.

'Don't move, Es, you might have broken something.'

'How many fingers am I holding up?'

Esme didn't think she'd broken anything. She didn't *feel* broken. 'I'm fine,' she said again though she was cold and, when she tried to sit up, she realised that she was trembling. 'Really, I'm fine. Get me up, please.'

Allegra and Muffin took an arm each and gently pulled Esme to her feet. Being vertical made the world rush past her at twice the speed of light and, if Allegra hadn't still been clutching her arm, then Esme might have ended up on her arse again. As it was, she swayed where she stood.

'You really will do anything to get out of my hen party.' Seren wasn't sniping but rather trying to make a very weak joke as she stared at Esme in dismay, concern making a concerted affect to bypass her ethically sourced tweakments so she could furrow her brow.

'Bit shaky but other than that I'm all right,' Esme wheezed because it still felt as if her lungs weren't getting enough oxygen. 'Don't get mad, but I think I probably will go home now.'

'Oh my God, you're bleeding,' Allegra suddenly gasped. 'Your head. OK, we are going straight to hospital.'

Esme gingerly touched the back of her head and her stomach lurched alarmingly. She felt something wet then looked at her fingers, which were now sticky with blood.

Esme steadied herself on the cab, so she could throw up a bitter stream of vodka, kefir and ice cream, as a debate raged about whether they should call for an ambulance but how long would it take to arrive and were they even allowed to call for an ambulance given the current strain on the NHS unless someone had suffered a life-threatening health event like a heart attack or been knocked out by falling masonry.

'Gordon Bennett, you girls don't half go on,' the cabbie intervened at last. 'Now, you young things are going to have to get out and I'll take this poor lady to hospital.'

There was some grumbling and backchat from the teenagers while the hens debated which was the nearest and best hospital but eventually Esme was back in the cab, on the proper seat this time, next to Allegra, who held her hand tightly. Kemi had offered to come too, but Esme had pointed out that it was a waste of her shimmery white jumpsuit not to go dancing in it. Also, she didn't want Kemi to get blood on said jumpsuit.

'You're very pale, Es,' Allegra pointed out.

'I was going to fake tan today but I really wasn't up to it after the dentist.' The sharp, twinging pain at the back of her head was very different from the nagging throb where her wisdom tooth had been. The ache in her arm from the effort it took to keep a bar towel (someone had run into the bougie club to get something to stem the flow of blood) to the wound couldn't really compete.

Allegra clutched Esme's hand even tighter. 'God, that cyclist didn't even stop. And he didn't just cycle into you, he *hit* you. We'll see if there's CCTV so we can identify him then

44

Oliver will have him charged with riding without undue care and caution, assault, GBH . . .'

Esme didn't doubt that if anyone could, her brother-in-law could. 'Funny, isn't it? All these years I've been cycling in London and not even a scratch, then this . . .'

'Your voice is really slurred. Do you think you might have concussion?'

'I don't know what concussion feels like. It's probably all that vodka and kefir.'

They were at the hospital in no time at all. Esme let Allegra help her out of the cab because her legs weren't quite sure what they wanted to do, and waited for Allegra to pay the driver. Then Allegra helped Esme to put a face mask on before they walked through a set of revolving doors into the A&E department.

It was early enough on a Saturday night that the joint wasn't jumping but it still looked pretty lively. Even though she was holding a towel to her bleeding head, Esme wondered if she was making a fuss about nothing. It *did* hurt, but she famously had a very low pain threshold and it might turn out to be just a graze. In the media there'd been a lot of horror stories about how hospitals, particularly A&E departments, were overrun these days due to staff sickness, recruitment issues and chronic underfunding. Trolleys lined up in corridors. A twelve-hour wait to see a doctor, even longer if you had to be admitted to a ward, if there was even a bed free.

'You know that this is going to take ages,' Esme warned Allegra, but as soon as they approached the reception desk a young man in royal blue scrubs was bearing down on them with a clipboard and a frown.

'Head wound?' he asked, rather unnecessarily.

'*Still bleeding* head wound,' Allegra corrected. 'She was unconscious for five minutes.'

Those were the magic words which meant that Esme was ushered straight through to a curtained-off bay where she collapsed into a chair.

Allegra had been left behind due to the Covid guidelines. Esme retrieved her phone with the hand that wasn't still clutching the towel to the back of her skull.

'You might as well go home, or rejoin the hens,' she said when Allegra answered.

Allegra wasn't for budging. 'I'll wait until you've been assessed. Make sure they give you a tetanus injection. When did you last have one?'

'I have no idea.' Thinking made everything hurt even more. 'Look, I might be here all night before I get seen.'

'I'll wait,' Allegra said firmly.

It wasn't all night. Just as the stale school dinner smell of the hospital was making Esme feel like she might throw up again, the curtain was pulled back by a woman in maroon scrubs. Most of her face was obscured by a mask but she had very tired eyes. 'Just come to take down your particulars,' she said. Esme managed to launch the NHS app on her phone and retrieve her NHS number and vaccination details, which was quite hard when her hand was shaking like a kite on a windy day.

'Someone will be along to triage you quite soon.' Esme was left alone. She tried to get up on the bed but it was too much effort. Instead she leaned over from her chair to rest her head on it while she peered at her phone. Somehow, even though she was freezing cold and shaking and her head was pounding and her mouth was in nine different kinds of fucking agony, she dozed off until she was woken up by a woman in bright blue scrubs. This one had glasses and close-cropped grey hair.

'We can't have you sleeping, darling,' she said. 'Let's get you properly on the bed so I can examine you.'

Standing up, shuffling two steps, sitting down and then swinging her legs up onto the bed made Esme feel like someone was hitting her skull with a sledgehammer. She sat back carefully so that her head wouldn't make contact with anything and panted for breath.

'Goodness me, you're not having a great Saturday night, are you? What's been happening?' the woman asked as she perched on the corner of the bed.

It took Esme a long time to tell her tale of woe. That she definitely had fallen backwards and she didn't know how long she'd been unconscious but also that she'd had a wisdom tooth ripped out of her mouth that morning and she hadn't eaten all day while knocking back co-codamol. 'I'm actually very worried that falling and hitting my head might have knocked away any scabs that were forming and I'm going to end up with dry socket,' she added. 'Do you think you could have a look? Also, is my head still bleeding?'

'Head wounds always bleed a lot. I wouldn't worry,' the woman said blithely. 'Right, let's take your blood pressure.'

The stranglehold of the blood pressure cuff was just one more thing that hurt. Then a light was shone in Esme's eyes. Did she know her date of birth? Could she name the months of the year in reverse order? And who's the prime minister? 'Well, generally, I call them fuckhead.'

Next, she was led out of the cubicle to be weighed in case she suddenly had to be rushed to surgery and anaesthetised. That should have been scary but it wasn't as scary as knowing how many kilograms she needed to lose in the next week so she could fit into the bridesmaid dress that had fitted pre-pandemic. Esme shut her eyes and asked not to be told her magic number because the experiences of the last twelve hours had been traumatising enough.

Then she was led back to the cubicle and asked to put her finger on her nose, which made her wince. 'Have I mentioned that I had a wisdom tooth out this morning?' she said.

Suddenly Allegra pushed back the curtain. She was pinch-faced behind her mask and accompanied by a man in darker blue scrubs. 'He's a doctor,' she said to Esme, who didn't doubt that Allegra had demanded to see someone of his pay grade or above. 'Now, she was unconscious for five minutes. At least five minutes,' she said forcefully. 'She needs a CT scan.'

'I probably don't,' Esme protested. 'As far as I can tell, I'm between fourteen and fifteen on the Glasgow Coma Scale . . .'

'Oh, you didn't say you worked in medicine . . .' the triage nurse exclaimed.

'She doesn't . . .'

'I have done some medical copywriting,' Esme reminded her sister.

'That was *years* ago,' Allegra pointed out.

'Also, I looked up head wounds on Google.'

'I wish Google had never been invented!' The nurse sat down on the bed again.

'It was very informative,' Esme explained. 'I was worried that I'd end up having brain surgery before the night was out but if I'm between fourteen and fifteen on the Glasgow Coma Scale I can just go home, right? Also, I fell down a bit of a rabbit hole while I was googling so I also know the correct treatment if someone degloves their penis . . .'

'It might seem like she has a concussion, but this is what she normally sounds like,' Allegra said wearily, dropping onto the chair.

'I still think you're more like a twelve to thirteen on the GCS and we'll have to clean out that wound. Probably pop in a couple of stitches.' The doctor tilted Esme's head forward and gently parted her hair. 'You'll need a local anaesthetic but as you've already had one of those today, I'll have to consult with the anaesthetist on call and I think she's in surgery right now.'

'Couldn't she have the stitches without an anaesthetic?' Allegra asked, glancing at the time on her phone. 'Then shove her in the scanner and we can go home.'

Allegra of course had private medical insurance so she could have a CT scan like she was having her passport photo taken. 'I have a very low pain threshold. I'm not having stitches without any kind of pain relief. Also, I only need a CT scan if I'm less than thirteen on the Glasgow Coma Scale, right?'

Esme looked to the actual trained medical staff for a little backup. 'We can't be handing out CT scans willy nilly,' the nurse agreed. 'We'll probably keep you in for a few hours. There might be a bed free on the observation ward,' she added doubtfully.

'Ally, go home,' Esme insisted. 'There's no point you staying if I'm going to pull an overnighter.'

'Well, if you're sure.' Allegra was already on her feet, grimacing as she remembered that she was wearing a vertiginous pair of heels. 'Call me if you need picking up in the morning.' She allowed herself a small smile. 'Thank you for getting me out of clubbing.'

'You definitely owe me one now,' Esme said and then, with almost indecent haste, Allegra was gone, along with the doctor who promised to be back soon with wound-cleaning *stuff*.

Only the triage nurse lingered. 'I'm knackered,' she sighed but it seemed more a statement of fact than anything she wanted Esme to reply to. Then she stood up with a pained little 'oof'. 'Oh well, no rest for the wicked. I'll try and sort you out a bed upstairs so you don't have to spend the night down here.'

'That's very kind of you.'

'It's more that I need the cubicle, darling . . . Pubs should be emptying out now and I give it an hour before it's absolute carnage.'

Esme sat cross-legged on the bed, propped up by pillows so she didn't accidentally lean back and knock her head. Now that everyone had left, she had nothing to do but focus on the pain. Mouth, head and actually, now that she was taking stock, there was something wrong with her shoulder. Not dislocated but Esme was pretty sure she'd pulled a muscle.

She couldn't even distract herself by mindless Instagram scrolling through other people's Saturday nights as she didn't want to drain her battery. All she could do was sit it out, closing her eyes against the roiling waves of pain.

'Not feeling sleepy, are you?' The doctor was back. 'I'd try and stay awake if I were you.'

That was easy enough for him to say. Esme watched through half-lidded eyes as he put on a plastic apron then snapped on gloves. 'Is this going to hurt?'

'I'll try to be as gentle as I can,' he said, in a tone which didn't really inspire much confidence.

The cut was at the base of her skull. 'Not a great place to have a head wound,' the doctor noted, like there were much better places to have head wounds. 'But you haven't got any bruising behind the ears.' He jabbed an instrument into Esme's ear without much ceremony, which made her yelp, then repeated the procedure on the other side. 'No blood around the ear drum and you said that the bruising round your eyes happened after your wisdom tooth extraction. Would you say it looks worse than it did?'

Esme took out her phone and peered at herself in the unrelenting glare of the front facing camera. She looked awful, like she'd recently been eaten by bears, and was grateful for the mask obscuring half her face. There was blood all down her neck. Her skin was the colour of mud. And she looked as if she hadn't slept in months. 'Hard to say really.'

'Bruising would indicate a skull fracture but I think it's just a nasty cut.' He pulled a handful of paper towels out of the wall dispenser. 'You'll need these.'

What Esme really needed was a general anaesthetic even to cope with the sharp and urgent agony of having her head wound flushed out with saline and then dressed temporarily until the anaesthetist could be tracked down and she could have her stitches.

Eventually a porter arrived to take Esme up to the observation ward. Then there was more pain with every heartbeat and every jolt of the wheels as they travelled the length of the hospital, went up in what seemed to be a goods lift, and finally reached their destination.

Esme was left in the chair at the ward reception like an unclaimed parcel. There was no one at the desk, so she waited. God, there was so much waiting. At last, a nurse appeared through a set of double doors.

'Goodness me,' she said in a warm Irish brogue. 'Where did you come from?'

Esme handed over the folder she'd been given. 'I'm here to be observed,' she explained forlornly.

'I don't know why they sent you up here, we don't have any beds free . . .'

'Also, I really need a wee and painkillers,' Esme said a little desperately, watching the woman look around as if she expected a bed to suddenly materialise out of thin air.

'If I could find you a bed, then I could get you a bedpan . . . My name's Marie, by the way.' Marie was failing to see the urgency of the situation.

'Marie, I don't think a bedpan is going to be viable. I'm wearing a jumpsuit!'

Once it was established that Esme was able to walk, Marie guided her to a bathroom. 'Pull the emergency cord if you feel like you're going to faint,' she said cheerfully and finally Esme was able to wriggle out of her jumpsuit, her frantic movements making her head feel like it was trapped in a vice. Then she yanked everything down and peed like it was an Olympic sport and she was going for gold.

Esme didn't want to look at herself in the mirror, but she couldn't resist the lure of her own reflection again. Now all she could see was the blood. The ends of her hair were matted with it. The mask that she'd put on what seemed like hours ago was also streaked with it. Pity it wasn't Halloween.

A sharp knock on the door. 'Are you all right in there?' asked a new voice.

Esme unlocked the door to see a short man in maroon scrubs outside. 'We've managed to find a bed,' he said in a weary voice, as if he'd had to assemble the bed from a flat pack himself. Though given the cuts to the NHS, Esme wouldn't have been surprised if that turned out to be the case.

It wasn't. It was an ordinary hospital bed, tucked into a space that wasn't quite an alcove, and wasn't quite a cupboard but something in between. An alboard. A cupcove. But already resting on the bed was a man in dark clothes.

He'd looked up as Maroon Scrubs had pulled back the curtain. The bottom half of his face was obscured by his mask and he had a huge dressing over his left eye so it was hard to tell what he was thinking about this sudden interruption. Or indeed what he actually looked like.

'Gaping head wound meet glassed in the face. There's one bed, one chair, you'll have to fight it out between you.'

6

'Oh, being glassed in the face sounds awful,' Esme said, holding out her hands in protest as the man sat up, wincing as he did so, and swung his long legs over the side of the bed. 'No, stay where you are!'

'I'm sure a gaping head wound trumps a minor facial injury,' he said, standing up, as Maroon Scrubs hurried away. He was tall. Esme had to look up, then wished she hadn't, because the world and the man in front of her rushed past her and she had to grip hold of the curtain to keep herself upright.

'I'm fine,' Esme insisted weakly.

'You're not fine,' the man said. He folded himself into the chair, not even a comfortable padded chair but a hard, plastic number, then patted the bed invitingly. 'Also giving you the bed means I've done my Cub Scouts good deed for the day.'

'Well, in that case . . .' Esme was only too pleased to collapse onto the bed. 'I always wanted to be a Brownie but my mother made me join the Woodcraft Folk instead.'

'If it's any consolation, I got kicked out of Cubs quite early on for being a disruptive influence,' he offered, and though he had his mask on, Esme was sure that he was smiling. He sounded like he was smiling.

Then Marie was back to crank up the head of the bed to an upright position, 'Because we can't have you falling asleep if it turns out you've got a serious brain injury,' she declared. 'I'll be checking on you.'

With her bottom lip caught between her teeth Esme wriggled up the bed, grateful for the thin blanket that she huddled under because she was still so cold that she was trembling. 'Any chance of some painkillers?' she begged.

'I'll ask the doctor on call,' Marie said. Somewhere in the distance they heard the buzz of another patient's call button. 'I should get that.'

'It's just I had a bad wisdom tooth extraction this morning and this head wound and I've had no pain relief . . .'

'I'll see if we can page someone.' Marie sounded distracted. 'Now, you make sure she doesn't go to sleep and you make sure that he doesn't rub his eye and I'll be back in a minute.'

Then she was gone and Esme was left alone to process how her ordinary Saturday had gone from bad to worse to whatever was worse than worse. Terrible. Catastrophic. Absolutely fucking awful.

'A wisdom tooth extraction *and* a gaping head wound? Life isn't treating you kindly, is it?'

Esme remembered that she wasn't on her own. She was sharing the cupcove with a fellow member of the walking wounded.

'I have had much better days,' she agreed, trying to steal a sideways glance at him even though it made her feel dizzy. 'So, if you don't mind me asking, who glassed you in the face?'

Yes, he was tall and he seemed to have a sense of humour and good manners, but there was a catch. There had to be. Esme waited for him to recount a lurid tale of some stupid fight he'd had because . . . because . . . because of toxic masculinity.

'I cut off an angry punter who was shouting at his girlfriend. Refused to serve him any more booze and he didn't take it very well.' He touched the gauze pad over his eye with one long finger, then lingered there.

'I hope you're not scratching your eye. Marie was quite clear about that,' Esme said. She thought she'd be alone with her pain but actually she didn't mind having company. It took her mind off things. 'Are you a barman then?'

He shrugged coat-hanger shoulders. 'Barman, bottle washer, front of house, sous chef, head chef, bookkeeper and, occasionally and unsuccessfully, a bouncer.' It was his turn to shoot Esme a sideways look with his one good eye. 'I run a pub.'

His accent wasn't the London accent that Esme was used to. That could slide from salt of the earth cockney when you were trying to keep it real to plummy, clipped vowels when speaking to the upper classes. He had a faint Mancunian timbre, the tone of his voice deep and dark like really posh chocolate made in small batches from free trade cocoa beans.

Weird. Esme looked down at her now bloodstained vision board, which she'd managed to cling on to despite the events of the last two hours. There was a picture of the Manchester Ship Canal right next to a photo of an artfully scruffy chef chopping an onion with his long fingers. The chef was covered in tattoos. Her cupcove companion was wearing a navy peacoat so Esme couldn't see if he was inked or not.

Even so, it was quite the coincidence.

'How did you get your gaping head wound?'

'I collided with a cyclist with anger management issues who shoved me in the chest so I fell backwards and hit my head.'

'What a dick. I'm guessing he didn't stick around to make sure you were OK.'

'You guess right.'

The man's dark, thick hair needed cutting because he was currently sporting a cowlick, which just wouldn't lay flat. He pushed it impatiently away from his face with long fingers, a couple of silver rings glinting in the fluorescent strip lighting.

The one eye visible was now shut, so Esme could see his long eyelashes, absolutely wasted on a man, flutter. She wondered what the rest of his face looked like. Would his lips be full and sensual, curved upwards so it always looked as if he was smiling, amused? When he was angry or really turned on, did they flatten into a tight line, like he couldn't even trust himself to speak?

'Hey! Don't go to sleep on me,' Esme said, because as distractions went, he was very distracting.

He opened his eyes, well, one dark, soulful eye, which looked heavy-lidded and weary, like sometimes he woke up in the middle of the night too and couldn't get back to sleep. 'It's just if I shut this eye, then I can shut my wounded eye and it doesn't hurt quite so much,' he said. Not whining. Just stating facts.

'Does it hurt a lot?'

'It feels like there's a massive piece of grit in it,' he said. 'My cornea's scratched and they think the retina is detached. I'm just waiting for a plastics consult, then they're whisking me off to Moorfields. Though when I say whisking off, what I actually mean is that it's going to be much quicker for me to get there in an Uber. Not that I'm complaining about the NHS. God, no! They do a wonderful job . . .'

'Especially considering how underfunded they are,' Esme agreed. She shivered a little under her thin blanket. 'Did the guy who attacked you get arrested?'

He nodded slowly, like any sudden movements would hurt. Esme could relate. 'He tried to do a runner but Greta, my bar manager, sat on him until the police arrived. I got a lift here in a squad car, which was actually quite thrilling.'

'Did they blue light you?'

'They didn't, which is something I'll regret until the day I die.' Again, Esme was sure she could *hear* him smiling.

'I'm very jealous that you might be getting plastic surgery.' Gaping head wound might trump being glassed in the face but being glassed in the face seemed to come with benefits. 'I would absolutely get the surgeon to do a quick nose job while he was at it. Maybe a brow lift too.'

'I can't see your nose because of your mask but I'm sure it doesn't need anything doing to it,' he said immediately, like his mother raised him right. 'And I'll see what the surgeon says but I don't fancy skin grafts and all that palaver. I'm more worried about my retina.' He sighed.

'Where's the cut that might need surgery?' Esme asked.

He pointed to the corner of his gauze pad. 'Just missed my actual eye.'

'You'll probably end up with quite a rakish scar if you don't have the surgery,' Esme said.

'Do women like rakish scars? Do you?'

Despite the fact that Esme was pretty sure she'd never looked worse, the unflattering light, the blood and the pain, it felt like they were having a moment. Like he was flirting with her.

Because that was what men did. They flirted with women just to flex a muscle, thinking that the recipient would be grateful for the attention. Doubly so if the woman they'd deigned to honour with their faux interest wasn't the sort of woman men usually flirted with.

It wasn't flattering. It was stale and predictable but she didn't have any reserves of energy left to let her hackles rise.

Instead, Esme shut her eyes because keeping them open made her feel like she was seasick. 'No sleeping!' Marie was back with a plastic beaker of water and, miracle of miracles, a tiny paper cup with two pills in it. 'Paracetamol. That's all I can give you.'

Esme gratefully swallowed the tablets, although even taking a couple of gulps of water felt like a bullet ricocheting through her skull.

'Are you in a lot of pain?' he asked very softly and very gently, like he was being sincere.

'Yeah.' Even getting out one syllable hurt now that she'd had to make several movements in order to take the paracetamol. 'Also, stop rubbing your eye.'

'I'm not!' He lowered his hand. 'Although, OK, I was think-ing about it. What's that?'

He gestured at the vision board, her handbag dumped on top of it. The conduit to manifest the man of her dreams, which probably wasn't the man currently sitting next to her, so close that she could feel his body heat. 'It's a vision board. One of the activities at a hen party I was attending before I was cut down in my prime. You're not into all that woo woo stuff, are you?'

'Not really. Occasionally I google if Mercury is in retro-grade just to see if there's a reason why my day has been full of minor grievances.' He shrugged. 'Like today for instance. But if you had a wisdom tooth out, then a hen party, then a gaping head wound, you're definitely having a worse day than me.'

'Your finger is dangerously close to your eye again.' Esme reached for his hand to pull it away, then flinched as her sud-den movement meant a world of pain.

'You're really not all right,' he said, and Esme wasn't even sure how but he was holding her cold, cold hand. His skin was warm to the touch. 'Do you want me to call the nurse back?'

'No, I'm fine. Well, not fine. But I'll live. Hopefully.' Even though Esme was in pain, shivering with cold, her eyes were closing because she was so tired.

'You're not meant to go to sleep.' He squeezed her fingers gently. 'We had a deal. I don't rub my eye and you don't go to sleep. We've talked a lot about me. Let's talk about you. What do you do when you're not at hen parties or being set upon by angry cyclists?'

He wasn't her vision board made flesh. No. He was a unicorn. A man who listened when Esme spoke and asked her questions and didn't just talk about himself. Plus, he was still holding her hand but in a comforting way that didn't set off her spider sense, which was rarely wrong.

'I'm a writer,' she said. 'Well, I used to be a writer. But now my bio says that I'm a content strategist.' The words felt cumbersome in her mouth. 'Me and my friend Lyndsey founded a content and branding agency when we got made redundant from the last magazine we worked on.'

'Do you like it?'

'I like that I still get to be creative,' Esme said, though she missed her old magazine days when she got paid to write about whatever she could get past the features director. 'And I love working with my friends. I don't love having to deal with the QuickBooks software though.'

'I hear you.' He gently squeezed her hand again. 'So, tell me, who do you think would win in a fight between a pirate and a ninja?'

'I'm never entirely sure what a ninja is so I think I'd go with pirate,' Esme said. It was her turn to apply pressure to his hand. 'This is so weird. This should be awkward, but it doesn't feel awkward?'

He quirked his one visible eyebrow. 'What? Meeting like this?'

'Yeah. Normally I wouldn't be so . . . so . . . ' All the adjectives Esme was thinking of – friendly, welcoming, even confiding – weren't ones she would use to describe how she usually behaved when she was meeting a man for the first time. 'I'm quite guarded . . . Because, apparently, I have very limiting beliefs.'

'Not entirely sure what limiting beliefs are but these circumstances, they're quite extraordinary, aren't they?' He leaned forward to rest his elbows on his knees. 'People think I'm really grumpy until they get to know me. Then when they get to know me, they realise that I'm not *quite* as grumpy as they originally thought.'

Smiling was another thing that made Esme's head hurt.

'I have resting bitch face, I can relate.'

She really wanted to go to sleep now, but he gave her fingers a warning squeeze and started to tell her about *his* terrible day because it had been terrible long before his face made contact with a wine glass. He'd woken up that morning to water pouring from the flat above through a light fitting on his ceiling. Five minutes after that, the ceiling collapsed. He was meant to be staying with friends tonight but they were currently in a maternity unit across town because their baby had decided to arrive a month early.

Even though he was having a bit of a moan, and who could blame him, Esme liked the sound of his voice. There was something so warm yet wry about the way he spoke. If running a pub didn't work out, he could definitely make a living narrating audiobooks. Even better, if they were very smutty audiobooks.

'Hey! You're not going to sleep on me, are you?'

'No! Of course I'm not,' Esme said indignantly because she'd only closed her eyes for a second. Not even a second. 'What were you saying about your upstairs neighbour?'

'That I think he's a spy. He's gone at odd hours and even though I've lived below him for five years . . . You're going to sleep again . . .'

'I am *not*,' Esme grumbled, fighting hard to keep her eyes open.

And then she woke up, though she didn't even realise that she'd been asleep.

She had no idea how much time had passed but there was no longer a tall, tousled, smiling-voiced man sitting by her side and holding her hand. She was on her own.

Also, she was in so much pain.

7

Sunday

Esme held out for a good ten minutes, checking the time on her phone, until she had to press the call button.

The intermittent buzz was like a swarm of angry bees and it felt like several days until Maroon Scrubs appeared. 'I'm really sorry but I'm in so much pain and those paracetamol . . . they didn't even touch the sides.'

His masked face was blurry and indistinct, but he still managed to look quite pissed off. 'That's because you haven't taken them,' he said, through what sounded like gritted teeth. He held up the little paper cup. 'They're here. You haven't been sleeping, have you? You're not meant to fall asleep.'

He stood there, arms folded, while Esme took the tablets, though she was sure that she'd already taken the tablets. In fact, she could have sworn that she'd taken the tablets.

'Where did the man in here go?' Esme asked. 'The one who'd been glassed in the face?'

'Look, is there anything else you need because I really have a lot of paperwork to do before we change over shifts?'

'Is it morning already?'

'It's nearly six o'clock.' There was a frown from behind the mask. Esme was getting used to the frowns behind the masks. 'You know, you really have to try and stay awake. It can be very dangerous to sleep if you have a concussion.'

Glassed in the face – she hadn't even asked his name – seemed to have gone. Though it was odd he hadn't said goodbye. Or stopped her from dozing off. But they'd held hands. Though come to think of it, Esme wasn't a hand-holdy type of person. And as for holding the hand of someone she didn't even know – that was completely out of character.

Could she have imagined him in the same way that she'd imagined she'd taken the tablets? She'd probably been lucid dreaming. When Esme was ten she'd had her tonsils and adenoids whipped out, and after coming round from the anaesthetic, she'd had a very detailed conversation with her parents about getting a kitten. Except it hadn't happened, because neither Debbie nor Gary had felt the need to take any time off work to be with Esme.

'Why are your eyes shut?' Maroon Scrubs switched on the overhead light, which made Esme blink and the pounding in her head rise to a crescendo. She was pretty sure that the next phase of keeping her awake would probably be a little light waterboarding. 'I've already told you, you're not meant to sleep with a head injury.'

At least it was impossible to sleep now that the ward was coming to life. More lights were switched on. The rumble and laughter of the staff and a plaintive voice from behind a set of open double doors, calling, 'Nurse! Nurse,' in a weak, reedy voice every few seconds.

There was the rumble of the cleaning trolleys, then the tea and coffee cart and finally breakfast. Esme wasn't allowed either tea or coffee or a piece of toast, though the thought of swallowing anything made her feel nauseous.

'Better keep you nil by mouth just in case you do need surgery,' said the ward registrar when she did her rounds. She

66

looked about twelve. 'Probably another couple of hours then we can discharge you.'

'So, I'm not having stitches?' Esme asked and then she had to explain all over again about her wisdom tooth and the local anaesthetic and the anaesthetist being AWOL.

'I'll make some calls,' she was told, and the registrar left, never to return again.

After a few hours when nobody even bothered Esme with a blood pressure cuff or wanted to know if she could remember her date of birth, a porter suddenly appeared to take her . . . well, she didn't exactly know where.

Back to A&E it turned out, where a doctor was waiting who'd spoken to the lesser-spotted anaesthetist. 'In a minute, you won't feel a thing,' he promised Esme as he came at her with an absolutely huge syringe.

'Ow. Fucking ow. Fuck,' was all Esme could say as a dose of lidocaine was injected into the back of her neck to dull the pesky nerves that kept putting pain messages on blast.

Then she really didn't feel a thing. Just a slight tugging sensation as the two sides of her six centimetres long and two and a half centimetres deep laceration were stitched together.

'You can go home now,' the doctor said, when he was finished.

'I don't need a CT scan? I'm fifteen on the GCS?'

'You seem pretty alert to me.' He paused from washing his hands. He was in his late twenties, masked but still fresh-faced, just come on shift and cocky with it. 'Who's the prime minister?'

'That absolute disgrace of a human being,' Esme said, because the PM's name was on the tip of her tongue but annoyingly just out of reach too.

'There you go. Absolutely nothing wrong with your brain.'

'So I can go home and go to sleep?'

'I don't see why not.'

'More importantly, can I wash my hair?'

'One of the nurses will hook you up with an information sheet on how to look after your wound and what not. We'll sort you out with some antibiotics just to be on the safe side. You'll have to have the stitches taken out in a week or so, but your GP can manage that.' Even though he was wearing a mask, Esme could tell that he was flashing her a bright but insincere smile. 'Anyway, I'll let you go. Bet you can't wait to see the back of this place.'

She really couldn't, but Esme didn't immediately make a bid for freedom. She sat down in the waiting room, aware that she looked like an absolute state in her bloodstained faux leopard fur and crumpled jumpsuit, but her head was numb and she wasn't in pain so it was all good.

She rummaged in her handbag for her phone and saw that she had countless missed calls, texts, messages and voice notes from the assorted hens. But mostly from Allegra.

Are you actually dead? Can't get a lick of sense out of any-body when I call the hospital. What is going on? read the last message.

Though she couldn't feel pain, Esme could still feel guilt, irritation and also a sense of weariness; the usual complicated mess of emotions that Allegra aroused in her. Especially when, once again, it seemed that Esme was making major demands of her sister's emotional bandwidth.

Maybe that was why she called Kemi first, but her phone went straight to voicemail. It was well past noon, Esme realised, and Kemi would still be in church with her phone turned off. Even if she'd been dancing until the wee small hours, Kemi never missed her Sunday morning appointment with the Lord.

The only other person she knew with a car was Allegra, who had offered to come and fetch her. But it was still better to message rather than call and get an inevitable bollocking about being incommunicado.

> Sorry, I turned my phone off because I didn't want to kill the battery. Only just had my stitches done. Don't need a CT scan. Is there any chance of that lift you offered? Also, sorry, but can you lend me a change of clothes? No worries if not!

Allegra being Allegra, her contact info went from a timestamp of ten minutes ago to immediately online. Next, blue ticks to show that she'd read Esme's message then 'typing'. That simple six letter word always felt quite ominous when Esme had imparted some unwelcome news to Allegra (which seemed to happen a lot) and was waiting for her reply.

> At least you're not dead, I suppose. We're actually on our way to have lunch with Oliver's godparents in Wimbledon. Can you not get an Uber?

It was very on brand of Allegra to promise something then snatch it back a few hours later.

> Fine. I'll get an Uber.

Esme waited for Allegra to ask for an update on her health, but even though the ticks were blue, Allegra was now offline.

Anyway, Esme *could* get an Uber and at least she wouldn't be beholden to Allegra, who would have spent the entire journey back to Gospel Oak sighing and saying passive aggressive things like, 'Well, I suppose we can have Sunday dinner instead of Sunday lunch even if it will cut into bedtime.' Or, 'Oliver jokes that I should start charging you petrol money.'

However, there were no Ubers in the immediate vicinity. Esme tried to download the Lyft app but couldn't get a decent Wi-Fi signal. She followed the signs out of A&E, staggering a little as the cold Sunday afternoon rushed to greet her.

The taxi rank opposite was empty. Esme was even resigned to bankrupting herself and getting a black cab home but as she squinted up and down the street, she couldn't see the welcoming orange light of a cab for hire. Ordinarily Esme would have got public transport, even though it involved changing tubes twice, then the bus, but she'd just had her gaping head wound sewn up and she really didn't fancy it.

All the while she'd been refreshing the Uber app and finally, success! Success and a twenty-eight-minute wait, which was nothing compared to the hours she'd already spent waiting in the hospital.

Already shivering in her matted faux fur, she approached a bench, eyes glued to her phone screen, where a little car icon was still twenty-eight minutes away.

'How's lunch service? Is it slammed? I could come in for the evening. I can't remember if we're fully booked or not.'

There was a man sitting at the other end of the bench, hunched over as if he was trying to shield himself from the cold.

Esme stared down at her phone, which wasn't making her Uber get there any quicker.

'Well, if you're sure you can manage without me. Thank God we're closed tomorrow. I feel like I could sleep for a week.'

He had a familiar Mancunian accent and, when Esme glanced over at him, she could see that he was tall, all knees and elbows. His hair was tousled and he kept pushing it back with long fingers so she could see the patch over one of his eyes.

He finished the call.

Esme wanted to say something. If nothing else she was desperate to know if they'd attached his detached retina. But their cupcove interlude had been an intimate moment out of time, what with the intense conversation and the handholding.

Whereas now, it would just be weird.

Awkward.

'Hey! Sorry I didn't get to say goodbye earlier.'

It was too late. He'd noticed her and had now swivelled around so Esme had his full attention.

It was going to be *so* awkward.

'Glassed in the face, we meet again.' Especially when that was her opening line.

'Gaping head wound. How are you doing?'

'I'm just head wound now, it's no longer gaping,' Esme said. 'And you, how's the detached retina and the facial laceration?'

'Turns out it wasn't detached. I just have a deep scratch on my cornea . . .'

'Ugh!' Esme couldn't help the full body shudder. 'Sorry, I'm not normally squeamish about eyes.'

'Don't worry about it. I, however, am always squeamish about eyes. I have these antibiotic drops but I don't know how

I'm going to put them in. How do people with contact lenses poke things in their eyes every day?'

Esme shrugged. 'And the facial laceration? Have they booked you in for plastic surgery?'

He shook his head. 'They just glued my face back together. My career as a model might be over, but someone told me that women think scars are rakish, so it's not all bad.'

He wasn't wearing a mask anymore. Neither was she. Esme could see the lower half of his face now. It was a very nice lower half. He had a good pair of cheekbones, his nose was perfectly inoffensive, firm chin and his lips *were* full and sensual, curved upwards, so it looked as if he was smiling, amused, even though there was now a pause in the conversation, which *was* a little bit awkward. He looked down at his phone.

Esme looked down at her phone too. Her waiting time for Jorge in a Toyota Yaris was now only seventeen minutes.

'I'm Theo, by the way.'

She looked up.

Nothing was going to happen. Meeting a man who didn't give her the ick within five minutes was just one more strange thing in a night full of strange things. But still, it was good practice in being open and positive.

'I'm Esme.'

They solemnly shook hands. His touch was still warm where she was cold and probably a little clammy.

'Like the J.D. Salinger stories? "For Esme – with Love and Squalor"?' He grinned a little sheepishly. 'I bet everyone says that.'

'They really don't. Most people aren't that well read and my mother actually named me after the French pen pal she used to have.' It was Esme's turn to smile a little sheepishly. 'I've always been grateful her pen pal wasn't called Clothilde.'

72

They were both still staring at each other and smiling like fools, as if they were having a moment, then they both looked down and realised they were still holding hands.

'Oh God . . .'

'Sorry . . .'

They snatched their respective hands back.

Esme had forgotten how exhilarating it could be to have that little spark with another human being which maybe, given time, would either fizzle to nothing or turn into a major conflagration resulting in third degree burns.

She looked down at her phone again. Jorge's ETA was now twelve minutes.

'I don't know what's wrong with Uber. I've been trying for ages, but it says that they don't have any cars available.' Theo held up his phone. 'Don't suppose you know the number of a good cab company?'

Then again, sometimes a spark could turn into something warm and glowing.

'I've actually got an Uber on its way.'

'Lucky you!'

Esme thought back to her affirmations. She might not be 'open and ready for love to pour in and make me whole', but she could be open. Maybe just a little bit.

'I'm going north. Gospel Oak. If that's any help.'

'I'm in Kentish Town.' He shrugged. 'I haven't sorted out where I'm going to stay tonight but there's a Travelodge in Belsize Park, right? I could walk there from Gospel Oak.'

'Maybe you could ring them now?' Esme suggested. 'Though I can't think that they're going to be at maximum capacity on a Sunday in February.'

Theo bent over his phone screen. 'I think I've got just enough battery charge . . . Fuck, no, I haven't.'

'Neither of us are having a good weekend, are we?'

'Worst weekend ever,' Theo agreed. But then he held her gaze with his one good eye and it wasn't just the upward quirk of his lips, he was definitely smiling at her. 'But there have been some high points.'

Esme nodded and she wanted to smile too but she didn't want him to get notions. He hadn't put a foot wrong so far, but he would, sooner or later. 'Yeah, at least bashing my head meant that I got to leave the hen party early and swerve dancing with investment bankers at some awful Chelsea nightclub.'

That just made Theo's smile widen as he sat back and folded his arms. 'A fate worse than death. Though maybe not worth risking actual possible death . . .'

'My options at the time were limited,' Esme said, and he laughed then winced.

'OK, so laughing really pulls on my glued-up laceration.'

'I'll be sure not to crack any jokes then,' Esme said. She looked down at her vision board, which she'd managed to hang on to despite the fact that the doctor who had stitched her up had said it was a biohazard.

Theo really did resemble a young James Stewart. The similarity was remarkable.

'Anyone ever tell you . . .'

She was saved by her phone. A triumphant chime to let her know that Jorge had broken all land speed records and lo and behold, there was a Toyota Yaris pulling up in front of them.

8

It turned out that Jorge liked a chat.

He wanted to talk about football or, rather, he wanted to deliver a quite boring monologue about Arsenal's chances in their match next Saturday.

Esme didn't bother to engage and shut her eyes though Theo, whose allegiance to Man City was met with hoots of derision from Jorge, listened and made the odd comment. Unlike, say, her colleagues Ant and Cedric, Esme could imagine that if she did end up watching a football match with Theo, he wouldn't wang on about boring footie statistics.

It was a damp, dreary afternoon and the traffic was so quiet that it wasn't too long before Esme came to with a start, realising that Jorge had already veered left onto Highgate Road. A minute later, she leaned forward. 'It's the next road on the left.'

She couldn't remember the last time she'd been so pleased to see the redbrick mansion blocks that lined the street.

'And anywhere here is fine.'

'If you give me your email address, then I'll PayPal you the fare,' Theo said, as they watched Jorge drive up the road with a little farewell toot of his horn.

'Oh no, you're all right. I mean, I'd still have had to pay the fare if it was just me.'

Esme hadn't realised that Theo had a bag with him, a big black leather holdall, which he hefted over his shoulder. 'Well, thank you for keeping me company last night.'

'Thank you for letting me have the bed,' Esme said.

She waited for him to say goodbye, to walk out of her life and towards the Travelodge in Belsize Park. Just the thought of it made her feel a little panicked. The same kind of fluttering dread as when she couldn't find her purse or keys.

'I guess I should be going then,' Theo said, but he didn't take so much as a single step away from Esme.

'Unless you wanted to come in for a cup of tea and to charge your phone.' Esme shrugged like it was no big deal and really, it wasn't. 'There's no point schlepping all the way to Belsize Park only to find there's no room at the inn.'

'That would be really kind. Also, I'm gasping for a cuppa,' Theo said as he followed Esme to the front door of her block. 'I was nil by mouth all night, in case I needed surgery, and it was only at the last minute that they decided I was just a malingerer.'

Esme couldn't remember the code for the door. It changed every week. She had to look it up on her phone from her block's WhatsApp group.

'I'm on the top floor and there's no lift,' she warned Theo once they were inside. The smell of beeswax polish on the wood panelling and some delicious cooking smells wafting out from Marion and Jacinta's flat were instantly comforting.

'I'd better save my energy for the long climb ahead,' Theo said, and he wasn't wrong.

Esme was up and down the stairs to her flat on the fourth floor at least twice a day. Sometimes she *ran* up them if she was feeling particularly energetic but this afternoon, by the time they reached the second floor, she felt like she was scaling the Matterhorn.

Theo wasn't faring much better. They hadn't discussed his fitness levels, but he was breathing hard and gave an unhappy groan when they reached the third floor and he realised that there was still further to climb.

'I think I'm having a relapse,' he panted once they'd reached the top. It wasn't so spacious on the fourth floor, but Esme adored her little attic flat with its sloping ceilings and slightly wonky floors.

Esme had worked very hard to afford the flat, although the inheritance from her maternal grandmother's estate, which had been held in a trust until her twenty-first birthday, had helped.

'It's not enough to put a deposit on a flat,' Allegra had advised Esme flatly. 'You'll never get a mortgage, not with what you earn.'

'You had enough to put a deposit on a flat,' Esme pointed out.

Allegra had smiled smugly. 'And pay off some of my student loans but it was eleven years ago, property was cheaper and I'm much more financially savvy than you.'

Esme still wasn't sure if she'd wanted to prove Allegra wrong or if she had really wanted to get a foot on the property ladder, but that was when she'd started copywriting in her spare time. Other twenty-one-year-olds were getting drunk every night and copping off with randoms, while Esme was extrapolating and summarising information on a blind study about the effects of Omega 3 oil on arthritis in rats. Though to be fair, she still got drunk and copped off with randoms on the weekends.

It had been worth it, though, to get the keys to her very own flat (granted technically the building society owned 80 per cent of it). It had also been worth it to have Allegra eat humble pie. Though being Allegra, when she'd turned up with a bottle of Prosecco and a bunch of flowers, the first words out of her mouth were, 'What were you thinking buying a flat with restricted head height on the top floor of an old building? Bet the roof leaks.'

The roof didn't leak but there were certain no-go areas of the flat if you were five foot eight or taller. 'You'll have to mind your head if you go into the bathroom,' Esme told Theo as she unlocked the door. There was also a sloping ceiling in her bedroom but he wouldn't be going in there. Definitely not. 'Bathroom's on the right,' she gestured to the open door and prayed to God she hadn't left any underwear scattered around. 'Living room is on the left. You can unplug the lamp on the end table for your charger. How do you take your tea?'

'Strong. Just a splash of milk. Literally just a drop. One sugar,' Theo said, dropping his bag on the floor with a grateful sigh.

Esme hadn't really appreciated how tall he was. How he seemed to fill up all the space in her tiny hall.

'I only have oat milk,' she said apologetically, though caring for the planet wasn't something she should apologise for.

'Cool. Are you vegetarian? Vegan?' Theo crouched down to unzip one of the pockets of his holdall.

'Vegetarian mostly, and, well I really like cheese. And butter,' Esme couldn't help but sound defensive because this stance was something that Oliver, her brother-in-law, was always particularly sneery about.

'Some of my happiest memories involve a large mound of cave-aged cheddar,' Theo said. He held up his charger. 'OK, so . . .'

Esme reached through the open doorway of the living room to switch the big light on, though normally she preferred to spend the evening in the dim shade of several small lamps. 'Make yourself at home. I'll stick the kettle on. Are you hungry? I could make toast.'

'I don't want to be any trouble,' Theo said, which was neither yes nor no. And actually, if he was anything like Esme, then he had to be starving.

Esme didn't even realise how hungry she was until she found herself stuffing a slice of dry bread into her mouth because she couldn't wait for the toaster to do its thing. She only just remembered to avoid the left side of her mouth and the scab that she hoped had formed overnight. That wisdom tooth extraction seemed very long ago and she no longer felt like that same person who'd woken up yesterday morning full of dread and anticipation.

Esme looked around her little galley kitchen to be reassured that actually, yes, all was just how she'd left it when she'd gone out last night.

Her 1920s Golden Age of Travel calendar was hanging from a hook by the window. There was the really fancy Dualit toaster currently full to capacity with four slices of bread, and coming up to the boil was the matching kettle that she'd inherited from Allegra. Her sister had had her kitchen remodelled and the pale green kettle and toaster no longer matched the new cabinetry. Allegra had planned to stick them on Facebook Marketplace but Esme hadn't been above begging for them, though every time she made herself a cup of tea, she remembered having to plead for the kettle and the smug look on Allegra's face.

She was calmed by the familiar movements of spreading butter on hot toast, letting the teabag stew for a minute before dunking exactly eleven times for the optimum strength cup of tea. Then she dug out a tray and carried her heavy load into the living room.

'I made toast but I wasn't sure what you liked to put on it, so I brought in, well, everything,' Esme said, staggering slightly as she bent down to put the tray on the coffee table. 'Peanut butter, jam, Marmite, honey.'

'This is great. You didn't need to go to so much trouble,' Theo said, leaning forward to take his mug of tea.

'It was putting some bread in the toaster. Well within my limited culinary expertise.'

Usually Esme would fling herself at her sofa after a long day and marvel that the springs hadn't collapsed, but now she settled herself decorously in her blue velvet bucket chair that her mother Debbie had found in a skip and had stripped and re-upholstered for Esme's thirtieth birthday.

It was maybe the nicest thing, apart from giving birth to her, that Debbie had ever done for Esme. And one of the worst things was the so-called mustard feature wall that she'd painted without permission when Esme had let Debbie stay in the flat while she was on holiday. Esme now turned her face away from it so she could look at Theo.

He wasn't man-spreading like he owned the place (one of Esme's pet peeves) but he wasn't perched right on the edge of the sofa, like he was apologising for his presence, either. In fact, as he took an appreciative sip of his tea, he looked both comfortable in his own skin and as if there was nowhere else that he'd rather be. Though maybe that wasn't too far from the truth.

'I'm not kicking you out but any luck with the Travelodge?'

'Apparently they're completely booked out with a large family come over from Ireland for a funeral.'

'Cheery.'

'But I'm trawling through local Airbnb listings and if worst comes to worst I can sleep in the office at work,' he assured her. 'I'll be out of your hair soon, don't worry.'

'I'm not worried,' Esme said, which was surprising because there was a man in her flat. She couldn't remember when this rare event had last occurred. 'Take as long as you need. Though talking of hair, I really need to wash mine.'

'Go ahead, don't mind me. I promise I won't steal the family silver.'

They both looked at her MacBook, which was hanging out at the other end of the sofa.

'Though you should totally put that away if you want, I won't be offended,' Theo continued, because he was the most considerate of house guests.

Esme wanted nothing more than to snatch up her Mac-Book. No, that wasn't true. She wanted to wash her hair more than anything else in the world.

'I think I trust you. Though generally I'm not a very trusting person,' she admitted.

'Those limiting beliefs again?'

'Yup, they get me every time.' Esme stood up and for a second felt so dizzy that she almost sat down again. Then the world righted itself and she had an urgent appointment with her shower and a bottle of baby shampoo. 'Look, I have to get this blood out of my hair. It's really grossing me out. Can you entertain yourself for five minutes?'

'I have tea, toast, various garnishes and a phone that's now on twenty-seven per cent battery, I'll be fine,' he said, with another of those smiles that even the dressing over his eye couldn't diminish.

Esme was hardly going to strip off and climb into the bath, though getting out of her grungy, bloodstained jumpsuit was another urgent thing on her to-do list. She read the care sheet she'd been given at the hospital: *Wash your hair with mild shampoo as soon as possible after treatment and then not again until after the stitches have been removed. Dry your hair gently and don't comb over that area.*

A whole week without washing her hair? A cruel and unusual punishment. Esme was determined to make this hair wash count.

She unhooked the shower attachment from above the bath and turned it on, waiting until the water was hot enough, then leaned over the edge of the tub. She couldn't wait . . . but oh! That dizzy, churny, sicky feeling was back and it only went away when Esme straightened up.

Maybe if she only tilted her head down slightly? But then she was getting water everywhere and it still made her feel as if she might pass out like a highly strung Victorian lady who suffered from nerves.

Having only managed to damp the ends of her hair, Esme turned off the shower and sat down on the rim of the bath to regroup. She could put the shower head back on its hook, strip off and wash both her hair and herself, but no matter how much Theo didn't set off her finely tuned Creep Alert, she didn't want to get naked with a stranger, a strange man, on the premises and no lock on the bathroom door.

She'd just have to kick him out. Something that Esme had never had a problem with when past gentlemen callers had outstayed their welcome. Sometimes she didn't even wait for the afterglow to be over and done with.

She took a deep breath then took the five steps which meant she was hovering in the living room doorway, where she was witness to Theo demolishing a piece of toast and peanut butter in four decisive bites.

He'd taken off his coat and was just wearing a black T-shirt so that Esme could clearly see the tattoos that curled around his arms, up to his neck, and even on his hands. Which was strange because last night she hadn't noticed his tattoos. He'd had his coat on but there had been an awful lot of handholding. Still, she'd had plenty of other things to worry about.

Theo glanced up to see Esme standing there. 'You decided not to wash your hair?'

This has been OK. You haven't managed to actively offend me and you seem kind and I like the way your face looks. However, I need you to go now but I'm not opposed to swapping details and meeting up at some later date when my head and your eye have healed.

'Every time I bend my head, I feel like I'm going to pass out or puke. Maybe both,' were the actual words coming out of Esme's mouth.

Theo stood up immediately, his expression soft and concerned. 'You should have said that you weren't feeling well.'

'I do feel well.'

'Really?' His expression might have been soft and concerned but the tone of his voice was dry and sceptical.

'Yes, I have a wound in the back of my head but it's still numb from the anaesthetic, it's just bending over that's the problem.' Esme was still holding the bottle of baby shampoo like she couldn't bear to let it go. 'If I don't wash my hair soon, I'm going to cry.'

She blinked rapidly because the threat of tears wasn't hyperbole but the God's honest truth.

'That bad?' Theo asked. He was close enough now that he could brush away Esme's tears before they'd even start falling, but he didn't.

There was a brief bottleneck in the doorway then Esme stepped back, but she could still feel the heat, the *leanness* of Theo as he squeezed past her to peer into the bathroom.

'Have you got a chair? A normal hardback chair?' he asked.

Esme didn't but she did have a fancy pink velvet one with a shell back from Oliver Bonas. It looked pretty, although it wasn't ergonomically practical as a work chair, which was why Esme's spine hated her.

It was a tight fit to get the chair in the bathroom in the narrow sliver of space between the bath and the wall.

'Just sit on the chair and tip your head back and see if that makes you feel dizzy,' Theo suggested from where he was sitting on the edge of the bath.

Esme wanted to point out that this was a ridiculous idea and that the chair wasn't the right height but when she sat down on it, and very carefully lowered her head, she could feel the edge of the sink against her neck. And she didn't feel as if she was going to pass out, which was an added bonus.

'But how am I going to wash my hair like this?'

'I thought I could wash it for you.' Esme lifted her head in time to see the realisation hit Theo full in the face. 'Is that weird? It feels weird, doesn't it?'

'It really does.' Esme folded her arms and wondered what kind of . . .

'I'm not some kind of pervert who gets his rocks off touching women's hair.'

It was as if Theo had plucked the words right out of Esme's brain.

'Which is just what someone with a hair-washing fetish would say.'

Theo nodded. 'I get that. But also, my mum has her own hairdressing salon. I've been washing hair since I was knee high to a backwash.'

'Your mum. . .' If he had a mother, and a good relationship with that mother, then maybe he wasn't so bad.

84

'Yeah, Sandra. And a dad too. Keith. He was a chef and I decided to follow in his footsteps, but I do still know how to wash hair and, if you're lucky, I'll throw in a head massage,' Theo said winningly.

'You seem really over-invested in washing my hair,' Esme said suspiciously, even though she was also over-invested in washing her hair.

'It's because I want to trade services . . . No! Nothing like that,' Theo said quickly as Esme's eyebrows shot up. 'I just need you to put in my eye drops. There's no way I can do it myself.' He flinched as if a phantom was coming at him with a laden pipette. 'A favour for a favour. Although what with the Uber and the tea and the toast and the phone charging, I think I'm going to have to shout you a free meal at The Harvey.'

'The Harvey? Is that your pub?' Esme asked.

'Yeah. The Harvey Arms. It's in Clerkenwell.'

Esme could already see it in her head. Because she'd imagined a man who looked a lot like Theo and had a creative adjacent job as maybe the landlord of a restored old pub. What a coincidence. Almost as if there was something in this manifesting malarkey.

But even Esme's febrile imagination couldn't have imagined the scene which unfolded five minutes later.

Esme had been more concerned about deploying towels so that she didn't get water down the back of her neck or, more importantly, on her pink velvet chair. And showing Theo exactly where her stitches were so he'd know to go carefully.

But then Theo had squeezed himself into the tiny gap between the chair and the wall, which meant he had to lean right over Esme first to reach for the shower hose, then to turn the bath taps on.

'How's the temperature?' Theo asked as he began to rinse the blood out of Esme's hair with a gentle stream of water that was perfect; hot but not too hot.

'It's good,' she assured him as he leaned over her again, the soft cotton of his T-shirt brushing her face. Considering where he'd spent the night, he smelled amazing. Woody, spicy, with wisps of tobacco and leather like really posh, really expensive aftershave. In fact, aftershave that was so posh and expensive, it was rebranded as cologne.

'OK, then. Let's get you properly wet,' he murmured, separating out strands of Esme's hair so he didn't miss any.

How Esme wished that she'd had her half head of Christmas highlights redone and that Theo was working with hair that didn't have a good four centimetres of dark roots.

Not that he seemed to mind. He was very intent on the job at hand. Usually the scent of Johnson's baby shampoo transported Esme back in time to her childhood and the Sunday evening bath. She'd wear a huge foam sunflower on her head to keep the shampoo out of her eyes as Debbie attacked her scalp with great vigour then briskly towelled her off. Her mother had never been blessed with a gentle touch. Unlike Theo.

'I think you're wet enough,' he said in that dark, treacly voice, and Esme was going to be adding this to her wank bank savings account and withdrawing it multiple times.

Then he poured a small amount of shampoo onto the top of her head and Esme could have cried tears of sheer gratitude as he started to work it into her scalp, making sure to avoid the problematic area at the base of her skull.

His touch was gentle but firm and it was all Esme could do not to moan rapturously. As it was she let out a little sigh of bliss.

'I'm going to rinse you off now.' Even his voice couldn't break the spell because his voice was one of the magic ingredients that had Esme in its thrall. Her little bathroom was now steamy from having the shower on and Theo was so close that if Esme turned her head she was confronted with his . . . his . . .

His pelvis.

His groin.

His loins.

His crotch.

Every word that she thought of for the *cradle of his hips* sounded as if it was imported straight from a smutty historical romance. Ordinarily, Esme got the ick from the word crotch, but not now when she could, oh my goodness, lean left and forward and she'd be mouthing his *cock* through his jeans.

No!

This was entirely down to sleep deprivation and painkillers and two lots of local anaesthetic. And nothing to do with the very good-looking, seemingly kind man whom she hadn't even known for twenty-four hours who was now washing her hair and making it feel like foreplay.

'Do you want conditioner?' Theo asked, entirely unaware that Esme was trapped in an erotic web and couldn't even flail a feeble limb to try and escape.

'Yeah,' she croaked.

'And I'll throw in that head massage I promised you.'

Esme didn't tell Theo that she only wanted conditioner on her ends. If she'd done that then he might not have felt the need to do what he was doing now, which was caressing various pressure points in her skull with a deft, uncompromising touch.

'Is this OK? It's not too hard?'

Esme rolled her eyes at Theo's crotch. 'No. It's good.' She hardly recognised her voice, which was both breathy and breathless. 'Um, you could go a bit harder if you want.'

He made a sound at the back of his throat, which to Esme's inflamed senses seemed very sexy. 'I can definitely go harder. Is that hard enough?'

'It's perfect.'

She shut her eyes, half in ecstasy, half so she didn't keep glancing at his *flanks*.

It was a salient reminder that, no matter how good and how vivid Esme's fantasies were, they couldn't compete with the real thing.

'OK, I think you're all done now,' Theo said, and Esme was snapped back to reality as a trickle of water squirmed its way down her back and Theo gently tucked a towel around her head. 'Does that feel better?'

'You have no idea.' He manoeuvred himself out from between the wall and the chair so that Esme was no longer tormented by the promise of his pelvis.

She raised her arms above her head and stretched. The painkillers and the numbing effects of the anaesthetic were starting to wear off and she was aware of all sorts of twinges and aches.

Theo was sitting on the edge of the tub again. He ran his fingers through his hair, silver rings glinting in the light.

'I should probably get going,' he said, the words ending in a yawn.

The thought of him going sent something piercing through Esme. Something that felt like regret.

'I haven't done your eye drops,' she reminded him. 'And how about some more tea?'

He nodded. 'Tea sounds good but then I really must get out of your newly washed hair.'

Esme stood up on wobbly legs. 'You go and make yourself comfortable in the living room. I'll just be a moment.'

As she moved past him he caught her arm, his fingers causing brushfires against her skin. 'Thanks for this,' he said, holding Esme's gaze with his one good eye. 'I really appreciate it. I'll leave you to it.'

Then he was gone.

Stripping off and having a shower still didn't feel appropriate. But Esme cleaned her teeth, which felt almost as good as the hair wash, then headed for her bedroom.

There were several piles of clothes on the bed courtesy of the clothes panic of last night. Not that Esme was planning to go to bed just yet, no matter how tempting it looked even with a mound of going-out tops and another heap of dresses obscuring the brushed cotton green tartan bedding.

She wanted to break free from her jumpsuit but settled for toeing off her trainers. Then Esme sat down on the bed because even that small exertion was making her feel dizzy. There was no harm in just lying back for a minute and being grateful to past Esme for changing the bedding on Friday and even spritzing with the lavender pillow spray, which was meant to facilitate a good night's sleep, but didn't really. It smelled nice though.

It took every ounce of willpower not to burrow under the duvet. It was still daylight outside, she hadn't closed the curtains, but the shadows were lengthening and dusk was creeping in.

Esme didn't fall asleep as soon as her head very carefully hit the pillow, but certainly seventy-three seconds after she carefully placed her head on the pillow, she was fast asleep.

It was a solid sleep. No dreams. No fitfulness. No tossing. No turning. No thumping the pillow. Just sleep.

Outside the night took over and all was silent, apart from the occasional wail of a siren and George in the flat directly below Esme watching *Antiques Roadshow* with the volume turned all the way up to eleven because he refused to accept that he was deaf as a post. 'I'm not deaf,' he'd say indignantly whenever Esme brought up the subject of his too-loud telly and if he could maybe try turning on the subtitles. 'It's just that people mumble. If they properly enunciated their words, then I'd be able to hear perfectly.'

That evening, Esme slept through *Antiques Roadshow*. She slept through Marion and Jacinta, on the ground floor, leaving their flat at 10 p.m. sharp to give their wheezy pug Buster his last walk. They always slammed the front door hard enough to be heard all the way up the stairs. Esme slept through Marion and Jacinta returning fifteen minutes later and slamming the door again.

Then she was suddenly jerked out of sleep. She could have sworn she heard someone moving around the flat. She listened out, wondered if it might be a serial killer and if she could actually be bothered to get out of bed and confront him. (Serial killers were usually men, weren't they?) She decided she couldn't be bothered and all it took was one yawn and rolling over on to her other side before she was asleep again.

9

Monday

The next time Esme woke up, it was morning.

It was a brand new day. Her mouth didn't hurt and, when Esme gingerly investigated with her tongue, she could feel the tender softness of new tissue where her wisdom tooth had once been.

Her head still hurt. But now it had downgraded to a dull throb, if she didn't make any sudden movements, which was sure to become more manageable when she took some tablets. Still, Esme made no move to get out of bed. She was quite content to lie there and take an inventory.

Mouth. Head. Shoulder still a bit achey.

Brain still there. Esme could remember all her times tables right up to the twelves and no one could be expected to know any more numbers after twelve times twelve equals one hundred and forty-four. She knew the fate of each of Henry VIII's six wives: Divorced. Beheaded. Died. Divorced. Beheaded. Survived. Most important of all, she still knew all the words to Baccara's 'Yes Sir, I Can Boogie', her song of choice at karaoke. It always brought the house down.

In short, Esme felt like herself. She *was* herself. A herself that was quite cross that she'd gone to bed with wet hair because, when she looked in the bathroom mirror, it was sticking up in fifty different directions.

She pulled on a shower cap because, although she'd been allowed to wash her hair yesterday, her wound management information sheet was quite specific (it involved capitals and underlining) that she wasn't allowed to get her head wet again until after the stitches were removed. God, there was going to be a lot of Batiste in her immediate future.

Having a shower felt like a religious experience. Then, after a quick recce of all the bruises on her body, Esme cleaned her teeth, cleansed her face and moisturised, all while still marvelling at how much she felt like herself again.

There was absolutely nothing wrong with her. Everything was good in her world, Esme thought as she walked into the living room in just a towel. She was alive and it was glorious and . . .

NO.

NO.

NO.

How could she have forgotten about him?

The handholding at the hospital. Sharing an Uber. The sexually charged hair washing.

And now, Theo was asleep on the sofa. Like some kind of creepy stalker, because she definitely hadn't told him he could stay. But there he was looking cosy and comfortable under the Welsh blanket that she'd painstakingly knitted during the first lockdown, with a lot of help from Jacinta.

Esme yanked the two ends of her towel tighter together, and stood over the still slumbering *squatter* on her couch, hands on her hips, fight on her face.

He didn't stir and Esme couldn't force any words out of her mouth. So she headed back to the kitchen again, then almost back to the living room and so on until she wondered if she was destined to spend the rest of her days hurrying back and forth along the hall while muttering under her breath.

'What is this? What is going on?' Esme whispered urgently. 'What is his deal? Is this some kind of cuckooing scam? Does he fake injury so he can befriend vulnerable women outside hospitals and inveigle his way into their homes? Oh my God, he could have murdered me while I was sleeping! I'm calling the police!'

Esme even went as far as getting her phone, which was buried at the bottom of her handbag and practically on zero charge. She was momentarily waylaid by the sheer number of notifications of missed calls, voice notes and messages obscuring the photo of her friend Grace's two whippets, Gilbert and George, on her lock screen.

Kemi Odu
OMG! You can't post a pic like that on IG then go no contact.

Lyndsey Shepherd
Call me. Seen your IG. Seriously freaking out over here.

Seren Dipity
Not to make this all about me, but really hope that bruising goes down before Saturday. Sending healing vibes xxx

Esme started charging up her phone and clicked on the first Instagram notification, which led Esme to her last post, a post which she didn't even remember making. It was a selfie taken from her hospital bed, the Clarendon filter completely unable to cope with Esme's blood-splattered mask, blood-soaked hair and sunken, bruised eyes.

> If you think I look bad, then you should see the other guy.
> #wokeuplikethis

No wonder her phone was blowing up.

> Re: Instagram pic. Sorry to cause panic. I'm fine. Really fine. Looks worse than it is.

Esme hated to be *that* person, she really did, but she sent the message to everyone in her contacts.

Then she tried to remember what she'd been going to do before she'd been distracted. Oh yes, she was going to call the police to report . . . what exactly?

That she'd befriended a man and willingly invited him into her home. Had tea and toasted him. And, now Esme was remembering, she'd never asked him to leave.

Gingerly, as if the floor really was lava, Esme tiptoed out of the kitchen yet again and back into the living room. Her heart was beating so loudly and so fiercely that she wouldn't have been surprised if it had burst from her chest and made a break for freedom.

He was *still* there. Snoring very gently. A long, lean lump under her Welsh blanket.

Esme approached the sofa with extreme caution; she had to remind herself not to hold her breath. She dropped to her knees so she could get a really good look at him. She held her hand up in front of his mouth and, as warm breath hit her palm, she could confirm that, yes, he was breathing. Which wasn't that helpful.

Esme inched further forward. Her eyes were growing accustomed to the shadows now and she could see the obstinate lock of hair falling into his face, the straight fuzzy lines of his eyebrows, his full mouth relaxed.

She didn't know how long she stayed like that, kneeling on the floor, eyes locked on the hard lines of his face, as she listened to the easy in and out of his breathing. It was quite soothing actually.

Then he opened his eyes. 'What the *fuck*?'

Neither of them did anything for a second, then another second, Esme still practically nose to nose with him. She thought she might be experiencing some kind of paralysis. But then he gave a start. Shouted, 'What the fuck?' again as he threw off the blanket so that Esme screamed and reared back in alarm, falling on her arse and flashing everything. 'What are you doing?'

Esme clamped her legs together. 'What are *you* doing?'

He stood up, all the better to tower over her, in faded black T-shirt and dark jeans, all of him wiry and spare.

'What are you doing here?' she asked again, and Theo seemed to shrink in on himself.

'Oh, shit! I'm so sorry,' he said, cringing away from her. 'I was waiting for you to come back and do my eye drops. Then I realised you'd fallen asleep and I didn't want to go into your bedroom . . . or wake you up. I was going to leave, I really was, but I think you must have locked your front door and then I must have . . . I was so tired.' He frowned so hard that his eyebrows almost met in the middle. 'I only meant to shut my eyes for a second. What must you think of me?'

Esme had thought a lot of uncharitable things about Theo since she discovered him asleep on her sofa but common sense was finally prevailing. Also he looked grey and tired and she was pretty sure that, if she really had to, she could have him in a fight. 'I fell asleep unexpectedly too,' she said slowly. 'And I do lock my front door, force of habit, because one time someone got in downstairs by pretending to be a Deliveroo driver and tried to break into several flats. Are you pissed off with me?'

'Of course not,' Theo said immediately, like nothing could be further from the truth. 'Though, as a friend . . . are we friends, would you say?'

'I think so. If the last twenty-four hours or so hasn't bonded us then nothing will,' Esme decided. But then she flash-backed to the hair washing of the night before, which had been more erotic than friendly. Or maybe that was just the fevered spin she'd put on it. 'Anyway, what were you going to say, as a friend?'

'It's nothing personal, but your sofa really isn't designed to be slept on.' Theo put a hand to the small of his back and Esme could almost hear the click of his aching bones. His eye patch was still attached but his other eye seemed shadowed, though that might have been because the curtains were still shut as they had been when Esme had gone out on that fateful Saturday night.

She took a step to open them then realised, with horror and a blush that seemed to start at the top of her head and travel swiftly all the way to her toes, that she was still wearing nothing but a towel.

'I need to get changed,' she announced, averting her eyes from Theo in the vain hope that if she couldn't see him, then he couldn't see her. 'You're welcome to have a shower or a bath. I feel much better since I've had a shower and cleaned my teeth.'

At that, Theo held his hand over his mouth. Esme had forgotten about the shit tattoos over most of his visible bits of skin. At least he'd managed not to ruin his face with ink. 'Morning mouth,' he mumbled through his fingers. 'Would love a shower.'

'I'll get you some towels.' Esme was already hurrying out of the room. She retrieved a couple of towels from the little airing cupboard between the bathroom and the kitchen then collided with Theo, who'd just come out of the living room. 'Here you are.' She shoved the towels at him. 'Shower's pretty simple to use but it does run cold for about a minute.'

'I really appreciate this,' Theo said, so close that his breath, which didn't smell at all morning-y, ghosted against her forehead. 'Again, so sorry for crashing last night.'

'It's fine,' Esme said, because weirdly, it was fine. His explanation was plausible. No liberties had been taken. His presence, even this morning, wasn't irritating her to the very edge of her nerves. His presence with her just in a towel was having a very different effect on her. 'Shower. You shower. I dress.'

She felt relieved to be back in the sanctuary of her bedroom again. The walls painted navy blue, the woodwork a soft, cheery pink, so that the space was restful but also a little fun, as all bedrooms should be. Though as Monday morning had rolled around again, it was also her office; a little desk pushed up against the window with her MacBook on it, her pink velvet chair none the worse for its bathroom adventure.

Esme sat down on the bed and started folding the going-out tops. She couldn't work in such a messy environment and, also, she wanted to make sure that Theo had finished in the bathroom before she ventured out again.

After she put her clothes away, she tidied up her bedside table. Straightened the tubes of hand cream and lip balm, the bottle of ruinously expensive facial oil that made Esme look fairly perky each morning, a tiny phial of CBD oil and her lavender-scented pillow spray. She flicked through the pages of the new Marian Keyes novel, a takeaway flyer wedged in it in lieu of a proper bookmark, as she listened out for Theo.

Esme heard the shower come on, a pause as she imagined him taking his clothes off, but no she shouldn't be imagining stuff like that. She didn't want Theo imagining her like that either, though the thought of it made her toes curl in the thick plush nap of the midnight blue rug by her bed.

Esme always worked from home on Mondays, which meant wearing an old T-shirt and an even older pair of what she called yoga pants, though she wore them even when she hadn't downward dogged in months. She usually accessorised this on-trend ensemble with an ancient baggy cardigan, thermal socks, fleece-lined Birkenstocks and no bra. It was a look that screamed, 'I haven't had sex since before the beginning of the pandemic and you know what? I don't even care!'

Now, Esme felt that she should make more of an effort. At the very least, she should wear a bra and maybe choose a T-shirt that didn't have 'Menstruate With Pride' printed across her chest (a promotional item from one of her copy-writing clients). She didn't want to repulse Theo. But then again, she didn't want to attract him either. Or maybe she did. God, she was off her dating game. Mo, whom she dimly recalled binning off on Saturday night, had never got her even a fraction as flustered as she was now.

As Esme struggled into her bra under her towel – terrified that Theo might burst in unannounced – it began to rain. Not a persistent drizzle but hard, driving rain that hit the windows horizontally. The world outside was just a grey and green blur. She was glad that she was working from home today, though even if she was meant to have been in the office, she'd have begged off.

Which reminded her that she really needed to take her antibiotics, and some more paracetamol couldn't hurt.

She emerged from her bedroom just in time to hear the shower shut off. It was Esme's cue to hurry to the kitchen. She resolutely stared out of the window, her back to the door, until she heard Theo leave the bathroom, pause for one second in the hall, then return to the living room and shut the door.

Esme let out a breath. She felt as nervous as if it were a real morning after. When she'd slept with someone for the first time and wasn't sure if they were going to make some lame excuses and leave, never to be seen again. Or worse, in the cold light of day she was the one racked with buyer's remorse and just wanted them gone as quickly as possible. It was very rare that there was a mutually appreciative outcome.

Her hands were actually shaking as she poured a glass of water then squeezed her antibiotics out of their blister pack. After she'd taken them, Esme busied herself by filling up the kettle, then opening the fridge and staring blankly at the contents, until she heard the living room door open and straightened up.

'Do you feel better for having a shower?' she asked.

'At least seventy-five per cent better.'

Theo looked different now he was awake, alert, his features no longer creased by sleep and confusion. He'd removed the dressing from his left eye, so Esme was seeing his whole face for the first time. It was quite a hard face, like life hadn't been kind to him, but his mouth was soft and his eyes were still dark and heavy-lidded, as though he was having all sorts of wrong thoughts. He was now wearing another thin black T-shirt with a looser neck so she could see a murmuration of starlings darting across his collarbone and neck then disappearing into his T-shirt.

He was *just* her type. Disturbingly like the man she'd spent years fantasising about. The actual reality of a man who looked as handsome and as sexy as she'd always imagined him was absolutely devastating.

In any other circumstances, though in what other circumstances would her fantasy boyfriend be flesh and blood Esme didn't know, they'd be kissing by now. Really going for it.

'How do you feel? You look quite flushed,' Theo said, taking one small step into the kitchen. 'I hope your wound isn't infected.'

That should have poured cold water over any X-rated thoughts that Esme might be having, and was also a salient reminder of her formerly gaping head wound, but he was closer now. She could smell the minty fresh toothpaste, the clean laundry smell of his new T-shirt and that heady scent of woodsmoke and spice.

'I've just taken my antibiotics.' Esme looked closer at the newly revealed quarter of Theo's face that had been hidden from her. Now she noticed the jagged line that marred the harsh beauty of his face. 'I thought that would look worse than it does,' she said. 'Your ocular area. Does it hurt?'

'It wouldn't be very brave and manly if I said that it did.' Theo's left eye might be under medical supervision, but he could still quirk his right eyebrow upwards. Because *of course* every boyfriend in Esme's imaginary canon could raise one eyebrow in a smirky, sultry way, so it stood to reason that this non-imaginary man, who was ticking every single one of her many boxes, could too. 'The cut doesn't hurt anymore and

I heal quickly. But my eye, I still want to rub it. It's all I can think about.'

'Once again, I'm so sorry for falling asleep like that. Shall we do something about your antibiotic drops?' Esme asked. 'And you should probably take some paracetamol. Might help with the pain.'

Theo opened one hand to reveal a small plastic bottle. 'Where do you want me?'

Even talking about their respective wounds couldn't kill the flirty atmosphere that seemed to sizzle between them. It wasn't helped when Esme, after washing her hands, directed Theo back to the living room so he could sit in an armchair and she could stand over him and stare deep into his eyes, even if one of them was incredibly bloodshot.

Then she switched on her reading light and Theo blinked rapidly. 'I feel like you're about to interrogate me to within an inch of my life.'

'I should probably be snapping on a pair of leather gloves and strapping you down,' Esme blurted out and Theo's one working eyebrow shot up again. 'Not that I would. I have a very gentle bedside manner.'

God, everything that came out of her mouth sounded like a come-on.

'I'll take your word for it.' Theo sounded huskier than he usually did, and Esme was startlingly aware of him as she squinted at the tiny instructions on the tiny, tiny bottle.

'Right,' she said, a little unsteadily because she was leaning right over him, could feel the heat of him even through her thick layers. 'I'm going to need you to tilt your head back. Shall we do a count of three?'

'Have I mentioned that I'm really squeamish about any-thing to do with the eyes?'

'You might have done once or twice.' His hair was damp from the shower but that obstinate cowlick was falling in his face so Esme had no choice but to smooth it back so it didn't get in the way.

Every time she approached with the phial Theo blinked, so in the end Esme had to use force. 'Count of three, remember? One, two . . .' She didn't wait for three but squeezed a couple of generous drops onto his eye and held tight when he tried to wriggle free of her hands, one of which was keeping his eye open, the other still in his hair.

'Oh! You didn't wait for three,' he complained. 'I expected better from you.'

'A foolish mistake,' Esme murmured. And then, because she didn't really have a gentle bedside manner at all, 'Stop being such a big baby.'

Even with one eye watering, Theo managed to look affronted.

'You're like the Nurse Ratched of North London.'

Esme had been called worse. A lot worse. And even when he was insinuating that Esme reminded him of the sadistic nurse from the lunatic asylum in *One Flew Over the Cuckoo's Nest,* it still seemed as if Theo were flirting with her.

So she stayed where she was, warmed by the BTUs coming off him as the rain beat hard against the windows and sounded as if some weather god was throwing handfuls of dried peas onto the roof. Esme peered down at Theo, ostensibly to check that the drops were evenly distributed but mostly because she liked being this close to him.

Esme hardly recognised herself. Seren would be cheering at how open and vulnerable she was. More likely it was because she'd recently suffered a vicious blow to the head and wasn't firing on all her usual cylinders.

But it was as if Theo liked being near her too, because when she did try to take a step back, he curled his fingers loosely around her wrist. He was always warm where Esme tended to be cold.

He looked up at her and Esme couldn't hear the rain anymore, just the slightly giddy rhythm of her breathing.

'Do you feel . . . ?'

Whatever Theo was about to ask her, and Esme was in a torment to know, was drowned out by the sudden and deafening rumble of her belly.

She wrenched away from him. 'Oh my God!'

Theo grinned. 'Was that thunder?'

'Shut up!'

'It was you?'

'Which part of shut up is giving you problems?' Esme put her cold hands on her burning face and backed away from Theo as, still grinning, he stood up.

'When was the last time you ate?' He gestured at the tray and plate on the coffee table. 'Did you have any toast last night?'

'Fell asleep, didn't I? I think I had a piece of bread while I waited for the kettle to boil. I didn't even have any tea!' Esme remembered with dismay. She couldn't even think of the last time she'd gone so long without a mug of Yorkshire Tea. Her stomach rumbled again to remind her that tea could possibly wait, food couldn't.

'Let me make you breakfast,' Theo suggested. 'It's the least I can do.'

If he was making breakfast, then Theo wasn't about to disappear into the rain-soaked ether.

'I don't have much in,' Esme warned him. 'I was going to do a big shop yesterday . . .'

'I'm sure I can rustle up a little brekkie. You'll feel even better once you've had something proper to eat,' Theo said confidently, because he hadn't seen the sorry contents of her fridge.

Esme couldn't think of the last time that someone had cooked for her.

Had taken care of her.

Or that she'd let someone take care of her.

It was years and years.

Not since Alex, and she'd learned her lesson there, but she still let Theo steer her out of the living room and into the kitchen as if he were ushering her to the best seat in the Ritz.

10

The first thing Theo did was wash his hands, so Esme didn't have a chance to worry about poor hygiene practices. He was at the sink, his back to her as Esme opened the fridge so she could retrieve bread and butter. She could have a quick slice while she waited for Theo to perform Jesus-like miracles with her scant supplies. She couldn't keep downing tablets on an empty stomach, even though they had little effect on the persistent, permanent headache she'd now had for thirty-six hours and counting.

'How hungry are you?' asked Theo from behind Esme. 'It's nearly ten now.'

'I suppose I am, actually, kind of starving,' Esme said, as she was gently shoved out of the way so Theo could take an inventory of the fridge.

'There's some elderly mushrooms and spinach that I can work with. And enough cheese to sink a battleship. Which would be a waste of good cheese.' He squatted. 'You keep your bread and eggs in the fridge? Were you raised by wolves?'

'There's only one of me,' Esme protested. 'If I didn't keep my bread in the fridge, then it would go mouldy and stale too quickly. Also, yes, I was raised by wolves or Gary and Debbie as I called them because, as they were always reminding me, they were people in their own right and their identities weren't wrapped up in being parents.'

'My mum would have given me a clip round the ear if I'd called her Sandra,' Theo said as he straightened up. 'I'll make us an omelette and resurrect this sourdough loaf so it's fit to be eaten.'

The sourdough loaf bought last Thursday was now rock solid. Though she hated food waste, Esme would probably have chucked it, but Theo ran it under the tap. 'Can I help with anything?' she asked.

Theo shook his head. 'My turn to wait on you. But you could tell me more about Gary and Debbie, if you like. Did you grow up around here?'

'Pretty much. I've lived in North London all my life,' Esme explained.

By the time Esme was ten, she'd lost count of the times they'd moved.

Never venturing out of a very parochial five-mile section of North London, Gary and Debbie would buy a rundown house, move the family in no matter how rudimentary the facilities were (and Esme counted herself lucky if there was a working loo) and do it up. Then, just as Esme was getting used to having all sorts of luxuries like hot and cold running water and non-rotting floorboards, the house would be sold at a good profit and on to the next dump.

People always said that moving house was one of the most stressful things in life after death and divorce, so that might be one of the reasons why Debbie and Gary spent most of their time sniping, shouting and screaming at each other, then having noisy make-up sex.

It was a relief when they finally decided to part ways when Esme was sixteen. Both of them intended to leave the country. Allegra had long moved out by then to her own flat, the deposit paid by the small inheritance from their maternal grandmother. Desperate to be rid of each other and their youngest daughter, Debbie and Gary browbeat Allegra into evicting her flatmate so they could move Esme in and pay her rent until she was eighteen.

'Then you're on your own,' Debbie had said. 'Old enough to stand on your own two feet.'

'I left home at fifteen and it was the making of me,' Gary had added, because this was the one topic they could agree on.

Allegra had grudgingly, resentfully, done as they asked, though she'd been so furious that she'd barely spoken to Esme for weeks. Esme had vowed then that she was going to be independent. Fiercely and gloriously independent.

Even so she'd once said to Debbie, granted before Esme's own divorce and all the horrors that had entailed, 'Could you two not have stuck things out until I was eighteen?'

'No,' Debbie had said immediately. 'I'd either have killed myself or him.'

'So, not the most ringing endorsement for marriage,' Esme said, casting a look at Theo, who was doing things with her sad collection of fridge items and rudimentary cooking utensils that defied belief. 'Probably why I was divorced myself by the time I was twenty-five.'

'You must have got married young,' Theo said, in a tone of voice that didn't indicate how he felt about Esme having been married and divorced.

This was unfamiliar territory for Esme. She rarely divulged her tragic marital history to new people in her life.

Yes, she might sleep with someone on a third date, sometimes even the *first* date, but Esme had to be months into something with a man before she admitted that one of her past relationships was actually a short-lived marriage that had ended in a very acrimonious divorce.

'I wasn't a child bride, but I was a twenty-three-year-old bride who thought she knew everything when really I didn't know my arse from my elbow,' she said. Why was it so easy to talk to Theo? Maybe it was because his attention was on what he was doing; chopping a handful of spinach with Esme's one sharp kitchen knife like he was on *Masterchef*. But then he'd look over his shoulder and smile empathetically, encouragingly.

'Being a dickhead at twenty-three is understandable. Being a dickhead at thirty-three is unforgivable,' he said.

'I'm thirty-three,' Esme pointed out, hackles on the rise.

'And you're absolutely not a dickhead, whereas six years ago, when I was thirty-three, I was working in a two-star Michelin restaurant and my salary barely covered my coke habit,' he said easily, but he'd stopped chopping spinach to look at Esme intently.

She didn't mind a man with a bit of history. And the coke habit explained the bad tattoos.

'I think all the best people have some demons in their past,' Esme said calmly.

'Hard agree. By the way, I'm making the omelettes French style and not American,' he added, like Esme even knew the difference.

'I much prefer French style anyway.' The least she could do while Theo slaved over a hot stove was sort out plates and cutlery. She was just taking slices of the resuscitated sourdough out of the toaster when Theo turned from the stove with the frying pan in his hand.

'Perfect timing.'

It was perfect, except for one thing that Esme should have mentioned earlier. 'Not to be difficult or anything but I can't abide a wet egg,' she confessed.

'That won't be a problem.' Theo arranged the folded omelette on her plate with a flourish. 'No wet egg on my watch.'

The omelette was just the right side of not runny and immediately in the top five favourite things that Esme had ever put in her mouth.

She was so hungry that it was hard to take lady-like bites rather than inhaling omelette and toast. Sitting next to Theo on her sofa – her kitchen, her flat, was far too small for a table to dine on – she could hardly believe that he was real.

Theo might be a stranger, but Esme felt so comfortable with him. Well, as comfortable as she could be when she was also experiencing the throb of attraction. 'Frissoning' as she and her friend Lyndsey called the flutters you got from being with someone and hoping that it was the start of something.

Also, Esme still couldn't get over how much Theo looked like her ubiquitous dream boyfriend, except now she noticed that his nose was slightly crooked like it had been broken and reset by someone who'd never reset a broken nose before. While she may have allowed her fantasy lover a couple of tattoos, she certainly hadn't given her permission for the murmuration of starlings swooping down one side of his neck or the letters on the back of his fingers. Not 'love' and 'hate' but it was too hard to decipher the words while his hands were in motion.

Then Theo looked up from mopping the last smear of melted cheese on his plate with a piece of toast and Esme was torn between running for the safety of the bedroom because this was all too much for her aching head to deal with, or staying right where she was because she just wanted to be near him for a while longer.

Her breath caught because the way he was looking at her, the tenderness in those dark eyes, threw her. No one had looked at Esme like that in a long, long time. Maybe ever.

'Are you working from home today?' he asked.

The mention of work reminded Esme that she was pretty sure she had a Zoom meeting scheduled for some time that morning. 'I am and very glad about that,' she said, glancing at the window that was so rain lashed, it was impossible to see the world outside. 'It really is the most Mondayish of Mondays. Outside the hospital, not that I was earwigging, but didn't you mention to someone that you had Mondays off?'

'Yeah, we're closed on Mondays. I should be making a move soon.' Theo looked out of the window too and it was only because Esme was staring at him, while trying to pretend that she wasn't, that she saw the tiny shudder he gave at the prospect of stepping out into a cold, very wet Monday. 'I've got admin to do. I can do that at the pub, even if we aren't open.'

'And then what? You haven't sorted out somewhere to stay yet.'

'I'm sure I can scrounge a sofa from a mate,' Theo said, putting his empty plate on the coffee table.

The thought of him leaving wasn't a happy one. Maybe Esme had imagined the frisson between them and Theo actually couldn't wait to leave. He might go through the charade of swapping numbers but then there was a possibility that Esme would never see him again.

Or she could be vulnerable. Ugh!

Open. Yuk!

Put her feelings out into the universe. Oh no!

'I mean, you don't have to leave. You could stay here, I don't mind. I know the sofa wasn't ideal, but it does actually fold out into quite a comfortable bed.' Esme ground to a halt and turned her head so she could pull an agonised face at the wall. 'If you wanted to . . .'

Theo sighed. It was impossible to translate that exhalation of breath, especially when Esme still couldn't bring herself to look at him.

Then, shockingly, he put his hand on her knee. Esme stared down at it. At the letters S-A-L-T etched into his skin. She'd never been so conscious of her knee before. Always thinking of it as a useful hinge connecting the thigh to the shin when now it seemed to be a very knobbly erogenous zone.

'That's really . . . I need to be straight up with you, Esme,' Theo said, his hand still on her knee, so he must have felt her cringe because she knew what was coming next.

Theo seemed to be that rare thing, a genuine nice guy rather than a self-styled nice guy who turned low-key evil when you wouldn't sleep with him. He was going to let Esme down gently because it was painfully obvious that she was into him, but he didn't feel the same way and . . .

'Look, your offer is really generous, but I should probably tell you that I fancy you.'

Esme could finally turn her head to look at Theo, who was looking back at her with that tender expression again.

'You fancy me?' Scepticism dripped from every syllable.

'Well, yeah. Why wouldn't I fancy you?'

There were many, many, *many* reasons. Even her own sister claimed that it was impossible to get close to Esme. 'I have quite a lot of baggage.'

'Me too. And I really respected the way you've been so open and vulnerable about your past,' Theo said, quoting Esme's own inner dialogue back at her. 'But you're also funny, very kind and even with a gaping head wound, you look hot.'

Esme had come so far in such a short time, that surely she could go a little bit further. 'I guess . . . I suppose . . . I quite fancy you too,' she said, shrugging her shoulders, the words almost ripped out of her mouth.

Theo's hand squeezed her knee for a brief moment. 'So, if I did stay today, I wouldn't want you to feel any pressure or obligation. I don't want things to get weird when we haven't even gone on a date yet.'

'Believe me, if things get weird, you'll be the first to know,' Esme said, which sounded a lot more like her usual acerbic self.

'Glad to hear it.' Theo was laughing as he took his hand from her knee so he could stand up. 'So, you're fine with me hanging out for today?'

Esme always listened to her gut and her gut was adamant that it was A-OK with Theo. 'I work in my bedroom, so you can have the living room and if you promise not to use it to download porn, I'll even give you the Wi-Fi password.'

'I never download porn during work hours,' Theo said primly.

Even though he'd cooked, he insisted on helping Esme clear up their breakfast things and then it was time for them to go their separate ways. Esme to her bedroom, Theo to the living room, but before that . . .

He took half a step towards Esme, who was at the sink. So close that they were almost touching. Then he took another half step, which meant that they were no longer almost touching, but very much touching. His chest pressed against Esme's back, his legs brushing against hers, and other parts of him intimately fused to other parts of her. She carried on concentrating on the washing up, the poor teaspoon in her hand had never been scrubbed so hard . . .

'It wouldn't be appropriate to kiss you when we haven't even been on a date.' He leaned forward so Esme felt completely surrounded by him but not crowded, his breath tickling her ear in a way that wasn't at all unpleasant. Neither was the way he took hold of her upper arms in a firm but soft grip, tipping her forward slightly so that he could nudge her hair to one side and uncover her neck.

Then his teeth scraped ever so gently across her skin, not hard enough to leave a bruise but hard enough that Esme's insides turned to liquid and, if Theo hadn't been holding her up, she'd have sunk to the floor in a puddle of gloop formerly known as Esme Strange.

'What are you doing?' she mumbled, amazed that she was still capable of speaking when all she could think about was Theo bending her over the worktop and doing unspeakably filthy things to her.

'Just a little something to remember me by,' he said, and by the time Esme turned round, he was no longer there.

11

It was more by luck than judgment that Esme was in front of her MacBook in time for the Zoom with a client to discuss final tweaks on the copy for their latest catalogue of home aids.

'Can you make sure the copy has a little more personality, a little more pizazz,' said Didi, the founder of Granny, Don't Take a Trip, who had more than a little personality and pizazz herself, with her exquisitely straight snow-white bob and her statement earrings which swayed emphatically when she talked.

'Absolutely,' Esme said, her mind very much *not* on how to inject some sassiness into the copy for a riser recliner chair upholstered in a shocking pink, but very durable, easy-wipe velvet.

How to explain *this?*

This was hearing Theo moving around the flat. When she was with him, it all made sense. But now, she couldn't quite believe that she'd asked a comparative stranger to spend a second night in her flat, even if he was a very personable and foxy stranger.

Esme had been here before and it hadn't ended well. Maybe she really did have concussion and that was why she was acting so out of character.

'Finally, I know it's a pain, but will you double-check the product numbers from the master list?'

'Absolutely, Didi. Not a problem.' Esme made sure to keep making eye contact with Didi and nodding but her mind was still dancing fandangos all over the place. When she wasn't being confused about Theo and his easy presence in her life, or thinking about whether she should Deliveroo a curry for dinner, Esme was also having angry thoughts about Allegra. Murderously angry.

The sisters rarely called each other casually, preferring to WhatsApp, though not usually during working hours. But for all Allegra knew, Esme could have suffered a brain haemorrhage since she came home from the hospital and she hadn't even bothered to check in. God, Esme was cross just thinking about it.

As soon as the Zoom finished, Esme snatched up her phone. Allegra answered on the first ring. 'What is it? Are you all right? Don't tell me you're back at hospital. Such a fuss about a little scratch.'

'It wasn't a little scratch. You described it as a bleeding head wound,' Esme reminded her tersely.

'That was only so you'd get seen quicker.'

'Oh my God, are you actually gaslighting me over my own head wound?'

'That's not the correct use of gaslighting,' Allegra said smugly.

Esme gasped. 'And now you're gaslighting me about gaslighting.'

'I thought we only called in work hours if there was an emergency.' Allegra sucked in a breath. 'Is there an emergency?'

'Only that I'm not dead, which you'd know if you'd bothered to get in touch to find out how I was . . .'

'You could have just WhatsApped me to relay that news. Honestly, what with work and Oliver and the children, I scarcely have a minute to myself.' Allegra always pulled out the very-very-busy-with-my-fulfilling-life card even though she had a full-time nanny and a cleaner who came three times a week. 'So, how are you, apart from not being dead?' she added in a vaguely conciliatory tone.

'I'm fine. I've got a bit of a headache and my stitches kind of twinge, but my mouth doesn't hurt at all now.'

'Well, I'm pleased you're alive but I've told you many times not to call me at work, unless it's something really important.'

Esme rolled her eyes. The way she made it sound, Allegra was employed finding a cure for cancer or a solution to world hunger. Not head of PR for some boring blue chip logistics company. It was a wonder that she didn't welcome the distraction. She certainly found time to post some not-very-amusing memes to the Seren's Hen WhatsApp group during work time.

'I could have been dead though. Just saying!'

'I have to go. I'm actually rushed off my feet. Are you all right to pick up the kids on Friday or do you think you'll still be having this existential crisis?'

Esme was stung at the implication that she might shirk on her commitment to provide free childcare on Friday afternoon. Or that she might not be emotionally well enough to look after her niblings, whom she adored, despite their parentage. 'Of course I'm fine to have the kids. Why wouldn't I be?'

'You tell me,' Allegra said, but she sounded distracted, and Esme could sense that she was losing her. 'Apparently you feel *fine* but I hope you're going to snap out of this before Saturday.'

'What's happening on Saturday?' Esme asked, because she was coming up with nothing.

'It's the bloody wedding of the year, isn't it? I wish I could forget it but I can't because, unlike you with your lack of responsibilities, I've got Debbie staying and Gary's now angry that she's staying with us because he has to prise open his wallet and pay for a hotel. I hope you're going to be around to entertain them . . .'

Esme would much rather have a serious head injury which necessitated major surgery than have to entertain either, or God forbid, both of her biological parents. 'Debbie's already making noises about staying for a while and Gary has faxed me over a list of Barbara's dietary requirements to pass on to Phyllida . . .'

Their stepmother Barbara was a wholly unremarkable addition to the family. She doted on Gary and saw any other women in his life, even his two daughters, as competition for his affection, which was very rarely given anyway.

'Why the hell did he send a fax?' Esme asked. 'I mean, we *are* in the twenty-first century, right?' It didn't do any harm to check.

'He's taken against email. Says that it's just a way for Bill Gates to spy on him.'

Esme snorted. 'I'm sure that Bill Gates has more important things to do than read Gary's emails and look at the borderline racist memes he posts on Facebook.'

'You'd think, wouldn't you?'

For maybe three seconds, the two sisters were in perfect accord. 'Anyway, don't call me at work again unless it's really urgent.'

And then they weren't, and Allegra was terminating the call without even saying goodbye.

As ever, Esme felt unsettled and moody after speaking to her sister. For want of anything better to do, like the work she was getting paid for, she started sorting through the pile of papers that were an almost permanent feature on her desk. She even filed some of them in the little one-drawer filing cabinet that lived under the desk. As if she were seeing it for the first time, she noticed that two files along after 'council tax' and 'credit card' was the file marked 'divorce'. Just seeing the word was enough to make goose pimples sprout painfully along her arms even though she was wearing a long-sleeved dress and a cardigan.

She didn't even know why she was bothering to look, but Esme pulled out the file: divorce petition, the decree nisi, the decree absolute, and a bunch of correspondence from their respective solicitors.

It was just paper now. But eight years ago, it had meant a lot more. Thousands and thousands of pounds. Months of heartache and stress. Every time Esme had seen a pile of post waiting in her mail slot downstairs, or heard a ping to alert her to a new email, her stomach would instantly knot and she'd feel sick.

They'd met when Esme had interviewed Alex about his role in an unexpectedly successful British rom-com for *Feisty*, the teen mag she worked on. He had floppy blond hair, elfin features and a way of holding her gaze that made Esme blush and trip over her words. He'd spent the entire allotted forty-five minutes flirting shamelessly with her, then asked for her number. It was only much later that she found out he'd flirted shamelessly and asked for the phone number of every woman who'd interviewed him.

But Esme was the only one foolish enough to text Alex a brief, bold message that she'd spent two days agonising over. Some nonsense about how much she'd enjoyed their conversation and would love to do it again, this time without her voice recorder on.

She'd never expected (though she'd hoped, how she'd hoped!) that Alex would text her back. But he had. Asked her out for a drink. After three vodka and cranberries and a lot of deep, meaningful looks, Esme went back to Alex's room in a shared house in Balham. It was the first time that she'd slept with someone on a first date.

But then her relationship with Alex was all about firsts. By the end of that first week, he'd moved into her flat. He was the first person to ever say 'I love you' to Esme. Certainly, she'd never heard either of her parents say it, or even Allegra. No wonder then that she'd fallen hard for Alex as he relentlessly lovebombed her for those first few heady months. As an actor he needed adulation like other people needed oxygen and Esme was only too happy to oblige.

So, a whirlwind romance.

Three months after that fateful interview, they were married. Even Esme's most feckless, flakiest, flightiest friends had begged her not to but that was because they were jealous. Esme had hit all her adult milestones ridiculously young: emancipated from her parents at sixteen, a full-time job on a magazine at eighteen, buying her first flat when she was twenty-two. So marrying a handsome actor at twenty-three was simply following the same glittering and upward trajectory.

The honeymoon period was good while it lasted. Until it became clear that Alex's brief brush with fame was over and it was time for him to go back to waiting tables at Pizza Express. Esme's starry-eyed devotion couldn't make up for the rejections he got after every audition and casting call. That was when everything, especially their repent-at-leisure marriage, fell apart.

Esme loved being a staff writer on *Feisty*, but it wasn't like she was making big bucks. As it was, she'd had to take on extra freelance work to support her new two-person household. Then there was the weekend when she hadn't slept at all but, fuelled by Diet Coke and Red Bull, had written a thirty-thousand-word unofficial biography of One Direction for two thousand quid, because someone had to pay the bills. Esme had pointed that out when Alex was bitching at her for buying supermarket own brand coffee beans instead of the very expensive coffee beans from Ecuador that he preferred.

It was their first argument and it had lasted *days*. Alex had been saving up months' worth of resentments and slights for just that occasion. It was around the same time that he'd started taking his phone into another room whenever he got a call. Then came the staying out late and refusing to tell Esme where he'd been. One night he'd come back and got into bed with Esme and she could smell another woman on him; not just her overly sweet, cloying perfume but the musky scent of sex clinging to his skin, his hair. When she'd told him this, in a voice that trembled with rage and grief, Alex had just laughed.

When Esme had had her epiphany, when she realised that she didn't love Alex anymore, it had been liberating. The thought of him with other women no longer had the power to torment her, to keep her up at night waiting for the sound of his key in the lock.

'I could have really loved you if you'd been a bit more lovable,' he'd said when Esme had told him it was over one sunny Sunday afternoon, when he finally crawled home sometime after midday.

'No, we're not doing that anymore,' Esme had said, proud of the way she hadn't even flinched at Alex's words. 'We're done. We both know it and it's not like we have children. We don't even have plants, there's nothing keeping us together.'

'Sounds like a plan,' Alex had said carelessly. 'I'll go and stay with a friend.'

'I'll speak to a solicitor, sort out what paperwork we need to fill in.' Esme knew that if she left it to Alex, they'd still be married decades from now. 'We can split our stuff up later on. I mean, you can have that collection of hunting prints that your father gave us, I won't fight you for them.'

'No way am I getting stuck with them.' It seemed impossible, but they were smiling at each other, the atmosphere in the flat almost as light and bright as the sun that poured in through the windows, yet Esme couldn't remember the last time they'd had a conversation that hadn't turned into a pitched battle.

Days had passed, then weeks. There didn't seem to be any urgency and Esme wasn't even sure if they needed to fork out for a solicitor but could just fill in the forms themselves and have them signed by a notary.

Then one morning, an A4 buff-coloured envelope arrived with a divorce petition in it from Alex, requesting a dissolution of their marriage on the grounds of Esme's unreasonable behaviour and, her heart hitched in her chest, a claim for spousal support.

Alex had moved back in that night. 'I'm not stupid, Esme. I took legal advice. You've been supporting me financially for the last two years and it's all very well deciding that you want out, but what am I meant to do?'

'I was supporting you because you're too lazy to get a job.'

'The fact that I'm unemployed is your fault. You drag me down. Drained the life out of me with your constant carping, so it's no wonder I can't get a decent acting job.' He flung himself down on the sofa that Esme had bought, like she'd bought pretty much everything else in the flat. 'Put the kettle on, there's a love.'

Esme hated going to Allegra for advice. Allegra, whose four favourite words were, 'I told you so.' But she had no one else to turn to.

'No, I'm not going to say anything.' Allegra had pursed her lips shut tight when Esme had delivered the news. She'd been avoiding Allegra for weeks, not that it was hard. As usual, it had taken a while to get Allegra to agree to meet even for a quick drink one evening. 'Oh God, how could you have been so stupid? Everyone else knew that he was absolutely, unequivocally no good.'

'I thought you weren't going to say anything?' Esme pinched the bridge of her nose. She'd been doing that so frequently since the divorce petition had arrived that the skin was red and inflamed. 'He wants me to sell the flat. Says he's entitled to half of what it's worth.'

'You bought the flat before you married him. Why should he get anything? He can work, can't he?'

'Well, because I supported him financially it's set a precedent. That's what my solicitor said.'

Allegra had folded her arms. 'Where did you find your solicitor? If you say Google, then I will smack you.'

'They have a lot of five-star reviews,' Esme had said weakly and it was decided, or rather Allegra had decided, that Esme should use the solicitors that had handled their parents' divorce. Which had been acrimonious in the extreme, but Gary and Debbie had managed not to kill each other.

It was good advice. Except Esme didn't make that much money even though she was now working on the more grown up *Skirt* magazine; she was still supplementing her wages by writing about boy bands and the efficacy of vaginal suppositories. Her only real asset was her little one-bedroom flat with its sloping ceilings and temperamental plumbing. So when Allegra had asked her how it had gone, Esme had shrugged and tried not to cry. There'd been a lot of shrugging and trying really hard not to cry lately. Alex's latest tactic had been to move in his newest shag, who'd forgotten she left a bath running and neither of them seemed duly concerned that the water had flowed down into the flat below.

'You know how, like, you go to the hairdresser with a picture of Michelle Williams sporting an adorable pixie crop and there's no reason why your hair wouldn't look exactly the same . . .'

'Except you don't have the bone structure for a pixie crop, adorable or otherwise,' Allegra had interrupted. Sometimes Esme wished she could divorce her sister for emotional cruelty too.

'No reason except all you can afford is the salon junior who's only very recently transitioned from washing your hair to doing this very intricate cut. Well, my solicitor is the legal equivalent of the salon junior.' The last word was broken in two by a sob. 'Honestly, Ally, he looks like he's twelve. I can't even believe he's qualified. He just says that unreasonable behaviour or emotional cruelty, even adultery, is very hard to prove. That it's a case of he said/she said and would it really be so bad to sell my flat and give . . .'

'He is not getting a fucking farthing out of you.' Allegra had called the solicitors to complain, then insisted on accompanying Esme to her next appointment.

Clearly Allegra had gone full scorched earth on the junior solicitor, because instead of meeting in a tiny little room, surrounded by filing cabinets and teetering piles of yellowing folders, they were upgraded to a conference room. Also when Eddie, her solicitor, arrived, the tips of his ears as pink as peonies in full bloom, he was accompanied by a strapping and coldly handsome man who didn't look like he was twelve. He looked like he'd never been twelve but had emerged from the womb wearing a grey suit and a superior expression.

'I'm Oliver Dickenson, one of the partners. I'm shadowing young Eddie as part of our mentoring programme,' he'd said smoothly, his eyes resting on Esme, who was already breathing deeply and trying not to cry, then moving to settle on Allegra. 'You'll hardly know I'm here.'

'I hope that isn't the case because I'm extremely concerned about the advice my little sister's been given so far,' Allegra had said crisply.

'I'm sure between the four of us, we can muddle along,' Oliver had said. What followed was maybe the worst two hours of Esme's life. Even worse than anything that Alex had put her through, although it was what Alex had put her through that led to her sitting in that conference room. Having to read out emails and text messages from Alex that proved that he'd been emotionally cruel, that he'd behaved unreasonably and that he'd committed adultery when he'd sent Esme pictures of a woman giving him a blowjob with the caption, 'It's a pity you only suck in other ways.'

It was humiliating. Beyond humiliating, especially when Esme had cried so hard that she'd had a choking fit and Eddie was despatched to get more water.

'This would be a lot easier if you'd stop getting so emotional,' Oliver had noted. 'I know it's a challenge but if you could look at this objectively rather than subjectively, it will be a breeze.'

'Esme's always had too many feelings,' Allegra explained, as she'd shoved another tissue in the direction of her sister.

In the end, because good things often happened to very, very bad people, Alex had suddenly landed a meaty role in a big bucks fantasy drama television series, which had been commissioned for at least three seasons. He didn't need whatever cash he could squeeze out of Esme. Oliver had said that there was a good case for Esme petitioning for some of his earnings, but by then she had nothing left in her emotional tank. Esme had extended her mortgage to pay her legal fees and, because she was so desperate for it to be over, as a gesture of goodwill, she'd paid Alex's legal fees too.

When Esme had vacated her flat for three hours as mandated by their lawyers so Alex could pack up his stuff, he'd taken everything he could. Just left her with the hunting prints, which she'd later sold along with her wedding ring and donated the money to Women's Aid.

It was done. Esme was divorced. She was never going to get married ever again. Never going to trust a man again. Never going to let herself be vulnerable and open and trusting and stupid enough to ever think that she was in love again.

'You can just put this all behind you now,' Allegra had said. 'I know it's been horrible but it's all in the past now.' In fact, the one good thing about the divorce was that it had brought Esme and Allegra closer. There'd been a definite thawing in their usually frosty relationship, so Esme was perplexed when Allegra had suddenly disappeared off the face of the earth. It seemed like they played phone tag for weeks. She was never in and her flatmate was very evasive when Esme popped across Kentish Town Road to Allegra's garden flat in Dartmouth Park. She could have just left it but Esme was still hopeful that, instead of being sisters with an eleven year age gap who argued a lot, they'd become friends.

In the end, she'd decided to surprise Allegra one evening and turn up at her offices with a bunch of flowers. It turned out that Oliver Dickenson had had exactly the same idea.

'I forbid you to date my divorce lawyer,' Esme had told Allegra when the three of them had awkwardly decamped to the bar at The Delaunay, which was just around the corner.

'What is wrong with you? Not only does he look like an Aryan breeding experiment and you could do *so* much better but your meet cute was the worst two fucking hours of my entire life.'

'You're completely overreacting.' Allegra wouldn't even look at Esme. She was too busy eyeballing Oliver's broad back in case he returned with their drinks while they were still hissing at each other like angry geese. 'Don't be so silly, Esme. It's not like it's going to go anywhere. It never does.'

Reader, six months later, she married him.

Not that Esme attended the wedding because she wasn't speaking to Allegra. Or Allegra wasn't talking to her. Either way, there was no contact for the next year until they bumped into each other at Parliament Hill Lido. It was impossible not to notice that Allegra was pregnant.

Of course, Esme was always going to turn up at the Portman with a teddy bear that was bigger than Oscar Lucien Dickenson, her new nephew – she wasn't a monster. Though she'd sworn off love, she fell head over heels with Oscar and his ten perfect toes and the way his eyelashes cast crescents on his chubby cheeks and the pleased noise he made when Esme picked him up. She fell in love with Fergus, when he arrived fifteen months later, and there was still plenty of room in her heart for Summer when she burst into the world three years ago.

It was just the children's parents that Esme had a problem with. Her relationship with Allegra, such as it was, had irretrievably shattered when she'd decided to get with Oliver and, though the sisters had made a half-hearted attempt to put it back together again, it was full of cracks and could break again at any moment.

'Oh my God, enough!' Esme said out loud. She shoved the divorce papers back in their file then slammed the door shut.

This entirely unpleasant trip down memory lane had served no purpose but to remind Esme that things with Theo were moving far too fast. Like they had with Alex.

She had to slow things down. Maybe see where they were, what kind of man he really was, after a few dates. Esme listened out but couldn't hear Theo in the other room, just the usual background noises; the faint gurgle of the radiators, George in the flat downstairs with his telly at full volume, the general creaking and settling of a building that was one hundred and twenty-five years old.

After she'd finished her work, Esme would put on her best fight face and explain to Theo that actually she'd been too hasty, too trusting and he needed to go. The rain had eased off slightly and he must have friends that he could stay with, and if he didn't have friends then that was a major red flag.

How had she got herself into this mess? It was as if Esme had forgotten all the hard learned lessons from her divorce. Esme groaned at her own foolishness as she lifted the lid on her MacBook. But as soon as she pulled up the latest iteration of the Granny, Don't Take a Trip catalogue copy, she felt a sense of calm come over her.

Life was much easier when it was laid out on the page. Correcting a spelling here, reworking a line, making every word earn its place, lingering over commas and semicolons, double-checking product numbers and prices. It was fiddly but immensely satisfying.

By the time Esme was finished, it was just gone six. She realised that she was sitting there in darkness and, also, she really needed a pee. She emailed the copy off to Lyndsey, who'd do a final read through.

When Esme stepped out of her bedroom the door to the living room was closed, though she always left it open.

12

Esme hung about in her own hallway for far longer than she should. Even though it was *her* hallway, in *her* flat.

It was all very deja eewww to those dark months with Alex when she'd felt like an unwelcome guest in her own home. All the more reason to march into the living room and tell Theo he had to go. That she wasn't a pushover. She'd been love-bombed before and she knew the warning signs . . .

She was still pacing and frowning when the living room door opened and Theo appeared, taking up every inch of space. Esme's space.

'We have to talk,' she said grimly.

He nodded, his face serious too. 'I know.' He tilted his head. 'Also, you've been holed up in your room all afternoon so, apologies if I'm overstepping the mark, but did you remember to take your antibiotics?'

Esme was just about to snap that she could take care of herself when she realised that she hadn't taken her antibiotics, and a couple more paracetamol wouldn't go amiss either as the back of her head felt like it was being repeatedly stabbed.

Theo followed her into the kitchen and declined the paracetamol that Esme graciously offered him but held up his tiny bottle of eye drops.

'Would you mind?'

Esme could feel all the fight fizzling out of her as she took her tablets then found herself back in the living room, gazing into Theo's soulful though still rather bloodshot dark eyes as he sat staring up at her.

This time, she only counted one before she squeezed the drops into his eye.

'Fuck!' Theo wrenched himself out of Esme's hold. 'Why did you do that?'

'I knew you were going to blink on two so I didn't give you the option,' Esme explained, without even a hint of regret. Sometimes, quite a lot of times, you had to be cruel to be kind. Which reminded her that once Theo had stopped blinking and shaking his head and being a drama queen over a couple of little drops, they needed to talk.

'I was going to build up to this gently but now you're going to think I'm mad at you,' he said, and all of a sudden Esme was on high, panicky alert.

'Build up to what gently?' she asked, folding her arms, all the better to completely shut down her body language. 'I don't like gentle. If something is going to hurt, I'd rather just get it over and done with.'

Theo nodded as if he were filing away that information for later use. 'It's not going to hurt,' he said. 'In fact, you'll probably be secretly relieved.'

'Right,' Esme said doubtfully. He had a girlfriend. She *knew* it. Or a wife. They'd had an argument. It was probably how he ended up nearly losing his eye but now they'd made up and he couldn't wait to get back to his entirely dysfunctional relationship. Esme had had a very lucky escape. 'Hit me with it.'

'I'm going to crash at a friend's place.' He winced either at his abrupt delivery or the prospect of spending the night on another sofa. 'I think it's for the best.'

This was exactly what Esme had wanted. What she'd decided herself. So she should be pleased. Relieved. Instead, she felt the icy cold draught of rejection like having a glass of water thrown in her face.

'Right. OK then. If that's what you want.' Esme was no longer folding her arms because she'd wrapped them around herself. Even when you thought you'd found the one good man left in the whole of London, it always turned out to be fake news.

'It's not what I want but I think it's for the best.' Theo gathered a handful of Esme's dress to pull her a little closer.

She grudgingly took two baby steps nearer. 'So, you don't fancy me anymore, then?'

Not that Esme was particularly fanciable at that precise moment. She could hear the churlish tone to her voice and feel the way that her bottom lip was jutting out in the mother of all pouts.

'It's because I do fancy you,' he said softly, tugging her even closer so their legs were knocking together. Esme, unresisting but stiff, let Theo pull her down onto his lap. 'Is this all right?'

'I don't know,' Esme replied truthfully, because right now, it seemed more awkward than anything else. Though he smelled so delicious that the part of her that wasn't confused and distrustful wanted to bury her head in the crook of his neck and take long, heady whiffs.

'I'm attracted to you. I hope you're still attracted to me and the manly way I handle myself while you're doing my eye drops.' That teased a reluctant smile from Esme. 'So, that's why I'm going.'

'I wasn't going to throw myself at you. I do have some self-control,' Esme said, still a little huffily, which she could admit wasn't one of her finest qualities.

'So do I. I mean, I would never do any throwing of myself.' Theo furrowed his fuzzy eyebrows at the thought. 'I'm very big on consent.'

'Well, I'm glad to hear that.' Esme allowed herself to relax a little, to settle back against Theo's arm instead of perching awkwardly on his quite bony knees. 'I'm a big fan of consent too. Always good to know where you stand. Or sit.'

Theo shifted his position so his arm was around Esme's waist and, now that they'd established consent, she swung her legs up so she could dangle them over the arm of the chair. 'So, that's why I don't think it's a good idea to stay. What with the mutual attraction.'

'I still don't get it.'

'Because I want to be the guy you've just met who you think could be the start of something special,' Theo said. 'Not the guy you've just met that could have been the start of something special, but he ended up outstaying his welcome and actually that was kind of creepy and now you never want to see him again.'

'I wouldn't think that,' Esme insisted. Although it sounded like a very possible scenario. 'I was starting to worry . . . Not that I think you have creep-like tendencies, but . . . it's hard to even say . . .'

Theo's arm tightened around her. 'Shall we establish my lap as a circle of trust? No judgement.'

'With Alex, my ex-husband, it all happened so quickly. We went from first date to living together, no pauses.' There she was, being all open and vulnerable again. 'It's made me a bit wary of taking things too fast.'

'I completely get that,' Theo said. 'And because of my past substance abuse, it's made me a bit wary of acting on impulse.'

'We really are a pair, aren't we?' It was weird but also quite reassuring that unwieldy emotional baggage was something that they had in common. 'Maybe that's why this feels so intense.'

'Well, we did meet in extraordinary circumstances. It's like those couples who meet in war zones . . .'

'I wouldn't say an observation ward was a war zone, exactly,' Esme pointed out. 'Though we both had significant injuries.'

Remarkably, Theo's wound seemed to have almost disappeared. It was only when Esme put her hand on his chin to turn his face towards the reading light that she could see the raised red line where his skin had been glued back together. Even so, it wasn't looking that raised or that red.

'I told you I heal easily,' Theo said, even though Esme hadn't voiced her thoughts out loud. 'Or did you just want a reason to put your hands on me?'

His voice was low, its pitch making all of Esme's nerve endings sing. She doubled down and raked her other hand through his unruly hair. All the better to bring Theo's face closer to hers so all that she could see was him.

'If you're going then we should probably have a goodbye kiss,' she said. While his had been low, her voice was high and giddy, shocked by her own daring.

'Not a goodbye kiss, a see you soon kiss,' Theo said firmly.

They came together, driven by an invisible force, until kissing was inevitable.

Instead, they bumped noses. Esme giggled, Theo smiled.

They drew back, regrouped, adjusted and leaned in again.

The first whisper-soft brush of lip against lip. Neither of them moving, just holding still. Holding steady.

Then Theo very gently threaded his fingers through her hair, far away from where Esme's stitches were still making their presence known, so he could tip her head back.

Esme sighed and imagined that little breath full of longing was making its way through the door, out into the corridor and down the stairs, to wisp through the ventilation brick. Once it met the cold night air, it would crystallise into a heart . . .

'I'm trying to kiss you and you're miles away,' Theo said, and Esme blinked up at him.

'No, I'm right here, waiting for you to kiss me.'

Esme didn't expect Theo's lips to feel so soft, even as his stubble slightly scratched against her face.

She kissed him back, both of them careful and cautious. Exploratory kisses, though the contours of Theo's mouth felt both like unknown terrain but shockingly familiar.

Then they didn't need to explore any longer, because they'd reached their destination. Esme wriggled on Theo's lap in a way that made him groan into her mouth and things became less heady and more heated. A flash of tongue and teeth and he tasted of butterscotch and all of the things Esme had lost or never had.

Basically, it was good kissing. Really, really good kissing. Until the kisses became softer again, slower, until they weren't kissing anymore, but both breathing heavily, their mouths very close together.

'I'm going to go now,' Theo said. 'I don't want to but I am.'

Esme reluctantly crawled off Theo's lap and curled up in the armchair, watching as he gathered his things: laptop, washbag, a small pile of dark clothing, and stuffed them in his holdall.

It made sense, good common sense, that he slept somewhere else, but now that they were no longer kissing the mood had shifted, and she was suddenly worried that this would be the last time she ever saw him.

As he shrugged into his jacket, Esme got to her feet then followed him to the front door.

'Why do I feel like I'm never going to see you again?' she asked as he did up his buttons.

'Because you've known too many bad men. I'm one of the good ones,' Theo assured her. 'And you will see me again. I'd put money on it.'

'But how, Theo, when I don't even . . . It's not as simple as that,' Esme said, because she knew hardly anything about him. They hadn't even . . .

'It doesn't have to be difficult,' he said. 'If you want to see me again, just tell me and I'll be there.'

There was just time for one brief, clinging kiss, then Esme was on her own in an empty flat.

13

Tuesday

Esme was woken early by her alarm. Or rather it felt early. She could have happily had a couple more hours' sleep. At least.

For a moment, she thought that Theo was still there. In her bed and spooning her. She'd had so many sleepy morning moments when she hit the snooze button and pretended that the arm she had wrapped round her midriff belonged to her fantasy boyfriend. That the weight of her full-length body pillow was the solid weight of him.

After what felt like a few seconds, the alarm went off for a second time and Esme remembered that she was in bed on her own. And that Theo wasn't a fantasy boyfriend. He wasn't her boyfriend at all. He was an interested party, maybe even a situationship. Also, he was very real.

When Esme got out of bed she was overcome with another wave of dizziness, as if the floor was about to rush up and greet her. She grabbed onto the corner of her bedside table for dear life until the head rush abated, and then all was fine. The floor was thankfully flat underneath her feet as she selected her outfit for the day.

It was a challenging cycle ride to Kentish Town. Then, weaving through the back streets, all with a slight but punishing incline until Esme nipped across Camden Road, then along York Way, veering right just before she reached Kings Cross. Even taking the back roads it was still a busy commute while also trying not to choke on exhaust fumes or, like, die. Esme never felt as alive as she did when she was on her bike, legs pedalling furiously, middle finger held aloft, screaming, 'Cyclists have right of way!' at any white van man who tried to overtake her as they approached a junction.

When Esme reached her destination, a co-working space just off the achingly trendy Granary Square, her legs felt like limp noodles. It was also a phenomenal effort to carry her bike down the steep set of stairs that led to the basement bike store. Usually Esme managed it without even breaking a sweat, but today she was out of breath as she made her way back up to ground level. She even thought about taking the lift up to the third floor, but decided against it. Instead, clutching onto the rail, she hauled herself up the stairs thinking of the porridge pot and mug of coffee that would be her reward when she reached the summit.

By the time Esme was in the kitchen with her porridge pot doing perambulations in the microwave, she was no longer panting for every breath, but wrestling with the hot water tap, which was where Lyndsey found her.

'Greetings, stranger,' Lyndsey said, her eyes already narrowed and fixed on Esme's face. 'I did wonder if you might not make it in today on account of being dead, but then you emailed the catalogue copy over last night so I assumed you were still alive.'

'Why would I be dead?' Esme finally succeeded in persuading the tap to put boiling water in her mug and not about her person. There had been several scalding incidents in the past. 'And if I was, the last thing I'd be doing is copy-writing from beyond the grave, right?'

Lyndsey gave her a look. Esme had been the recipient of that look many times over the years that they'd been friends.

In fact, the first time they'd ever spoken was when Lyndsey had first given Esme 'The Look' some ten years ago. They'd both been working on *Skirt*, a now defunct fashion and style magazine. Esme had just arrived as the new Features Writer from *Feisty* on the floor below in their grotty Marble Arch office building. Lyndsey was already in situ as the Chief Sub. It was quite the culture change from One Direction and Primark to spa breaks and Gucci. Though that wasn't the reason why Esme had emerged from one of the toilet cubicles after a crying session that had been noisier than she'd intended. It hadn't been anything work-related though Beth, the Features Director, gave such brutal edits it was like having your skin peeled off with a rusty penknife.

No, Esme had been crying because of Alex. Back then, ninety-nine per cent of her tears were down to her husband. The week before she'd been flown out to LA to interview the star of a big-budget costume drama, which was thrilling. Alex had been furious, just as he'd been furious about Esme's new job. They were in different professions; actor and writer, so there was no reason why he shouldn't cheer his wife's triumphs as she always cheered on his successes.

Esme suspected that Alex was seething because he was between jobs (he was between jobs more than he was ever *in* jobs) and he felt that by rights he should be the star of a swanky costume drama ensconced in some fancy LA hotel on a press junket. Even when Esme had explained that LA had turned out to be Pasadena and she never got the chance to leave (the admittedly quite luxurious) hotel but had done the interview, then holed up in the business suite to transcribe the interview and write up the piece before flying home, because it was on a really tight turnaround.

'For all that I saw of LA, I might just as well have been in Wigan,' she'd told him. 'And I was in economy class, which was rammed. So it sounds really glamorous but actually it wasn't at all.'

'I can't even believe that they sent you,' he'd sneered. 'Interviewing boy bands is more your level. Not that it matters, you probably won't even pass your probation period.' That was the last thing he'd said to her before he decided that he wasn't actually speaking to Esme, which was why she'd been crying in the toilet and had then come out to see Lyndsey standing by the sinks, giving Esme that look in the mirror.

'Beth's edits aren't worth crying over,' she'd said wearily, like it was something she'd said a lot to other *Skirt* features team newbies who'd had their dreams crushed under the weight of Beth's red pen.

'Nothing to do with Beth,' Esme had mumbled.

'Well then *he*, whoever he is, or it might be she, they're not worth crying over either. Nobody is worthy of a cry in a work toilet.'

'OK, fine. I'll do my crying at home instead where I can't be given unsolicited advice from strangers,' Esme had snapped.

'So you do have a backbone.' Lyndsey had smiled at her own reflection. 'I don't want you crying when I'm standing over you because your copy's late on press week.'

'Just so you know, I might cry about that too.' But Esme had found that she was smiling at Lyndsey's reflection too and, though she hated it when Allegra was getting all Big Sister on her, she never minded when it was Lyndsey. It was all in the delivery.

There was always a glint of mischief in Lyndsey's blue eyes. She'd have made a terrible poker player because whatever Lyndsey was thinking, it was writ large across her pretty, expressive face. There had been times in editorial meetings when Beth was tearing someone's ideas to shreds, literally, or Kiki, the Fashion Director, was frothing at the mouth because the advertising team wanted to showcase more high street brands when Esme didn't dare even look in Lyndsey's direction as she knew she'd start laughing.

Even her masses of dark hair, tightly plaited today, seemed to crackle with energy. But mostly today Lyndsey was giving Esme 'The Look'.

Then she pulled her phone out of her jacket pocket. 'I'm saying this from a place of love, but don't ever post another picture like this at three o'clock on a Sunday morning otherwise our friendship is over.'

Esme took the phone and was once again confronted by possibly the worst selfie ever taken. 'Wow! I look really rough. I still can't believe I shared that with everyone I know.'

'It's just as well that you eventually sent a follow-up message. I was so worried I nearly turned up on your doorstep and you know how I feel about North London.'

'Nice place to travel through but you wouldn't want to visit.' Esme had heard this contentious statement many times and no longer rose to the bait. She had been to Herne Hill, where Lyndsey lived, on several occasions and though it was quite nice, she was happy with her own picturesque patch of North London, thank you very much. 'I'm sorry. I haven't been ignoring you but there's been a lot going on. Like, a hell of a lot.'

Lyndsey nodded, but didn't seem that eager to get into it. 'So, when does Didi want to sign off on the catalogue?'

Yesterday's Zoom was but a dim and distant memory. Esme hoped that she'd made a note of the sign-off date. 'I'll check my notes.'

'I need to clear the decks as much as possible now, because you know I'm off for most of April,' Lyndsey said. 'We need to talk about that today with the boys.'

Unlike Esme, who liked to eke out her holiday allowance in scattered mini-breaks and maybe a week somewhere sunny once the schools had gone back at the end of summer, Lyndsey liked to take a three-week chunk during the first half of the year. Not so she could sun herself on a beach with frozen daiquiris on tap either. She used the time to volunteer at animal sanctuaries in India, Bali, Singapore, Romania, all over. It was why half of their mutuals owned a dog who'd previously lived in one of these rescue centres. Esme had lost count of the number of her friends who'd been unable to resist the heart-tugging pictures that Lyndsey would post on her Facebook page.

Her greatest achievement had been persuading Grace, *Skirt's* former Fashion Editor-at-Large, to adopt two bonded whippets with demodex mange at the start of the pandemic. Grace had been adamant that she was going to spend thousands of pounds on an Italian greyhound puppy whose pedigree could be traced back to the sixteenth century. But now, free from mange, Gilbert and George were Instagram influencers with their own range of doggy clothing and accessories, and Grace and her terrifying art dealer husband were absolutely besotted with them. Esme knew that it was only because she lived in a top floor flat without direct access to a garden that she hadn't been browbeaten into rehoming some scruffy mutt.

'Let me have my porridge pot first,' Esme said now as the microwave pinged. 'With blueberries and honey, I think. God, I love office days!'

'It's not like your breakfast comes free of charge. Those fresh blueberries and the honey and that boiling water tap, which is a lawsuit waiting to happen, are all included in the not inconsiderable rent we pay,' Lyndsey reminded Esme. As ever, she was the voice of reason.

'But it's still cheaper than when we used to rent those offices in Shoreditch, right? And there are no rats here and the toilets don't smell of raw sewage,' Esme said, as she followed Lyndsey out of the kitchen, through an open plan office and into a smaller space sectioned off with a large screen featuring a Yayoi Kusama mural.

Esme had always known that she wanted to be a writer, even before the days of the Harry Potter fanfic. She imagined that she might be a novelist of award-winning, ground-breaking fiction or a hardened journalist reporting from war zones and holding the government to account. Then, aged fifteen, she'd done work experience at *Feisty*, the teen mag for baby feminists, and Esme realised that all she wanted in life was to skewer manufactured boy bands through the medium of the written word and write about first kisses, best friends and ten ways to smash the patriarchy without getting grounded. She'd loved those two weeks on *Feisty* and returned every school holiday.

They in turn had loved Esme because she was keen, able to follow instructions and the living, breathing embodiment of the *Feisty* reader without the features team having to go out and do vox pops.

In the summer after she'd done her A levels, with a place on a Magazine Journalism degree course at Thameside University dependent on getting three Bs, Esme interviewed for and was offered the position of Features Assistant on *Feisty*. It was a no-brainer.

'It's not a no-brainer. You *have* to go to university,' Allegra had said wearily, as if Esme was deliberately trying to goad her. 'You'll live to regret it if you don't.'

But what was the point of spending three years being taught how to write for magazines, then graduating with a metric tonne of debt and having to do unpaid internships for years until Esme had enough experience to maybe get the same job she was being offered now?

Absolute no-brainer.

Esme had had ten good, often wonderful, occasionally terrible years working on magazines and doing something that she loved. So when *Skirt* and all the other magazines folded, unable to compete with the Internet, she'd decided to take up copywriting full time and just work to live. She hadn't reckoned on having more work than she knew what to do with, so she'd sent a lot of clients Lyndsey's way. It quickly transpired that companies didn't just want copywriters, they wanted the full package: copy, design, branding.

Esme and Lyndsey had soon worked out they could charge more money if they were their own agency, instead of working on a day rate. They'd drafted in Cedric, who'd been on the art desk at *Skirt,* and Jupe was born. Skirt in French, because Cedric was from Paris by way of the Ivory Coast and they didn't want to get sued by their former employers. The last of the gang was Cedric's friend, Ant, who'd been languishing in the marketing department of a second division football club and hating every second of it.

Esme had never imagined being her own boss. It felt very grown up to have your own business. To register at Companies House and open a business bank account. She'd worried a lot during the first year of Jupe's existence that the work would dry up and they wouldn't be able to pay their VAT and business rates and end up in debtors' prison.

However, the work didn't dry up. Of all the many people they knew who'd worked on magazines that had gone to the

great newsagent in the sky, a good half of them had their own
start-ups. Art editors now ran stationery companies, food editors were involved in micro-breweries and zero waste bakeries.
Most of the fashion peeps had started sustainable clothing
brands and the former beauty teams were all about SLS-free
haircare and vegan make-up. The Health and Well-being
Director from *Skirt* had even founded Oh My God!, a high
end, zero carbon sex toy company, and was coming in later
for a brainstorm.

It had happened quite organically that Jupe gathered a ros-
ter of clients who created the kind of products and services
that Esme and her colleagues believed in. They'd been asked
to pitch for big, corporate accounts but the four of them had
agreed that they didn't want to work for people who polluted
the environment or preached inclusivity and diversity when
their shareholders were all middle-aged white men.

Esme knew that she'd made a lot of mistakes in life. That
she certainly wasn't the best person that she could be, not
even close, but she was very proud of what they'd created
with Jupe. Not least because they donated ten per cent of
their profits to charity. Profits, which had increased each
year, despite the pandemic, especially when they'd realised
just how much money they were wasting renting office space.

Now they split the week; three days working from home
and two days in the co-working space so they didn't all go stir
crazy and, also, fresh blueberries on tap.

'Greetings, esteemed colleagues,' Esme said now, through
a mouthful of porridge as she stepped past the screen to the
table where Cedric and Ant were sitting opposite each other,
eyes glued to their laptops.

'She's not dead then,' Ant announced, barely looking up
from his screen. 'Mate, that selfie. Not cool.'

'You are all right, though, Es?' Cedric did Esme the honour of actually making eye contact. Then he shook his head and pulled a face. 'Don't take this the wrong way but you've looked better.'

'The only way I can take that is the wrong way,' Esme grumbled as she sat down. Cedric was ridiculously good-looking. He was tall, muscular, had lashes and lips that Esme would have killed for and the most exquisite bone structure ('Those cheekbones could have been carved by Michelangelo,' Beth used to sigh every time Cedric sauntered past the features desk). Esme had been out with him on three separate occasions when he'd been stopped by model scouts. But the combination of killer good looks, spending his formative years in Paris, and English being his third language meant that he wasn't very good at winning friends and influencing people. When you got to know Cedric he had a heart of gold, but still a very unfortunate manner. 'Most of the bruising is from having my wisdom tooth wrenched out of my mouth.'

It was Ant's turn to pull a face. 'Can we not talk about this?' He had a notoriously delicate constitution. 'But seriously, how are you?'

'I'll live,' Esme said, though she'd definitely felt better. There was a ridge in the padding of her cycling helmet that Esme had never paid much attention to, but today it felt as if it were digging right into the tender patch where her stitches were meant to be knitting her head back together. Actually, there was no good reason why she was still wearing her cycling helmet. She started to unbuckle it. 'I tell you, Saturday night did not go to plan at all.'

'I still don't really know what happened to you on Saturday night, only that at some point you were taken to hospital,' Lyndsey pointed out. 'Like, having your wisdom tooth taken out wasn't bad enough.'

'The dentist had to break it in two to get it out. My roots were embedded,' Esme said proudly, because her wisdom tooth extraction now felt like a restorative break on the French Riviera. Ant winced once again and made a big show of putting his ear buds in, while Cedric just grinned and leaned forward to hear the gossip. 'So I was at the hen, which, FYI, needs a whole debrief of its own, but heading to the second location . . .'

'Never go with a hen party to a second location,' Lyndsey said with a shudder. 'A life rule that's served me well.'

'Well, I wish you'd shared it with me because as we got to the second location I was mown down by a rogue cyclist, who punched me in the chest so I fell backwards and cut my head open,' Esme explained with some relish as both Cedric and Lyndsey's eyes widened impressively at the dramatic denouement.

'You probably have brain damage, yes?' Cedric asked. 'How many fingers am I holding up?'

'You know exactly where you can put that one finger you're holding up,' Esme said, and he grinned again.

Lyndsey was much more sympathetic. 'Did you get your head X-rayed? Did you have stitches? Did it hurt?'

'No, yes, not really but the numbing injection before the stitches did. There was swearing. But apart from that . . .' Esme indicated her body, currently dressed in denim shirt-dress, black tights and boots. 'I'm fine. My head hurts a bit but that's only to be expected, right?'

Lyndsey peered at her friend. 'Your face is really bruised. We'll have to try and push back your *Vogue* cover shoot.'

'Like Esme would ever be on the cover of *Vogue*,' Cedric scoffed. 'She's attractive but she's *nowhere* near *Vogue* cover beautiful.'

'Wow. Thanks for the validation, Cedric.'

He waved one elegant hand. 'Don't mention it.'

'Ignore him.' Lyndsey paused in booting up her laptop. 'So, apart from a headache, no side effects then?'

In a way, Theo was a side effect. That is, if she hadn't had a gaping head wound, then they'd never have met. 'Well, there is one thing . . .'

'I'm not NOT interested in Esme's well-being, but your mate is coming in at eleven with her *devices*,' Ant reminded them. 'Can we talk about the cauliflower pitch before that?'

'Those cauliflower people make me want to eat rare steak,' Cedric said. Though Esme hadn't eaten red meat in years, she knew what he meant.

Because their clients' brands tended toward the eco-friendly and the holistic, the sustainable and the carbon-neutral, they inevitably wanted some happy clappy, be the best version of yourself that you could possibly be ethos as part of their branding.

The people from the Cauliflower Consortium UK were no exception. Plus, they'd been getting notions ever since cauliflower had become repurposed as a low-carb pizza crust. Now that cauliflower was also a low-carb alternative to rice, they'd become absolutely unbearable. It might just have been that she hadn't had one sip of coffee yet and her porridge was already lukewarm, but Esme couldn't muster any enthusiasm for multi-tasking brassicas.

'I thought we were going to riff on that Internet meme,' she said. 'You know, if cauliflower can be pizza, you can be anything.'

'Yes, that has legs,' Lyndsey agreed. 'If cauliflower can be rice, then you can be the first woman on Mars. Other uses for cauliflower? Ant? Anyone?'

'I had it deep fried in a tempura batter in a restaurant in Paris,' Cedric offered half-heartedly. 'I'd much rather talk about vibrators.'

'Wouldn't we all,' Esme muttered but they kept up with the cauliflower chat until eleven o'clock when Marianne, their ex-colleague, turned up with her husband Jonty.

'Darlings, have I got some goodies for you,' Marianne said, once they were all seated in a conference room. She was as effervescent as a bottle of champagne given a good shaking. During the last awful months at *Skirt*, with the threat of redundancy hanging over their heads and daily cost-cutting edicts issued from the management suite on the top floor, Marianne had been so thin that she was verging on haggard and so stressed that she was constantly necking Bach Flower Remedies by the bottle. Five years later, she was no longer dressed in head to toe black but favoured vibrant prints and had stopped straightening her glossy brown hair so it was now as curly and full of life as Marianne herself. Yes, freed from the yoke of corporate publishing, Marianne looked sleek, well-rested and much, much happier.

So did most of Esme's ex-colleagues. Esme wondered if she was happy. Was she happier than she'd been back then? Happiness was so hard to quantify.

' . . . you'd like to try this one, Esme? You said last time I saw you that you liked vaginal penetration even if you couldn't necessarily orgasm that way.'

That brought Esme back into the room and away from her existential musings. 'You what?' Her face felt hotter than the surface of the sun. 'I'm sure I never said that and I'm not going to try it *here. Now.*'

She'd forgotten that while Cedric, who'd just cracked his knuckles in glee, had an unfortunate manner, Marianne had no filter. 'You mentioned it when we grabbed a drink before Christmas,' Marianne said, absolutely unperturbed, as she held out a vibrator, which Esme gingerly took from her. 'Our first dual vibrator in our trademark black silicone with rose gold accents promises the user both clitoral and G spot stimulation. I went off like a rocket first time I tried it, didn't I, Jonty?'

Jonty, who resembled a ruddy-faced, blond-curled cherub from a Renaissance painting, albeit a fifty-something cherub with a penchant for checked shirts and corduroy trousers, nodded eagerly. 'Like Niagara Falls. And of course, it comes with our luxury, embossed vegan leather travel case.'

'Great. And charger included too, like your other products?' Esme asked, desperately trying to assert some control as Lyndsey tried not to laugh, Cedric didn't even attempt not to laugh and Ant disappeared into the neck of his grey jumper.

'Of course,' Marianne said, pulling out a wand-shaped object from her box of delights. 'Now I'm sure you can all tell from its slim design that this is primarily for anal use . . .'

There were three other items to be added to the Oh My God! range, including a tiny clitoral vibrator, which Esme eyed with interest. Though if things continued with Theo as they'd started, maybe she wouldn't have to source her own orgasms.

Marianne wanted the latest additions to be part of a relaunch for the brand with new packaging and branding, a bold redesign of the website and a general repositioning in the market.

'Our branding has been rather serious thus far,' Jonty explained. 'But it's fun, isn't it? Sex.'

'Well, it should be.' Esme couldn't even remember the last time she'd had sex with someone who wasn't made of black silicone with rose gold accents, or her own hand. 'We could definitely look at bringing in an element of playfulness without losing your luxe look and feel.'

'If we do a new shoot then a lot of that will be down to the styling and the models we select,' Cedric said, which led to a spirited discussion about what the Oh My God! woman represented and, half an hour later, they were having a quick brainstorm to come up with a line that encapsulated fun sexy-times but also the eco-sensibilities of the brand.

'We put the oooh in carbon neutral,' Jonty suggested, though there wasn't an actual 'oooh' anywhere in carbon neutral.

Usually Esme loved a brainstorm. It really brought out both her competitive and creative sides. Invariably, she ended up shouting over everyone else but today, trying to think of a tagline was like trying to cut through steel with a pair of nail scissors. That sparky, quick-witted part of her brain was dull and sluggish. Maybe she was simply having an off day or maybe there really was something sinister going on behind her stitches. Although in herself, she felt fine. Perfectly fine.

'Something about climaxes and climate control?' Lyndsey wondered aloud.

They had a rule that when they were brainstorming, there were no bad ideas. Every contribution was valid, even the really rubbish ones, but Esme felt as if they were really scraping the barrel. Not that she was being much use herself.

The words she wanted were just out of reach and though she tried to grab at them, they evaded her until, suddenly, they slotted into perfect formation.

'Everybody shut up and listen to me! I've got it!' she shouted over whatever Ant was trying to say. 'What about this? You don't need to frack to feel the earth move.'

There was a moment's silence and Esme wondered if the words hadn't actually been in perfect formation after all, if she'd lost her ability to makes words do clever, sparky things. After all, Cedric was rolling his eyes but Cedric rolled his eyes a lot . . .

'It's annoying how good you are,' he said to indicate that, in this instance, the eye rolling signified grudging respect.

'Oh, she's very good. I love that,' Marianne agreed warmly. 'I think we might name the dual vibrator The Esme in tribute. What fun that would be! Now, we have to go. We've got a lunch in Battersea at half one.'

Although she was all about the sex positivity, Esme didn't particularly want women putting something named after her up their hoo-has. She was about to tell Marianne that, but the other woman had already pushed her chair back and was handing out her samples. 'What can I tempt you with, Esme?'

'If you leave the three new models, that will really help on the creative side,' Esme said, as she discreetly pocketed the clitoral vibrator. She was ovulating next week, which always gave her the raging horn.

'I'll email you over a precis of what we discussed, and Cedric and Ant will start working up some ideas for a new look and feel,' Lyndsey said, but she had a gleam in her eyes, which Esme knew only too well. 'Before you go though . . . Jonty, you were going to message me about that dog I posted on Facebook.'

'Were you, Jonty?' Marianne looked at him askew, while Jonty squirmed under her scrutiny. 'You didn't mention that to me.'

'I did say if we got a dog, we'd want a beige one because we've just had new cream carpets put in,' he blustered.

'You are not choosing a dog based on colour,' Lyndsey said firmly, then seemed to melt where she stood. 'Then again, there's Rusty. He's a golden retriever whom we rescued from the meat trade in China. Marianne, he'd be the *perfect* dog for you.' She was already scrolling through her phone. 'I have pictures.'

By the time Jonty and Marianne finally left, they'd agreed to a meet and greet with Rusty and Lyndsey was looking incredibly pleased with herself.

Esme stretched her arms above her head, aware that the background throb of her wound had upgraded to something a little more nagging. Lyndsey had offered to get her lunch from Pret and as soon as she returned, Esme took one bite of her smoky carrot and falafel sandwich then swallowed her antibiotics and a couple of paracetamol with a large swig of her Vitamin Volcano smoothie.

'Are you sure you're all right, Es?' Lyndsey asked with some concern. 'If we have just a brief catch-up about where we are and what we have on for the next week then maybe you should go early.'

'I'm fine,' Esme said, though it was less that she was fine and more that she couldn't quite face cycling home just yet.

'You are pale. You look quite sickly,' Cedric added and, rather than being annoyed, Esme realised that this was the moment and the cue she'd been waiting for.

'Well, I did bang my head quite hard. I'm really lucky that there were no serious side effects, no concussion, though you'll never guess what happened to me when I was in hospital,' she said in hushed tones so the three of them gave her their full attention. 'Something quite odd.'

'Can you only see in black and white?' Ant asked.

'No! So, I met this guy at the hospital, Theo. It's early days but, well, I'm feeling quite optimistic.' Esme glanced at her colleagues' faces but none of them seemed that impressed at her good news. 'He runs a gastropub, he's funny, kind and perceptive. Fantastic kisser. Well fit. The only downside is he has these shit tattoos, but that's hardly a deal breaker.'

'Aw, is he taking good care of you?' Lyndsey cooed. 'I'm glad he has a caring side because usually your fantasy boyfriends are all about the absolutely filthy sex.'

'Yes! Do you remember the one who always turned into pizza after they'd shagged?' Ant recalled a particularly surreal character in Esme's fantasy boyfriend canon, however . . .

'No, this is a real . . .'

'How I wish I did not know anything about Esme's many different make-believe boyfriends,' Cedric snapped with an extravagant eye roll. 'Or Lyndsey's imaginary dog, Mr Waffles . . .'

'Mr Woofles *actually*,' Lyndsey snapped back.

'This is nothing like Mr Woofles. Theo is real . . .'

'Mr Woofles is very real to me,' Lyndsey said of the fake dog she had because her cat Tigger was allergic to dogs. Though having met the Machiavellian moggy, Esme was of the opinion that Tigger was just pretending to be allergic to dogs. 'Next, you'll be telling Ant that Donna isn't real.'

'This is not like Mr Woofles and Donna though . . . yes, I have had fantasy boyfriends before, but now . . .'

'You're talking about my first born there, Es,' Ant said in a tone of mild censure because he and his girlfriend Clara had an imaginary five-year-old daughter called Donna, who was a successful grime DJ and swore a lot.

Oh! Esme could see what the problem was.

She loved working with very creative people with lively, some might say overactive, imaginations, but it had been Esme herself who'd completely normalised having make-believe characters with detailed backstories in their lives. In fact, she'd positively welcomed these fantasy figures because it meant that she wasn't the only freak.

'Theo is different. He's very, very real. I met him at the hospital on Saturday night and then we spent the next twenty-four hours together in my flat . . .'

Lyndsey made a very unattractive scoffing noise. 'You met some random and then let them stay in your flat? Yeah, right!'

'I know it sounds out of character but at the hen party, brace yourselves, I vision boarded my perfect man then I repeated all these affirmations to attract love into my life,' Esme explained earnestly though, even to her ears, the actual person who had done these heinous things, it sounded quite implausible. No wonder Ant and Cedric shared a disbelieving, mocking look. 'I made a promise to the universe that I was going to let myself be open and vulnerable, so when I met Theo instead of . . . well . . .'

'Telling him to do one?' Lyndsey suggested archly because that was Esme's usual MO when she met a man in the wild rather than having vetted him thoroughly on a dating app first.

'I don't tell every man I meet to do one,' she groused. 'Theo and I, we just have this connection. Like we already know each other. It's a bit freaky actually because he embodies pretty much all the criteria on my vision board of my perfect man.'

Esme stopped because she'd forgotten all about her vision board. She wasn't even sure where it was. But now that she thought about it, it really was a near note perfect representation of Theo.

'Honestly, I can't take any more of this white person bullshit,' Cedric said wearily, as if he was the only one of the four of them that didn't believe in a multiverse. Even Cedric had admitted, while under the influence of several Aperol Spritzes, that he sometimes pretended he was Didier Drogba when he played football on Thursday nights with a group of other designers who called themselves Artboys United.

'It's not bullshit,' Lyndsey said. 'We just have *layers*.' She gave Esme an exasperated look. 'You almost had me going there, until you started wanging on about affirmations and the universe. You're *such* a wind-up merchant. But it's a pity Theo isn't real. You could do with someone to administer to you while you're feeling poorly.'

'He is real . . .' Now Lyndsey and Ant shared an indulgent smile and Esme didn't know what else she could say to convince them. When she got home, when she saw Theo again, she was going to take a picture of him and post it on the office group chat. But for now, Esme realised that she was hoist by her own petard, as her grandmother used to say.

'Why don't you go, Esme?' Ant asked. 'You look done in.'

'Very pasty,' Cedric added. 'You and your vibrator are not needed here.'

'I'm fine,' Esme insisted, but after another two hours, during which they met with the cauliflower people then put together the work schedule for the next few weeks, all she wanted to do was rest her head very gently on the table. Maybe even find a comfy sofa (there were many, many sofas dotted about the co-working space) and have a little nap.

'Well, I'm going early,' Lyndsey announced with another concerned look at her friend. 'I've got an osteopath appointment at five that I absolutely can't miss. Come on, Es, I'll walk you out.'

Esme didn't even argue but packed away her laptop and her notebook, and followed Lyndsey down the stairs.

'I don't want you coming in on Thursday like usual, I think you should take it easy. Save yourself for Saturday when we'll have a proper catch-up, in between the speeches.'

Esme looked up from her phone, which she'd been checking to see if anyone (Theo) might have left her a message. 'Why? What's happening on Saturday?'

Lyndsey treated Esme to another outing of 'The Look'. 'It's your mate Seren's wedding. I agreed to be your plus one and I will be calling in that favour at a later date.'

'You know, Lyns, Theo is . . .'

'Really got to hustle, Es.' Lyndsey was already striding towards the street door. 'My shoulders start to crunch if I miss a session with my osteopath. I'll see you Saturday.'

Esme continued down the stairs to the basement and winced as she put on her cycling helmet and that little ridge in the padding rubbed right where she was sorest. As she carried her bike up to street level, she contemplated leaving it at the office and getting the Tube instead, then walking home from Kentish Town at the other end. She even thought about cycling without her helmet, but instantly dismissed that idea.

The quicker she got on her bike, the quicker she'd get home.

By the time Esme was hefting her bike onto its wall rack in her allocated basement storage space, it took every ounce of strength that she possessed. Walking up the many, many flights of stairs to her flat felt once again like she was climbing the Matterhorn. Some of the mansion blocks in their little street actually had lifts – how Esme longed for such unparalleled luxury and convenience.

It wasn't until she was unlocking the front door that Esme realised she was holding her breath. She let it out again when she remembered that her flat didn't have a Theo in it.

He was, hopefully, well enough to be hard at work in his gastropub.

Not even bothering to take off her coat, Esme collapsed on the sofa with a tired little grunt. One day, not even a full day, in the office had really taken it out of her. She was also quite annoyed with her friends and colleagues, who could maybe do with a lesson in being open and vulnerable themselves.

Yes, she'd hurt her head. But concussion had been ruled out and Esme knew the difference between real and not real.

Theo was real. She'd touched him and he'd touched her. She'd felt his breath tickle her ear. She'd stared into his blood-shot eye as she'd administered his antibiotic drops.

He had parents, Sandra and whatever his dad was called. He had a backstory. A whole life that wasn't dependent on Esme's imagination or whims. Yes, there were startling similarities to the vision board and all the ideal qualities Esme would like in a partner but so what? After one failed marriage and years and years of dates ranging from the indifferent to the indefensible, was it really so strange that, just this once, Esme had found the man she'd been half-heartedly looking for?

Anyway, you could have the most gratitude in your attitude of anyone who'd ever lived, be so abundant in your mindset that you attracted only good things in your life, from vast amounts of money to little bluebirds that perched on your windowsill and chirped at you like you were the heroine in an old school Disney movie. But no one, not even bloody Gwyneth Paltrow, could conjure a whole other person out of thin air. If that were a thing that people could do then there'd be, at the very least, a Netflix documentary about it.

Maybe meeting Theo would have been nothing but a brief chance encounter if Esme had been as closed off and suspicious as she usually was. Having a head wound had resulted in her being off her game, though maybe that wasn't such a bad thing if it meant that she'd been a little more trusting and receptive than usual. Except that, three days later, her head currently felt like it was on fire. Mind you, she was *still* wearing her cycling helmet.

Esme took it off and almost cried out as the pressure was removed from the tender spot at the base of her skull. She should really sort through her notes from today and make a start on working up some cauliflower ideas. Or playful copy for Oh My God!'s new range of vibrators. Anything to stop thinking about Theo . . .

Esme decided it could all wait. Shedding clothes as she went, like a snake shedding its skin to become something shiny and new, she headed for the bedroom. She wasn't the kind of person who ever day-napped, unlike Lyndsey who was a big fan of what she called 'retiring to the soft office'. Sleep Esme had during the day was sleep she wouldn't have that night, but this afternoon she couldn't resist the siren song of her bed.

She didn't so much slide between the covers as collapse onto the mattress. Esme was going to set her alarm clock to wake her up in exactly an hour and fifteen minutes' time. She'd once read somewhere that was the optimum amount of time for a nap; long enough to restore you, short enough not to send you into a deeper sleep and mess with your circadian rhythms or whatever.

She really did plan to stretch out an arm and make contact with her alarm clock, but she fell asleep before that could happen.

14

Esme wasn't sure what had woken her but the room was shrouded in the velvet darkness of late night, so she'd obviously slept a lot longer than one hour and fifteen minutes.

Her mouth was dry and stale and her head, as per Esme's new reality, was aching. She got out of bed, clutching onto her bedside table, then the door, because her legs were wobbly and the room was spinning.

As Esme stepped out into the hall, she heard a noise just outside her front door – probably Aidan who lived at the other end of the corridor and kept late hours. Then Esme heard the scrape of coir as something was placed on her doormat and the faint beeping of someone who hadn't turned off keyboard sounds on their phone. It seemed very late for a courier to be dropping something off and she couldn't remember any recent drunken ASOS or eBay sprees.

Esme grabbed her towelling robe from its hook on the bathroom door and pulled it on quickly. She realised it was back to front because she was still stupid with sleep, but unlocked the front door anyway, just in time to see a shadowy figure about to disappear down the stairs.

If it was a choice between fight and flight, then Esme chose violence every time. 'Who is it?' she called out belligerently. 'What do you want?'

The figure paused. Esme looked down to see a thermal bag on her doorstep, then took a step towards the downlight that had come on when her door had opened so she could get a proper look at him. Her whole body was suddenly suffused with a warm glow.

'I'm so sorry,' the man said in a frantic whisper. 'I know it's late. Did I wake you up?'

'Theo.' Esme swallowed and ran a tongue over her filmy teeth. She wanted to smile at him but she also very much wanted to keep her mouth closed. 'What are you doing here?'

'I just dropped off a few things to say thank you,' he said, coming closer. 'Your fridge was empty and I didn't know if you'd had time today to do a shop so I brought you . . . well, if I say leftovers, it conjures up half a sad tuna casserole in some Tupperware but these leftovers are a bit fancier. There's even a portion of dauphinoise potatoes.'

He was talking a lot, rambling, as if he were nervous. Unsure of his welcome. But all Esme could think about was how lovely it was to see him; that kind, hard face that seemed kinder and less hard the more often she looked at him.

'Hi,' she said simply and softly.

He smiled. 'Hi.'

Then the downlight switched off, plunging them into darkness.

Esme swung her front door back and forth until lo, there was light! 'Do you want to come in?'

He shrugged, shoulders almost touching his ears. 'It's late.'

'But do you want to come in?' Esme repeated, trying to keep the hope out of her voice.

'I'd love to,' he said, and she stepped aside to let him pick up the bag of gastronomic goodies, then enter. Another wave of giddiness almost knocked Esme off her feet at his warm aroma of leather and woodsmoke, the chill of the night still clinging to him.

'Make yourself at home. Even better, put the kettle on,' she said as he hesitated in the hall. 'I really need to clean my teeth. I only meant to nap but I've been asleep for hours and my mouth tastes foul.'

Too much information. Far too much, very unattractive information.

'Tea?' Theo asked.

'I could murder a mug of tea,' Esme said before slipping into the bathroom. When she'd finished brushing her teeth she stared for long moments, with some despair, at her still bruised and swollen-eyed reflection in the mirror. Then she hurried to her bedroom to pull on her nicest pyjamas, the black ones adorned with brightly coloured birds of paradise, and emerged just as Theo came out of the kitchen with tea and toast.

'I thought, if you've been asleep, then you probably haven't taken your antibiotics,' he said casually. Not as if he was telling her what to do or being controlling, but just a thoughtful gesture from someone who had her best interests at heart, so there was no need for Esme to bristle. She willed her bristles down.

'I haven't,' she said. 'And have you had someone come at you with the eye drops?'

Esme took one corner of the sofa, and Theo put the tea and toast down on the coffee table in front of her.

'I haven't.' He shot her a sly, sideways look. 'No one has your way with a pipette and a count of three.'

He'd made her a grilled cheese sandwich, which far surpassed any grilled cheese sandwich that Esme had ever had.

'It's applying heat to cheese on bread. Not exactly splitting the atom, though there is a science to it,' Theo explained as Esme tried to take delicate, bird-like bites but ended up horsing it down. 'I don't add the Worcestershire sauce until *just* as the cheese is starting to bubble. And that would be a really generous dollop.'

'Heavy carbs and cheese before bed. That's asking for indigestion and nightmares.'

'Absolute myth that cheese gives you nightmares,' Theo said very firmly, folding his arms. 'Cheese should sue.'

'Cheese needs to get a better publicist,' Esme agreed and, in between mouthfuls, she told him about the uppity people from the Cauliflower Consortium UK and how things had got quite icy when Lyndsey had gently pointed out that cauliflower wasn't the new avocado because you couldn't really put it on toast and have done with it.

'You can put anything on toast if you're really determined,' Theo argued. Then he shrugged. 'Though I guess you'd have to take it through a couple of cooking processes until it was spreadable. Maybe a cauliflower hummus?'

'Two words that don't belong together,' Esme pointed out, but her sentence got lost in a yawn.

'I should go. I'm keeping you up,' Theo said, though he'd only just got there.

'I haven't fooled you with a fake count on your antibiotic eye drops yet,' Esme reminded him. She saw that his holdall was on the floor at his feet. 'Where did you sleep last night?'

Theo grimaced at the memory. 'On my friend's airbed. It had a slow puncture.'

'And where are you sleeping tonight?' Esme asked.

'I thought I'd go back to my flat. My bedroom and bed are a write-off but now that the insurance people have been, I can clear up some of the mess and then sleep on the sofa,' he said.

Even in the dim light coming from a side lamp, Esme could see how tired he looked. Shadows and hollows carved deep around his eyes. He probably hadn't had a decent night's sleep since the night before his ceiling caved in.

'This is ridiculous.' It came out a lot more harshly than Esme had intended. 'Technically this is our what? Fourth date? You can stay the night here, you can even sleep in my bed but we're not doing *anything*. I can't stress that enough.'

'Of course we're not doing anything. It's Tuesday. It's a school night,' Theo said in scandalised tones. Then he yawned. 'Are you sure it's all right?'

It *was* all right. They hardly knew each other, but Esme knew that she could trust him. Not because she was a starry-eyed idiot like she'd been with Alex. This felt deeper, more profound. All her atoms and molecules recognised that Theo was a good person. That he wouldn't take her faith in him and stamp it under his feet.

'Absolutely all right,' she said casually, as if her having faith in someone, a man, was no big deal. 'I'm going to clean my teeth again, then the bathroom is all yours. But first I'm doing your eye drops.'

To mix things up, Esme put the drops in after a count of five, the hand in Theo's hair now more caressing than medicinal, his hand on her hip, though that might have been so he could push her away and glare at her from leaking, blinking eyes.

'You're a monster,' he said, but he couldn't have thought her that much of a monster because while Esme was in the bathroom, he kindly cleared up the kitchen to a standard never before achieved. Not even on the day that Esme had moved in.

Then, as if they'd lived together for years and had their own set routine, Theo headed for the bathroom as Esme went into the bedroom. Even though she'd just carb-loaded and had already had nearly six hours' solid sleep, she was pretty sure, if it weren't for the fizzle of nerves in her stomach, she could sleep for eight hours more.

When Theo came into the bedroom, Esme was sitting up, pillows propped behind her. She was overcome with a blushing, paralysing wave of shyness.

Esme opened her mouth to say something, to puncture the silence before it could become weird, but then shut it again as Theo sat down on the bed and took her hand in his. All the better to confirm that the tattooed word that she hadn't been able to decipher was definitely 'Salt'. She lifted his other hand, let him thread his fingers through hers, so she could see the word 'Acid'. When she turned his hands over, he had 'Fat' and 'Heat' across his wrists. Very cheffy. Also, unbelievably *not good*.

'Your tattoos . . .' she murmured.

'I know.' He smiled faintly. 'If I lasered away every bad inking I had from the days when I was off my tits on cocaine, I wouldn't have any skin left on my upper torso.'

'They're not *that* bad,' Esme said, because they certainly weren't worth the pain of being lasered off. Kemi had had a very ill-advised, full-colour butterfly tattooed on her shoulder, which looked like an evil jack-in-the-box. She'd spent a lot of money on laser removal and the numbing cream that she slathered on before each session. It had been three years, and it was still quite visible. 'I suppose some of them are quite . . .' She looked at the murmuration of starlings rising from the collar of his T-shirt. Normally she found neck tattoos quite unsavoury but these were . . . 'you know, sexy.'

They were having a moment by lamplight, with the hand-holding and the dark, intent way Theo was looking at Esme, especially when she suddenly felt compelled to lick her lips, which had gone quite dry.

'How's your head?' he asked.

Esme was almost used to the background throb where her stitches were. Not the sharp agony it had been, twinging and nagging. Now it was probably between a two and three on the pain scale. Anyone could live their life perfectly well if they stayed between a two and three on the pain scale. She'd been doing it for years.

Esme shot him a sideways look that some people might call coquettish. 'How's my head? Well, I've never had any complaints before.'

He raised an eyebrow, like he wasn't in the mood for coquetry or even a little light flirtation. 'We're not doing anything. You were quite clear about that and I was quite clear that I respected your wishes.'

'Sorry, I don't know what came over me.' God, try as she might, every word out of Esme's mouth seemed like an invitation for sexy fun times.

Maybe that was why Theo lifted one of her hands to his mouth so he could press a hot, open-mouthed kiss to her wrist. It made Esme wonder what it would be like to kiss him again.

Then he stood up and Esme saw that he was ready for bed. He was wearing a pair of black and white plaid pyjama bottoms with his white T-shirt but he still managed to look rangy and a little bit dangerous as he slid in beside her.

Both of them were sitting up, duvet tucked under their armpits, like an old married couple. Esme couldn't remember the last time she'd shared a bed with a man. No wonder her bedside etiquette was a little rusty. She wriggled down the bed until she was lying down. 'You ready to turn out the light?' she asked, which didn't sound remotely sexy when it was punctuated by a gigantic yawn.

167

Theo reached over to turn out the bedside lamp, then shifted to get more comfortable. His legs brushed against Esme's and she gave a nervous start. If she wasn't acting like a sexpot, then she was doing a good impersonation of a terrified Victorian bride on her wedding night.

Best to aim for something in the middle.

'I hope this is better than the airbed with a slow puncture,' she said.

Theo 'hmmm'ed in agreement, then he turned over and pulled her close, as if it was something that he did every night. Both the assurance and the reassurance of his touch was very, *very* alluring. 'The thing is, Esme, technically we're not on our fourth date. We haven't even had our first date,' he said.

'Wasn't our first date on a hospital ward?'

'That wasn't a date, that was an introduction. It wasn't even a meet cute,' Theo complained. 'After all this, the head wounds, the facial gashes, the calamities, our first date is going to have to be one for the record books.'

'That's a lot of pressure to put on a first date,' Esme said. 'I think we should do something low-key. Like pizza and a film, maybe?'

Theo moved against her restlessly. 'We have to do better than a four-cheese pizza and an evening at the Everyman,' he said. 'Go big or go home. Or rather don't go home. We should go away.'

'On a mini-break,' Esme murmured, stifling another yawn, even though the conversation had taken a riveting turn. 'I love a mini-break.'

'I was thinking Lisbon,' Theo said. 'We can have custard tarts for breakfast every day.'

Theo had it all planned out. Especially the food. The *Time Out* market, and the ricotta, honey and walnut gelato that

Esme would love. The night when they'd both have an inexplicable craving for Chinese food because he knew a place that did incredible dim sum.

'Then there'd be a couple of days when they'd laze on the beach, though neither of them were really lazing on the beach people. 'But we can't be rushing about all the time. Also, I tan really easily and I'm hoping you'll be even more attracted to my swarthy good looks,' Theo said.

He described walking up a massive hill to the Castelo de San Jorge de Lisboa and when they reached the top, the stunning views: the terracotta rooftops of central Lisbon stretching all the way to the Tejo Estuary. How the water was impossibly blue and three shades deeper than the sky. There would be peacocks too 'and a lot of moaning,' Theo explained wryly. 'Mostly while we're walking up that bastard hill.'

'Moaning from you, you mean,' Esme said, because she cycled everywhere so a steep hill wouldn't be unduly taxing.

'Well, I'm sure I'll moan in a manly way,' Theo conceded, and went on to rhapsodise about buying beer and chips from the food vans in the courtyard so they could sit on a bench to watch the sunset.

It sounded wonderful. The best first date ever. It also sounded very familiar because Esme had gone on a mini-break to Lisbon with Lyndsey last year and they'd done all of the things that Theo was describing so well. *All of the things.* From the dim sum to the food trucks to the beach-lazing, though Esme didn't tan easily and despite the factor 50 had burned the back of her legs.

What were the chances that they'd both been to Lisbon and done the exact same things? Maybe the Castelo. Maybe the beach. But knowing the exact flavour of gelato that Esme had become addicted to? That she'd had a custard tart for breakfast every day? Or that there'd been a peacock who sexually harassed female tourists?

That seemed way more than a coincidence.

'So, you've been to Lisbon a lot then?' Esme asked in a croaky voice.

'Last year on a stag weekend in May but it would be more fun to go with you.'

'I went to Lisbon last May too . . .'

'Did you love it?'

'Well, yeah . . .' Esme sighed. 'Don't you think it's a bit odd that we both went to the same place at the same time?'

'Not really. It's a capital city that has a beach as well as all the usual capital city stuff. Three-hour flight. And they relaxed their Covid regulations the week before we went . . .'

' . . . so we hustled and got a last minute, really cheap deal,' Esme remembered, and when she'd been in Lisbon with Lyndsey, as usual her world had been split in two. Between what she was doing in the here and now, and what she was doing with the man who existed only in her head, but resembled Theo so much. Because that was how she lived her life; with a shadow fantasy existence constantly running in the background like a back-up program on a computer. It was only now Esme realised that since she'd hurt her head, or rather, since she'd met Theo, she'd stopped fantasising and was living wholly in the real world.

And in this real world, Theo's voice wrapped around her in the dark. They'd shifted position again. He was spooning her, his arm around her waist, his fingers tucked into the waistband of her pyjama bottoms. Now he slid his hand up and under her pyjama top so he could cup her breast and rub his thumb over her nipple, which immediately and obediently hardened.

'Is that all right?' he asked.

'Oh, yes . . .'

Consent had never felt so sexy.

'Do you want to know what we're going to do after hours on our mini-break first date?'

Now all Esme could think about was Theo's tongue, his fingers, his cock driving into her again and again.

'You are a very, very bad man,' she said.

Esme could feel him laugh, his body shaking silently where it was pressed against hers. His thumb still causing havoc. 'Did you want to wait until the third or fourth date then?'

'Serve you right if I did,' Esme grumbled. Theo laughed again and took his hand away. She could feel his dick against her, half hard, and she waited for him to make a move on her, really wanted him to, but he didn't. He just held her as he described how you couldn't move for people taking pictures for Instagram on Lisbon's famous pink street. She didn't have the heart to tell Theo that she knew about the Rua Nova do Carvalho, she and Lyndsey had spent *hours* taking selfies there until they finally had one where both of them looked good enough that they could post it on Instagram.

Eventually Esme fell asleep, lulled by the stroke of Theo's callused thumb against her hip bone.

15

Wednesday

Another morning, another loud noise disturbing Esme and her sleep.

She rolled over, grabbed her phone, which was ringing rather than pinging, and was half tempted to turn it off until she saw the name on her screen.

'Hi Marion, what's up?' she said thickly, though she was trying to sound awake and perky given that it was . . . she squinted at her phone again . . . God, it was past nine. She must have forgotten to set her alarm last night.

'Oh, have I woken you up? So sorry,' came the plummy tones of Marion from downstairs.

'No, no, I've been up for ages,' Esme lied. She heard a rumble behind her and looked over her shoulder to see Theo there, still half asleep but entertained by her prevarications. 'Are you all right? Does Buster need a walk?'

'Would you mind? Jacinta's already left for a hospital appointment and my hip is really playing up today. Barely slept a wink.'

Esme sat up, fully awake now. 'I could go to the chemist too. Do you need painkillers?'

'I have a heating pad and paracetamol. It's just poor old Buster.'

Esme was already out of bed. 'Tell him to cross his legs and I'll be twenty minutes tops.'

'I'd love a tea,' Theo grunted as Esme grabbed clean clothes. Clearly, he wasn't a morning person, though Esme supposed that he did work late nights. She wasn't a morning person either and could never understand those insufferable people who got up at 4 a.m. to spend an hour meditating then an hour working out and then another hour writing in their gratitude journals.

She switched the kettle on after she'd dressed her still shower-damp body, but before she brushed her teeth, so it was just coming to the boil as she finished.

Esme sucked in a breath before she toed open the bedroom door, which was slightly ajar, but Theo was just where she'd left him, lying on his front now, face hidden in the pillow. She ruffled his hair, then wondered if that was too much. 'It's fine if you wanted to stay here tonight. What time do you finish work?'

'Not so late,' he said, his voice muffled. 'Bye.'

Apparently, they weren't going to be one of those couples that kissed each other hello and goodbye. Esme felt a little sad about that as she hurried down the stairs to the ground floor.

She had a key for emergencies, but she knocked on the door and heard Buster barking wheezily then a heavy shuffling sound before Marion opened the door.

'Are you OK?' Esme asked.

Marion was tiny – she barely came up to Esme's shoulder – and insisted that it was because her mother had smoked all the way through her pregnancy and that there'd still been rationing, though her wife Jacinta was the same age and towered over Esme. But she'd grown up in Jamaica, where apparently there'd been no rationing.

'I've felt better.' That was Marion-speak for, 'I'm in some considerable pain.'

'Shall I make you a cup of tea?' Esme asked, but Buster was already nosing her shins. 'Or I'll make you a cup of tea when I'm done walking young sir.'

Walking Buster wasn't a lot of fun. He was a ten-year-old pug, idle as well as elderly, with breathing problems. He shuffled along until they reached Parliament Hill. There was a large patch of grass, Duke's Field, with a children's playground to one side, before the running track, the bandstand and the cafe.

Esme let Buster off his lead to do a slow perimeter sweep, wheezing at any dog that dared approach him. He did a couple of wees and a very unpleasant runny poo, which Esme had to scoop up as best she could. Then Buster did what he always did, which was why Esme hated walking him, not that she'd ever tell Marion and Jacinta.

He came to a halt, plonked his well-upholstered bottom down on the grass and refused to walk another step. Esme half-heartedly tugged at his lead, but this wasn't her first time at the Buster rodeo. As he started to scream (and the screams of foxes having sex were nothing compared to the screams of a pug who was done with that morning's perambulation) people turned to look with concerned expressions, as if they thought Esme was beating Buster, though she was at the other end of his lead.

With an anticipatory sigh, Esme hefted Buster up. 'You weigh a ton,' she told him, but he just breathed hot, fetid air on her, his big pink tongue lolling out of his mouth. 'Also, you have halitosis.'

Jacinta was just coming down the road as Esme was coming up it. You could spot Jacinta a mile off. She'd worked in fashion – she and Marion had met at art college in the seventies – and always wore the brightest colours. Today it was a fuchsia wool coat, royal blue trousers and black and yellow, acid wash high top Nikes. Esme felt distinctly *de trop* in her black athleisure wear, though she had no intention of doing any kind of athleisure. They met at the entrance to their block. 'Cheeky bugger, he never does that with us,' Jacinta said of Esme's pug parcel.

'Buster does not respect my authority,' Esme panted, as she followed Jacinta through the door. 'He's done everything he needs to do. If you want me to walk him this evening, just give me a bell.'

She waited until Jacinta had got her front door open before she lowered Buster gently to the ground then straightened up.

'Goodness me!' Jacinta exclaimed, as she stared at Esme. 'You look *dreadful*! You didn't look like that when we saw you at the farmer's market on Saturday morning. Have you been in a fight?'

'I had quite an eventful Saturday night.'

'Well, I'm all ears.'

Esme had planned to deposit Buster and leave but she nodded at Jacinta, who was now in their kitchen, holding up a mug in a silent question. 'Coffee, please. Have you got any non-dairy milk?'

'No, because we're boomers,' Jacinta said. 'Also I've seen you wolf down a whole baked Camembert so you're clearly not lactose intolerant.'

Esme wandered into the living room where Marion was sitting in state in the turquoise velvet recliner chair from Granny, Don't Take a Trip, which Esme had got her at a sizeable discount. The walls, in fact every wall of the flat, were covered in framed pictures of all sizes, most of them original works by Marion, who worked with paint and collage.

Every time Esme visited Marion and Jacinta, and she was always popping in to see them, they seemed to have added another *objet d'art* to their huge collection of *things*. This time it was the two Staffordshire china dogs on either side of the fireplace. Hanging above them were Jacinta's prized collection of plates from the Queen's many jubilees.

Esme had spent several nights in their spare room during the most vicious moments of her short-lived marriage. She'd had to share the space with Jacinta's clothing rails (her 'overspill wardrobe' as she called it) and a life-sized cardboard cut-out of David Bowie in his Aladdin Sane phase, which had given her a minor heart attack every morning when she'd woken up to see him looming over her.

They had one of the prized three-bedroom ground floor flats, and unusually for mansion blocks, had their own private back garden instead of communal grounds. Even before she'd become friendly with them, Esme had known of Jacinta and Marion, who were the undisputed queens of 23 to 45 Parliament Hill Mansions, trumping even Gilda, head of the Parliament Hill Mansions Residents' Committee. They were famous for having very loud, very legendary parties, which is how Esme had first met them.

Also during the most vicious moments of her short-lived marriage, Alex would lock Esme out of the flat. Her own flat. She'd alternate begging him to release the deadbolt and let her in with sitting on the stairs and crying. Which is how Jacinta had found her when she'd come upstairs from another fabulous party to see if anyone had any ice.

Marion and Jacinta weren't honorary mothers or grandmothers. They'd have hated the very thought. Instead, they were Esme's older, wiser friends, who'd always given her good counsel and somewhere to stay when she'd really needed it.

So now she didn't stand on ceremony but flopped onto their well-worn sofa, which was covered in a clashing and eclectic collection of cushions and throws.

'I didn't notice before, but you have been in the wars,' Marion said, raising her reading glasses so she could peer at Esme. 'My niece got mugged at a cashpoint last weekend. You know, there's no point in being a hero. You should just hand over your phone and your purse.'

'I wasn't mugged. Remember? I had a wisdom tooth out last Saturday. That's why I've got so much bruising around my eyes.'

'I still have all my wisdom teeth,' Jacinta said, coming in with a laden tray on which were two mugs, one delicate bone china cup and saucer, and a plate of chocolate Hobnobs.

'Which is why you're so wise.' Marion took her cup of Earl Grey. 'So it couldn't be you who forgot to add Buster's favourite treats to the pet shop order.'

'In my defence, those treats do make him fart a lot,' Jacinta said, sitting down next to Esme and scrutinising her young friend's face. 'Apart from the bruises, you still don't seem yourself.'

Esme really didn't want to get into it though Marion and Jacinta never made her feel, like Allegra did, as if her life was one long stream of catastrophes that she needed to be rescued from. But then again, she *was* among friends. 'I got into an altercation with a cyclist on Saturday night. Banged my head. Had to have stitches.'

That about covered it, though she then had to explain that no, she hadn't had a CT scan and no, she didn't have concussion but happily that led to a long, impassioned conversation about NHS cuts and how the health service was on its knees, though the staff were doing their best and Marion was hopeful that her hip replacement, which had been put back twice already, might happen before summer.

'We really want to go back to Paxos,' she explained a little wistfully, because pre-pandemic, they'd always spent September in the same villa on the small Greek island that was an hour's ferry ride from Corfu. 'But to get down to the beach involves a roughly hewn mule path. We could stay in a hotel, but it wouldn't be the same.'

'Maybe we could get a villa with a pool this time,' Jacinta mused. 'I really don't want you haring down roughly hewn mule paths even with a new hip.'

'Or we could hire an actual mule.'

'Do they have actual mules?' Esme asked, but they both shook their heads and laughed. She made a gesture as if she was going to get up but couldn't quite manage to get her brain to pass on a message to her legs. 'I really should be going. I've got a meeting with our accountants at lunchtime.'

'You won't have another coffee?' Jacinta asked.

Esme was tempted but she noticed that Marion was casting longing looks through the open living room door, which meant that she was keen to get down to some work in the largest bedroom, which had been repurposed as her studio when they first bought the flat in the eighties. Esme couldn't bear to know how little they'd paid for it; she suspected it was probably five quid and a fish supper. The flat next door to them had gone for well over a million last year.

'No, I won't keep you,' she said decisively, getting up as Jacinta held out a hand to help Marion out of her chair. Then she raised the hand to her lips for a kiss.

Marion and Jacinta were the only two people that Esme knew in such a long-term relationship. Nearly fifty years of being together. It wasn't just their togetherness. It was the way they were with each other: caring, silly, loving. The sort of love that Esme had never seen in the wild. Certainly never between her parents, and it was also far removed from the chilly companionship of Allegra and Oliver.

Esme couldn't begin to imagine how other people would view the vibe between herself and Theo . . .

'Are you just going to stand there for the rest of the day? We don't mind but you'll have to move when *Countdown* comes on so we can see the telly . . .'

It was on the tip of Esme's tongue to tell Marion and Jacinta that she'd met someone. That she thought it could be the start of something special. But then she remembered how the same news hadn't gone down too well at work. Although Marion and Jacinta weren't quite so *au fait* with Esme's rich inner life.

Also, it was rather lovely to have a Theo-shaped secret. There'd be time enough to introduce him to everyone once she'd worked through all the complicated, conflicted, confused feelings she was having about relationships and her own sorry history. So, for now, Theo belonged solely to Esme.

She realised that Marion and Jacinta were both still looking at her expectantly just as the back of her head gave a warning twinge. Had she taken her antibiotics this morning? 'I just remembered that I need to make a doctor's appointment for Monday to have my stitches out,' Esme muttered vaguely. 'I should be off.'

'Good luck with that. There's one receptionist who must have been a member of the Stasi in a former life,' Jacinta said darkly, while Esme gave Buster a goodbye scratch as she walked down the hall.

16

Esme barely had time to head back up the stairs to her own flat to grab her bags and change. The effort of changing her tight black athleisure wear was more than she could bear, and their accountants had lots of creative types on the books, so Esme was sure that they'd seen a lot worse than her in her Sweaty Betty finest.

'I'm back, but not for long,' she called out when she opened her front door, but she was greeted with silence.

Theo had obviously left for the day but as Esme stood there in the hall, there was something about the stillness of the empty rooms that made it seem impossible that he'd ever been there.

Aimlessly, Esme walked into the living room and scowled at the mustard feature wall, as if she were seeing it for the first time. She really needed to do something about it. It had been over three years now and it made her angry on a weekly basis.

Esme's thoughts were like a trail of breadcrumbs that she couldn't quite trace back to their original source and it didn't help when her phone beeped with an incoming message.

Hope you're feeling all right. See, I do care that you're not dead. Can you definitely still take kids on Friday afternoon, as per usual? If not, please let me know ASAP as it's getting very late to make alternative arrangements.

Allegra clearly only cared that Esme was not dead so she could carry out her usual weekly auntly duties, which she'd already told Allegra she was fine to do. She'd barely missed a week, come rain, come shine, come snow.

Hissing with annoyance, she texted back a very terse, 'I'm fine. It's still fine,' as she left the flat, slamming the door with great force.

For once, Esme didn't cycle into town and when she left her accountants' offices in Soho after a very long, very boring meeting about company pensions and tax allowances, she wandered through the tiny, crowded streets until she found herself outside a DIY shop on Brewer Street. She'd walked up and down Brewer Street hundreds of times and had never noticed the shop before, but there it was. It had to be a sign. A sign that Esme should go in and buy a tin of paint to cover up the mustard abomination.

The man behind the counter wanted to talk about undercoats and sugar soap but Esme didn't have time for that. She wanted the mustard gone in one coat, two tops, so bought a tin of a dark, smoky grey eggshell emulsion. Then, apparently, she needed a paint tray and roller, brushes for the precision work, white spirit and masking tape. By the time she left, she was fifty pounds poorer.

As soon as she got home, Esme went straight to work. Her mind focussed on the task at hand rather than Theo's whereabouts. She grabbed a couple of old towels, a chair to stand on and set to work.

The man in the shop had said it was best to paint in daylight, but it was a grey day at the very end of February. If Esme waited for daylight, she'd still have a mustard feature wall come June. She turned on the big light, then turned on all the lamps too, cleared the mantelpiece of half-burned scented candles and the two small art deco figurines she'd inherited from her grandmother and set to work.

The first coat of paint took hardly any time at all. Esme only had to slow down when she was doing the fiddly edges. She took a step back to admire her handiwork. There didn't seem to be any mustard showing but after a couple of hours with the central heating going full blast, and after she'd done some work that she was actually getting paid for, Esme put on a second coat.

As she carefully painted the last strokes just above the skirting board, it occurred to her that by getting rid of the mustard wall, she was also getting rid of the last vestiges of her old life. If there was no mustard paint, then she was welcoming in the new, being open to the changes that had happened in the last few days.

Esme would never fully understand why Theo was as attracted to her as he seemed to be, but she was grateful that he was. Even though she was still as prickly and as defensive as she'd been ever since her divorce. Even though she hadn't done the work; hadn't had to spend the last few years becoming a better person who was ready for a relationship.

The strange thing was that Esme hadn't even realised that she wanted a relationship. But after these past couple of days, she now realised it wasn't just about the hot, chef boyfriend with the bad tattoos and the promise of some really good sex. Without even knowing it, Esme had also been *craving* the cosiness of cohabitation, the comfort of being with someone who just *got her*. Maybe that was why the universe had given Theo to her, even though she'd done nothing to deserve him.

It was properly dark now and had been for some time. It wasn't until Esme went into the kitchen to find an old glass to soak her brushes in that she saw it was past seven. The sudden, determined rumbling of her stomach reminded her that she hadn't eaten since the chocolate Hobnobs of this morning.

Esme could have sworn that there were still plenty of gastro-pub leftovers in the fridge, but it was more or less empty. Still, she always had a couple of cans of Heinz tomato soup in the cupboard for emergencies and she heated one up, toasting a couple of slices of granary bread she found in the freezer.

She wasn't sure what time Theo got home from work, but he'd said it would be late. He probably stayed until closing time, which would be what? Eleven? Did he help the staff get the place ready for lunch service the next day? Did he cash up? Then he had to go from Clerkenwell to Gospel Oak. It would be midnight, at the very least, before he was there.

Just thinking about Theo's return made Esme's stomach clench painfully. What if he wasn't coming back? What if it was over before it had even started?

She couldn't believe she was doing this, but after Esme had run herself a bath, because she'd managed to get a lot of paint on herself as well as the feature wall, she lit some candles and fetched her crystals. She even put them on a nice soft towel on the bathroom windowsill and . . . and . . . and . . .

Esme wasn't even sure what she was meant to be doing with them, despite the constant crystal tutorials from Seren. She picked up the big smooth hunk of black obsidian, because it was the most pleasing to the touch. Also, according to a quick google, it was a root chakra stone, which banished negative thoughts. She leaned forward so she could hold the obsidian against the base of her spine (Esme was pleased that there were no witnesses), where her root chakra was apparently located. She tried to think positive thoughts about her and Theo but it was an awkward position, not at all relaxing, so she kissed the stone and put it back on the towel, then picked up a lump of rhodonite.

It was pink and spiky, reminding Esme of pictures of a virus cell, but it was also a heart chakra stone, which healed emotional scars and nurtured new love. Esme could place it just above her left boob while she lay back in the warm water and welcomed in nurturing thoughts about Theo and their relationship. At the same time, she had a small piece of garnet tucked between her thighs, which would connect with her sexual energies. That might have been why, instead of the nurturing thoughts, her mind wandered to the night before and Theo's hand on her breast, his voice dark and amused as he alluded to what sounded like it would be a very fulfilling sex life.

It had been ages since Esme had had sex with another person. Now, as she thought about having sex with another human being – no, not just another human being, Theo – she could feel herself getting hot in a way that had nothing to do with the fact that she'd had to lower herself into the bath practically centimetre by centimetre, her skin instantly reddening.

They'd only kissed once but it had been a near perfect kiss and it was obvious that Theo was good with his hands; Esme had seen him finely chopping up spinach after all. She'd also felt the promise of his dick against her and, when she put her hand between her legs to retrieve the garnet, she wasn't surprised to find that she was wet. The bathwater couldn't wash away the sticky liquid heat at the heart of her.

Esme felt so restless, so . . . might as well call a spade a spade . . . so skin-twitchingly horny, she was sure that she'd jump Theo when he returned, before he'd even taken his coat off. Would wind and curl herself sinuously around his lean frame so he'd have no choice but to put his hands on her, press her between the wall and his body . . .

The bathwater, once punishingly hot, was now rapidly cooling. Esme yanked out the plug with her toe, then heaved herself out of its depths. Her reflection was blurry and indistinct in the misted mirror above the sink. She wiped away the condensation to see her face, flushed and wanting. Her eyes looked bigger, her lips fuller as she bit down on her bottom lip and lifted her hair. OK, she was now on day three hair and was as desperate to wash it as she was desperate to get fucked, but she applied more dry shampoo and hoped that it looked tousled and sex kittenish.

Then she moisturised with care so she didn't miss a millimetre of skin and remembered to pluck the one solitary hair that grew just below her navel. With great daring, she walked from bathroom to bedroom completely naked, half dreading, half hoping for a tread on the stair, a gentle knock on the door, but no such luck.

Esme pulled out her bottom drawer to retrieve a black satin slip that she hadn't worn for longer than she hadn't had sex. Probably why it was a little tight over the hips, but the overall effect was still 'come hither and put your hands on me right now'.

Although she was on antibiotics and couldn't drink alcohol, Esme poured a ready-mixed can of clean gin and tonic left over from when she was doing a very miserable Dry January into a fancy glass and hoped the placebo effect would mean she got slightly tipsy. Then, arranged artfully on the sofa, she waited.

The waiting wasn't so bad to start with. Since Theo had breezed into her life, Esme had neglected many of the other parts of that life.

The Seren's Hen WhatsApp group had been particularly lively in the run-up to Saturday's nuptials. Esme had forgotten that it was only three days until the actual wedding. Probably because there'd been such a build-up to the original date just before the first lockdown, then the subsequent pencilled-in but cancelled new dates, plus the two other weddings. Now that the all singing, all dancing, four hundred guests extravaganza in a Park Lane hotel was finally upon them, it didn't seem quite real.

With seventy-two hours to go, Seren had abandoned any kind of inner calm and was demanding that each hen put on the black designer dresses that had been fitted and purchased two and a half years ago. 'Although I would have expected that everyone would have lost their pandemic pounds by now, knowing that my special day was imminent.'

Cue a mass of pictures of the hens looking willowy and ethereal in their black dresses (Allegra looked particularly smug) because, unlike Esme, they clearly hadn't spent most of the last two years stuffing their faces. Allegra had been very scathing when they'd arranged a socially distanced meet-up on the Heath because Esme hadn't seen the kids in weeks and Esme had pulled out a Tupperware box of homemade chocolate chip banana bread. 'Not for us,' Allegra had said in her most condescending voice. 'I don't think a pandemic is a good enough reason to eat refined sugar. You always did eat your feelings.'

Sadly, this was true. By the time her decree absolute had come through, Esme was two stone heavier than she'd been on her wedding day. Not that she wanted reminding of that, but with Seren and Isaac's wedding day looming, it was inevitable that Esme's thoughts would take an occasional unhappy turn.

Only Kemi was a lone voice of dissent.

> **Kemi Udo**
> Can't believe you're trying to fat shame us days before the wedding. If my dress is tight, then this is why God and Kim Kardashian invented shapewear.

Big knickers, check. Esme wrote in the chat. Then, because she had at least four people who swore by manifesting and crystals at her fingertips, she seized her chance.

> **Esme Strange**
> Btw, you'll never guess what happened as a result of all the vision boarding and tarot and what not on Saturday night?

No answer. Just tumbleweed. Though Seren replied to Kemi to say that, if she had to wear shapewear, then it had to be black.

There was a bit more back and forth about what time they were due to assemble on Saturday. Then a run-down on *exactly* the look Seren wanted, which would be provided by a battalion of make-up artists.

> **Seren Dipity**
> Dewy, soft. No smoky eyes. I hope you're all drinking plenty of water this week. Tomorrow is the very last day that you can safely exfoliate your face.

Esme put the group on silent. It was eleven. Still at least an hour before Theo might be back, unless the pub was quiet. Though did gastropubs get quiet in the same way that restaurants did? Weren't they bound by licensing laws to stay open until eleven?

Usually Esme didn't mind being alone with her thoughts and she still had that delicious frisson of anticipation, a pulse beating out its siren song between her legs. She distracted herself with a delicious little daydream about Theo finding her prototype mini vibrator and using it to tease and torment, edging her, until it was Theo who lost control first, desperate to be inside Esme, and all the while his voice was in her ear telling her what he was doing, what he was going to do next . . .

Esme shifted on the sofa. Eleven thirty now. She attempted to marshal her thoughts because if she had any more X-rated fantasies, then she'd have to take matters into her own hands when, tonight, she wanted Theo to take her in his hands. Never mind going on an actual first date. She already felt as if she'd known him for months so why not skip straight to the sexy fun times?

She tilted her head back and winced as the tender spot at the base of her skull came into contact with the arm of the sofa.

Ten minutes later Esme was mindlessly scrolling through Instagram, liking random posts and reels. Then, even though she always swore that she wouldn't, she logged out of Instagram so she could pore over Alex's feed safe in the knowledge that she wouldn't accidentally like a post from months before. Even though Alex had people who manned his social media for him and Esme was sure they had better things to do than scroll through thousands and thousands of likes to see if her name cropped up.

If it was true that karma got you in the end, then her ex-husband was the exception that proved the rule. Since he'd landed a plum role just before they finally parted, Alex's star had been firmly in the ascendant.

He might not have made it quite to A-list leading man status, but he was firmly B-list, playing second leads in big budget films and the title character in a Netflix show about a serial killer. Esme hadn't seen it, but she was pretty sure that it hadn't been a stretch for Alex. Psychopathy had always come naturally to him.

His Instagram was a beautifully shot, heavily curated selection of photos. Pictures of Alex on the red carpet with his co-stars, always in a Prada suit, as he had a special relationship with the brand. Relaxing in his New York loft apartment, sun streaming in through the floor to ceiling windows, a glossy brown spaniel looking up at him adoringly. There was an actress, fifteen years younger than Alex, who gazed up at him adoringly too. They were rumoured to be engaged.

In his official biography, on IMDb, on Wikipedia, it was common knowledge that Alex had been married and was now divorced but Esme's details had been expunged from the records. Once, when grilled about his past relationships in an interview with *Esquire*, he said, 'I got married young. I knew I'd made a terrible mistake before the ink was even dry on the marriage certificate. Then, thank God, I got divorced young too.'

He hadn't been *that* young. He'd been thirty, but he'd knocked five years off his age since then, and Marion and Jacinta insisted he'd had some work done.

Esme didn't mind that she'd become an anonymous if cautionary tale on Alex's CV, but it galled her that he was doing so well. It wasn't fair. If revenge were a dish best served cold, then the revenge would be coated in permafrost by the time Alex finally got served.

Esme wondered about the girlfriend too. If Alex had love-bombed her as well for those first giddy months so she believed him when he said she was the funniest, cleverest, most beautiful woman he'd ever met. If they'd spent those early days unable to keep their hands off each other and, like Esme, she'd mistaken sexual intimacy for love.

Then, when the first flush of being together had worn off, did he make her suffer the way he'd made Esme suffer? Did he cheat on her? Did he lie to her? Did he cut her down with the terrible things he said because, in his mind, by his tally, her star was eclipsing his?

Did she wait, like Esme had waited, long, long nights for Alex to come home? If pressed, he might promise to be home at a certain time, but the hours would pass and he never came. Sometimes he'd turn his phone off, but it was even worse when he left his phone on. Her texts would go unanswered. Her calls would roll over to voicemail. And though her WhatsApp messages would be blue-ticked and Esme could see that Alex was online, he wouldn't reply.

So Esme had done exactly what she was doing now.

Waited.

Ears alert to every noise; a distant car alarm, someone shouting in the street below. Her heart would thud when she heard the front door slam and then it would sink when the footsteps on the stairs stopped at the first floor because it wasn't Alex.

She'd forgotten about the waiting, which was odd because during that time in her life, it seemed to Esme that all she did was wait. She'd never felt so alone and so lonely as she had when she'd been Alex's wife.

When you loved someone, you handed them all the weaponry they needed to hurt you. So what did it matter if you met someone and it felt like you were meant to be together? Sooner or later they'd end up breaking your heart, and then you'd be left on your own to try and patch yourself back together as best you could.

In the space of three or four days, Esme had fallen back into bad, old habits. Tears were trickling down her face and gathering pace now. This was why imaginary boyfriends were a safer bet than real ones.

Esme still couldn't help but listen out for Theo, but it was hopeless. She already knew that he wasn't coming back, and then she was properly crying and wouldn't have been able to hear anything over the sound of her own sobs anyway.

17

It took a while before Esme heard the soft but insistent tap at her front door. Still sniffing, she got up to answer the summons and was surprised to see Theo standing there, though who else would it be at this time of night?

She turned her damp, crumpled face away from him.

'What's the matter?' he asked, not angry, not weary of her emotions like Alex always had been. There was nothing but concern in his voice. 'Did someone upset you? Are you in pain? Is it your head?'

'It's not . . .' It was hard to speak when Esme hadn't quite got rid of the last of the sobs. 'I thought you weren't coming. You're so late.'

Theo frowned, his brow well and truly furrowed. 'But, sweet girl, I said I'd be late as . . .' He looked around as if a clock might suddenly materialise. 'What is the time?'

Esme walked back into the living room to pick up her phone from the coffee table, then folded herself into a small, irregular shape full of stiff lines at one end of the sofa. 'It's nearly one.'

'That's not so unprecedented,' he murmured, crouching down in front of Esme to brush away what was left of her tears with the pads of his thumbs. 'Had a party of twelve who wouldn't leave and didn't really feel I could kick them out when we're so quiet at this time of year.'

Esme took hold of his wrists to keep his hands on her face. 'I was sure you weren't coming back,' she whispered.

Theo pressed his forehead against hers. 'Why would you even think that?' he asked. 'I'll always come back.'

'Do you promise?'

'I promise,' he said, and he took his hands away from her face but only so he could place one above his heart and make the promise legally binding. Then he rocked back on his heels and sniffed the air suspiciously. 'What is that smell?'

Esme's despair quickly became indignation. 'This perfume is very expensive.'

'Not perfume.' Theo stood up with a wince like he was getting too old to spend much time on his knees. 'It's paint.' He turned round to face the feature wall. 'You old goth, I can't believe you painted it black.'

'It's not black. It's actually a very dark grey.' Esme swung her legs round so she was sitting on the sofa, not slumped on it in abject misery. 'It's called Coal Scuttle.'

Theo's face was still screwed up at the paint fumes. 'I thought you *liked* the mustard.'

'What are you talking about? I *hated* the mustard. I thought it looked like baby poo.'

'It did, but it would have been rude to point that out.' Theo held out his hand so he could haul Esme up from the sofa. 'It was the one con pitted against a very long list of pros.'

'Well, that con was all my mother's doing.' Esme had taken a step towards the door but now she came to a halt. 'I would never.'

'Come on! Keep moving.' A light tap on her arse and then Theo's hand was at the small of her back to guide her out of the room. 'Anyway, I decided that your baby poo feature wall wasn't going to be the hill I died on.'

'I can't believe you'd think that of me,' Esme said, but her voice was thick with tiredness and she was glad of Theo supporting her because the walk from living room to bedroom felt like trekking in the Hindu Kush. 'Anyway, it's all fixed now.'

Theo pushed her in the direction of the bedroom. 'Go on. I'll be ten minutes.'

Esme should probably have kept to one side of the bed but, as she listened to Theo clean his teeth, she couldn't resist stretching out right in the centre then ran her hands down her sides. Her satin slip had been cool when she put it on, but now it had warmed to her body heat. Her existential crisis over, she was back to feeling horny. What was the point of spending time with a sexy man who seemed quite tolerant of all your foibles if you didn't take him out for a test drive?

She was just wondering if her breasts were shown to their best advantage if she was lying on her back (maybe she could make a cleavage if she pressed her arms together) when Theo walked into the room.

'Budge over,' he grunted, which wasn't very romantic, but instead she rolled over so as he got into bed, they collided. He was wearing just black boxer briefs, so they were immediately skin against skin. Theo was cool where Esme was so hot that she felt as if she might combust.

Such a lovely way to burn.

She just needed to tangle her legs with Theo's, tug one of his hands onto her breast while her other hand pulled at his hair, making it even wilder, so she could bring his face closer and closer.

'What's got into you?' he asked against her lips.

'Hopefully, you will,' she whispered, because anything louder would break the spell. 'Before I got upset, I was, well . . .'

'Desperate for a shag?' Theo said knowingly and a little smugly. He hooked a finger into one of the thin shoulder straps. 'Why else would you be wearing a fuck-me slip?'

When Esme opened her mouth to protest that she would never be that obvious, he stopped her with a kiss.

It wasn't a gentle, preparatory kiss, taking time to learn the contours of Esme's mouth. Soft and slow to start with until he'd worked out what turned her on, like their first kiss. This was a kiss from a man who knew exactly what Esme liked, what she wanted and what she needed in this exact moment. Something fierce and demanding, the scrape of his teeth on her bottom lip, his tongue driving into her mouth.

Esme was weighted down by Theo's body, wrists pinned over her head when usually there was no way, no fucking way, she would ever let a guy do this first time out of the box, or even the tenth or twentieth time, without a very long conversation about consent and boundaries and 'if you do anything that we haven't discussed, then I reserve the right to twist your balls until you're crying for your mother. And not in a good way.' The men that Esme met on dating apps, even the men she met through friends who came with some kind of recommendation, seemed to think that choking was the new second base.

But not Theo. And Esme wasn't panicking or struggling to get free. Because for some reason that she didn't fully understand, she trusted him.

'How is it that you know exactly what I want?' she murmured, arching against him. It was as if Theo had accessed her deepest, darkest fantasies.

'Because we both want the same thing. Which is why I know that if I do this . . .' Theo lowered his head and through her slip sucked one aching nipple into the warm cavern of his mouth so Esme bucked her hips against the hard jut of his cock and moaned '...it will get you wet.'

Then he did the unthinkable.

He stopped.

'Nobody likes a tease, Theo, especially not me,' Esme murmured, but he shushed her.

'Your head.' He brushed the hair back from her face, so sweetly, so tenderly, even though he'd just kissed her like he was already fucking her. 'Probably be more comfortable if you weren't on your back, so you're not putting any pressure on your stitches.'

Esme felt the fierce prickle of tears. He really was too good to be true. 'You . . . God, you . . . This is just . . .'

'You're already incoherent just from a kiss?' Theo swooped down to take her mouth again. 'I've barely even got started.' Another soul-sucking kiss. 'So, how do you want to do this? On your side? On your knees? On top?'

'What do you think I like best?' Esme asked with a hint of challenge that tipped her chin up and made her meet his gaze in the soft lamplight of the room.

'That's an easy question.' Theo rolled her over again, so she was on her side, facing away from him. She heard the soft rustle of fabric as he got naked. Then he was pressing himself against her, his dick nudging against the curve of her hip. 'You like a little tease, then a little darkness to really get you off.' His hand slid into her knickers. Esme wriggled out of them so he could rest his hand, heavy and warm, between her legs.

'So I know that if I do this, then your clit will throb even though I barely even touched you . . . yet,' he drawled, circling that deliciously sensitive nub with the tip of his finger.

'Don't stop,' Esme gasped as he sped up. 'I knew you'd be good with your hands.'

'And I also know that when I do this,' two fingers pushed inside the damp heat of her cunt, 'you're going to beg me to fuck you.'

'No, I don't. I mean, I won't,' Esme said mutinously, clamping down with everything she had in the way of internal muscles because he was withdrawing his fingers and she was going to die if he didn't stop teasing her. 'I never beg. Never! Now, fuck me!'

It was Theo's turn to moan and whimper when Esme reached back so she could clasp her greedy fingers round the warm, thick length of his cock. She didn't plan to let go any time soon.

'Any time you'd like to beg, Es,' Theo gritted, as she rubbed her palm against the wet head of his cock. 'Just ask me nicely and I'll fuck you.'

'Or there's this thing I can do with my tongue,' she suggested sweetly, because in her head she'd done the thing with her tongue on her imaginary boyfriends countless times. 'Do you want me to tease you for, say, a good half an hour before I even start sucking?'

'That sounds great, but I want to be both giving and receiving pleasure,' Theo said softly, and now Esme's heart was quivering too. She turned over, her hands still on him, and wriggled even closer so they could kiss hotly, wetly.

They didn't speak after that. Too busy kissing, their hands stroking, and Esme thought that she'd be happy with just that but then Theo slid a hand down the back of her thigh so he could drape her leg over his hip and Esme guided his cock into her soaking wet pussy.

Theo sank into her like he was coming home. Her cunt welcomed him in with a rush of sensation, which made Esme gasp and clutch Theo's shoulders. Like so much else with Theo, it was entirely new but also very familiar.

'God, you feel amazing,' Theo rasped, unable to move fast and hard like Esme had thought she wanted, but actually slow and deep was even better. They were nose to nose, almost kissing but not quite, breathing in time with each of Theo's steady thrusts. Esme felt as if she was drowning in him. Then, when he picked up the pace just enough that she had to bury her face in his neck, and she reached down to touch her clit, Theo's hand was already there. It was then that she decided to just let the current claim her. She squeezed Theo tighter with her legs, her arms, her everything, screwed her eyes shut and took a dive so she was freefalling.

And just as she got to the bottom, he caught her.

★

They lay there for long minutes. Theo softened, but still inside her, Esme's hand on his chest so she could feel his heart begin to steady. His lips pressed against her forehead.

Finally, they broke apart and Esme curved into his side because she didn't want to stop touching him. That might have been the best sex she'd ever had. It was God tier sex.

'I wonder if it will always be like that?' she asked him, smoothing her thumbs across the permanent shadows under his eyes.

Theo was silent for a bit, then he turned his head to kiss the underside of Esme's wrist. 'Not always. Otherwise we'll never get anything else done.' His gaze held hers. 'What we have, this is something special, right?'

'I hope so. I really hope so.' Esme wasn't sure if she said the words out loud or if they were a silent, heartfelt prayer. She ran her fingers down Theo's cheek and frowned. 'How is it that there's barely a mark on you?'

Theo moved slightly so that his face was caught in the glow of the bedside lamp, and though she could have sworn that five seconds ago, his skin was blemish-free, now she could see the mark that had been left from having a glass smashed in his cheek. It was thinner, a lot less red and angry than she remembered.

'I told you, I heal quick,' Theo said. He smiled slowly. It wasn't a kind smile, but Esme liked it all the same. 'Although I'm going to need at least an hour's recovery period after what we've just done, but if you're good to go again, we can always improvise.'

'Hands, tongue . . .' Esme said a little dreamily, then ruined the possibility with a massive yawn. 'I think I need at least another hour to regroup too. Maybe a little power nap would be good.' Her eyes were already closing as Theo curled his arm around her waist and shuffled her across the mattress because she was taking up most of his side.

18

Thursday

The ache was the first thing Esme noticed when she woke up the next morning. Not a headache. Or a toothache. It was a languorous sort of ache in parts of her which hadn't known the touch of anyone in quite some time.

Not just the touch of anyone, the touch of Theo, who was still there. Would Esme ever take it for granted that he was just *there*?

This morning she was spooning him because, apparently, they were equal opportunity spooners. Even though the curtains were still drawn it was light enough to see that, apart from the murmuration of starlings that swooped down from his neck and across his left shoulder, the rest of his back was a blank canvas. Smooth, olive skin broken up only by a half moon of freckles, which Esme traced with the tip of her finger, then pressed her lips to the perfect imperfection.

'Far too early for you to be putting the moves on me,' Theo murmured sleepily, but when Esme slid her hand down his chest, his cock was already stirring and so was she. That ache between her legs was now more urgent than languorous.

'Are you sure about that?' Esme stroked up the length of his hardening cock, her grip firm as she reached the head and squeezed gently.

Theo sucked in a breath and covered her hand with his, guiding her motions so they were faster, a little rougher. 'It's my day off. I always have a lie-in on my day off,' he said, but he already sounded a little out of breath.

'You could slip it in and go back to sleep . . .'

'What? Just the tip?' Theo's voice was thick with tiredness, but he also sounded amused, aroused.

'Maybe a bit more than the tip.' Esme pressed open-mouthed kisses against his warm skin as their hands moved faster, until Theo squeezed her fingers so they stilled. But his dick, now properly hard, pulsed under her touch.

'You keep doing that and it will be game over. You're going to have to come over to my side of the bed if you're determined to have your way with me.'

'You could just roll over,' Esme pointed out, trying to rub his cock again but Theo prised her fingers off.

'I'm tired, Es. Got no energy,' Theo groaned dramatically.

'Fine,' Esme snapped, climbing very ungracefully over him and only feeling a little bit guilty when Theo 'oof'ed because she'd caught him in the ribs with her elbow.

But she didn't really care about that because now Theo was spooning her, his cock nosing between her legs, his hand smoothing down her flank then parting her folds. He made an approving, appreciative noise when he discovered how wet she was.

He bit down hard on her neck at the same time that he eased his cock into her. 'Just the tip,' he whispered in her ear and Esme shuddered with the tiniest orgasm just from that. 'Now go back to sleep.'

'I can't. Not when you're doing that,' Esme protested, wriggling her hips to try and get another inch of him inside her, but Theo's hands were suddenly tight around her waist so she couldn't move.

'I'm not doing anything,' he said, biting down ever so slightly on the plumpness of her earlobe. 'Seriously, go back to sleep.'

There was no way she was going back to sleep when she could feel his dick, just the tip, twitching inside her, the walls of her pussy fluttering in response, but then one of Theo's hands started stroking the hair back from her face very slowly and very rhythmically and Esme genuinely thought that she might drift off . . .

Then she gasped because Theo's hand was on her breast, his finger and thumb lightly pinching her nipple as he thrust into her.

'No sleeping on the job,' he said, worrying at her neck again, teeth lightly scraping so that Esme shuddered with another not-quite-all-the-way-there-yet. 'I thought I might mix things up a little.'

'How were you going to do that?' Esme hardly recognised her voice, it was so needy, so dark.

Theo didn't answer but he leaned forward, his dick drilling deep into her and making Esme squeal in delighted surprise, his arm tightening round her waist as he reached for something on the nightstand. 'I saw this and felt inspired,' he said. Esme could hear the rattle as various things knocked against each other but then Theo was leaning back and Esme had no choice but to lean back with him so his cock went deep again.

Then she heard a familiar buzzing sound and she opened her eyes, which had been tightly shut, to see a bulbous black silicone device, shaped like a very small, oval egg, vibrating in Theo's hand.

'How did you even know what that was?' Esme asked, even as she realised that wasn't something she cared about.

'I'm a man of the world.' He thrust into her a couple more times, a lazy back and forth, then he took the vibrator and put it between her legs so it was maddeningly, frustratingly, just out of reach from where she wanted it most.

'It's doing nothing for me there . . .'

'Don't be so impatient,' Theo said, moving the vibrator up just a centimetre more so it was glancing against her clit. 'If you dare let this drop, I'll stop. You know I will.'

Esme didn't doubt him. He tucked the little device into her folds so it was pulsing rhythmically against her clit but she had to close her legs to keep it there. It meant that Theo couldn't fuck her deep and slow like he had the night before, but fast and hard more than made up for it, one of his hands playing with her nipples again, the other tight around her hips, anchoring Esme in place so she could hardly move.

Not that she needed to do much because she was already coming and coming hard. The force of her orgasm made her part her legs so the vibrator fell away, but she could grind herself back against Theo.

'I said I'd stop,' he reminded her huskily, but he was still thrusting into her.

'You wouldn't fucking dare,' Esme managed to say, and she was right because he scooped up the egg and held it in place against her clit so Esme was coming again, or maybe she hadn't stopped coming. It was just wave after wave of sensation, pushing and pulling her this way and that, while all the time Theo was everywhere. Around her, on her, in her, until she didn't know where he ended and she began.

19

The third time that Esme woke up that morning, it was to the persistent shrill of her phone because someone, clearly of the older generation or wanting to know if she'd recently been in an accident, was calling her.

It was neither. It was Lyndsey, who really should have known better.

'I'm only phoning because I've exhausted all other avenues of trying to get in touch,' she said when Esme asked what was wrong with WhatsApp or email. 'I even sent you a DM via Twitter.'

'I've been away from my phone,' Esme said, which wasn't a lie as she'd managed to knock her phone off her bedside table, probably during the throes of passion. Speaking of which, Theo pressed a kiss to her shoulder then slipped out of bed, making the universal sign for 'do you want a cup of tea?' and giving Esme a thumbs up when she nodded frantically. 'Sorry about that, Lynds. So, what's up?'

'It's one o'clock . . .'

'It can't be that late,' Esme said, holding the phone away from her so she could see the time. 'Wow. I don't know where the time's gone.'

She knew exactly where the time had gone. Sleeping off the multiple orgasms that she'd remember when she was on her deathbed. She didn't feel she could tell Lyndsey that, especially as Lyndsey was far more concerned about the concept document that Esme had apparently promised the Cauliflower

Consortium UK she'd have done and emailed by nine this morning.

'Are you sure you're feeling all right, Es?' Lyndsey asked gently after an 'I'm not angry with you, but I am disappointed in you,' lecture, which made Esme low-key squirm.

'I'm feeling perfectly fine in myself,' Esme said, as she heard the shower start and then a muffled 'fuck' as Theo immediately stepped under the spray because he'd forgotten that it took a minute to heat up. She'd read somewhere that a cold shower in the morning released all kinds of endorphins and was character building, but Esme already had plenty of character without the need for that kind of masochism first thing.

' . . . are you even listening to me?'

'Yes! Of course I am,' Esme said quickly and hoped that Lyndsey wasn't going to ask for a verbatim account of what she'd just said. 'I'll send them an apologetic email and get the document done this afternoon.'

'Also, didn't you see the email from Didi with the very last changes to the Granny, Don't Take a Trip copy?'

'I swear I'll get on that this afternoon too,' Esme promised. 'I'm sorry to have dropped the ball. I've just had, well, *a lot on* this week.'

She heard the water turn off and Theo step out of the bath.

'Well, it's not surprising. You should probably have taken the week off,' Lyndsey was saying. 'How's your head?'

Esme considered the question. 'A bit throbby still.' There was an ache where the stitches had gone in but Esme was used to that now. 'Also, I'm desperate to wash my hair.'

'You can't wash your hair?' Esme thought that Lyndsey had sounded appalled while she was telling her off for her bad work ethic but that had obviously just been a dress rehearsal because now she sounded absolutely *fucking* appalled.

'Not allowed to get the stitches wet.'

'But what are you going to do for Saturday then?'

There was a sound behind her and Theo, wearing only a towel so all that lean muscle and all those shit tattoos were on display, came in with a steaming mug of tea, which Esme took from him gratefully.

'Esme? God, what is wrong with you today?' came Lyndsey's increasingly peevish voice.

'Sorry. What?'

'I asked what you were going to do on Saturday if you can't wash your hair?'

Esme tried to focus on Lyndsey's question and not on Theo, who was collecting clean clothes from his holdall, which seemed to have the same kind of mythic capacity as Mary Poppins's carpet bag. 'What's happening on Saturday?'

There was a growl of frustration from down the phone. 'Seren's wedding.'

'Oh yeah, *that*,' Esme said without much enthusiasm. 'Clearly, I'm in denial about the whole thing. I hope the grub's good at the very least.'

Lyndsey rung off after Esme promised that she would get all her outstanding work done by Friday, tomorrow lunchtime, at the latest.

Then she wandered into the kitchen to see Theo at the stove.

Esme could get used to this. The thought popped unannounced into her head and needed further investigation. Could she really get used to sharing her life, her home, all her messy, baggage-laden bits, with someone else? Could it be that the fantasising and rich, inner life-ing had been because, on some subconscious level, she'd wanted to be in an actual, long-term, fully committed relationship?

Not that being in a relationship the first time had had much to recommend it. And Esme didn't have that many great examples of relationships that she wanted to emulate. Debbie and Gary's marriage had been less a joining of souls and more open warfare. However much Esme squinted, she didn't see Allegra and Oliver as love's young dream either; it was more that Allegra's critical faculties had been silenced by the deafening tick tock tick tock of her biological clock and, much as she denied it, she'd been secretly furious that Esme had got married before her.

Who else was there? Seren and Isaac? Seren claimed that they'd been lovers in a past life but she'd also joked that, when she was manifesting wealth, Isaac had swiftly come into her life with his annual bonus, his share portfolio and a three-bedroom lateral apartment in Westbourne Grove. There was Marion and Jacinta – what they had looked a lot like love, but maybe they were the exception that proved the rule.

'Nothing fancy I'm afraid. Just making some French toast with the ends of a brioche I brought home last night,' Theo said, not even turning round. 'You've got time for a quick shower.'

'I really could get used to this,' Esme said, low enough that she thought she was talking to herself but Theo glanced over his shoulder.

'I hope so.' He brandished the frying pan, wafting up a delicious scent of butter and cinnamon. 'Because I intend to treat you like a queen.'

'You don't have to do that. Just treating me like a princess or a minor European royal would do,' Esme said. But as she stood in the bathtub, showering away the last traces of him, she knew they couldn't go on like this.

There weren't enough superlatives in the world for how amazing the sex had been but if that hadn't been so good, then Esme wouldn't be quite as suspicious as she was. Yes, she and Theo had a connection. There was a spark between them that just kept glowing brighter, but he understood her too well. Knew things about her, deeply hidden, secret things, that it wasn't possible for him to know after just a handful of days.

That someone lightly scraping their teeth against her skin made Esme lose all reason. That, as Theo had said last night, she needed a little edge, a little darkness, to really get off. But she hadn't met a man that she could trust to give her those things because a little edge, a little darkness could quickly transform into someone hurting Esme, trying to control her, to dominate her and not in a fun, mutually consensual way.

So she'd only trusted her fantasy boyfriends with her actual fantasies until Theo had rocked up in her life and just seemed to know who Esme was and what she needed.

When she was back in her bedroom, Esme hunted for the vision board from Saturday night. It had got shoved under the bed so as well as being blood splattered, tear stained and crumpled, it was now home to a couple of dust bunnies.

Making a mental note to vacuum under the bed occasionally, Esme blew them away and studied the collage. The young, lanky, anarchic looking James Stewart with his stubborn cowlick of dark hair. The tousled chef with tattoos covering his arms and his exceedingly talented fingers. The Manchester Ship Canal. Even, and now Esme recalled mentioning something about mini-breaks and her last mini-break in particular, a picture of the red and white rooftops of Lisbon set against an azure blue sky. And in big silver glittery writing was 'Absolutely filthy' arching over the top of the page. Those two words confirmed all the suspicions that were niggling at her, because last night had been both absolutely filthy but also very, very familiar.

In fact, the only thing that hadn't come to pass was the Labrador puppy being cradled in the arms of yet another scruffy sexy man, but there was still time.

The vision board and all that had come with it explained the extraordinary circumstances that Esme now found herself in. Not just extraordinary but unprecedented. Things, men like Theo, didn't happen to people like Esme. Because men like Theo didn't even exist. Not in the real world.

But how to even bring it up? Esme didn't know where to begin.

It was Theo's day off, which only meant that he wasn't at the pub. He still had work to do. 'Invoices and orders and menu planning,' he groaned as they sat side by side on the sofa with their laptops open.

At four, when Esme's head started to pound, or rather pound harder than usual, she decided to suggest going for a walk on the Heath before it got dark. It felt like a conversation that was easier to have as they were walking slowly up Parliament Hill, their breath crystallising in the air, like little puffs of dragon smoke. Maybe when they got to the crest of the hill, the rooftops and church spires and skyscrapers of London on the horizon, they could sit on a bench and she could break the news to him.

'Shall we get some fresh air?' she asked, her voice so strained that she nearly choked.

Theo didn't even look up. 'If I take a breather now, I'll lose all my momentum,' he muttered, his attention on the very boring looking spreadsheet on his screen. 'I just need to focus until I'm done.'

Sarra Manning

It was very hard for Esme to focus on fucking cauliflowers when Theo was next to her. Living, breathing and emitting body heat so she didn't need to wear her baggy cardigan and was even thinking about turning the thermostat down.

'Right, I'm done,' he said a couple of hours later. It was dark now – at one stage Esme had got up to turn on the big light – past six. 'Shall we order pizza?'

The thought of pizza made her feel vaguely nauseous. 'Maybe later. Hang on.' Esme quickly saved her thoughts about cauliflowers then emailed them off as an attachment. She closed her MacBook and took a deep breath. 'We need to talk.'

Theo instantly stiffened. 'Four words that lead to nothing good. What have I done?'

'You haven't done anything,' Esme quickly assured him, patting his knee in a way that was meant to be comforting but actually felt a lot like she was smacking him. 'It's nothing bad. Not really.'

Theo put his laptop on the coffee table so he could stretch out his legs and fold his arms, his body language far from encouraging. 'Go on, then.'

'Well, it's so bizarre that I can hardly explain it,' Esme said slowly, putting her hand on Theo's knee again – his very knobbly, needlessly complicated knee – and marvelled at how she'd willed this knee and all the other parts of him into being. 'There's no easy way to say this, Theo, but I'm pretty sure that I invented you.'

Theo screwed up his face as if Esme had just made him lick batteries. 'Sorry, what the *fuck* are you talking about?'

'What I'm talking about is that you *were* my imaginary boyfriend until, I think it was that Sunday morning in the hospital, you suddenly became real.'

Esme paused there because, really, she didn't know how to continue, but Theo nodded like he understood.

'OK, I suspected something like this,' he said in a much calmer voice than Esme had been anticipating.

She let out a deep sigh of relief. 'I'm glad you think the past few days have been weird too and it's not just me.'

'So, I'm your imaginary boyfriend?' Theo queried gently.

Esme nodded. 'Well, more like a composite of several imaginary boyfriends that I've had.' She looked at Theo from under her lashes as he gazed steadily back at her. 'I must say, you're taking this much better than I thought you would.'

'Well, there's a simple explanation, isn't there?' Theo shrugged.

'Yes!' Esme snapped her fingers, making Theo blink. 'It's Occam's razor.'

'It's like you're speaking in tongues,' Theo drawled, forehead still scrunched up. 'What has my razor got to do with anything?'

'Not an actual razor, I don't know why it's called that, but it's like, a philosophical rule that the simplest explanation is usually the best one.'

Theo sighed and it was his turn to rest his hand on Esme's knee, long fingers with their crap tattoos splayed against the black cotton and spandex of her leggings. 'The simplest explanation, and I don't like it any more than you will . . .'

'I don't *not* like it . . .' Esme said because yes, it was weird turned all the way up to eleven but . . .

'The simple explanation,' Theo repeated with grim emphasis, 'is that . . .'

'I manifested you!'

'. . . You've got a concussion.'

20

'But I haven't,' Esme protested, covering his hands with hers. 'For a start, I can still remember the words to "Yes Sir, I Can Boogie" . . . Surely song lyrics would be the first thing to go if . . .'

'That's because it's a disco classic,' Theo said slowly, like he was trying to explain Pythagoras' theorem to a five-year-old. 'I mean, my favourite artist is Tom Waits but "Yes Sir, I Can Boogie" is a bop.'

'It really is.' Esme shook her head. They were getting side-tracked. 'Anyway, if I'm concussed, then how come I can remember all of my times tables?'

'I don't think that's how concussion works,' Theo said, looking at Esme now like she really was talking in tongues.

'Five times six? Thirty!'

'Doesn't count. That's an easy one.'

'Eight times nine? Seventy-four! Eleven times twelve? One hundred and thirty-three!' Esme nudged Theo with her elbow. 'Honestly, if my brain was having a hard time it would dump the boring maths stuff straight away, and it also doesn't explain the fact that you're a figment of my imagination who's suddenly become real. The only explan-ation is . . .'

'Concussion . . . and we're getting you a head CT, stat,' Theo said flatly, like it wasn't even a suggestion but a state-ment of fact.

Esme glared at him. It was odd how glaring at him always gave her such a sense of déjà vu. 'No. The simple explanation is that I manifested you.'

Even as Esme said it, she was riddled with doubt. How had she, a non-believer, manifested an actual fucking human being?

Esme thought back to that eventful, fateful Saturday night and the events leading up to what she now knew to be Theo's manifestation. She'd been in a highly charged emotional state as she'd assembled the vision board. She'd been crying as she recited her affirmations, imbuing them with the same kind of meaning as if she'd been reciting her marriage vows. The crystals had been resting on the board and she'd cried on them, coated them with her tears, until the candles had all suddenly roared into life then snuffed themselves out. Plus, she'd had that weird electric shock. Then, later on, she'd coated the vision board in a fine layer of her blood, and Esme had watched enough *Buffy the Vampire Slayer* to know that blood was the bulk ingredient in any standard ritual.

But probably the most important element had been the crystals resting on the vision board.

'Where's your phone?' she asked Theo.

He patted himself down. 'I don't know. Maybe I left it charging in the kitchen.'

'Don't go anywhere,' Esme said, because it would just be typical if now he decided to disappear in a puff of smoke.

But when she came back into the living room with her phone, Theo was still there. Head back, eyes closed but they opened immediately when Esme sat back down next to him.

'Right,' she said, looking down at the Google search results and clicking on 'Seventeen Crystals for Manifesting Love'.

'So, at Seren's hen we made these vision boards to represent a specific goal or dream and I vision boarded you . . .'

'Oh, did you?' Theo rolled his eyes and Esme could tell he was trying to humour the sad woman with the alleged concussion. Not very successfully either.

'It's not like I just poofed you into existence on Saturday night. I've already said, you've been in my head for years. Like a fantasy boyfriend. A sweet smorgasbord of all the qualities I'd want in an ideal man.' How to explain this? 'The thing is, Theo, I have a very rich inner life.'

'Well, I definitely want to know *all* about your rich inner life.' Esme could tell that he was trying to hide his smile again. After all, it was a look she'd seen on his face, his imaginary face, countless times. It was also very sexy.

'Let's not go into *that* right now,' Esme said, her face burning at the thought of just how many times she'd fired up her vibrator while a very detailed fantasy of a man who closely resembled Theo and exactly what he was going to do to her played in her head like her frontal lobes were directly hardwired into PornHub. After all, they'd visited the highlight reel of those fantasies last night, which had coalesced all of Esme's suspicions that Theo hadn't been independently living his life for thirty-nine years.

He was just too perfect to be real.

So he must have sprung fully formed from her cerebral cortex in the early hours of Sunday morning.

'I'm just a figment of your imagination?' Theo asked, stroking his fingers down her flushed cheek. 'You can't feel that?'

'Stop it,' Esme said weakly, though she didn't really want him to stop. 'All I'm saying is that you're not a figment of my imagination anymore and it's obvious that the crystals played a key part in your manifestation. One of them was rhodonite, which apparently harnesses forgiveness and helps you move past stagnant cycles.'

'They're just coloured stones, Es,' Theo said, closing his eyes again, head tipped back so Esme could appreciate his bone structure. The similarity to a young James Stewart was uncanny. It sounded ridiculous to claim that she'd manifested Theo, but how else to explain that she was now sitting next to a living, breathing embodiment of the fantasy figure who lived had rent-free inside of Esme's head because she liked him far too much to ever charge him £900 pcm, plus his share of the bills? 'You really didn't strike me as someone who believes in any of that crystal bullshit.'

'I didn't. I don't. I never recharged them in moonlight as per Seren's instructions, but kept them stuffed in my knicker drawer. That's bound to have some kind of significance to do with sex and passion, blah blah blah. Then I definitely had rose quartz on the table, which is the Big Daddy of love crystals, and then there was black obsidian, which helps you feel worthy of love . . .'

'But you've always been worthy of love . . .'

'In your reality or wherever you've come from maybe, but in this reality, I'm only worthy of fuckboys.' Esme scrolled past pictures of the other crystals until she came to a photo of a jagged lump of yellow citrine. She showed it to Theo. 'Now, this one . . .'

Very gently, he took her phone from her. 'I think you should have a CT scan tomorrow morning.'

'You know they don't just hand out CT scans on request and I *know* the Glasgow Coma Scale,' Esme said a little pompously. 'I haven't forgotten that, and I do not meet any of the criteria of a) a serious head injury or b) needing a CT scan.'

'We haven't been together long, but you never mentioned that you had a medical degree.' Theo pressed his lips together to hide the smirk that Esme was sure he had good to go.

'Maybe I haven't manifested you,' Esme admitted, poking Theo in the ribs with a finger, a move which made him hiss in irritation. 'I'm pretty sure I wouldn't have manifested someone so annoying.'

Theo was made of sterner stuff, apparently. 'You have no idea how annoying I'm going to be until you get your head checked out,' he said, picking up Esme's phone from the coffee table.

'My head is fine. I still have every single word from *Hamilton* committed to memory and I can remember all the stuff that I made up about you and it kind of tallies with the memories that obviously got implanted in you during the manifesting . . .'

'I get it, Esme, you're stubborn. Well guess what? I'm more stubborn.'

'Not possible,' Esme insisted, but Theo shook his head and held her phone out to her.

'I'm not going to drop this. If you won't phone 111, then you need to phone your GP. At the very least make an appointment to get your stitches taken out.'

'But it hasn't been a week yet . . .'

'You should never take any chances with head injuries,' Theo said implacably, like Esme could actually steamroll all over him and his flattened pancake of a body would still be insisting that she sought medical advice.

'But I have the kids tomorrow and then there's something important happening on Saturday,' she said as she reluctantly took the phone from him.

'So make an appointment for Monday.'

'It's late. The surgery will be closed now.'

'Aren't some GP surgeries open until eight on Thursdays? Mine is. It's only just gone seven now.'

Esme put the phone on speaker as she wouldn't put it past Theo to accuse her of ringing up the speaking clock. Still, she'd be waiting hours in a queue to actually speak to someone and by then the surgery would be closed and she'd have to . . .

'You're number one in the queue,' said the automated voice annoyingly, and then there were only a couple of bars of Handel's Water Music, not great if you were calling about a UTI, before an actual human woman answered the phone and asked Esme for her name and date of birth.

'It's nothing serious,' Esme said, turning her back on Theo, who didn't even bother to hide the fact that he was listening intently. 'It's just a follow-up to a very minor head injury.'

'Oh my goodness! In that case, do you want to come in now?' asked the receptionist, which sent a little wisp of panic curling through Esme's insides.

'Head injury is probably overstating it.' Theo tutted but Esme ignored him. 'I just need some stitches taken out after a week, but they only went in on Sunday morning. Have you got any appointments free for Monday?'

They did. Esme confirmed the appointment, then it was her turn to hiss in annoyance as Theo rested his chin on her shoulder to watch as she put the details in her calendar.

'And don't forget the two alerts. Oh, and also, you'd better set some alarms so you get up on Monday too.'

'You are *so* infuriating,' Esme gritted, but Theo just grinned like he was fine about that and kissed her on the cheek. 'You know, you weren't the only man to feature in my rich inner life. Harry Styles was there too and I'm starting to wish that I'd stuck him on my vision board instead.'

Theo seemed supremely unbothered that he had a rival for Esme's affections. 'Whatever. Now that we've got that sorted, shall we order pizza?'

They didn't talk about Theo's manifestation or Esme's alleged concussion for the rest of the evening. Instead they watched some old episodes of *Taskmaster* and had a very long, very animated discussion as to the velocity needed to hurl a shoe into a bath from some distance away, using a homemade catapult.

It wasn't until they were getting ready for bed that Theo brought it up again. He was brushing his teeth at the bathroom sink while Esme sat on the edge of the tub and worked her serum in with her rose quartz roller (now that she thought about it, crystals were omnipresent in her life) when she realised that Theo had stopped brushing and was staring at her in the bathroom mirror.

'What?' she asked as she went at her neck and hoped it would be a good few years before it went crepey.

Theo puffed out his chest like a pigeon. A pigeon with shit tattoos. 'I'm the perfect boyfriend, am I?'

He really kind of was. 'Not that perfect it turns out. You're very argumentative and why haven't you put the top back on the toothpaste?' Esme demurred.

'Too right, I'm argumentative. I'm bloody-minded. I'm grumpy but I've actually been on my best behaviour these last few days.'

Esme didn't mind grumpy. She was hardly Little Miss Sunshine herself. 'Why have you been on your best behaviour?' Her eyes narrowed, because she'd been here before. 'What do you want?'

Theo's eyes narrowed too. 'I don't want *anything* but I've been on my best behaviour because I've been trying to impress you. I really like you Esme. In spite of the fact that you think you magicked me up with a few lumps of coloured stone.' He ran the cold tap, solely so he could flick a few drops of water at Esme, which made her roll her eyes as she rolled the underside of her chin. 'Could a figment of your imagination do that?'

'Maybe this is all a Patrick from *Dallas*-style dream?' Esme mused. 'I'll wake up tomorrow and none of this will have happened.'

The thought of it made her feel not just sad, but immediately bereft. Like her life would suddenly become monochrome. That there'd be a hole right through the centre of it that it would be impossible to fill.

'We shouldn't have . . . I shouldn't have . . .' He pushed his hair back from his face and Esme wondered yet again what the difference was between a cowlick and a widow's peak '. . . we shouldn't have had sex.'

That brought her back into the room. 'Why the hell not?' Of all the bizarre things that had happened since Saturday, the sex had been the absolute best. Number one with a bullet.

'How can you give consent if you've got concussion?' Theo sat down next to her on the edge of the bath, mainly so he could slump forward, his elbows on his knees. 'What if all that toing and froing jolted something?'

'It did jolt something and I was very pleased when it did.' Esme was sick of theorising about it: concussion or manifesting? No wonder she had a permanent headache.

'Bed,' Theo announced firmly. 'You should be in bed.'

She liked the authoritative tone he got, which managed not to be patronising but still quite sexy. Her vagina definitely needed some R & R, but there were other things, all sorts of delicious other things, they could do. 'I thought you were worried that I might have jolted something?' Esme asked flirtatiously, even throwing in a little flutter of her lashes, but Theo stood up as quickly as if the porcelain rim of the bathtub had suddenly become electrified.

'We're not doing any of *that*,' he snapped, managing to look both affronted and regretful. 'Not until you've had the all clear. Possibly even a doctor's note.'

21

Friday

Theo was as good as his word. He didn't lay a finger on Esme all night, though when she woke up at a respectable hour, because she'd remembered to set her alarm, his arm was around her waist. Like he was trying to anchor her in case she slipped away.

Esme slipped out of bed carefully so as not to wake him. It was still early enough that the sun was struggling into position. As she waited for the kettle to boil, the world outside the kitchen window was soft and smudgy, the mist wisping and curling over the hedges of the little green directly opposite her block.

Fingers warmed by a mug of tea, even though her baggy cardigan wasn't doing much to warm the rest of her, Esme sat down at her desk, opened her laptop and vowed that, apart from hydration and the inevitable pee breaks, she wasn't going to move from that spot until she'd finished all her work for the week.

At one stage, Theo came in with tea before he had to leave for work, dropping a kiss on the top of Esme's head and not even mentioning the fact that her hair was starting to smell. For all the snark and swagger, he was really nice. Really nice was a very overlooked quality in a man.

'See you later,' he murmured against her rank, greasy hair. 'Try to avoid making any sudden movements.'

'I will,' Esme said, raising her head for a kiss, which Theo willingly gave, his lips clinging to hers for several sweet seconds before he straightened up.

'I can't believe you think that I didn't exist before you manifested me,' he said a little sadly, and before Esme could tell him that she was very glad that he did exist now, he was gone.

She sent off the last piece of work at just before two and only had time for a quick shower, swapping her pyjamas for jeans, jumper and walking boots. Then she pulled on her bulbous puffer coat and raced down the stairs to collect Buster before heading out into the wider world for the first time in two days.

Buster had a couple of wees then looked at Esme expectantly until she heaved him up into her arms. As usual, he was a heavily panting dead weight as she crossed over Highgate Road and braced herself and her thigh muscles for the uphill walk ahead of her.

Dartmouth Park was one of those minuscule areas of London known only to its residents and local estate agents. It was tucked away in between Parliament Hill and the far less salubrious Archway, its houses getting bigger and grander the further uphill you went.

Allegra and Oliver lived in a massive three-storey redbrick Victorian house built when middle class people had large families and at least a couple of maids who could sleep up in the attic. Their attic now housed the master bedroom with en suite wet room, walk in wardrobe and a gym area with a Peloton bike and a full set of weights. Their neighbours included Ed Miliband and Benedict Cumberbatch, as Allegra was wont to remind Esme at regular intervals though, quite frankly, you couldn't live in their part of North London without bumping into Benedict Cumberbatch every time you popped out for a packet of biscuits.

Esme was still struggling up the steep set of steps that led to the fashionably grey front door when it opened.

'You're late,' lamented Jean, the Dickensons' nanny, as she manhandled the pushchair through the front door while Summer tried to climb into it. Jean had been in situ ever since Oscar first came home from the hospital. She was a tiny, tiny, doe-eyed creature with masses of chocolate brown pre-Raphaelite curls and a broad Glasgow accent. She didn't speak French or Mandarin or have a black belt in Krav Maga like some of Allegra's friends' nannies, but she was regarded in the Dickenson house as being precious above rubies. 'Summer, you have to wait until the pram is on the pavement. We've been through this.'

'Otherwise you'll tumble out of it like a sack of potatoes and no one likes bruised spuds,' Esme said. It was the same every Friday handover. Summer hated walking almost as much as Buster. So much so that Allegra had taken her to see a child development specialist because she was so slow to walk and had been incensed when the diagnosis had come back as sheer, bloody laziness.

'Bruises on my bum!' Summer shouted excitedly, which made Esme wince for her poor head. It didn't bode well for the rest of the afternoon.

'You doing anything nice for the weekend?' Esme asked Jean, as she put a protesting Buster down so she could help with the pushchair.

'Well, I'm babysitting tomorrow night while they're at the wedding,' Jean said in a low voice. 'Got to pick the kids up from the reception.'

'Hope you're getting time and a half,' Esme said.

'Double time, a Deliveroo and an Addison Lee car there and back.'

'Good for you.' The irony was never wasted on Esme that she got on better with her sister's nanny than she did with her sister. 'At least you've got this afternoon off.'

'Daren't even go out on the lash tonight because those three tomorrow when I'm hanging . . .' Jean tailed off because Summer was now clinging to her legs and all of Jean's reminders about being a tattletale always fell on deaf ears. 'Look! There's Buster! Are you going to say hello to him?'

Summer eyed the wheezing pug with disdain. 'No. He stinks.'

'Fair enough, he really does.' Esme made sure the pram brakes were on and then held out her arms. 'Are you going to say hello to me?'

Giggling and still clinging to Jean, Summer shook her head. 'You stink too.'

'Rude!' Esme exclaimed and pretended to cry. 'Shall I spritz the stink away?' She pulled a bottle of hand sanitiser out of her coat pocket and sprayed her hands, because Buster really didn't smell too fresh. 'Better?'

'I come with you now,' Summer agreed, already hurling herself at Esme. It was like making full body contact with a cannonball. Summer was small, compact and sturdy with straw blond ringlets and huge blue eyes. A quick hug then she climbed into the pushchair. She could even clip herself in. 'OK. Let's go!'

'Their snacks and water are in the front pocket,' Jean said and, just as Esme thought they were done, the door opened again and her heart sank, expecting either Allegra or Oliver, who sometimes still worked from home.

It was neither of them, but someone almost as bad. Or worse. Esme could never decide.

'Well, there she is,' was all she got by way of a greeting from her own mother.

'Yes, here I am,' Esme said. 'Are you all right?'

'Can't complain,' said her mother, which was a lie because all she ever did was complain. She looked well though, standing at the top of the steps. She was tall and spare looking, capable, as befitted a woman who could tile and grout a bathroom in a day and rewire a lamp without having to watch twenty YouTube videos first. Or paint a feature wall a disgusting colour without being asked. She was wearing a taupe jumpsuit, socks and Birkenstocks, her long white hair fluttering in the early March winds. 'I'll grab my coat.'

Esme sighed. She might bitch about providing free weekly childcare but that was only because Allegra rarely thanked her for it. The reality was that she liked spending time with the kids and it was always a joyful way to end the week. Whereas Debbie did nothing but kill joy wherever she found it.

'No, don't grab your coat, you're not coming,' Esme said flatly, when usually she'd acquiesce then spend the rest of her time with her mother quietly seething.

Debbie was so taken aback that she took an actual step back. 'Don't be silly. Of course I am.'

'I don't want you to come. I don't know why you even want to . . .'

'To spend time with . . .'

'I don't like you, you don't like me, so let's not,' Esme said, and she didn't wait to debate it but started walking. 'Have a good weekend, Jean.'

'You too,' Jean said faintly.

Even Buster got the message that Esme didn't want to hang about because he shuffled along next to the pushchair at what was a breakneck speed for him.

Esme couldn't quite believe that she'd been so . . . rude? Was it rude when she'd been telling the truth? Debbie didn't like Esme. Her mothering style could be loosely described as benign neglect. She didn't care much for Allegra either.

Whenever Esme thought back to her childhood, her memories weren't happy ones. She couldn't ever remember Debbie hugging her or comforting her when she had a nightmare or even telling Esme that she loved her. Not that Gary was blameless. He was only nice to Esme when he was sending her off to the corner shop with a note and a fiver so she could buy him cigarettes.

And whatever rundown property they were living in was always full of Debbie's horrible friends. She described herself as a collector of people, interesting, fascinating people: artists, writers, singers, activists. When in reality they were simply a lot of people who drank too much, took too many drugs and liked to talk about themselves at the top of their vocal range. Gary had always complained that the house was full of 'fucking nutjobs'. He'd had a point.

Then there were the ferocious arguments because Debbie and Gary both had main character energy and wouldn't accept second billing. Her parents' relationship had been tumultuous at best. Two absolutely incompatible narcissists who should never have even gone on a date, let alone get married. They'd met when Debbie had bought her first house, a near derelict two-up two-down in Tottenham, and Gary had arrived by way of a card in a newsagent's window to install a new sink and toilet.

'Five minutes after showing him where the bathroom was, we were fucking on the upstairs landing,' Debbie had recalled when she was giving Esme the most brutal facts of life talk that any thirteen-year-old had ever suffered. 'Just because you're ridiculously, mindlessly sexually compatible with someone doesn't mean it's a good basis for a relationship. They might be able to satisfy you in bed but that doesn't mean they can nourish you emotionally or intellectually.'

No wonder Esme's formative years had been so miserable that she'd sought solace in her own imagination. She'd never really felt safe, settled or loved. So, when Esme thought about that and about all the times that Debbie had never once put Esme first, then it was perfectly OK to tell her mother that she didn't like her. Quite frankly, it was long overdue.

22

Esme was determined to put Debbie out of her head. By the time she reached the boys' posh little prep school in the very heart of Dartmouth Park, her smile wasn't at all forced as she caught sight of Oscar first, then Fergus, who each waved, then raced towards her.

'Ooooof!' Straight into her like they were playing All Nations rugby. 'Steady on!'

'We thought they'd have shaved all your hair off,' Oscar said with genuine dismay.

'Can we see your stitches?' asked Fergus.

They looked up at her expectantly.

For a second, Esme didn't know what they were talking about. Then she let herself become aware of the ever-present headache, that distinct twinge at the back of her head.

'I don't think you can even see them,' she said, as she steered the pushchair and her nephews past the school run hordes. Well-polished North London mums and slightly less polished North London nannies were handing over snacks to small children who couldn't go less than an hour without a wholemeal pitta bread strip dipped in organic hummus. By now, Buster had given up walking and was snoozing away in the shopping basket beneath Summer's seat.

'We could *try*,' Oscar said. 'It's the most exciting thing that's ever happened to you, Es.'

'Lots of exciting things have happened to me,' Esme protested, though a lot of them weren't things she was prepared to share with two boys aged seven and only just turned six. They'd reached a comparatively quiet corner, so she stopped and put the brake on the buggy. 'OK, I'm going to part my hair and you can look, but *do not touch!*'

'My hands are clean!' Fergus said in injured tones, holding up a pair of grubby hands that looked like he'd been digging for potatoes just before the end-of-school bell had rung.

Esme leaned forward and gently tugged her hair out of the way so the two boys could peer at whatever her cut looked like now after six days. She could have sworn that she felt their hot breath on her scalp, probably containing all manner of dodgy bacteria, so she quickly righted herself, gripping on to the pushchair for support as she had another one of those almighty head rushes.

'Can hardly see anything,' Oscar complained. 'No wonder Mum said you were making a fuss about nothing.'

'Oh, did she?'

'She said you were a drama queen from way back,' Fergus added because, like their grandmother, neither of them had any filter. 'That if it had been really serious they'd have given you a cat scan.'

'Why do they scan cats if you've hurt yourself?'

'CAT scan is actually an acronym.' They stared at her blankly. 'It stands for computed axial something or other but basically it's a fancy word for an X-ray.'

'Have you got snacks?' Oscar was already clearly bored of the conversation.

Esme pulled the ubiquitous Tupperware box out of one of the pushchair's many compartments and handed it over as they started walking back down the hill towards Highgate Road.

Oscar prised open the lid, fending off Fergus, to uncover their Friday afternoon treats. A mini bag of lentil curls apiece, some apple slices and a fun size bar of dark chocolate.

'Gross,' Fergus summed up, with a sideways look at Esme. 'So gross,' she agreed. 'You know what to do.'

Their spoils were carefully left on top of the next street bin. Not thrown away, because food waste was bad, but left there so that if a passer-by was hungry, they could help themselves to the lentil curls.

That done, the boys raced off down the street, though they knew to wait for Esme if there were any roads that needed crossing.

Soon they were back in her neighbourhood and joining what seemed like hundreds of other primary school-age children who were racing across Duke's Field, the little patch of grass where Buster preferred to do his ablutions, and descending on the playground.

Esme wheeled the buggy into the playground enclosure and set up camp by the most toddler-friendly equipment so she could keep an eye on Summer. The boys had already abandoned them in favour of climbing the huge wooden structure, which resembled a fort and featured many towers and slides. It would keep them busy for fifteen minutes tops.

Whereas Summer had a couple of goes on the smallest slide then was happy to sit in the sandpit and do nothing.

'Excuse me! Excuse me!' Esme took her eyes off her niece long enough to look at the querulous face of a woman who was suddenly looming over her. 'Dogs aren't allowed in the playground!'

'He's asleep in a basket,' she muttered, rolling her eyes.

'But they're not allowed.' The woman was really thin, very bulgy of eye, very tattered of nerve. 'It says no dogs allowed very clearly on the sign.'

'He's asleep in a basket,' Esme repeated. 'What do you want me to do? Leave my three-year-old niece and her brothers unattended?'

'You shouldn't be in here with a dog.' The woman was practically vibrating with outrage as she pointed a finger at Buster, who was sleeping through all the *sturm und drang*. 'I'm going to the keeper's office to report you.'

'Go on then, off you fuck,' Esme said, sitting back on the bench and folding her arms. 'FYI, he's my emotional support dog for when I have to deal with arseholes.'

Then, because the whole thing was ridiculous and, also, because Esme was very amused with her own last line, she laughed. The woman huffed so hard in speechless fury that Esme was amazed she didn't take off.

'I'm going to call the police,' she said when she could speak again.

'Why? So you can report your face as a hate crime?' Esme asked and the woman stalked away, muttering under her breath, just as the boys came running up.

'Hungry,' they said as one. Esme was only too happy to leave before she was arrested. Though, to be fair, the woman had been rude first and she needed to get her nose out of other people's business.

Of course, this was the one occasion when Summer didn't want to get back in the pushchair. 'I'm playing,' she insisted, while mindlessly letting handfuls of sand trickle through her pudgy fingers.

'But we're going to get cake,' Oscar said cajolingly. Summer shook her head, her bottom lip jutting out, two telltale signs that she was seconds away from a meltdown.

'We could just leave her here,' Esme suggested. 'What's the worst that could happen?'

The two boys thought about it. 'She could be taken by a paedo,' Fergus said eventually. 'What *is* a paedo, anyway?'

'A bad person,' Esme said. Maybe leaving Summer on her own to think about the errors of her ways wasn't a great idea. 'Come on, Sum, you love cake. Or how about I get you an ice cream?'

Summer flopped on her back. 'I hate ice cream.'

'She's lying,' Oscar said anxiously. 'She loves ice cream. We *all* love ice cream.'

With a deep sigh, Esme stood up and walked over to Summer, who stiffened every one of her limbs in anticipation. Esme picked her up and Summer obliged by screaming as if she really was being abducted.

'You'll have to manage the buggy,' Esme said to the boys as she carried their spluttering, squealing sister out of the playground by her armpits. 'Christ, Sum, you weigh a fucking ton.'

'You're not meant to say fucking. It's the rudest word!'

'Not the rudest word.' Esme hefted Summer up higher in her arms as the boys tried to get the pushchair through the gate. 'There are much ruder ones. I might start saying them if your sister doesn't shut up.'

'That would be thrilling,' Fergus said. 'We wouldn't mind if you wanted to say them.'

'We would, it's wrong to swear,' Oscar said, thumping Fergus on the shoulder, which meant that Fergus began to cry, even though it was a puny punch, and whacked Oscar back.

While seven-year-old Oscar had both elfin looks and physique (Esme always thought that he should be kitted out in full choirboy garb complete with a piecrust collar as he warbled '*Pie Jesu*'), Fergus was eighteen months younger but stronger, stockier and quicker to anger. His punch landed with great force right in Oscar's stomach and then they were rolling about in the grass, pummelling each other. They spent a lot of time pummelling each other, but Esme didn't have either the energy or patience for it this afternoon.

She put the still screaming Summer down on the ground, then dropped to the ground herself. Esme shut her eyes and actually, even though she was lying on damp grass, it wouldn't take much for her to fall asleep. If only Summer would stop making that awful racket and the boys would stop fighting.

'Oh no, are you dead?' exclaimed a tearful voice, and she looked up to see Oscar and Fergus looking down at her, Fergus biting his bottom lip to keep himself from crying.

'I'm not in the mood to be fucked with,' Esme explained kindly.

'We promise we won't fuck with you,' Fergus said, a little gleam in his watery eyes that he'd got to say the f-word without being told off or having his mouth washed out with organic dish soap. 'You have to look after us, so we don't get taken by paedos.'

'I might just stay here,' Esme said, only half joking.

'You can't,' Oscar said in a scandalised tone. 'You're the grown-up.'

'I don't want to be the grown-up!'

'Well, tough! You are!' Oscar sounded alarmingly like his father and, with an unhappy groan, Esme sat up and held out her hands so that Fergus and Oscar could take them in their hot, sweaty clutches and haul her to her feet.

'Are you going to be good?' Esme asked them.

'We're going to be very good,' Oscar promised, wrapping his arms around Esme's waist.

'And I love you,' Summer said winningly from the push-chair, where she'd put herself after she realised that she was working her aunt's last nerve. She had several rivulets of snot hanging down from each nostril. Esme retrieved tissues from the buggy and wiped her nose.

'I'm not sure that I do love you guys,' she mused. 'I'll have to think about it.'

'But you're our favourite grown-up,' Fergus insisted.

It wasn't like Esme had much competition there but she appreciated the sentiment, especially when both boys hugged her again and even Summer felt moved to unclip herself from her buggy and wipe her nose on Esme's legs. It was a good feeling to be hugged by three small people that she did actually love a lot. 'Shall we go to the cafe then?' she asked, and the three of them let go of her pretty quickly so they could run the short distance to the cafe.

Dogs weren't allowed inside but they covered Buster up with the spare blanket from the buggy. Esme liked to think that this small act of rule breaking was teaching the children to think outside the box. Not that they cared. They were already queuing at the counter, Oscar lifting Summer up so she could see what cakes were left.

Esme realised that she was ravenously hungry. She hadn't eaten anything since last night's pizza, and it was four o'clock now. She ordered sausage, chips and beans, a mug of tea and a can of lemon San Pellegrino to wash it all down.

There was a happy silence at their table as the three children polished off their cake, crisps and fizzy pop (three items that were strictly verboten in the Dickenson house).

Fergus gulped down the last of his Coke and then burped long and loud, much to the admiration of his brother and sister.

'Better out than in,' Esme said, and they giggled again. Now that they were all in good moods, earlier upsets forgotten, she fixed Oscar and Fergus with her sternest look. 'I really wish you two wouldn't fight so much. It's not nice.'

'He's always bossing me about, just because he's the oldest,' Fergus said, jerking his head in Oscar's direction.

Oscar, given his eighteen months of seniority, considered the matter for a moment. 'It's just . . . you *are* really annoying, Fergs.'

'I'm not . . .'

'No, you *really* are . . .'

'The thing is if you keep doing this, arguing and fighting, then eventually you won't be able to come back from it,' Esme said, as she mopped up some of the bean juice with a chip. 'Your mum and I argued all the time when we were kids and now we're not friends and that makes me very sad.'

'It doesn't make Mummy sad,' Oscar said. 'She seems quite happy. Anyway, she has lots of friends so maybe she doesn't want any more.'

'Well, I have a lot of friends too,' Esme said a little curtly, because it wasn't like she was so desperate for friends that even Allegra would do. Rather, she wished their circumstances were different, that their relationship hadn't always been defined by dissent, because now they couldn't move past it.

It was quite hard to explain that to the boys, especially as Oscar was giving her one of those looks he must have learned at Oliver's knee. 'I thought you were a vegetarian. Why are you eating a sausage?'

'I am a vegetarian,' Esme said, as she suddenly became aware of the piece of highly processed meat by-product shaped like a sausage that was on her plate. 'I was so hungry that I forgot I was a vegetarian.'

'You're so silly, Es,' Fergus said.

Oscar nodded. 'Very silly.'

While Esme was pleased that they were in agreement about something, she wished it wasn't her own shortcomings.

It was getting dark now and they were the last set of stragglers still in the cafe. Esme finished her chips, Oscar sucked the last drops of Coke out of his can, while Fergus bent his head to lick cake crumbs off his plate. Summer had chocolate smeared all over her face, even in her hair, but shied away when Esme came at her with a wet wipe.

'You can do it yourself,' Esme decided because, much as she loved them, the three of them were very pampered and had absolutely no real-world skills. As she wheeled the buggy out of the cafe, she was hit by another wave of exhaustion, which made her want to lie down on the damp grass again.

Luckily, it was only a short walk home. Jacinta and Marion were still out – on the first Friday of every month they met up with friends in town for a long, boozy lunch – so she made sure that Buster had fresh water and a couple of biscuits to keep him going, then folded up the pushchair and left it in the lobby.

'You going to walk up the stairs?' she asked Summer, who very firmly shook her head.

Esme hauled Summer up and slung her over her shoulder, then started the long climb up to her flat while the boys raced ahead, already giddy at the prospect of at least an hour's TV with very little adult supervision.

Oscar and Fergus pawed at the door as Esme struggled to unlock it. As soon as it was opened a mere crack they pushed through, straight into the living room – and came to a halt.

With a grateful sigh, Esme put Summer down and wondered why the boys were frozen to the spot.

'Um, what's happened in here?' Oscar asked, his eyes wide.

Esme followed his gaze to the . . . 'Oh yeah, I painted that wall dark grey. Looks good, doesn't it?'

Oscar and Fergus eyed the wall, then each other. Clearly primary school-age children were no arbiters of taste. They'd probably have preferred it if Esme had painted a Minecraft mural.

'Well, it's different,' Fergus offered at last.

'It's awful,' Summer said scathingly. 'What a mess!'

'Well, I think it looks great,' said a voice from the doorway and Esme looked round to see Theo standing there.

Would Esme ever not get that fluttery feeling when she saw him? Not just because he was ridiculously good-looking but because she still couldn't believe that he was nothing more than a trick of light.

'Are you going to say hello to Theo?' Esme asked the children hoarsely, something deep in her fluttering again as she realised that this was the first time it wasn't just her and Theo. Now there were independent witnesses to corroborate his existence.

'Hey kids,' Theo said easily, not at all daunted by their presence, while Oscar and Fergus turned to the doorway with the same faces full of disbelief as when they'd looked at the feature wall now repainted a very on-trend dark grey.

'Theo's a new friend of mine,' Esme explained as Theo came into the room so he could put his arm around Esme and kiss her forehead.

'I like Theo!' Summer said, ever a girl with strong opinions, and Esme let herself relax a little. 'He's funny.'

Theo pulled a face at Summer, who responded by grabbing hold of Esme's leg and hiding her face like she was shy, when in fact she was one of the boldest kids Esme had ever met.

'Yeah, right, hi Theo,' Oscar said with a shrug, trying to play it cool as befitted a seven-year-old.

'Hi,' Fergus muttered.

'This is just a drive-by, left my laptop here, but next time you come round, we'll make brownies,' Theo promised, dropping another kiss on Esme's forehead and trying to tug on one of Summer's curls but she ducked her head away from him.

'You love brownies, don't you, boys?'

They both shrugged, like she hadn't just seen them demolish a brownie, a doughnut and a blueberry muffin each.

'Have you got brownies?' Fergus looked hopeful though he couldn't *still* be hungry.

'No, Theo just said that he'll make brownies with you next time,' Esme said, but she was talking to her younger nephew's back as he was retrieving the TV remote from the coffee table, while Oscar still stood there with his hands in his pockets.

'I'd better go,' Theo murmured. 'Don't wait up for me, but I hope you don't mind if I wake you up with a little treat.'

His voice was dark and purry so that now the fluttering was right between her legs. 'What kind of a treat?'

He winked and leaned down to whisper in her ear. 'I shaved this morning so I can eat you out without giving you stubble burns.'

'I thought you didn't want me to get jolted.'

'Oh, I'm going to be very, very careful with you,' he promised.

'Well, I look forward to that,' Esme said primly as if they were discussing taking tea with the vicar, especially as both boys were eyeing her disapprovingly. 'I'll leave the front door on the latch.'

'I bet you will.' Theo smiled and he put a hand on her arse, fingers tightening meaningfully in a preview of what was to come. Then he was gone.

Oscar and Fergus were now sitting on the floor and watching some loud Manga cartoon in complete silence, which was very unlike them. Only Summer seemed unaffected by Theo's presence and when Esme stretched out on the sofa, she climbed on board, snuggled under Esme's arm and was asleep in seconds.

23

'Wake up! Esme! Wake up!'

'Is she dead?'

'No, she's not dead. She's dribbling. Dead people don't dribble.'

'I'm not dead, not dribbling either,' Esme managed to say as she struggled to wakefulness to find Oscar and Fergus staring down at her. 'Sorry, didn't mean to have a snooze.'

'It's very late. We should probably have been home *hours* ago,' Oscar said, sounding both accusatory and worried.

Esme was still wearing her coat. Her fingers fumbled over the smooth waterproof material to retrieve her phone from one of the pockets.

It wasn't *that* late. It was . . . gone eight. She always had them back by six. 'Shit! Why didn't you wake me?' Esme was already scrambling to her feet. 'Fuck! Your mum and dad are going to kill me.'

'So much swearing,' Fergus said admiringly. 'We wanted to watch the end of our movie.'

'Then we couldn't wake you. Fergus wanted to throw a cup of water over you, but I said that was a bad idea.'

'No, you wanted to do it too but you said I had to take the blame and I said . . .'

Esme let them rattle on as she considered the missed calls, the voicemail messages, the God knows how many WhatsApps and texts.

She rang Allegra's number and winced as her sister answered before it had even rung once.

'Where are you?' she all but screeched so that even Oscar and Fergus, who didn't have the phone pressed up to their ears, winced.

'Sorry. So sorry. We were having too much fun and time just ran away . . .'

'Time doesn't just run away,' Allegra snapped.

'Yeah, I've said I'm sorry, we're on our way to you,' Esme said, though the thought of the stairs and carrying Summer and wrestling with the buggy and the uphill walk made her want to cry.

'No need, Oliver will come to you,' Allegra said very tightly, like her lips were so pursed that it was an effort to force the words out.

Esme sat back with a little sigh of relief. 'Well, if you're sure.'

'He's leaving now. Make sure you're out front and waiting for him.' There was an angry intake of breath. 'I can't believe you. We've got a lot to do this evening to get ready for tomorrow and you pull a stunt like this so . . .'

'What's happening tomorrow?' Esme asked, rolling her eyes at the boys, but they were obviously used to Allegra kicking off so they didn't seem unduly bothered. Probably because, for once, they weren't in trouble.

It sounded like Allegra had taken the phone away from her mouth so that she could have a little scream but then she was back and angry as ever. 'It's Seren's bloody wedding. The group chat has been blowing up all afternoon but you're not concerned about that, are you? Just because you don't like weddings, you're determined to make sure that everyone else has a stressful time . . .'

'Oliver's on his way, right?' Esme cut right through her sister's invective. 'I'd better get the kids downstairs.'

'And what on earth did you say to Debbie when you picked up Summer? I came home from work early to find her in *tears* . . .'

'I just told her that I didn't like her. It's hardly a newsflash.'

'We are going to be having words tomorrow,' Allegra promised grimly, as if Esme wasn't dreading the wedding anyway.

'Well, it's been lovely to chat, but I really have to go,' Esme said, and she cut Allegra off mid-whatever bitchy thing she was planning to say next.

'Come on! Let's move, move, move!' she said to the boys, who were very slowly picking up coats and bags. Summer, uncharacteristically, was already waiting by the front door.

'I need a wee.' She assumed a pensive air. 'I think I had a wee.'

Esme knew more about Summer's toilet training than she'd ever wanted to. 'In your pull-ups?'

'They're *wet*.'

'Mummy will sort that out when you get home,' Esme said firmly, snatching up Summer's coat from the hall floor where she'd apparently dropped it. 'Boys! Have you got everything?'

As they went down the stairs, Esme was sure she could hear the toot of a car horn. Probably Oliver idling impatiently at the kerb, all ready to give Esme a telling off too. Speaking of which . . .

When they got to the ground floor, Esme grabbed hold of Fergus and Oscar by their coat sleeves. 'Now, remember. What do we say about Friday afternoons?' she asked them urgently.

'What happens on Friday afternoons is nobody's business but ours,' Oscar parroted back.

Esme nodded. 'That's right. It's our little secret and if any-one else found out about the cake and fizzy drinks . . .'

' . . . and the crisps,' Fergus added.

'Them too, then our Friday afternoons would have to stop and we don't want that, do we?'

All three of them shook their heads. Then there really was the unmistakable sound of a car horn right outside. Typical of Oliver that he always managed to find the optimal parking space.

Esme pushed the three of them out of the door, yanked the pushchair out of the little alcove behind the stairwell where she'd left it and hurried out into the chilly night.

Oliver was leaning on the car but straightened up as his off-spring appeared. 'I'm wet,' Summer said by way of a greeting, and he frowned.

'Not Esme's fault,' Oscar said supportively as he got into the back of the car. Esme took advantage of Oliver having to strap Summer into her seat to open the boot and put the pushchair away herself.

'We do appreciate you having the kids on a Friday but really, Esme, we expected you back two hours ago,' Oliver said in his best barrister voice, like he was just about to call a witness for the prosecution.

'I love having the kids and I know what a *big* help it is to you.' Esme smiled sweetly as she backed away. 'You've got a lot to do this evening, so I won't keep you.'

'Two hours, Esme! You weren't answering your phone. We were about to call the police.' There was a sharp note of real anger in Oliver's voice.

'I told Allegra, I was sorry. I'm *sorry*, all right? Stop going on about it.' Esme was at the street door, which was on the latch so she could bump it open with her bum. 'I'll see you tomorrow.'

'This isn't on . . .'

'Oh my God! Allegra said you had *loads* of stuff to do tonight, so why are you still here and busting my balls?' Esme demanded. 'I said I'm sorry. What more do you want? Blood? Do me a favour!'

Oliver looked positively Robespierre-like under the street-lights. Like a man who wished that they still had the death penalty and knew a sympathetic judge who'd order that his sister-in-law be taken to a place of execution and hanged by the neck until she was dead.

Esme was sure he had more to say but she couldn't be bothered to hear it so, with one last wave at the children, who were staring at her forlornly, she slipped through the door and quickly shut it.

Once she was back in her flat, Esme didn't even have the energy to stay mad at Allegra and Oliver. They were such drama queens. They knew the children had been with her and if they'd really been that concerned, they could have come over a lot sooner. It was only a five-minute drive. Not even five minutes!

She retrieved her phone from the sofa then ran herself a bath. Seren was going wiggy in the chat about shapewear and how she expected them all to wash their hair tonight because it was easier to work with hair that hasn't been freshly washed.

> **Seren Dipity**
> Also, no facial oil as part of your morning skincare, otherwise your make-up won't sit right. Just cleanser, serum then a light moisturiser.

Seren Dipity
Also, black underwear. If you haven't got black shapewear then you're going to have to Amazon Prime some now.

Seren Dipity
And black shoes.

Seren Dipity
Esme, why have you gone AWOL for the hundredth time this week? Allegra, I need you to make sure Esme turns up tomorrow with all the items on the list.

Allegra Dickenson
Esme is big enough and ugly enough to take care of herself.

Seren Dipity
Well, evidently, she's not and I do not need this kind of negative energy when I'm just about to have a cleansing gong bath.

That had been at four o'clock this afternoon. Esme was glad she'd missed it.

Then there were several emails and calls from Lyndsey about bloody cauliflowers and a long, rambling email from

Debbie with loads of randomly capitalised words. Esme was tempted to throw her phone in the bath.

It felt like everyone in her life expected her to do better. To be better. The only person who accepted Esme for who she was, imperfections and all, was Theo.

After a long soak in the bath and a long overdue catch-up with her personal grooming regime, Esme laid out what she'd need for tomorrow.

The bridesmaid dress, paid for by Seren, or rather Seren's parents, was the most beautiful and expensive dress Esme had ever owned. Unfortunately, it had been fitted in 2019 for the following March. Who knew then that the whole world would be in lockdown and that Esme would eat quite so much chocolate chip banana bread in a futile attempt to deal with it?

She tentatively unzipped the garment bag, caught a glimpse of layers of black ruffled, frothy tulle, and quickly zipped it back up again. Then she dug around in her drawers for gut-buster knickers – if need be she'd double Spanx – and a sturdy black bra.

Then Esme got to work assembling all the other items she'd need for a wedding. Her make-up bag, which hadn't been updated in a good three years. Blister plasters and gel pads for feet that would be crammed into heels all day. Tampons, paracetamol, hair clips, a miniature sewing kit, a packet of oat cakes and a packet of chocolate buttons, because once Esme had been to a wedding and they'd taken so long to do the photos, without so much as a *vol-au-vent* for the assembled guests, that she'd nearly passed out. Travel size Savlon, mouthwash, deodorant. A bottle of clear nail varnish for spot repairs.

She was probably the lowliest member of the bridal party and yes, Esme had entirely sacked off the group chat this week, but she was prepared for any emergency and eventuality. She was showing up.

It turned out that preparing for showing up was almost as tiring as actually showing up. Not wanting any more furious phone calls from Allegra, Esme even remembered to set her alarm. Or rather she set six alarms at five-minute intervals then ordered a car to pick her up an hour after the last alarm.

It was like she was back to being organised, mostly unflappable Esme. Only the headache and that strange sensation at the back of her head were the relics of what had happened a week ago.

Then, as if he were standing behind her, Esme felt the phantom touch of Theo's hand on her arse. The words he'd whispered in her ear. The last week had given her much more than a permanent headache.

She was still in her towel and Esme thought about pulling on . . . what had Theo called it? Her fuck-me slip? But she didn't need that kind of advertising. She'd already given Theo the green light to wake her up in the most delightful way, so she draped the towel over the radiator and slipped into bed naked and full of anticipation.

Esme wasn't going to stay up waiting. The deal was that Theo would wake her up when he got in. And Theo wasn't Alex. There was no artifice, no malice to him. She hadn't known that there were men like Theo in the world.

She wriggled against the soft brushed cotton of her winter sheets and even though she knew that Theo would wake her up, she was sure she was too excited, a dark kind of thrill already snaking out its tendrils, to fall asleep. But Esme hasn't even thought of five breeds of dog that begin with the letter A (Alsatian, Airedale Terrier, Afghan Hound, Akita . . .) before her eyes closed.

★

Esme woke up with a gasp to see a shadowy figure standing in the open doorway of her room. 'You frightened me,' she mumbled.

'I don't want you to ever be frightened of me.' As Esme's eyes grew accustomed to the dark, she saw Theo come into focus as he stepped closer. 'How are you feeling?'

'Suddenly not as sleepy as I was,' Esme said, because she'd gone from REM sleep to raring to go in five seconds. 'Wide awake, in fact.'

Theo smiled. The smile wasn't as gentle as his words or the tone of his voice. A wicked, knowing smile that felt like foreplay. 'Head all right?'

'Well, it's still attached to my neck so, yeah.' Esme had a headache because she always had a headache now, but she'd once read somewhere that orgasms helped to relieve pain, and she'd rather have a couple of those than yet more paracetamol. 'You made certain assurances before you went out.'

'So I did.'

He pulled away the duvet so he could slither down her body, skimming cool hands across her breasts, her stomach, no need to part legs that were already open.

'I thought I'd have to unwrap you first,' he drawled against her skin.

'Didn't want you to have to waste time,' Esme said in a voice that was still a little fuzzy around the edges.

'So considerate.' Theo pressed a kiss against her inner thigh and even though he said that he'd shaved, Esme could feel the rasp of his stubble against her. Not that she minded; she liked that he was rough where she was smooth. But one thing was bothering her. 'How did you get the street door open? Did someone let you in?'

'Never mind that,' he murmured against her skin. 'Now, let me ruin you.'

It was pitch black in the room so all Esme had to go on was touch as Theo hooked his arms under her knees so she could drape her legs over his shoulders, feel the tickle of his hair as he bent his head. Then he was tracing patterns on her clit with the tip of his tongue, silent, reverent poetry until she could feel herself grow damp and heavy. She heard Theo's approving moan as she got wetter still, how the hum of it vibrated against her clit and made her arch her hips and twist her fingers through his hair and press herself closer and closer to his mouth because she wanted him to devour her.

But Theo's lovemaking wasn't fierce or frantic. It was a hazy, unhurried pleasure as he spent what seemed like years with his head between her thighs. All his attention focused on her and her needy, ravenous cunt.

'You can't stop coming, can you?' he murmured in wonder, because once Esme had come, with the right kind of stimulation, the insistent suck of his mouth, two fingers twisting in her, she could just keep going.

'You can fuck me now,' she decided, because he had to be in agony and she was going to die from this if he kept on doing what he was doing, the tip of one finger pressing a spot inside the walls of her pussy that made her clench down hard and wonder if she'd just seen God.

'I'm not going to last long,' Theo warned her as he rose on his knees. Esme let her legs drop but then his hands were on her hips, hauling her close so he could sink his cock into her and she was so liquid and hot that she could hardly bear it. 'It's going to be hard and fast.'

'I love hard and fast,' Esme panted as he set a relentless rhythm. She managed to lever herself upright, so their chests were pressed together and God, they hadn't even kissed.

She could taste her own tart juices as she thrust her tongue into his mouth, one hand clutching onto a taut bicep, the other hand curling in Theo's hair as he angled himself deeper inside her.

'I need . . . I'm going to . . .' she breathed into his mouth. 'I just . . .'

'I know exactly what you need,' Theo said, his fingers suddenly right *there*, where they were joined so he could rub her clit as hard as he was fucking her until Esme was scoring her nails into his arms, whipping her head back and sobbing as she came one last time. Theo, his rhythm lost, driving into her in a series of determined thrusts until he was coming too.

They stayed like that for long, shuddering moments, sitting up, torsos pressed together, arms around each other.

Then Esme was wriggling free and Theo sighed and swayed. They both flopped onto their backs. Esme took Theo's hand and brought it to her mouth so she could press kisses against his knuckles, the letters that he'd inked onto his skin.

'I love you,' Theo said simply, as if telling someone you loved them was the easiest thing in the world, when actually it was maybe the hardest.

The silence that followed wasn't necessarily awkward, but it was charged.

'It's too soon to say it, I know that,' he admitted, entwining his fingers with hers. 'But it also feels right. There are too many people in the world who never say what they really mean and I don't want to be one of them.' It was his turn to lower his head and kiss Esme's hand, which was still clasped around his. 'Have I scared you off? Are you about to run for the hills?'

'After what you've just done to me, I don't have the energy to run anywhere. In fact, I'd be happy to stay like this, with you, holding hands, for a long, long time.' She took in tiny sips of air. 'For what it's worth, I like you a lot.' Esme had made a vow to herself, after declaring her love for Alex far too soon and before she even knew what love was, that she'd never say that word to another human being until she was absolutely sure of not only them, but herself too.

'I like you a lot too,' Theo said immediately, and it was another sugar-dipped arrow piercing her heart that he wasn't angry with her for not declaring her love right back. He turned on his side so he could curl his body against Esme and brush the hair back from her heated face. It was such a precious moment that Esme wished she could trap it under glass. 'Christ, it's at times like this that I wish I still smoked.'

The moment was done. Basking was over. 'No smoking,' Esme insisted in a breathless voice, because he'd really taken it out of her.

Theo kept stroking her hair, even though it was now even more tangled and damp than ever. He nuzzled against her neck and Esme's eyelids were growing heavy and the last thing she heard before she fell asleep was Theo whispering in her ear, 'Now, tell me, could Harry Styles do that?'

24

Saturday

Esme was not woken up by any of the alarms she'd set.

Instead, she was woken up a whole hour before the first alarm by her phone ringing. Not an uncommon occurrence this week but its ring seemed particularly shrill and no wonder because it was a particularly querulous Allegra on the line.

'Why are you calling me? I nearly didn't answer. Thought it had to be some scam merchant pretending to be from my bank . . .'

'I'm calling because you can't be trusted to be where you're meant to be at the right time,' Allegra said, in a voice positively dripping with condescension. 'Not that I want to help you out, but it *is* Seren's special day.'

What a horrible way to be woken up. Still, Esme wasn't going to rise to the considerable bait. Instead she pulled a face at Theo, who had his hands over his ears and was doing a good impersonation of Edvard Munch's *The Scream*.

'Appreciated,' Esme said; the effort nearly killed her. 'Though, technically speaking, Seren has already got married twice and had two special days. How many special days does one bride need?'

'No, Esme. I won't have you bitching and complaining. You're not the first person whose marriage didn't work out and you won't be the last. I'm so sick of your bitter divorcee routine,' Allegra snapped. 'You'd better be on your best behaviour or God help you.'

'I'm happy for Seren but I've also been happy for her on two other occasions. That's all I'm saying and I'm not . . .'

'Have you got plain black underwear sorted? What shoes are you wearing? Don't forget your make-up bag and your phone charger. Are you still on antibiotics? Probably best you don't drink at all today.' Allegra was like a Sherman tank, obliterating everything in her path in her determination to ruin the day for Esme before it had even started.

'For fuck's sake, I'm not five. I don't need you bossing me about and trying to run my life . . .'

'Because you're doing *such* a great job of that all by your-self,' Allegra said. Esme could hear the sound of the children in the background. In particular, she could hear Fergus shouting, 'I don't care if they're breeches and not knickerbockers. I'm still not wearing them!'

As so often happened when Allegra was being particularly overbearing, Esme forgot that she was a fully paid grown-up with her own home, her own business, who hadn't even been overdrawn for years. Instead, she felt herself transform into the sulky, recalcitrant sixteen-year-old she'd been when Debbie and Gary went their separate ways and decided that Esme could mostly look after herself and Allegra would do the rest.

How she longed to channel that sixteen-year-old and scream, 'I didn't ask to be born!' down the phone.

Instead she pulled another face at Theo, who shook his head and mimed cutting his throat.

'Look, Ally, I don't have time for this. Sounds like you don't have time for it either. I'll see you later,' Esme said crisply, then hung up so she could lie back on the bed and flail her limbs in sheer frustration and fury.

'So your sister is . . .'

'Whatever you're going to say, I've already thought it but with more swearing,' Esme said, letting Theo pull her into his arms and kiss the scrunched-up lines of her forehead.

She wished that she could stay in bed, in his arms, for the rest of the day but he was already pushing her away then rolling over with a satisfied sigh because he didn't need to get up for a good couple of hours.

Theo was fast asleep when Esme, showered and dressed, brought him a mug of tea. She didn't have the heart to wake him. But as she retrieved her phone charger, and yes, she was low-key fuming that if Allegra hadn't reminded her, she'd have definitely forgotten it, he opened bleary eyes.

'You look like you're about to witness an execution,' he mumbled.

'Well, that's one way of looking at a wedding, isn't it? The murder of someone's hopes and dreams . . . the death of expectation . . .'

Theo frowned. He was so adorably crumpled at all times but especially first thing in the morning.

'You don't really believe that, do you?' he asked, carefully picking up the mug of tea then taking an exploratory sip.

Of course Esme did. It was her go-to rant. That marriage was a tax break at best. A con, at worst. Fooling impressionable women into believing in fairy stories when in reality they were condemning themselves to a lifetime of having to pick up someone else's dirty underwear and always making themselves a little less because God forbid that they be too much.

But Theo didn't leave his dirty underwear lying around. Or he hadn't, so far. He didn't want Esme to be less or more or anything other than what she was. 'You wouldn't murder my hopes and dreams, would you?'

'I wouldn't,' he said solemnly. 'Why would I ever want to?'

'Some people would,' Esme said, one knee up on the bed as she packed her wedding day essential kit into an overnight bag. 'But I'm very glad that you're not one of them.'

Men were bad. You couldn't even know how bad until you married one. So best not to let them get too close. But these last six days with Theo had changed something quite fundamental for Esme and she hadn't even realised it until now.

That didn't mean she was turning cartwheels at the thought of spending the whole day in the grip of The Wedding Industrial Complex.

'I wish you could come with me,' she said longingly. 'I mean, Lyndsey's my plus one but . . .'

'I have to work today. I've been slacking off all week and Saturdays are so busy. We're soft-launching our new spring menu,' Theo said, taking another appreciative sip of tea. 'God, you make a great brew, Es.'

Esme nodded in acknowledgement of that fact. Then she zipped up her holdall and made absolutely no progress in moving towards the door, even though she'd just heard her phone chime with a message, which had to be an alert that her Uber was incoming.

'If, by some miracle, you're not that busy this evening, maybe you could swing by the reception just for an hour,' she suggested with a crooked smile. 'I mean Clerkenwell and Mayfair aren't so far apart.'

They might just as well have been continents apart if you were trying to get from one to the other on a busy Saturday night, but Theo didn't point that out. Instead, he took hold of Esme's limp, cold hand, his own fingers warmed by the mug of tea, and tried to squeeze some life into her.

'I'll try,' he said, and he sounded very sincere, though Esme knew that come eight o'clock he'd be up to his elbows in hungry punters.

25

It was a personal, and quite a smug, triumph for Esme that she arrived at the door of the Princess Grace suite at one of the grandest hotels in London a whole five minutes early.

The door was opened by Phyllida Dickenson, Seren's mother and Allegra's mother-in-law, who was exquisitely dressed in an understated dove grey coat dress accessorised with a chic Juliet cap with veil and her usual wintry smile.

'Hello, Phyllida, you look absolutely *beautiful*,' Esme said, leaning in for the customary double kiss, a displacement of air as lips never met cheek. 'You must be *so* happy that the big day has finally arrived.'

'Well, yes, it did seem at one point that we'd never be able to celebrate Sarah and Isaac with all our family and friends,' Phyllida conceded. She was a chilly woman by nature but she did warm up eventually, so Esme was pleased to see that she already had a glass of champagne in one impeccably manicured hand, her nails a discreet greige, as she ushered Esme into the five-room suite.

Even though, technically, she was early, a quick headcount proved that Esme was the last one to arrive, which was no reason for Allegra to glare at her.

'Hello, everyone!' Esme cried in a good impersonation of a perky, peppy sort of person who just lived for all things wedding. 'Isn't this *exciting*?'

'Have you already started drinking?' Kemi asked, as she detached herself from the throng of women arranged on

261

three plump sofas, all chintzy and gilty and beswagged and tasselled.

'Only if a mug of Yorkshire Tea counts as drinking,' Esme said. She lifted her holdall and garment bag. 'Where shall I get changed? Where's Seren?'

'She's in the master bedroom having a massage,' Kemi said, now close enough to whisper in Esme's ear. 'We've already had three meltdowns. I'd steer well clear and I wouldn't get changed until you've done your make-up. Did you bring a robe?'

Of course Esme had forgotten something. 'Fuck! No!'

'I'm sure we can find you something,' Phyllida said with a little wince as Esme defiled the sanctity of the Princess Grace suite with her foul language.

Soon enough Esme was swathed in a towelling robe the colour of spilled salt, so plush it felt like velvet, waiting for the attentions of one of the three make-up artists on call.

'We're going to divide you into groups of four,' said a woman called Davinda, who was apparently Seren's deputy wedding planner. The big cheese wedding planner was closeted in the main bedroom with Seren and now Phyllida – apparently there was some crisis to do with the wedding photos. 'Your personal aesthetic architect will get to you as soon as they can.'

'It will be my turn and they'll suddenly realise that their darkest shade of base is still ten shades lighter than my skin,' Kemi muttered to Esme, who did a quick look around the room. She hadn't realised before but . . . 'Yes, Esme, I'm the only brown person here, apart from the two women from Housekeeping who keep turning up every time someone summons them on an app.'

'Sorry,' Esme said, because she didn't know what else to say. She always wanted to be a good ally but was aware that sometimes she fell short. 'Where's your mum?'

'In a suite on another floor with all my aunties and cousins and no, I wouldn't be happier there because the conversation would mostly be about why I'm thirty-five and not married.' Kemi shrugged, an elegant roll of her shoulders. Her hair was already pulled back in a sleek chignon and, even without make-up, she was still all eyes and cheekbones.

'You know what? Even if you decided to accompany Seren down the aisle in that fancy tracksuit . . .'

'It's a cashmere lounge ensemble, Es . . .'

'Whatever, you'd still be the most beautiful woman in the room. But don't tell Seren that.'

'Of course I'm not telling Seren that. She'd kneecap me with her nail file.'

Esme wasn't sure why she'd been dreading this day. While she was waiting to have her make-up done, she could hang out in this luxurious lounge, its windows looking out onto Park Lane. Through the plane trees, she could see the lush green expanse of Hyde Park. Even better, there was an all-day buffet set up in one corner.

Esme loved finger sandwiches and mini pastries. But despite the champagne bottles waiting in their ice buckets, she decided that she'd only drink for the toasts. It had nothing to do with Allegra's express instructions (her sister was still giving her the evil eye), but it was her last day on antibiotics and she *still* had a headache. However, there was a huge assortment of non-alcoholic drinks, the ubiquitous kefirs and kombuchas, and also a very thirst-quenching organic elderflower pressé.

'Right, you're next,' the make-up artist a.k.a. aesthetic architect pointed at Esme with a tail comb. 'I'm Danii with two I's. We'll do your hair first. Chignon, with a side parting.' She was a pretty girl who had absolutely no need of the industrial amounts of make-up she'd laid out on a table. 'It's going to be a very tight do and it's going to hurt. If I were you, I'd pop a couple of aspirin now.'

Esme sat down in the grey velvet bucket chair in front of the make-up station. Her worried face stared back at her. 'Maybe you could make mine less tight? It's just I banged the back of my head last weekend and I have stitches.'

Danii pointed her tail comb at the ornate gilt-edged double doors that led through to the inner sanctum. 'Your bride was very clear about what she wanted.'

Esme just had to get through today. It was eleven now. It had said on the invitation, very pretentiously, carriages at eleven. Twelve more hours. She could do twelve hours with painful hair and painful shoes and a painful twinge in her heart, because being at a wedding would always remind her of the vows she'd said so hopefully and how they hadn't meant a thing.

She was going to be on her best behaviour. Company manners. Unimpeachable. Not just because Allegra, who was now sitting in a matching bucket chair across the room, was still managing to shoot daggers in Esme's direction despite currently having her eyes done.

No, because it *was* Seren's day. Yes, she'd had two other wedding ceremonies, one of them legally binding, but she had also waited two years to be able to waft about in a £10,000 dress in front of her family and friends and declare her love for Isaac. Who really was quite sweet for an investment banker and who'd brought Kemi into Esme's life. Before Isaac, Seren had loved a Piers who was an absolute rotter and very rude to wait staff.

With all that in mind, Esme still pulled an unhappy face as Danii picked up a wide-toothed comb. 'Also, word of warning, what with the stitches and all, I haven't washed my hair since Sunday so you might want to wear gloves.'

It hurt. It really hurt. Enough to bring tears to Esme's eyes as Danii tried to brush out the tangles at that tender spot where her stitches were still knitting the skin back together.

'Sorry!' Danii kept trilling, as she yanked Esme's hair this way and that, digging hairpins into her scalp and asphyxiating her with the fumes from both dry shampoo and lacquer. Obviously Seren's wrath if her bridal party, even the bin tier of the bridal party, didn't have the exact same side part chignons that she'd specified was far greater an incentive than Esme's agony.

There was a brief respite between courses. Esme was sent off to put her dress on before Danii started on her make-up. 'It's going to take a lot of base to get rid of those bruises,' she said as she worked her comb through the silky, tangle-free hair, like a knife slicing through hot butter, of one of Seren's university pals.

In a pink marble bathroom modelled to the former Grace Kelly's personal preferences, Esme unzipped her garment bag with great trepidation. Even before the pandemic, the dress had been a little on the snug side. And this week alone, Theo had fed her all sorts of delicious and calorie-laden dishes like he was fattening a goose up for *foie gras* season.

Esme stared at herself in the mirror in her firm control bra and knickers then, with a fervent prayer to a God that she really didn't believe in, she eased the dress over her agonisingly coiffed head.

The dress slipped down like an oyster without coming to an abrupt halt at Esme's hips. She didn't even have to ask for the assistance of another woman and a coat hanger to get the concealed side zip done up. The dress fitted perfectly. If anything, it seemed as if Esme had lost weight, which just wasn't possible.

She swayed back and forth as the ruffles of the black dress floated delicately and the light sparkled on the tiny crystals sewn onto the fabric. It was short-sleeved and high necked with a tight-fitting bodice, the skirt made up of undulating waves of frothy tulle. It was serving goth Miss Havisham realness and Esme was here for it.

She'd never been a bridesmaid before. When she was little, none of Debbie's friends were the kind to marry, let alone want several pint-sized bridesmaids in meringue dresses in attendance. Once Esme was grown up, her friends knew better than to ask. Besides, her friends were very much the kind of people who got married in a registry office or a country barn and would never force their friends into hideous dresses so as not to eclipse the bride. Lyndsey had an awful dark purple sheath dress in an unforgiving satin at the back of her wardrobe that she'd been bullied into wearing by her overbearing friend Emma.

Seren, for all her faults, had wanted her bridal party to look chic in the photos. Also, Seren had a healthy ego and couldn't even perceive that anyone would look more beautiful than she did on her wedding day.

And she was right. An hour later, after Danii had concealed, then contoured Esme's face until it didn't even look like Esme's face anymore and she was carefully sipping water through a straw, Seren emerged from the master bedroom.

There was a mutual and audible gasp. Seren was swathed in acres and acres of ivory silk and ruffled tulle. Her train entered the room approximately five minutes after she did. Her wedding dress nodded to their black dresses but then wouldn't deign to speak to them, because the wedding dress was in another league. Transported from another realm, or rather a designer's atelier in Paris.

It wasn't just the dress or Seren's hair, pinned up and studded with diamond flower clips. Or her impeccable make-up.

Or the willowy figure built by yoga and a vegan diet. It was the radiant look on Seren's face. Esme didn't think she'd ever seen anyone look as happy as Seren did in that moment; her smile seemed to come with its own magnetic force field.

'You look so beautiful,' Ngaire murmured reverently.

'I'm so happy that I don't know whether I'm going to laugh or cry,' Seren said, tipping her head back as if the tears weren't that far off. 'I'm finally getting the wedding of my dreams with the actual love of my life. It doesn't get any better than that.'

'It really doesn't,' Allegra agreed with a warm smile, though stodgy, priggish Oliver was very clearly not the love of her life. He'd just been the right man at the right time. It was hardly the same thing.

Esme tried to remember how she'd felt the day that she got married to Alex. She'd been quite hungover and couldn't tell if it was that or the nerves making her feel so sick. But she'd been happy, excited, a little smug that all her friends were looking at her with such awe because Esme was always the one who reached her life milestones first. The first one to get a glamorous media job. The first one to buy her own place. The first one to go to New York. The first one to date someone famous. The first to get married. Not a boring church or registry office wedding either. They were getting married onstage at the Royal Court Theatre.

Esme had also been annoyed because Allegra had spent the whole day with a look of utter disapproval on her face. She'd even had the nerve, just as Esme was about to walk on stage, to pierce Esme's bridal bubble. 'I think you're making a mistake. He's just . . . He's not going to take care of you.'

Esme had reeled back in her Terry de Havilland gold platform sandals. 'You decide that this is the perfect time to say that to me? *Now?*' She'd smoothed down her vintage white sixties shift minidress; she'd been trying to channel Jane Fonda when she'd married Roger Vadim. 'I don't need him to take care of me. I can take care of myself.'

Then she'd marched onto the stage, determined not to let Allegra ruin any more of her day. But as Alex had laughed his way through the vows, playing to his friends in the stalls, rather than speaking to Esme with his heart, all she could think about was Allegra's warning.

'He's not going to take care of you.'

In the most literal sense, Alex hadn't taken care of Esme. He'd been careless with her love, her life, her dreams and, thanks to Allegra's warning, that had been painfully evident on their wedding day.

Esme's unhappy reverie was interrupted by two members of the hotel staff wheeling in a trolley full of gift bags. Esme wasn't at all mercenary, or rather she hoped she wasn't, but she perked up as she saw the sizeable stiff white bags with their silver and blue ribbon handles. Who didn't love a gift bag?

Seren sank carefully into a chair, like a flower dropping gently to the ground under the weight of its petals. 'Just a little something to thank you all for being part of today and I promise this is the last wedding I'm having,' she said as the gift bags were distributed.

Esme had to restrain herself from rifling through it with indecent haste. Instead, she carefully burrowed through the pale blue and silver tissue paper to reveal a Frédéric Malle scented candle in *Un Gardenia La Nuit*. 'My wedding scent,' Seren explained. 'There's a voucher for a massage at my favourite spa because I know we're all going to need one after dancing the night away. And one last thing . . .'

In a presentation box was a corsage in a delicate Wedgwood blue and silver. 'Oh, this is beautiful,' Allegra murmured.

Seren blushed. 'When we had our Nigerian wedding with Isaac's family, they all wore aso . . . aso . . .'

'Aso Ebi. It means family cloth,' Kemi said parrot-fashion, as if she anticipated having to explain this many, *many* times. 'It's a way of family and friends coming together at special occasions to show their unity and support.'

'Different colours have different meanings, so Isaac's family chose blue to signify harmony but it also means loyalty and trust, and the silver represents opulence, excellence and royalty,' Seren said, preening a little. 'Isaac always calls me his little princess.'

'We wanted Seren and Isaac's marriage to be based on solid foundations but also to turn a profit,' Kemi said, taking her corsage and carefully pinning it on the shoulder of her black dress. 'It means a lot to us that Seren wanted to include some Yoruba traditions in the big fancy wedding . . .'

'Of course I do,' Seren said, holding up her bouquet of tightly budded white roses, which were tied with the same blue and silver ribbons. 'It's my something borrowed and my something blue.' She fingered the petals of one flower. 'It's silly. We've been properly married for over a year now but I still feel as nervous as I did the first time round. I've got literal butterflies at the thought of seeing Isaac in his morning suit even though we've only been apart for less than twenty-four hours.'

Seren had her faults. She was silly, selfish and very spoiled but even she seemed to know the value and meaning of love.

'These presents are so thoughtful, so generous,' Muffin cooed as everyone pinned their corsages on their dresses. 'You are such a good person, Seren, you deserve all the happiness.'

There were murmurs of agreement. Esme took a delicious whiff of the scented candle. 'Definitely. This almost makes up

for all the hissy fits you had in the group chat. Right ladies?'
she said loudly.

Not right. Very wrong. Allegra's looks in Esme's direction
were now positively demonic and even Kemi shook her head
like she was very disappointed with Esme.

It was a relief when Seren floated out of the room in a
gardenia-scented cloud to be driven around Hyde Park for
her bridal photo opportunities, Phyllida and the top tier
bridesmaids going with her, including Allegra and Kemi.

Esme was left with two women who'd been at school with
Seren, a couple of second cousins and Seren's personal assistant, Laura, who seemed terrified by all the pomp and the
circumstance and the £400 dress she was wearing.

'Do we go downstairs?' she asked. 'What did the itinerary
say?'

There was an itinerary? 'I'd leave it to the last minute,'
Esme said. 'The quicker we go downstairs, the longer we're
going to be standing in our heels.'

Esme hadn't even put her heels on yet and she did wonder
aloud if she could wear her trainers instead. 'The dress is long,
who's going to see them?' but the other women didn't think it
was a good idea and were quite strident with their opinions.

It was another hour of desultory chat until, according to the
so-called itinerary, they were to make their way downstairs to
the entrance of the Park Suite, where they'd meet Seren stepping out of the car with her father for some pre-match photos.

Esme had quite clearly gained a reputation as a trouble-
maker, though surely she'd only said what everyone else had
been thinking. The other women gave her a wide berth, even
in the lift. As they assembled in height order on the grand
sweeping steps that led up to the wedding venue, Allegra was
opposite Esme. All the better to keep on glaring at her.

Esme made the universal sign for 'what the hell is your problem?' then couldn't help but shiver. Seren was lucky that there were blue skies but it was the first Saturday in March, and far too cold and windy to be standing about in a short-sleeved dress with a simpering smile as the photographer took pictures of Seren and her father Dickie, looking dapper in morning coat, silver waistcoat and blue cravat, on the steps.

Then they were corralled into a holding room, where the other women fussed with their dresses and the make-up artists provided last minute touch-ups.

'Game time,' Kemi said at last.

They assembled by a set of double doors, half hidden by a huge swathe of chintzy white and gold drapes, to be chivvied out one at a time by Leonie, the actual wedding planner, who had an in-ear microphone like Madonna and an ego to match.

'Down the aisle, slowly, and then disperse,' she hissed. When Esme missed her cue, Leonie gave her an almighty shove forward. 'You're to disperse right.'

26

Esme stepped out into a beautiful room with more park views out of more huge picture windows, which were swathed in yet more intricate drapes, like Victorian ladies wearing bustles. The scent of gardenias hung heavy in the air. There were rows and rows of gilt-encrusted chairs lined up on either side of the room, the men in dark suits, the women keen to have an opportunity to break out their formal finery. One woman four rows from the front was wearing a huge cerise hat which obscured the view for the people seated behind her, who were all craning their necks to get a good view of the dais. There stood Isaac in the most impeccably cut pearl grey tailcoat, visibly shaking with nerves, with Punter (so-called because his family had made their fortune with a chain of betting shops) his best man, who kept turning to leer at the bridal party.

Performance anxiety made Esme disperse left, though she could have sworn she'd dispersed right. When she realised her mistake and tried to correct herself, the guests tittered.

'Just stay where you are,' Allegra hissed at her from further up the line, so all Esme could do was plaster on a smile and try not to shift from one foot to the other to relieve the pressure of her shoes, which were already pinching.

There was a brief moment of light relief when Summer, in a baby blue and silver poufy flower girl dress, was suddenly unleashed from wherever she'd been contained. Followed by a sullen Fergus in his silver knickerbockers, Summer pirou-etted through the chairs, rose petals flung to the far corners, while she shouted, 'It's all right! I've had a wee and a nap!' Everyone smiled indulgently. Oh, to be three.

Summer stopped when she got to Esme and barrelled into her aunt, which nearly toppled Esme off her heels. 'Are you going to stand still and be very quiet?' Esme asked her. Summer shook her head and ran back the way she'd come. Fergus eyeballed her unhappily, his shoulders slumping when Esme gave him the thumbs up.

A little orchestra had been tucked away in a corner playing a selection of greatest hits from classical composers. Now it struck up the opening chords of 'Songbird' by Fleetwood Mac and everyone stood up as Seren floated down the aisle in her cloud of silk and tulle. Dickie smiled proudly as he was congratulated on all sides.

Punter whispered something to Isaac, who turned round just as Seren reached the dais. He held out his hand to lead her up the three steps and Esme saw him mouth, 'You're so beautiful.'

'So are you,' Seren whispered back, and though Dickie was bringing up the rear and the celebrant (even he was wearing a suit that must have started life in Savile Row) was shuffling his papers, they took a moment to just stare at each other, goofy grins on both their faces.

Nobody had ever looked at Esme like that.

Or they hadn't, until Theo. These last few days she'd been the recipient of several carefree smiles. Not even when she was gussied up, because he'd only seen her in pyjamas, working from home clothes or stark naked. But it was still enough for Theo to look at Esme as if she made everything all right in the world, much as Seren and Isaac were looking at each other now.

'Shall we do this thing?' Seren asked.

Isaac shrugged in his usual laid-back manner. 'Third time's the charm, isn't it?' It set a light mood that was live, laugh, love personified as they said their own vows then the celebrant went off on a long, meandering speech.

'I'm so bored,' said Fergus in a loud stage whisper. He hadn't known where to go after he'd walked down the aisle so he'd ended up next to Esme and was leaning heavily on her.

'It can't be much longer,' she whispered back, giving him a little nudge. 'Look, they're going to exchange rings now.'

Seren already had an eye-wateringly expensive, ethically mined diamond solitaire engagement ring, and more ethical diamonds on her pave wedding ring, but now she completed the set with what she called an eternity ring.

Esme couldn't imagine how many tens of thousands of pounds were resting on the third finger of Seren's left hand.

'Now, they're going to kiss,' she said to Fergus, who squinched up his face.

'Gross!'

'And, I think, yup, we're done.'

The orchestra started playing 'All You Need Is Love' to accompany them back down the aisle, Seren holding her bouquet aloft like it was a football trophy, Isaac grinning from ear to ear and looking dazed.

'If everyone would like to make their way to the reception room where champagne and canapés are being served while Isaac and Seren have their photos taken.'

'What are canopies?' Fergus asked as people began to get to their feet.

'Canapés,' Esme corrected him gently. 'Little things to eat. Like, mini salmon tarts and stuff.'

'Gross!' Fergus said again, as Allegra bore down on them.

275

'Fergs,' she said cajolingly, while completely blanking Esme. 'You need to be in the photos. We talked about this.'

'It's not fair that Oscar gets to wear normal trousers. You made me wear his breeches that he got too big for, even though my ones didn't fit either,' Fergus said, casting a look down at his monstrous silver bottom half. Esme hadn't really paid attention to the buckled shoes and white tights until now.

'Oh, mate,' she said sympathetically. 'I feel sorry for you.'

'Esme!' No one else but Allegra could growl her name like she hated everything to do with it, including the person. Then she turned back to her son. 'I'll give you five pounds to be in the photos, with a smile.'

'I wouldn't do it for less than fifty,' Esme said, because it was the absolute truth, even though she did slightly quake at Allegra's narrowed eyes.

She'd never been so pleased to see Lyndsey, who was walking very slowly towards them. Obviously she was also in agony being back in heels again, but Esme wished that she'd pick up the pace.

'Hello!' she called out enthusiastically. 'You're a vision in green! Gorgeous!'

'We are going to have words later,' Allegra promised in a doom-laden voice before bearing away her unfortunate middle child.

Esme made a mental note to avoid Allegra, and Oliver too, for the rest of the day.

'You look beautiful,' Lyndsey said, falling onto the nearest chair and gasping as she took the weight off her feet. She was wearing a forest green jumpsuit with silver platform sandals, her long hair teased and waved, make-up on point. She'd even managed to flick out her liquid eyeliner. 'Really lucked out with the bridesmaid's dress.'

'I know,' Esme agreed, collapsing gratefully into the chair next to Lyndsey's. 'But I'm now on six-day hair, more make-up than whatever the collective noun for a group of Kardashians is . . .'

'A hashtag of Kardashians, a sponcon of Kardashians, a buttload of Kardashians . . .'

Esme licked the tip of her finger. 'Sizzling word skills, Lyns.'

'Speaking of which, that cauliflower pitch you worked up yesterday? Did you attach the wrong file to your email?'

'I don't think so. Why?' Esme asked, though she was off the clock and she really didn't much care. Lyndsey was far more conscientious than she was.

'It was gibberish. Like you'd written it in Zapf Dingbats instead of your usual Avenir Medium.'

'My favourite font!' Esme clasped her hands to her chest in rapture. 'Though I'm a big fan of Helvetica too.'

Lyndsey raised her eyebrows. 'How many glasses of champagne have you drunk already?'

Before Esme could say, rather sanctimoniously, that she was only going to drink for toasts, they were interrupted by Davinda, the deputy wedding planner.

'There you are!' she exclaimed, her hand already wedged in Esme's armpit so she could haul her to her feet. 'We need you for photographs.'

★

The photos were taken in a charming roof garden with spectacular views across the London skyline. Seren had her love to keep her warm but the other women, in their short-sleeve dresses, black ruffles flapping in the breeze, looked like a gaggle of very pissed off goths.

Esme's smile was frozen on her face in a rictus grin. Her headache was piercing, the foot pinching was excruciating and Allegra's furious glances now had all the subtlety of a pantomime villain.

As soon as the photographer was satisfied that he'd got the last shot – bridesmaids and groomsmen fanning out on either side of an ornamental fountain, Seren and Isaac at the centre – Esme was hobbling back inside as fast as she could.

She was the first one in the lift, which looked like the inside of a Fabergé egg, and quickly pressed the button to close the doors so that she wouldn't have to share the journey with anyone. Especially if anyone was Allegra.

Esme did think about heading back to the bridal party suite to change into her trainers or, even better, to have a nap but decided to brave it out and look for Lyndsey in the throng of guests milling about in the reception room that led to the ballroom.

It was quite hard to find Lyndsey amid so many women in bright jewel-like colours but eventually Esme tracked her down to a quiet corner where her friend had found a sofa . . . and Esme's father and stepmother.

Before she could back away, Gary caught sight of her. 'Here she is!' he announced in his usual barrow boy tones. He'd been a newly qualified plumber struggling to get by when he'd met Debbie, who'd schooled him in the ways of property development. Now he had several flats that he rented out in North London and the Costa del Sol, and lived in a luxury apartment in an exclusive gated community in Malaga. But he still sounded like a man born and bred in Edmonton. 'I was just saying, you girls all look like crows! Don't know what that Sarah was thinking of.'

'Her name's Seren,' Esme said, leaning down to air kiss Barbara. She was a tiny, timid woman with a weak chin who Gary had rescued, aged forty-five, from what she'd thought was going to be a lonely life of spinsterdom. In return he had her undying devotion. For them, it was a fair swap, but Esme didn't know how Barbara could put up with Gary.

Whenever anyone asked her what her father was like (thankfully the question didn't come up too often), Esme always said, 'He lives on the Costa del Sol, doesn't speak a word of Spanish and voted for Brexit.' That sentence was Gary in a nutshell.

Gary had also packed on the pandemic pounds, his belly straining over the waistband of his suit trousers and against the buttons of his shirt, but he still managed to look inordinately pleased with himself.

'Bet this whole affair cost an arm and a leg,' he noted sagely, as he helped himself to another flute of champagne from one of the circulating wait staff. 'Thank God you only asked me to put five hundred quid behind the bar when you married that useless tosser.'

'Can we just not?' Esme begged, with a desperate look at Lyndsey. She threw a desperate look back, as if to say she was so sorry that she'd got cornered by Gary and Barbara.

One year, when they were both broke, Esme and Lyndsey had holidayed chez Gary and Barbara, although free bed and board really hadn't been enough to put up with the daily diatribes about 'bloody foreigners' and how they should bring back national service, imperial measurements and the death penalty.

'You can say what you like about Phyll and Dickie but they're not tight,' Gary continued. 'They forked out enough on Ally's wedding, even if it was just close friends and family at Kenwood. Now *that* was a classy affair.'

'It was a very tasteful wedding,' Barbara simpered. She was wearing a lilac dress that out-ruffled even Seren's designer wedding frock. The lilac clashed with her flushed complexion. 'Such a pity you weren't there, Esme. I still can't believe that you didn't go to your own sister's wedding. I said at the time, didn't I, Gaz? That you only have one family. As I like to say, blood is thicker than water.'

Unfortunately, that was the truth. 'Oh, that's ancient history,' said Esme.

Lyndsey nodded. 'Esme and Allegra are friends now. Sort of.'

'They never got on, even as kids. Though who could blame Ally? She'd been an only child for eleven years until this one came along.' Gary gestured with his thumb at Esme, who knew only too well that she'd been a surprise baby and an unwelcome one at that. 'We all had to do a lot of adjusting. A lot. If your mother and I hadn't been on the outs by then anyway, you would definitely have finished us off. Talk about hard work. You didn't stop crying for the first six months.'

'God, who could blame me?'

'Have you had a look at the seating plan?' Barbara interrupted, because she'd had a lot of practise at changing the subject when people were sharing a few home truths that no one wanted to hear.

'I haven't,' Esme admitted, her heart sinking at the thought of what horrors might lie ahead.

'It's OK, we're together,' Lyndsey said, taking Esme's limp hand in hers.

'Oh, like that, is it?' Gary's rheumy blue eyes took in the handholding. 'Seems a waste. Two pretty girls like you . . .'

'Just friends, not that there's anything wrong with being gay . . .' Lyndsey said, but the last thing Gary had posted on his Facebook was a very weak and entirely unfunny meme that declared 'my pronouns are lbs/oz/Fahrenheit/miles/yards/him' so Esme body blocked her.

'We'd probably better circulate,' she said, squeezing Lyndsey's fingers. 'I'm sure we'll see you after dinner.'

'We're meeting Ally and the fam tomorrow for a late breakfast, early lunch,' Barbara said. 'Or as I like to call it, brunch. We can catch up then.'

'We could catch up then but I'm NFI,' Esme said tightly, though the last thing she wanted to do tomorrow morning was brunch with some of her least favourite people. 'Which stands for Not Fucking Invited, and by the way, Barbara, *everyone* calls it brunch.'

'There's no need for that kind of tone,' blustered Gary, his face reddening, as he brushed back the few straw-coloured strands of hair that were all that was left of his comb-over these days.

'Oh, I think there's every need for that kind of tone,' Esme said as Lyndsey dragged her away. 'Oh my God, they're *so* annoying . . .'

'I know but Barbara doesn't deserve it, even if Gary does,' Lyndsey said as she pulled Esme through the crowd.

'Shall we go and find Debbie next and get that unpleasant confrontation out of the way?' Esme suggested, but Lyndsey shook her head.

'We're going to get you a glass of water, maybe even a bottle, to dilute some of that champagne,' she said, scanning the heads of the guests for a waiter.

'But I haven't had any champagne,' Esme protested as Lyndsey gave her a knowing look. 'I really haven't.'

Lyndsey looked as if she were about to argue the point, but they were interrupted by a man in red tailcoat and bib and tucker who announced, with the help of a microphone, that the ballroom was open and they were to take to their seats.

27

It could have been worse. Esme could have been on the top table with Allegra and Oliver shooting her furious looks just for breathing.

She wasn't stuck with any obscure relatives either. Instead, she and Lyndsey were on one of the three singles tables at the back of the room, where they could cause the least havoc.

'Although I'm not actually single,' Esme pointed out to Lyndsey as they took their seats, unfortunately with a seat in between them.

Lyndsey tilted her head. 'I know, babes. Such a pity that Harry Styles couldn't be with us this afternoon.'

'But I have Theo now,' Esme said. 'I told you all about him on Tuesday. He'd be here today if he wasn't working.'

'Let's get some water in you. Still or sparkling?' Lyndsey gestured at the array of bottles on the table.

'Still, sparkling makes me burp.' Esme was very thirsty and gulped down two glasses of water that probably cost what she'd normally spend on a bottle of wine.

They were quickly joined by the other singles. Sitting in between Esme and Lyndsey was Tristan, a junior member of Isaac's team at the bank, who looked about fifteen. As soon as Lyndsey introduced herself he gulped, 'I already have a girlfriend, actually.'

'Like we'd even be interested,' Esme snorted as Lyndsey shook her head and turned to the man on her left.

The man on Esme's right was Odin, Seren's Reiki master, who had a plaited beard, and when he shook Esme's hand he tickled her palm with one overly warm and moist finger. Both of those things made her want to throw up in her mouth. She shot a longing look at the kids' table where Fergus had recovered from his knickerbocker shame and was wearing his napkin on his head, to the amusement of his peers, while Summer was lying on the floor so that the waiters bringing round the first course had to adroitly step over her.

Esme realised that she was ravenous. Her first course, a Jerusalem artichoke carpaccio, barely touched the sides. Then she had to listen to Odin try to one up her in the vegan stakes . . . 'Of course, soy milk and oat milk are the best for the planet. Though they both release a lot of emissions. Which one do you prefer?'

'Look, Odin, I'm not a vegan,' Esme said through a mouthful of bread roll. 'I really like cheese. I'm just trying to do my best.'

'There are some very good vegan cheeses available now,' Odin insisted, as they were served their second course of a winter vegetable salad that contained far too many pickled mushrooms for Esme's liking.

The braised asparagus shut Odin up for one minute but then he was wanging on about the time he'd stayed in a shepherd's hut on an island in the Outer Hebrides and foraged for his own breakfast every morning.

'How do you know when someone's a vegan?' Esme announced to the table at large.

'Um, do they wear Birkenstocks?' ventured the woman on the other side of Odin. 'Not that there's anything wrong with wearing Birkenstocks.'

'Wrong answer!' Esme shouted so she'd be heard over the hubbub of conversation. 'You know they're a vegan because they won't shut up about being a vegan.'

There was a deathly silence. Odin fingered his plaited beard pensively.

Esme realised she'd ruined the punchline. 'No, that's not right.' She decided to go again. 'How do you know if someone's a vegan? Don't worry, they'll tell you within thirty seconds of meeting them.' She chortled to herself. 'No offence, Odin.'

'None taken,' he said icily, then turned to the woman on his other side so that Esme was forced to take refuge with Tristan. She nudged his elbow so he spilled pea puree everywhere.

'Sorry, Tris. I'm very bored, so you're going to have to entertain me,' Esme demanded, but he turned his back on her.

Luckily, Esme was soon demolishing her main course of Hen of the Wood risotto then there was a break for the speeches before pudding was served.

Dickie was no stranger to an after-dinner speech. He understood the assignment. First he hit some highlights from Seren's Greatest Hits. 'Phyllida and I might not have known what an influencer was but we knew Seren would be successful because she always managed to exert influence on me whenever she wanted a new pony.'

He was fulsome in his praise of Isaac and his family. 'Not only does Isaac love my daughter as deeply and as patiently as she deserves, he's also introduced us to Jollof rice, Kendrick Lamar and my investments have seen a fifteen per cent year on year rise since he took them over.'

Then he ended on a lighter note. 'So, welcome to the family Isaac. We've gained another son and not only have you gained a wife, you've also gained a yogi, a Reiki master, a lady who'll do your tarot and you've lost . . . well, all of your wardrobe space. To Seren and Isaac!'

Everyone dutifully toasted. Esme thought she'd be pleased to have a taste of champagne, but it tasted like old socks, so she gulped down more water.

Isaac stood up to do his speech, which borrowed heavily from Kanye West's 'White Dress', and got everyone to join in on the last refrain. Esme was all for a bit of audience participation by this point and enthusiastically whooped and whistled, until she caught eyes with Kemi sitting at the top table who mimed zipping her lips shut.

Esme thought that Seren might do a speech. It was the twenty-first century after all and Seren was a woman of many opinions, but it was Punter who stood up to do his best man's speech. Esme settled back in her chair because, knowing Punter, it was bound to be full of crass jokes, heavy innuendos and stories about what had really happened on their stag weekend in Vegas.

No such luck. Punter had known Isaac since they'd met aged five at prep school and he proceeded to describe all the major (and some of the minor) events of their thirty-year friendship at great length.

At one point Esme put her head on the table and pretended to fall asleep, but she was playing to a tough crowd and Lyndsey was giving her the full and unexpurgated 'Look', so she got up to crash the kiddies' table instead.

Fergus and Summer, who gave up her chair in favour of sitting on Esme's lap, were thrilled to see her, although she barely got a grunted 'wotcha' from Oscar. Best of all, they had bowls of Haribo, which Esme happily tucked into as Punter wittered on.

'Who is this guy?' Fergus demanded. 'I wish he'd go away so we can have pudding. It's molten chocolate cake.'

No doubt Esme's pudding would be some dry, non-dairy vegan fare so she decided she might as well stay put. The quicker that Punter was done, the quicker they could get to the fun stuff. Alas, Punter had only reached the university years, so he could well be hogging the microphone for another hour.

'Come on, Punter! None of us are getting any younger,' Esme shouted. 'Can you start wrapping things up?'

The children looked at her with a mixture of awe and horror. Fergus high-fived his aunt and Summer whispered in her ear, 'Mummy's going to make you sit on the naughty step.'

'I'm a grown-up. I don't ever have to sit on the naughty step,' Esme said, though judging from the looks Allegra was giving her from her raised vantage point at the top table, her sister didn't just want her to sit on the naughty step but would like to schedule in a little light whipping too. 'Isn't this dull?'

'Haven't you got your phone? Can we play a game on it?' Fergus asked hopefully, but Esme's phone was in her bag, which was on her table, and she couldn't face Odin or even Lyndsey, who was being an absolute buzzkill.

Thankfully, Punter got the message and fast-forwarded from the May Ball to fifteen years later when he and Isaac met Seren at a beach party in Mykonos.

Then it was time for dessert. Esme promised Summer a whole pound if she let Esme have her chocolate pudding. 'We can share the ice cream and anyway, you've got loads of Haribo, haven't you?'

Finally, coffee and petit fours were brought round. Then there was the first dance to a very unoriginal 'At Last' performed by a lady in a gold sequinned gown who'd joined the mini orchestra from earlier. Esme hoped they would push off soon and there'd be a proper DJ.

What was a wedding without a packed dance floor and everyone singing along to 'Come On, Eileen'? A waste of everyone's time, that's what.

As soon as Seren and Isaac had finished their clearly choreo-graphed slow shuffle, people gratefully rose from their chairs to join them as the band moved seamlessly into 'I Get A Kick Out Of You'.

'Right, Oscar, you're dancing with me,' Esme decided, as she staggered to her feet.

Oscar reared back in alarm. 'I am not.'

'You are or I'm never buying you another can of Coke ever again,' Esme said. Oscar flinched as if he'd taken the threat seriously.

'Go on then,' he said ungraciously.

'You have to twirl me,' Esme insisted, but once they were on the dance floor her eldest nephew resisted all her attempts to get him to do anything more than a side-to-side lumber.

'Are you all right, Es?' he asked, his choirboy face suddenly anxious. 'We were quite worried about you yesterday. You seemed . . . like, a bit odd.'

'I'm fine,' Esme said, twirling herself, though she could hardly remember yesterday when today had been so full-on. 'Nothing wrong with being a bit odd. Theo doesn't mind that I'm a bit odd.'

'Yeah, so, Theo . . .'

'Oh, here comes Summer!' Esme grunted as Summer ran at her full pelt then wanted to be picked up and spun round. Esme was only too happy to oblige, though it gave her one hell of a head rush.

This was why she was their favourite aunt; accept no substitutes.

The next hour was a blur. The orchestra packed up and was replaced by the longed-for DJ, who knew exactly why he was there and launched straight into a Motown medley, much to Esme's delight.

'Please stop punching the air and whooping,' Kemi begged when Esme jumped up and down at the opening bars to The Supremes' 'You Can't Hurry Love'. 'And go easy on the champagne.'

'I've barely touched a drop,' Esme shouted, grabbing hold of Kemi's hands. 'Come on, Kemi, dance! Dance like no one's watching!'

'The whole room is watching,' Kemi said, the usual wicked twinkle gone from her eyes. 'Can you dial it down a bit?'

It was hardly as if Esme had turned things all the way up to eleven. She'd turned things up to a six, or a seven tops, until the DJ played 'Gangnam Style' (it had reached that part of the evening) and Fergus appeared at her side, already galloping on the spot.

'Sexy lady!' he shouted through fits of giggles.

They weren't even halfway through their much-rehearsed dance routine when she saw Oliver striding towards them, Summer hanging around his neck.

'Sorry, old chap,' he said to Fergus. 'Jean's here. It's time for you tiddlers to go home.'

'Can't I stay?' Fergus asked as Esme galloped around them, twirling an imaginary lasso. 'I don't want to go.'

'Oh, let him stay!' Esme pleaded, pushing between father and son. 'I mean, Christ, you made the poor kid wear silver knickerbockers.'

'They're breeches!' Fergus protested.

'Knickers!' Summer shouted gleefully.

'It's getting late. There's a car coming in five minutes,' Oliver said over Esme's head, like he wasn't even going to bother to acknowledge her presence. Well, Esme was soon going to change that.

'Jesus, Oliver!' She jabbed her finger in his chest for maximum emphasis. 'Why do you always have to be *so* boring?'

Oliver's lips thinned out, then he turned his back on Esme completely and took Fergus by the arm. 'Come on,' he said briskly. 'Let's not have any more of this nonsense.'

He marched a still protesting Fergus off the dance floor as Esme shouted after them, 'Boring! Boring! Boring!'

She was about to go after them and drag Fergus back, he was definitely the funnest of all her niblings, but then 'Dancing Queen' came on and Esme knew where her priorities lay.

As she danced and chatted to anyone and everyone, Esme realised how much she'd missed *this*: the going out, the getting merry, meeting new people, losing herself on the dance floor. It wasn't until you had a taste of how things used to be that you realised what had been lost.

She even managed to be civil to Debbie when they bumped into each other in the powder room. Esme came out of the loo to see her mother at the sink reapplying the bright pink lipstick she always wore for special occasions, though it did absolutely nothing for her complexion and made her teeth look yellow.

That said, Debbie did look spectacular in a draped dress in a blue and pink tropical print, her long white hair pinned up and wedged in place with a pink fascinator. She had a tall, rangy body that always looked good in clothes, though her features were strong and uncompromising. People always said of her, 'She's a very handsome woman.' It was hard to believe that she was going to be seventy next birthday. Esme could only hope that she'd inherited some of those age-defying genes.

'You look good,' she said to Debbie as she washed her hands at the neighbouring sink. 'Enjoying yourself?'

'I'm surprised you can even bring yourself to talk to me when you hate me so much,' Debbie said sorrowfully.

Esme looked up to the heavens, literally. There was a Renaissance scene painted on the ceiling, which featured fluffy clouds and fat little angel children. 'I don't hate you.'

'That's not what you said yesterday,' Debbie reminded her as she snapped the lid back on her lipstick.

'Can't even remember that far back.' Esme peered at herself in the mirror. She felt flushed but she actually looked quite pale. Her make-up bag was upstairs in the suite but she wouldn't have dared interfere with all the contouring. She realised that Debbie was still standing there, arms folded and looking at her reproachfully when usually her mother looked at her with something close to disdain. 'OK! I'll bite. What did I say?'

'You said that you didn't like me and that I didn't like you,' Debbie said in a heated rush. 'Which was very hurtful. You're my child. Of course I'm fond of you.'

'You're not fond of me. You tolerate me. Barely,' Esme said, and whatever she might have said yesterday, she now realised that she hadn't really understood the dynamic between herself and her mother until that very moment. 'I was the baby you had to save your marriage and when that didn't work you resented me for keeping you married for another sixteen years. Not that I'd have minded if you and Gary had called it quits earlier, but then I guess neither of you wanted to get stuck with custody.'

Debbie drew herself up to her full and impressive height. 'Well, that's simply not true.'

'The pair of you buggered off for fairer climes literally the minute I was sixteen so Allegra got lumbered with me, when she'd never liked me either because I put paid to eleven years of her being the only child.' It was all so clear now.

'I had my own needs, my own desires . . .' Debbie tucked her lipstick away. 'You'd understand what the push and pull is like if you had children of your own.'

'Why would I want to have children when you were hardly the poster girl for motherhood?'

'Well, I'm sorry that I wasn't a better mother,' Debbie said, her nostrils flaring dramatically. 'I suppose I should have stayed home and baked cakes and taught you how to knit and . . .'

'I don't give a flying fuck about any of that stuff but what kind of mother says to their soon-to-be son-in-law's agent at my actual bloody wedding, "I give it six months. Esme never was the sharpest tool in the box."?' It had been ten years and Esme still wasn't over it. She didn't think she ever would be.

'You were getting married to some jumped up little twat who was clearly going to break your heart. It was the very definition of stupidity!'

'I thought I loved him probably because I had no idea what a normal, healthy relationship looked like thanks to you and Gary,' Esme snapped back. There really was something to be said for getting this all out in the open once and for all. 'Also, you painted my living room wall a disgusting shade of brown that looked like baby shit without even asking me. Every time I walked in, I felt violated!'

'You're just being silly now,' Debbie said, striding towards the door. Then she paused mid-stride. 'Oh! I get it now. Esme, why did you even come today when you hate weddings so much?'

'What?' Esme gasped at the unfairness of the accusation. 'I'm happy to be here. I've been having a wonderful time . . .'

'You've been divorced, what? Six years now?'

'Eight, actually.'

'Well, do what I did and get over the ex by getting under a new man,' Debbie all but shouted so that Isaac's mother, who'd just walked into the room, did a sharp turn and walked straight out again. Debbie's words were a grim reminder of Stefan, a pretentious, puffed-up peacock of a performance artist, whom Debbie had rebounded with before she'd left for France and her new life. 'Get under several new men, if you have to. Hell, try it with a woman, but brooding and sulking over the past after all this time has just made you bitter. It's not a good look on you, darling.'

'I am not bitter,' Esme said defensively. Maybe she was a *little* bitter still but none of the men that she'd got under, or even got on top of, since her divorce had been enough to erase the memories.

Apart from Theo, of course. How Esme wished that she was back at her flat and it was just the two of them. Only when she was with Theo, did Esme feel safe. Like the rest of the world ceased to exist or matter.

'I'm not going to say sorry for speaking so bluntly,' Debbie said, but she had her hand on the door handle now so hopefully this very unpleasant scene was drawing to a close.

'Why change the habits of a lifetime?' Things could have been different between them, could still be different, if Debbie broke the cycle. Pulled Esme into a hug. Stroked her hair. Told her, gently and kindly, that it was silly to live in the past when she had a bright and happy future ahead of her. But she never did, so here they were.

'You really are a very difficult person, Esme, you always have been,' was Debbie's pithy summary before she stalked out.

Left on her own, Esme could feel all the fire sizzle out. All of a sudden, she felt exhausted. God, she couldn't remember a time when she didn't feel bone weary. Her head was aching and her shoes were like size six torture devices so she kicked them off as Isaac's mother, Lola, walked back in. Usually Lola was a charming, good-natured sort of person who always made Esme feel like she was warmed by sunlight. The first time they'd met at Seren and Isaac's engagement party, Esme had been intimidated by the chic woman in the Chanel suit, but a smile and a hug later, she'd been smitten. Now, though, she could feel the icy gusts of disapproval emanating from the older woman.

For a moment neither of them said anything, then Lola made sure to look Esme straight in the eye. 'It's very disrespectful to speak to your mother like that,' she said in a clipped voice.

'You kind of caught us in the middle of . . .'

'The way you've been behaving today, you've disrespected your family, *our* family, even yourself, Esme. I'm ashamed that Kemi calls you a friend.'

Esme had to suck in a sob because this was so unexpected, so unjust. Also, the way that Lola was looking at her, her features set and tight, like she'd never gift Esme one of her sunny smiles again.

'Sorry,' Esme said reflexively, though if she could explain things to Lola, it would become clear that she didn't actually have anything to apologise for.

'Go home,' Lola said, and she stood there, holding her ground, until Esme slunk out of the door. 'Sleep it off.'

She leaned back against the wall and sniffed a couple of times before deciding that she wasn't going to cry. *She* wasn't the one who'd done anything wrong. But still, Esme wasn't going to stay where she was so unwelcome.

She'd go back to the ballroom to fetch her bag and phone, then up to the suite to retrieve the rest of her belongings before heading back to her flat, her safe space.

Esme hadn't even taken two steps when she saw a familiar figure at the other end of the corridor. If her flat were her safe space then, in the space of a week, he'd come a close second. *Theo.*

28

He was too far away for Esme to be able to see his face but then Theo held out his arms and she was happy to run to him, like every romcom cliché there was.

'You made it!'

'I did and I'm praying that our sous chef won't burn the place down in my absence.'

The sheer relief of being able to bury her face in the crook of Theo's shoulder, feel him solid and utterly dependable, made Esme want to cry again. But she didn't, not even when Theo pulled back from her enough so that he could get a good look at her. She could get a good look at him too.

'You look just as fine in jeans and a T-shirt as the posh boys in there in their Savile Row suits,' she jerked her head in the direction of the double doors that led to the ballroom. 'In fact, you look a million times better.'

Theo grinned and ducked his head. 'This old thing,' he said mockingly as he tugged at his Ramones T-shirt. 'I just threw it on.' Then his face softened. 'Anyway, you've made enough effort for both of us. Look at you, sweet girl.'

It was Esme's turn to look embarrassed. She swished the skirt of her black ruffly gown. 'This old thing? I just threw it on.'

He lightly caressed the side of her face with one calloused thumb. 'Sometimes I forget how beautiful you are, then it hits me all over again.'

'I'm so glad you're here. In fact, how did you know where to come? I don't remember giving you the address,' Esme said.

Theo suddenly went very still. 'Well, would you listen to that?' He took Esme's hand and began to pull her nearer to the ballroom.

'Listen to what?'

Theo pushed open one of the doors. 'They're playing our song,' he said, throwing out his arm so that Esme was sent skittering away from him, until he pulled her close again.

'Are you dancing?' she asked him with a grin.

'Are you asking?'

Esme nodded, smiling so wide that her face hurt. The threat of tears was long gone. 'I'm asking.'

'Then I'm dancing,' Theo said, tugging her right into the middle of the throng on the dance floor who were throwing their best (and worst) moves to Baccara's 'Yes Sir, I Can Boogie'.

Theo was the perfect dance partner. He had a great sense of rhythm, though God, she already knew that, and his moves were knowing and playful during even the cheesiest wedding tunes. He was practically interpretative dancing to 'I Will Survive', but when the DJ shifted the mood and Al Green started to croon 'Let's Stay Together', Esme was back in Theo's arms, as he expertly manoeuvred her around the floor, one arm around her, his other hand holding hers, his lips moving across her forehead.

Everyone was looking at them but Esme didn't care. Yes, she might be all of the things that she'd been accused of – bitter and stuck-up and disrespectful – but in spite of all that, Theo wanted to be with her.

She was so happy the universe had delivered him to her exactly when she'd needed him most, but she was even happier that Theo had come with his own free will fully installed and he didn't want to go anywhere. He liked being with Esme. In fact, he loved being with her.

He loved her.

Though Esme had sworn that she wouldn't let her heart have a deciding vote in her life ever again, it wouldn't be that hard to be in love with him too.

It was definitely the slow smooch end of the evening. Now the DJ was playing 'True' by Spandau Ballet and Theo and Esme weren't even pretending to dance but just standing there, occasionally shuffling their feet, but mostly locked in a tender embrace.

It was absolutely perfect, until someone tapped Esme on the shoulder like they were trying to drill for oil.

'You're coming with me,' Allegra said, her voice tight with fury once again. What a surprise!

'I'm not going anywhere with you,' Esme said as she snuggled tighter into Theo's arms. 'Why should I?'

'Well, for starters, we're all going upstairs to help Seren get changed.'

Esme was unmoved. 'She's an actual adult, I'm sure she can get ready without the help of ten other women.'

Allegra's hiss could be heard even over the dulcet tones of Tony Hadley. 'You are being absolutely fucking impossible, even for you.' She tried to pull at Esme's arm. 'How much have you had to drink?'

Trust her sister to kill the mood. With a sigh and great reluctance, Esme stepped back. 'Are you not even going to say hello to Theo?'

Allegra's eyes swept over him like he wasn't even there. She turned back to her younger sister with an air of extreme disdain. The lip curl alone. 'Oh Esme,' she said, every word a chip of ice. 'Why are you wasting my time with this?' She sniffed contemptuously. 'I'll expect to see you upstairs in the next ten minutes if you know what's good for you.'

Then she stuck her nose in the air and walked off with a very deliberate flounce. Some things never changed. If Esme's childhood had been soundtracked by Debbie and Gary screaming at each other, the bassline had been provided by Allegra stomping up the stairs and slamming any door which got in her way.

'Rude! She's so fucking rude!' Esme smoothed her hands down Theo's chest to reassure him that she would never blank him. He'd always be the most important person in any room that she was in.

'It's all right,' Theo said, though it was very, very far from all right. The mood had shifted after Allegra's interruption. 'I should be getting back now anyway. I've stayed too long but you're very hard to resist.'

'I'll come back with you,' Esme decided, but Theo shook his head.

'Don't do that, go and sort things out with your sister,' he said, pressing a kiss to Esme's forehead, which was very clammy by now. He gave a gentle push to get her moving on unwilling feet towards the doors.

Esme turned round for one last glimpse of him as he stood there on the dance floor, a point of perfect stillness to the conga line that was winding round him to the strains of 'Treat People With Kindness'.

'I'll see you at the flat?' she called out to him, and he nodded.

Then he was gone.

*

At various points during the evening, Esme had lost her shoes, her evening bag and her phone, but she just couldn't find it in herself to care very much.

All that she cared about was the pounding of her heart as she went up in the lift to the bridal suite, where Allegra and Lola and goodness knows how many other people would be waiting to tell her off. It wasn't even as if she'd been drinking. A couple of swallows of champagne hardly counted as drinking.

But when Esme entered the toile and chintz wonderland the outer rooms were empty, and when she poked her head round the door of the master suite, she was surprised to see Seren, all by herself, lying in the centre of a huge bed in a silky dressing gown. Esme was pretty sure that it had the word 'Wifey' embroidered on the back.

'Are you all right?' Esme asked tentatively.

There was no answer at first, then Seren raised her head. 'Just taking a moment to centre myself,' Seren said. There was a brief period of silence, no more than ten seconds, then she sat up. 'OK, I'm done with centring myself.' She patted the bed next to her. 'Everyone keeps forgetting that I'm meant to be the focus of attention and they've left me all on my own. Come and hang out with me.'

Esme didn't need to be told twice. Every bit of her still ached and she was happy to climb up on the bed and sink into the softness. It was all her *Princess and The Pea* fantasies come true.

'Have you had the best day?' she asked Seren as they lay side by side.

'I know that everyone thinks I'm so extra having three weddings . . .'

'Nah! You're not extra, they're just basic,' Esme said, though she had been guilty of that very crime.

'I thought that at least with today being the third time, I could really enjoy it, make those core memories, but the whole day has gone by in such a blur and I got stuck talking to all sorts of boring people . . . My uncle Malcolm tried to tell me about his gout. I mean, on today of all days!'

'And Punter's best man speech . . .'

Seren groaned. 'He was told not to make any shagging jokes or make any reference to Isaac's past girlfriends, but nobody thought to mention that his speech should be ten minutes.'

'It felt like ten hours,' Esme said. 'I did try to get him to speed things along.'

'Yes, we all heard you.' Seren didn't seem at all angry about it. 'How much have you had to drink anyway?'

'I don't know why people keep asking me that.' Esme tried to sit up, but the effort was too much. 'Allegra's been awful to me.'

'Whatever! If I don't want to hear about Uncle Malcolm's gout, I certainly don't want to hear you and Ally bitching about each other,' Seren said, stretching languorously. 'I'm meant to be getting changed. We're booked into the penthouse suite for tonight but I can't move.'

'What has Allegra been saying about me?' Esme demanded.

'Nobody cares, Es. You need to sort it out between you.' Seren sat up and tugged at her silky robe. 'Do you think it would be OK if I transitioned to the penthouse suite like this?'

'Considering how much this must have all cost, I reckon you can do what you like,' Esme said vaguely.

'It's just that to get to the penthouse, you need to go all the way down to the lobby and . . .'

'You know, she didn't even say hello to Theo.' Just thinking about it made Esme twitch her fingers and toes in anger. 'She looked at him like he was a piece of chewing gum stuck to the bottom of her shoe.'

Seren threw Esme a coy look. 'Oooh! Who's Theo?'

'I've met a man. The perfect man.' Esme prodded Seren's leg with her foot. 'Guess there was something to all that manifesting bullshit after all.'

'You manifested a Theo!' Seren put her hands in the prayer position. 'Is he dreamy?'

'The dreamiest,' Esme said with a happy little sigh. 'I've been dancing with him for ages, even though to look at him you wouldn't think he'd be much of a dancer. But he's got all the moves.'

Despite her fatigue, Seren seemed newly energised by this development. 'This is thrilling! Who is he? Is he one of Isaac's mates from the firm?'

'Oh, please! As if I would ever get with a finance bro . . .'

'You'd say that to me? On my wedding day?' Seren was getting a little too *The Godfather* for Esme's liking.

'*Third* wedding day and no he doesn't work with Isaac. I honestly did manifest him. The universe really came through for me. I think it was crying on the crystals when we were vision boarding at your hen that really did it.' Esme paused because Seren was staring at her like she didn't even know what vision boarding was.

'*What?*'

'What?' Esme echoed back. 'You're the one who's into the woo, not me.'

Seren shook her head. Her wedding hairdo was coming a little undone. 'Seriously, Es, how much have you had to drink?'

'Stop asking me that!'

'But it's a very good question,' said an acid drop voice from the doorway, and Esme looked over to see Allegra advancing on her with an acid drop face to match. 'You and I are going to have a talk.'

'Not here, guys.' Seren scrambled off the bed. 'Please take it somewhere else.'

Esme didn't have a chance to get off the bed too then make for the nearest exit because Allegra had already grabbed her arm with a pincer like motion and was dragging her towards the bathroom.

'Not that bathroom,' Seren called out. 'That's my special bridal bathroom. There's another one off the salon.'

'Let me go!' Esme tried to shake herself free from Allegra's grip, which was just short of bruising, but her sister held on fast until Esme was back in the pink marble bathroom of earlier and Allegra was slamming the door behind them. 'What? What the hell is your problem?'

'You are,' Allegra said, with real venom, then released Esme with a little push that had her stumbling back and knocking her hip on the edge of a towel rail. 'Congratulations! You've outdone yourself today.'

Esme rubbed her arm reproachfully. 'What have I done that's so terrible?'

Allegra's mouth fell open in disbelief. 'Where to even start? You were rude to Seren when she gave you your gift bag, you fidgeted all the way through the service, you *heckled* the best man . . .'

'It was hardly heckling and anyway, everyone else was thinking it. I just talked to Seren about it and she wasn't at all mad . . .'

'You constantly wind the children up until they're uncontrollable and, yet again, you've been unforgivably rude to Oliver,' Allegra said, as if that was the worst crime of all. 'That's just for starters.'

'I was hardly rude to Oliver.' Esme couldn't keep the sneer off her face as she said her brother-in-law's name. 'How was I rude to him? Did I swear at him? No. So . . .'

'It's not just about the way you behaved towards him tonight, Esme, it's about the last eight fucking years,' Allegra said and, unlike her younger sister, she rarely swore so the expletive was enough for Esme to take a step back and bang her other hip against the sink. 'You roll your eyes every time he walks into a room or dares to open his mouth. You can't even muster any attempt to be polite. Enough is enough!'

Everyone was so concerned with how much Esme had been drinking, but no one had thought to limit Allegra's alcohol intake, which was why she was now very drunk. Her face was red and shiny, and each new hurtful set of words was accompanied by a tsunami of spittle.

Esme was backed up against the sink but she still presented her best fight face. 'Get over what?'

'Your divorce!' Allegra practically screamed the words. 'And the fact that yes, I married your divorce lawyer, but I love him and that's not going to change any time soon.'

'You don't really love him, Ally. You wanted kids, you wanted financial security, I don't blame you for that. Oliver was the best candidate at the time, so you settled.' God, it felt so good to finally get it off her chest. 'It wasn't a love match and so if you were going to settle, then, yes, it was vile of you to do it with my divorce lawyer.'

'That man . . . that man . . .' Allegra's voice shook with the weight of her words. 'He's the love of my life.'

Esme couldn't help the short, sharp bark of laughter that erupted out of her. 'Oh, please! Oliver? Honestly, Ally, you could have done *so* much better.'

'I didn't want to do any better. I fell in love with him and yes, I wanted a family and I wanted security, someone to look after me for once because God knows, I was fed up with having to constantly take care of you,' Allegra flung at her.

'I didn't need taking care of then, but I had just got divorced so forgive me for wanting some support from my sister. Instead, you were too busy sneaking around with him.'

'I'm not going to apologise, yet again, for falling in love.'

'You have never, ever apologised, not even once, for what you did,' Esme reminded her darkly.

Allegra folded her arms. 'And you have never once thanked me for looking after you . . . I was twenty-seven when you were dumped on me. I shouldn't have had to take responsibility for you . . .'

'Dumped! That says it all, doesn't it? And I don't remember you looking after me. What I do remember is you banging on and on about what a burden I was. You made me feel so unwelcome.'

'You were a brat!'

'I was sixteen. Being a brat goes with the territory. Anyway, if I'd taken all your stupid advice, I'd have ended up doing a degree that I didn't want, saddled with debt and then having to use Granny's inheritance to pay just a fraction of it off.' Esme nodded because it was all so clear now. 'You're just angry that I followed my own path and I didn't shy away from the opportunities that came my way.'

'Oh, Alexander was *such* a great opportunity, wasn't he?' Allegra smiled vindictively. 'That was one piece of advice that you should have taken. Then maybe you wouldn't have spent the last eight years being angry and jealous of anyone who had the audacity to fall in love.'

'*With my fucking divorce lawyer!*' Esme shouted because, just once, she wanted Allegra to acknowledge that it had been a shitty thing to do.

'Honestly, I can't keep having this same conversation with you. You need to change,' Allegra insisted, her face less red, her words and the spit back under control. 'Seren's right. You give back what you put out and you don't put out anything but bitterness and bad vibes.'

'That's not true,' Esme said, because if she were nothing but bitterness and bad vibes then why would Theo love her . . .

'It is true and I'm not doing it anymore.' Allegra closed her eyes, took a deep breath, and when she opened them again, there was something resolute and final in her expression. 'Esme, I don't want you in our lives . . . You're horrible to Oliver. You're a bad influence on the children . . .'

Esme couldn't believe what she was hearing, though it was hard to hear anything over the rushing sound in her head. She clutched hold of the edge of the sink as a wave of dizziness threatened to overtake her. 'What have they been telling you? About the cake?'

'What are you talking about?' Allegra sat down heavily on the edge of the tub, as though saying completely horrible things to her little sister had shattered her. 'Actually, I don't even want to know.'

'It's probably for the best that I don't see you and Oliver,' Esme said, because actually that would be no great hardship. So why did she feel as if the world had just turned to cinders and ash? 'It's funny because all I ever wanted for as long as I can remember is for us to be friends, like the Fossils in *Ballet Shoes* or Laura and Mary Ingalls . . .'

'They're just stories. We were never going to be friends. There's a huge age gap and we couldn't be more different,'

Allegra said flatly. 'We have nothing in common, except we lived under the same roof for a few years.'

'You've never even tried to be my mate instead of my older sister. I reckon we could have been really good friends when Debbie and Gary left if . . .'

'No, we wouldn't have been,' Allegra said, as if the topic wasn't even up for discussion.

Esme could see that there was no point in trying to argue her case. She was shattered. Not least because Allegra was shattering. 'Fine, I'll stay away from you and Oliver. Like, I hardly ever see you when I'm dropping off the children on a Friday . . .'

Allegra held her hand up. 'No! I don't want you near the children either.' She sat up straighter, a flush quickly mottling her chest and neck as if she was getting angry all over again. 'You were two hours late to bring them home yesterday!'

'But you knew where they were and, obviously, they were safe if they were with me,' Esme pointed out, her head pounding now.

'Well, we didn't know that because you weren't answering your phone.' Allegra's posture was rigid now. 'And when we did finally get them home, something had happened. I don't know what because they wouldn't say . . .'

'Nothing happened,' Esme insisted, because the dumping of the middle-class post-school snacks and the buying and consumption of fizzy drinks and junk food had been going on for years. They weren't unsettled by it; they bloody loved it.

'I know my children,' Allegra said sanctimoniously, as she did when she was pulling out the mother card to prove that she was a far more evolved and fully rounded adult than Esme. And as proof that, because Esme wasn't saddled with children, it meant that she was an inherently selfish person.

'They were *so* subdued. It's the first time that Fergus has ever gone to bed without arguing and it was obvious that Summer had been wet for hours . . .'

'What do you think I was doing to them?' Of all the accusations that Allegra had chucked her way, this was the one that was most unfair and was heating Esme up like an old-fashioned kettle on a hob, shaking as it came to a piercing boil. 'I love those children.'

'I don't think you're capable of loving anyone,' Allegra said, standing up and smoothing down the ruffles on her dress as she looked at her younger sister. 'And you don't make yourself very lovable either.'

'That's a horrible thing to say,' Esme choked out. 'I'm not like that.'

'You are. You're exhausting, Esme. All our lives would be better if you weren't in them. Now go home, nobody wants you here,' said Allegra, stalking out of the bathroom like she'd just delivered a death sentence.

29

Esme's only satisfaction, small as it was, was that she burst into tears *after* Allegra had gone. So it was a while before she heard the tap at the door and it wasn't until Kemi poked her still perfectly chignoned head in that she realised where she was and that there was still a wedding going on outside.

'Oh Esme . . . what a state you've got yourself in,' Kemi said a little sharply as she slipped through the door. 'Come on, time to pull yourself together.'

Esme shook her throbbing head. 'Allegra . . . she's been . . . I'm never going to forgive her,' she said through her sobs.

'You two will make it up. You've been arguing for as long as I've known you,' Kemi said, as if it were no big deal when it was the very biggest deal.

She sat Esme down on the edge of the bath and wiped her face with a towel dipped in cold water, which came away smeared with make-up because Esme ruined everything.

Kemi's phone beeped and she sighed with relief. 'Right, that's Lyndsey. She's got your phone and evening bag. She's going to order you an Uber and meet us in the lobby.'

Esme was still crying; the shuddering, hiccupping, snotty stage of crying. 'You want me to leave?'

'You can't stay here.' There was that sharpness to Kemi's voice again. 'Look, we all know that weddings are hard for you, but no one forced you to get this drunk, Esme.'

'But I haven't . . .'

'Now, let's get your stuff together and get you out of here.'

Esme let Kemi take her by the wrist and guide her out of the bathroom. The suite was now full of black ruffled bridesmaids, who all averted their eyes as Esme emerged lest they be turned to stone. Someone had already packed up the holdall Esme had brought with her, which they handed to Kemi as they made their way out of the door, Esme still quietly sobbing.

As they waited for the lift, Kemi manipulated Esme's stiff arms into the sleeves of her puffer coat. 'Look, everything will be different tomorrow,' she said as they heard the welcome ding of the elevator arriving. 'You're going to have the mother of all hangovers.'

Esme didn't have the energy to explain, once again, that she'd barely touched a drop of alcohol. Instead, she let Kemi bundle her into the lift and lecture her all the way down to the ground floor.

'. . . and if you want to get back into my Mum's good graces, then it's going to take flowers and a handwritten letter of apology,' Kemi said as they reached their destination and the lift doors opened to reveal Lyndsey standing there with 'The Look' writ large all over her face.

'I know!' Esme rasped. 'I'm a terrible, awful, vile person. The whole world hates me.'

Lyndsey and Kemi shared a long-suffering look. 'Nobody hates you, Es, but my God, you really have tried everyone's patience today.'

Kemi was pleased to hand custody over to Lyndsey, who took Esme and Esme's bag and steered her to the ornate double doors that led out onto Park Lane. 'Where are your shoes?'

Esme gazed down at her feet just poking out from beneath the hem of her dress. 'I don't know.'

'Shall we go and find them?' Lyndsey sounded as if she was grinding on her back teeth. But then Esme supposed that today hadn't been much fun for Lyndsey when she was the plus one of The Most Terrible Woman in London. And now she was stuck with babysitting duties.

'Do you hate me too?' Esme asked with a phlegmy sniff.

'I don't hate you at all,' Lyndsey said, quickly enough that Esme hoped she was telling the truth. 'Though you're not exactly my favourite person right now. You must know where your shoes are.'

Esme shrugged. 'I don't know. I don't care, I couldn't walk in them anyway.'

'Shall we put your trainers on?' Lyndsey started unzipping Esme's holdall but then came the distant chime of a phone. 'Oh, that will be your car.'

'I can go out like this,' Esme said as a uniformed doorman, his expression impassive, held the door open for her. 'I just want to go home. Everything's better with . . .'

'Babes, today was always going to be hard for you, I know,' Lyndsey said as she followed Esme out into the cold, damp March night. 'But it has been eight years now. You have to get over the fact that your marriage didn't work out. Shit happens. Life goes on.'

She was right. Esme knew she was right. Surely her life was better, happier, now than it had ever been? Then she thought of Allegra saying that she was unlovable, that she'd never see the kids again, and although she could have sworn she was all cried out, a fresh wave of tears, a new round of sobs, were ready for an encore performance.

Lyndsey waved at a car that was idling at the kerb. 'You're a dick sometimes but I love you,' she said, as she helped a weeping Esme into the back of the Toyota Prius. 'I'll see you Monday and after you've apologised for being a dick, we'll have a full debrief. With cake. All right?'

She shut the door before Esme could reply, though talking was almost impossible when she was crying so hard.

'Parliament Hill?' the driver asked and Esme yelped something that sounded enough like a yes that he pulled out into the Saturday night traffic.

They drove in silence, the familiar London landmarks – Hyde Park, Marble Arch, Madame Tussauds, the edges of Regent's Park – a blur outside the windows.

It was only as they were drawing up outside 23 to 45 Parliament Hill Mansions that the driver spoke again. 'Whoever he is, my dear, he's not worth it,' he said in a heavy Middle Eastern accent, as Esme fumbled with the door handle.

★

She pretty much crawled up the stairs then took long minutes to find her keys. There was a white hot moment of panic when Esme thought they were lost and she'd have to wake up Jacinta and Marion or, worse, call Allegra, who had a spare set, when she remembered that Theo would be here soon. Theo would make everything better.

Then Esme found her keys in a side pocket of the holdall and didn't so much open her door as fall through it. She threw off her puffer coat and left it on the hall floor, pulled at the hairpins that were jabbing into her skull and threw them on the floor too, then stumbled blindly into the bedroom, not bothering to switch on lights.

Esme had never been so ready to burrow under the covers of her bed and hide away from a world that was cruel and careless. She pulled the duvet over her head and curled herself into a ball, trying to shrink her body as much as possible.

She was still crying when she drifted off to sleep.

And she was still crying when Theo got into bed and pulled her gently but firmly into his arms.

'Hey, hey,' he said softly, his lips soft like gossamer wings as he kissed the damp track of her tears. 'What's the matter?'

It was hard to say. Instead, Esme wrapped her arms around him and Theo didn't pester her for explanations but held her until the sobs died down and she stopped trembling and was quiet and still.

'Allegra hates me,' she said in a tiny voice. If she said it any louder, then the truth of those three words would be even worse; although deep down, hadn't Esme always known it?

'She doesn't hate you,' Theo said.

'She hates me and she doesn't want me in her life and I'm not ever going to see the children again.' Her voice broke and though Esme thought they couldn't get any closer, Theo pulled her even tighter, so nothing and no one could get at her.

'She doesn't mean it.'

'She does,' Esme said, and it wasn't as if this hadn't happened before. There had been two whole years when she and Allegra had been dead to each other. Esme had often wondered what would have happened if she hadn't bumped into a pregnant Allegra at the Lido. If she hadn't wormed her way back into her sister's life, once Oscar was born.

It had been Esme who needed Allegra, not the other way round. Allegra was Esme's only family, whereas Allegra has replaced the little sister that she'd never really liked with a new family of her own. Would probably quite happily have carried on through the years with no thought of welcoming Esme back into the fold.

'She can't stop you from seeing the kids,' Theo said. 'We'll get a lawyer.'

'She's already got a lawyer. *Him.* Oliver.'

'We'll get better lawyers,' Theo insisted.

'She said that I was incapable of loving anyone and that I was so unlovable that nobody would ever love me,' Esme repeated in a rusty voice.

'Well, you know that's not true, because I love you.' Theo kissed the top of her lank six-day hair. 'I don't think I've ever loved anyone the way I love you.'

'If I manifested you, have I just put those words into your mouth?'

'Still ninety-nine per cent sure that you didn't manifest me and that I mean every single thing I've said.'

'I've said it once, I'll say it again, you really are too perfect to actually be real,' Esme decided, and she felt rather than heard the rumble of Theo's laughter as he stroked the tight spot between her eyebrows over and over again with his thumb until it was impossible to stay awake.

30

Sunday

It turned out that there were worse things than a hangover brought on by too much drinking. A hangover from too much crying was similar but also much more evil.

Esme woke up very, very late the next day. Theo had already left for the pub, though she hadn't even been aware of him getting out of bed or heard any of those now familiar morning noises of the shower, the toothbrush, the kettle.

Her throat was drier than the Sahara, the Gobi, the Kalahari, any desert in the world. Her head felt as if someone had removed it, taken a sledgehammer to it, then reattached it to Esme's neck but the wrong way round. Her eyes were gunked up and swollen.

Esme got out of bed, clinging to furniture and door handles as the dizziness overwhelmed her. Once she'd managed to leave the bedroom, she thought about having a shower then thought better of it. Instead she brushed her teeth then stood at the kitchen window, gulping down a glass of water as she watched the sun set over the tennis courts and paint the sky gold.

She remembered the time last summer when she'd tried to teach Fergus how to play tennis but he'd got into a rage because he couldn't get the ball over the net. He'd thrown his racquet down in a fit of temper that would have had John McEnroe suing for copyright. Humphrey, a stalwart of the

Parliament Hill Mansions residents' committee and self-styled *gauleiter* of the tennis courts, had happened to be walking past and had banned Fergus for life from ever setting foot on the tennis courts again.

Esme had laughed and laughed all the way back to her flat until Fergus had got over his grump and laughed too.

'I bet he's written your name in his little black notebook and it will be passed down to every member of the residents' committee for years to come in case you ever try to sneak on to the courts to practise your backhand,' she'd told him over a consolatory Magnum. 'Even when you're sixty. Even when you're eighty. A hundred!'

'You really aren't like a proper grown-up at all,' Fergus had said in wonder and Esme had basked in his approval. In being the cool aunt who taught the children important life lessons while corrupting them slightly. It wasn't as if she had favourites, but if she did, then it would have been Fergus with his chaotic second child energy. Esme could relate.

That was all over now though. As the tears started to descend again, though Esme was sure her tear ducts were as dry as a shallow riverbed during a drought, she gave what was left of the day up as a bad job and went back to bed.

Esme woke up again when Theo came home from work. She drank another huge glass of water and, when he slid into bed, she was ready for him to chase the shadows and the darkness away with his mouth and his hands and his cock until she wasn't crying but gasping out his name.

Although Esme had trained herself not to be a snuggler, she thought the post-sex cuddling was a very close second to the actual during-sex sexing. They just seemed to fit together. Her head tucking under Theo's chin, his arm around her waist, her legs entwined with his.

'I never said this yesterday . . . not when you were so upset, but I can't believe you know a man called Punter.'

'I reluctantly know him. If it's any consolation he has never said one word to me in five years – all his remarks are addressed to my tits.'

'Well, they are great tits.' Theo kissed her shoulder. 'Speaking of reluctance, have you set an alarm on your phone so you don't miss your doctor's appointment?'

'I have. I'm sure I have,' Esme muttered sleepily, but Theo pinched her arse so she was forced back to the present.

'Where is your phone?'

It was still in her holdall that she'd dumped in the hall the night before, and almost out of charge. The dizziness was back as Esme crashed around the bedroom and made several attempts to plug in her charger, then plug the phone into the charger.

She had several missed calls and messages, but none of them was from Allegra so she decided that they could wait. Besides, Theo had other plans for her phone.

Although she'd set a reminder for her doctor's appointment and several alarms, he made her set yet more alarms.

'I know what you're like about getting up early,' he said when Esme finally settled back into his arms with an aggrieved little huff. 'You'll keep hitting snooze until there's no more snoozing to be had and you've missed your appointment.'

Esme frowned. That wasn't right. 'I'm not that bad. I get up eventually,' she said.

'First time for everything,' Theo said a little too smugly for her liking. 'But not tomorrow because I'm going to make sure you make your doctor's appointment.'

There had been a time, only a week or so ago, when Esme had always managed to get out of bed and turn up for any appointments she'd made. OK, she was usually five to ten minutes late but that was industry standard.

Now though, with her hand on Theo's chest so she could feel the steady beat of his heart, it was getting harder and harder to imagine the life she'd had before.

The life without him in it.

31

Monday

Though she would never have admitted it to Theo – although it was hard to talk to him when his head was buried under the pillow and he kept groaning as her alarms kept going off – Esme suspected that, without those multiple alarms, she wouldn't have got out of bed after all.

She didn't feel much better for sleeping so much. Could a person actually sleep too much Esme wondered as she made a mug of tea for Theo, who was fast asleep again when she took it in to him.

For a second Esme was tempted to crawl back into bed, but then another alert shrieked on her phone and she hurried out of the door. The quicker she got to the doctor's and had her stitches removed, the quicker she could get back home and wash her hair.

Her head was banging as she strapped on her cycle helmet and set off for the surgery. A cacophony of car horns and catcalls serenaded her as she cycled down Highgate Road, an indication that it was going to be one of those days. Esme was fed up with Those Days.

Of course, even though Esme was on time for her appointment – five minutes early actually – the waiting room was full and she had to wait nearly an hour before her name was called. She'd also forgotten to bring a mask and the one the receptionist gave her reeked of TCP, another reason why she wanted to get out of there ASAP.

Esme had expected a doctor, but she was greeted by a middle-aged nurse with purple hair and a nose stud, who stared at Esme unblinking for one long moment, then led her to one of the treatment rooms.

Esme shrugged off her puffer coat and tried to drape it over the back of a chair but couldn't quite do it. 'The material's so slippery and I'm all fingers and thumbs,' she said as the nurse gathered the supplies she'd need to remove the stitches.

In the end, Esme threw her coat on the floor and sat down on the chair.

'Is this going to hurt?' she asked, looking at the metal tray, tweezers and a wicked pair of scissors that were waiting for her. 'I don't handle pain very well.'

'It's nothing compared to having the stitches in the first place,' the nurse said. 'You won't even need an anaesthetic, though you will need to take off your helmet.'

No wonder Esme's head was so sore. She had trouble removing her helmet too until the nurse gently pushed her hands away and unclipped it herself.

'You just stay here for a minute. I'm going to ask one of the doctors to check in on you.' She hurried towards the door then turned to fix Esme with a stern look. 'You're absolutely not to leave this room.'

'Wasn't planning to,' Esme mumbled as she slumped back in the chair. All this fuss just to take out some stitches.

It felt like a very long wait. Esme must have nodded off because the next thing she knew there was a cool hand on her forehead.

'I wasn't asleep,' Esme said, looking up into the face of one of the more senior doctors whom she always hoped she'd see when she booked an appointment. Doctor . . . Doctor . . . Doctor Short gave every appearance of brisk efficiency but had been very kind when Esme was mid-divorce and suffering with a series of stress-related UTIs. 'I had a very early start this morning.'

'Before we take out your stitches, I just want to have a look at your notes and ask you a few questions,' Doctor Short said, sitting down at the desk and logging into the computer while the nurse perched on the edge of the bed. 'So it sounds like you had a pretty eventful time of it last Saturday night. Can you hit me with the highlights?'

Esme launched into her tale of that Saturday night, which now seemed to pale into insignificance compared to the latest Saturday night. Probably she should just stop going out altogether.

'So no CT scan, then?'

'No, because I didn't need one,' Esme said firmly. She couldn't believe that she was saddled up and at this rodeo again.

'How have you been feeling this week? Anything out of the ordinary?' Dr Short asked, with her eyes fixed on the monitor. Esme was tempted to fudge the truth, because really, she felt perfectly fine in herself, but it couldn't do any harm to mention that . . .

'Well, I've been very tired this week and also very head-achey, but that's normal after a *very minor* head injury, right?'

'It can be,' Doctor Short said, swinging her chair round so she was looking directly at Esme. She had a very forthright gaze. 'So, would you say you've experienced mood swings or a loss of inhibition?'

Esme snorted. 'I haven't been dancing the merengue naked down Kentish Town Road.' She'd just been herself. Bossed it at work. Got on with stuff despite the headaches. If any-one was suffering from mood swings, it had been the people around her. 'I went to a wedding on Saturday and everyone accused me of being drunk though I only had half a glass of champagne with the toasts. And it all seemed to get quite out of hand. I mean, any reasonable person would have heckled the best man, his speech was so long and boring.'

The doctor nodded like she understood and Esme waited for her to ask a leading question like, 'Have you been experiencing hallucinations?' Or, 'Has a tall, dark, handsome stranger appeared fully formed in your life?' Then, Esme would have had to be truthful, but Doctor Short didn't ask any leading questions, just wheeled her chair a little closer.

'I'm just going to shine a penlight in your eyes,' she said, holding up a small wand with an illuminated end, which made Esme flinch away when it was held up to her face. 'Any dizziness?'

'Now? No.'

'And during the week?'

'Maybe a couple of head rushes every now and again.' Esme could feel the first strands of worry starting to knot in her stomach. None of this was sounding good. It was sounding as if maybe there was something sort of wrong. 'What number do you think I am on the Glasgow Coma Scale?'

'Speech is very slurred,' the doctor said to herself, then she gave Esme a disarming smile. 'Head injuries can be tricky things. You're displaying a few symptoms that I think we should investigate so I'm going to write you a letter to take with you now to the Queen Anne Hospital . . .'

'OK, so are you going to take my stitches out though?' Esme asked. 'Because I really want to go home and wash my hair, then I need to go to work. Could I maybe pop to the Royal Free later this week?'

'You have to go to the Queen Anne now,' the nurse said gently, sharing a look over Esme's head with the doctor.

'But I have my bike. Should I cycle there? Where is this hospital?'

'It's in Bloomsbury,' Doctor Short said, standing up and picking up Esme's bike helmet. 'But your bike can stay in the cycle rack in our car park. Let's order you a car and we can have you on your way.'

★

The nurse actually stood over Esme to supervise as she ordered an Uber, then led her by the wrist to the reception area where she beckoned to one of the staff.

'This young lady has a car coming to take her to the Queen Anne,' she said brightly. 'Can you wait with her until it arrives?'

'I don't need to be babysat,' Esme protested but the man, who was a dead ringer for Bradley Walsh, said that he could do with some fresh air. They waited outside on a bench and he explained how he got mistaken for Bradley Walsh all the time. When Esme's phone pinged with a text message to say that her Uber had arrived, he stopped her from getting in the back of the wrong car.

'Good luck!' he said as he waved her off, as if luck was something that Esme needed. 'Don't forget to give them that letter when you get there.'

Esme very gingerly fingered the back of her head where her stitches were still very much in residence. It was tender to the touch as it had been all week, though she didn't know if that was of any dire significance.

She could feel panic rising in her like mercury in a barometer on a hot day. Even though she was in her puffer coat and the driver had the heating going full blast, she was icy cold. That didn't mean anything sinister. Just that the shock of suddenly finding herself in a car being driven to a hospital that specialised in people's brains was causing Esme to freak the fuck out.

What if? What if? What if?

What if her stitches had become infected because Esme couldn't swear on a bible that she'd remembered to take the complete course of antibiotics?

What if the accident had caused irreparable brain damage?

What if she actually had a brain tumour that she hadn't even known about and the accident had knocked it loose?

There was no point in catastrophising and what if-ing. She could call Theo and he'd tell her that it would be all right.

Oh God.

What if Theo wasn't a manifestation but a symptom?

That felt like the worst catastrophe of all. Even worse than a brain tumour.

Esme thought about calling Lyndsey to say that she was going to be late to start work but mostly just to hear a kind voice.

She even thought about calling Allegra, but to say what? 'I might have a brain tumour and I'm scared, and now aren't you sorry for what you said to me?' Then it would turn out that Esme didn't have a brain tumour at all and Allegra would be even more furious with her.

'Front entrance all right, love?'

Esme blinked and realised that they were already at the hospital and there wasn't time to phone anyone.

She got out of the car and stood there for a moment in the weak sunshine. The hospital was situated in a pretty Bloomsbury square. Beneath a blue sky, cotton wool clouds slowly

326

drifting by, was a fresh green lawn and flowerbeds where clusters of egg yolk yellow daffodils swayed in the breeze. Spring was coming but Esme felt as if she was still in the dark of winter.

There was no one babysitting her anymore. She could order another car to take her home so she could go to bed, pull the covers over her head and pretend that everything was going to be all right. Maybe everything *would* be all right and these symptoms were normal. Besides, Esme didn't think her speech was slurred at all, and anyone would snap their eyes shut if someone came at them with a bright light.

Esme could just go but, as if they were acting independently of her possibly damaged brain, her feet took her nearer to the entrance, then through the doors and walked her to the reception desk, where she handed over her letter.

32

Esme had a sense of déjà vu from the last time she'd visited a hospital. This time too she hoped that everyone, herself
included, was needlessly panicking and she'd have a long wait
only to be told she was fine.

Instead, she was directed up to the imaging department
where she handed her letter to the receptionist. She was given
a form to fill in but barely had a chance to complete it before
her name was called. Everyone who was already waiting sent
her resentful looks.

Esme was led into a large airless room with the scanner in it.
Then into a smaller anteroom to change into a robe and to make
sure she removed her bra in case it had any metal fastenings.

'And you're definitely not pregnant?' the radiographer
asked. He was a tall, lanky man with a comfortingly bored air
to him, like he did CT scans all the time and wasn't likely to
stuff the procedure up.

'Not as far as I know,' Esme said, because even though
she'd had unprotected sex with Theo, which actually she'd
never normally do, it was too soon to know if she was pregnant. Could he make her pregnant? Could manifested people
have babies? Then she realised that the man had just asked
her something else. 'You what?'

'No tattoos? No dentures?'

Esme shook her head, her mind going to that murmuration of starlings across Theo's shoulder and neck and how she
wished she was one of them and could fly away.

She wasn't though. So she put on the gown and made a half-hearted effort to tie up the back, but knew it was inevitable that she'd be showing her pants as she walked back into the scanner room.

Then she lay flat on a bed that would transport her into the scanner, a huge ring-shaped X-ray machine.

'Are you all right in there?' came the radiographer's voice.

'I'm fine. Just fine,' Esme said as she lay there. Then the bed moved backwards so that Esme's head was directly under the ring. The scanning started. It was noisy but not frightening and seemed to last no time at all. Then Esme was being helped off the gantry and directed back to the anteroom to put her clothes on and return to the imaging reception.

There was another 'blink and miss it' wait, then Esme was given a series of directions to a room on another floor where she'd be able to talk to a doctor. Maybe there really was something wrong with her because she had to ask the receptionist to write the details down on a piece of paper so she could navigate her way through a labyrinthine series of corridors and stairwells.

Going to be late. Still at doctors. Sorry. Your dickish friend. Esme messaged Lyndsey as she sat on a chair outside the appointed room, next to a withered old man who looked and sounded like he was in the last stages of emphysema. There was no point telling Lyndsey that she'd been sent to hospital when, hopefully, it was nothing.

Just to be on the safe side, Esme crossed her fingers as she waited. Someone came out of the room and emphysema man shuffled his way in. Esme sighed and tried to tamp down the panic that was still eddying up. She'd once done a breathwork class, but had been too annoyed by the wind chimes at the window to really focus on her breath. Now she tried to slow her breathing. Hold in each inhalation for a count of ten, like she did when she was smoking a spliff, then let it out for a count of ten, but it just made her head spin.

Or maybe that was the brain tumour that she hadn't even realised was there.

She looked up as the door opened and emphysema man came out. 'Said I've got the brain of a twenty-year-old,' he announced, which Esme very much doubted.

She expected her name to be called right away but instead she waited and waited and waited. Probably the long wait was because she wasn't that urgent, Esme reasoned. There were lots more urgent cases in front of Esme before she could be told that she wasn't a major priority and to toddle off home.

The door opened and a fresh-faced young woman stepped out. 'Esme Strange?'

Esme waved her hand. 'That's me!'

She was shown into a bog-standard doctor's room. Examination table. A poster on the wall of a cross section of the brain. It looked very complicated. At a desk was a slight, slender, middle-aged man who smiled gravely at Esme. He had kindly uncle vibes.

'I'm Mr Choudhury. I'm a consultant neurosurgeon,' he said, gesturing for Esme to sit down. 'These are two of my team.' He indicated to Miss Fresh of Face and a tall man with a luxuriant head of brown curly hair, piercing green eyes and the kind of cheekbones, which would normally have Esme going a little weak at the knees, before she remembered that no good came of men with chiselled cheekbones. 'Doctor Palmer and Doctor Nowak.'

Esme smiled but it was more of a grimace and waited for Mr Choudhury to get to the point.

He held up an X-ray. 'I've been looking at your scan and there's a large subdural haematoma at the base of your skull. I'd like to do an MRI scan so we can have a more accurate idea of the margins.'

Subdural haematoma. Neither of those seemed to be cancer words. Esme tried to recall the medical copywriting knowledge that she'd acquired all those years ago. 'Haematoma. That's blood, right?'

He nodded. 'You've got quite a significant bleed on the brain.' He frowned. 'Obviously we can't be sure that you sustained the injury when you hit your head, but I'm very surprised you weren't given a CT scan when you were admitted to A&E last weekend.'

'It was very busy,' Esme murmured. Her hands were shaking, so she slipped them under her thighs. 'So, is that serious then?'

'You shouldn't worry,' Mr Choudhury told her gently. 'You've obviously had a guardian angel looking after you this week. Of course, there's always going to be an element of risk, but we'll have a better idea of what we're dealing with once you've had your MRI.'

'Then we'll decide on the best course of treatment,' Doctor Palmer said, even though she seemed very young to be in charge of those kinds of decisions.

'So, what? Like, I'll go on blood thinners to dissolve the clot?' Esme asked, because the three of them all looked very serious but if she could just take some pills . . .

'My dear, you will have to have surgery. But until we've been able to establish the extent of the bleed, I won't know if we can avoid a craniotomy.' Mr Choudhury looked at her X-ray again, pointing to a small shadowed mass with the tip of his finger. 'We might be able to drain it by drilling a small hole . . .'

'In my brain! You want to cut into my brain!' Esme's hand shot up to cover as much of her head as possible in case Mr Choudhury decided to whip out a scalpel there and then.

'Ms Strange, you must have realised that something wasn't right,' said Doctor Novak in a silky, somewhat patronising voice. 'The letter from your doctor says you've been suffering from headaches, extreme lethargy, mood swings. Even speaking to you now, it's clear that your speech has been affected.'

'Maybe I always spoke like this,' Esme insisted. 'What other symptoms indicate a bleed? Like would I be seeing things, people, that weren't really there?'

'Have you been seeing people that weren't there?' Fresh Face asked softly.

Of the three of them, she was definitely the most sympatico, the most likely to understand where Esme was coming from.

'Maybe,' Esme prevaricated. 'Or maybe the perfect man really does exist. It's hard to tell.'

Was Nowak of the cheekbones smirking? If he was then Esme was tempted to garrotte him with his own stethoscope.

'Look, mate, you try being a single woman in her thirties. The dating pool is so murky that it's no wonder I thought I'd manifested the perfect boyfriend when I met Theo. But if I can touch him, then he's real, right?' She was blushing now to think of just how she had touched Theo and he'd touched her back. 'And it wasn't just me. Other people have seen him. Spoken to him. So he couldn't have been a hallucination, unless . . . are hallucinations a symptom of subdural whatevers?'

'Not a common symptom, but it wouldn't be unprecedented,' Nowak said a little pompously. 'The brain is a very delicate, very complex organ.'

'No shit, Sherlock,' Esme said. She refused to believe that Theo really was just a symptom. You couldn't have deep and

333

profound feelings for a hallucination brought on by a head injury. He was funny. He was kind. He was also grumpy. He had layers. Hallucinations didn't have layers. 'So, what happens now then? Do I book an appointment for an MRI?'

'You're already booked in for an MRI but we'll admit you first,' Fresh Face said. 'Now, can you remember how long ago it was that you last ate something?'

'Why do you need to know that?' Esme asked, feet braced on the floor, because she could just . . . she could just get up and walk the few paces to the door and leave. Maybe get a second opinion. Because she couldn't have a bleed on the brain. She'd be able to tell if she had . . .

'So we know what time to schedule your surgery for,' Mr Choudhury said. 'I'd prefer not to delay.'

'You're going to cut into my brain today?' You worked up to this kind of activity. Prepared for it. Said goodbye to your nearest and dearest and made sure you had a legally binding will, just in case. You didn't just trot along for a head X-ray one morning then end up in an operating theatre while someone tinkered about with your cerebral cortex or wherever the fuck this supposed bleed was. 'I can't. I'm not ready. I thought there were very long NHS waiting lists. I'll come back next week!'

Mr Choudhury reached over so he could pat Esme's clenched fist. 'I know it's a lot to process but you really must appreciate the severity of the situation.'

'You could have had a brain haemorrhage at any moment this past week,' said Novak, his piercing green eyes glinting at the thought. He really needed to work on his bedside manner. 'Even just sitting here, there's every likelihood of an aneurysm and fifty per cent of them are fatal.'

'Even if you did survive, sixty-six per cent of survivors experience permanent neurological deficit,' Fresh Face parroted, like she'd done the assigned reading too. 'So, we really do have to admit you straight away.'

Esme felt as if she should be committed rather than admitted. What if *this* was the hallucination, the delusion?

'Can't I just go home and pack a bag, say goodbye . . .'

'I wouldn't recommend it,' Mr Choudhury said. 'Once you've been admitted, you can contact someone. Now did you have any questions about the surgery?'

Esme couldn't think of a single question to ask. Or rather there wasn't a single question that she wanted an honest answer to. But the three of them were back to looking as serious as *the grave*. 'I'm not going to die, am I?'

'I operate on subdural haematomas several times a week. It's the most common neurological surgery,' Mr Choudhury said, which wasn't a yes, but it most definitely wasn't a no.

'Let's get you settled on the ward.' Doctor Palmer stood up and stared at Esme until she stood up too. 'Then you can phone someone.'

It was almost as if they didn't trust Esme not to bolt like a panicked racehorse approaching Becher's Brook. Doctor Palmer whisked her down corridors and up in a lift and said that Esme wasn't to worry because brain bleeds were ten a penny and that last week they'd operated on some poor soul who'd had a tumour the size of a golf ball. 'He'd had every diagnosis thrown at him to explain the changes in his behaviour: schizophrenia, bipolar disorder, multiple personality disorder, and all the time he had a humongous brain tumour. Incredible.'

They weren't the comforting words that Esme wanted and needed. So she was relieved when they finally reached yet another reception desk and, beyond that, the neurosurgery wards. 'If you sit there where I can see you and I'll find someone who can help us with the paperwork.'

Esme was left sitting on a chair. She felt entirely outside of herself. As if this was all happening to someone else.

She hadn't had time to even consider what lay ahead when Doctor Palmer was back with a man in a blue nurse's uniform clutching a clipboard.

'Hi Esme. I'm Adam, the ward manager. Just need to go through some Covid protocols with you,' he said, sitting down in the empty chair next to Esme's, as Doctor Palmer left with vague assurances that she'd be back. 'I see you're up to date with your vaccinations. When was the last time you did a lateral flow?'

Esme shrugged. Why hadn't she done a lateral flow before the wedding? She was usually a stickler for testing before any kind of social occasion, so she didn't unwittingly infect any-one.

'I think I did one last week before I went to a hen party.' If only she'd tested positive then. Surely Covid was less of a risk, statistically, than brain surgery?

'I'm going to get you to do a PCR test. You don't mind having one, do you? It's just, until I know your status, I don't know which protocol we'll have to follow.'

'No, that's fine,' Esme said, because doing a PCR test was the very least of it.

'Right, I'll be back in a tick,' Adam said.

There'd been so much waiting this morning on uncomfortable plastic moulded chairs. Esme watched Adam disappear through a set of doors and, when she was sure that he was out of sight, she got to her feet and followed the signs that pointed to the way out.

33

As luck would have it, and like something out of a movie, as Esme walked briskly out of the hospital, there was a black cab pulling up outside.

She waited for the passengers to disembark, then held up her phone. 'Do you take ApplePay?'

It was as simple as that. Not thirty seconds later, Esme was being driven home. The streets were busy even though it was that odd lull of a morning. Too late for commuters. Too early for the lunchtime crowd.

Camden High Street was bustling. Esme watched out of the window as two young women, their hair dyed glorious pastel colours, negotiated getting a supermarket trolley piled high with what looked like all their worldly possessions across the road.

It was such a peculiar feeling to be so in the midst of life, driving past M&S, Boots, Camden Town Station, but to know that you could drop dead at any moment. It was an even more peculiar feeling, fear clawing at her insides, to know that dropping dead at any moment felt like the lesser of two current evils.

Esme had never been so glad to see the 'red brick gloom' of Parliament Hill Mansions as the cab turned into her road.

'It's the third block on the right,' she said in a rusty voice, as she pulled out her phone to pay the fare.

While she was tucking her phone back into her coat pocket, it began to ring. Esme glanced down at the screen to see the number of her GP's surgery flash up. She declined the call, turned her phone off and retrieved her keys.

She supposed that she shouldn't really be making any sudden movements, but she still raced up the stairs to her floor, then came to a halt. She placed her palm flat against her front door and stayed like that, quite still, apart from the thundering of her heart, for a moment. Then Esme unlocked the door and stepped inside.

The flat felt quiet and undisturbed, as if it had been empty for quite some time. Of course it was. Theo would be at the pub. He wouldn't be here, waiting for her . . .

'Sweet girl? Is that you?' Esme glanced right, into the living room, where Theo was sitting on the sofa. Because he was always there when she needed him the most. 'Are you all right? How did it go?'

He was wearing the same dark jeans and faded black T-shirt that he always seemed to be wearing, his dark hair tousled, his face creasing as he looked at Esme. Esme liked the grim, forbidding angles of Theo's face; they were like a secret that only she knew. If someone didn't know him, they'd draw the conclusion that there was something hard about Theo's personality too. But they hadn't noticed how soulful, how kind his eyes were, or that, when Theo smiled, properly smiled, it softened a lot of the hardness, but not all of it.

'It didn't go well,' she said, her voice thickening with tears though she could have sworn that the last thing she wanted to do was cry. 'I've got a bleed. They want me to have brain surgery.'

Saying the words out loud didn't make them sound any more real or any less ridiculous.

'What are you doing here then, you silly thing?' Theo asked, holding out his arms so Esme could collapse onto the sofa, sink into his embrace and cry, the force of her sobs turning her inside out, while he made 'shush'ing sounds and stroked her back. 'It's going to be all right. Everything's going to be fine. You're going to be fine.'

'I don't think I am,' Esme mumbled into his shoulder. She rubbed her damp face against the soft cotton of his T-shirt. 'I'm always crying on you.'

'That's what I'm here for,' Theo said softly and with the greatest of efforts, Esme managed to pull herself out of his arms. She swung her legs up, so she was sitting cross-legged facing him and she could take Theo's hand and entwine her fingers through his.

'I think . . . I'm scared that you're not real,' she whispered. 'That you're just a hallucination, a delusion, because there's blood leaking around in my skull.'

Theo pulled Esme's hand to his chest where, once again, she could feel the steady thud of his heart. 'I feel real.' His smile was crooked. 'Why don't we go with the theory that I had all along? That I am real, and I'm not going to say I told you so, that's not my style, but there's something going on with that busy head of yours.'

The brain *was* a very complicated and delicate organ.

Theo *could* be real.

Then again, he could just be a figment of Esme's imagination. She'd always thought of it as her greatest asset, but it could have been malfunctioning ever since her head had hit the road nine days ago.

Esme stretched out her legs and wasn't that surprised when Theo grasped her ankles and settled her feet in his lap. He unlaced her trainers and pulled off her socks then started doing something with his thumb and her instep that hurt but in a really good way. He always knew what she needed before she even knew it herself. 'I mean, the last few days have been amazing. More than I've ever dared dream about, but deep down I think I knew that I could never live this sort of life.'

Theo's fingers worked down her left foot in a way that made Esme feel envious of her left foot. 'Hate to break it to you, but you *are* living this life.'

Esme wished that she were. Because yes, she'd felt fulfilled by all the time she'd spent dreaming of foreign travel, drama and hot sex, but she'd never dreamt about this . . . domesticity, companionship, along with the hot sex. But also, love? Like losing her virginity at sixteen to a twenty-five-year-old bloke with questionable personal hygiene and questionable morals just because he was the drummer in a minor indie rock band, now Esme could see that she wasn't emotionally ready for the life she'd stepped into.

'I don't deserve this,' she said softly, so Theo had to lean closer to catch every word. 'I don't deserve someone like you. I've trained myself to not want any of these things that we have. I've made myself heartless and hard . . . I had to because those years with Alex, the divorce . . .'

'It nearly broke you,' Theo said, but that wasn't right.

'It did break me and I had to put myself together again but the pieces I had left didn't match the picture on the box any-more.' Esme tipped her head and pinched the bridge of her nose, like she hadn't done for years. 'I don't let anyone in.'

'You let me in . . .' Theo moved onto the other foot now that Esme's left foot was doing a good impersonation of a limp noodle.

'That's why I know this isn't real, because if it were real, I'd never have let you get close and you wouldn't have wanted me to.' Esme tried to pull her foot free because this wasn't the kind of conversation you had while someone was giving you a foot rub.

Especially when you were explaining why you didn't deserve the kind of man who'd give you foot rubs. 'Everyone, Seren, Allegra, says that you attract what you put out and I put out bad vibes only. I haven't done the work on myself to be capable of a good, healthy relationship. Never felt the need to. Until now. Until you. And now it's too late and you're not even real.'

'I'm as real as you want me to be,' Theo said, and he took Esme's hands again, their fingers threaded.

'You're everything that I've always wanted in a partner and, I'm sorry, but it doesn't matter how many affirmations you send out, the universe is never that obliging.'

'I'm not *that* perfect,' Theo insisted.

Suddenly there was a hammering at the door, which made Esme give a nervous start then clutch Theo's hands tighter.

'Esme? Are you in there?' Allegra's voice was so shrill that it barely sounded like her. 'The hospital called your GP and they called me, I'm your next of kin . . .'

Esme tuned out her sister's voice and turned back to Theo. 'What if I have the surgery and then I wake up and you've gone? I can't risk it.'

'I won't be gone . . .'

'You need to go back to the hospital, Esme! I am sorry about our argument but that's not important right now. You . . . you're important. Will you *please* let me in?'

Esme rolled her eyes. 'Typical! *Now* she's being nice to me.'

Theo laughed then he looked at Esme, eyes scanning her face as if he was committing each feature, even the scar that nicked the end of her left eyebrow, legacy of a roller skating incident, and the smattering of freckles across the bridge of her nose to memory.

'She's right though, Es. You do need to go back to the hospital. Have the surgery. I know it's scary . . .'

'It would be scarier to go back to a life without you in it . . .' Esme told him, because when she thought about her life even two weeks ago, it wasn't the happy little existence that she'd pretended it was. Yes, she had friends, a job she loved, a home to call her very own. But also she'd been closed off, empty, a hollow girl, and she hadn't even realised it.

'I will always be in your life, I promise you,' Theo said, but his words were drowned out as Allegra redoubled her efforts to knock the front door off its hinges.

'There wasn't time to go home for our spare set of keys. Your downstairs neighbours are looking for theirs. Or you could just let me in. We can talk about this. What I said on Saturday . . . I was too harsh, OK? It's just . . . We are such different people, Esme. I don't know if it's the age gap or because you always made it so clear that you didn't need me . . .'

'What is she talking about?'

Theo shrugged. 'I guess she's finally seeing the many errors of her ways.'

Esme couldn't help but snort. 'Yeah, right.'

There were three more thumps from outside. 'Esme, I don't want to have this conversation with you through your front door,' Allegra shouted. 'Even when we weren't speaking, even when you didn't come to my wedding and I hated you for it, I always knew that you were just a phone call away, that you'd always be *there* if I needed you. You *have* to be there, Esme. That's the deal. Even though you can be super annoying at times, even when you haven't got a personality-altering brain injury . . .'

'Super annoying?' Esme repeated in an angry hiss.

'It would be super annoying if you didn't have the surgery,' Theo said. 'I can't believe we're even discussing this. You have to go back to the hospital, sweet girl. You'll have your operation and everything will be fine. Nothing but happy days ahead.'

'But you don't know that for certain,' Esme said, and she was wrong-footed and blindsided because he seemed so real. She could just reach out and . . .

'Esme! Have you got someone there with you?' Allegra shouted through the door. 'I just want to make sure you're all right. Esme, please . . . Look, there are times, a lot of times, when I don't like you, but I do love you and if anything happened to you . . . it would destroy me.'

It took Esme being on the verge of death for Allegra to admit, under duress, that maybe she did love her infuriating younger sister after all. It was everything Esme had ever wanted to hear from Allegra, but today it didn't seem as important as the man in front of her.

Now, it was her turn to study Theo's face like she was seeing him for the last time. The harsh lines softened by his beautiful mouth, the kindness in those heavy-lidded brown eyes, the little furrow between his eyebrows as he stared back at Esme, like she was a complicated puzzle that he'd made it his life's work to solve.

She lowered her head so she could kiss Theo's hand, the knuckles where his shit tattoos reached peak awfulness. 'What if I have the operation and then you're gone?'

To have him *gone*. Worse than death or divorce, because he'd never been real in the first place. Just a phantom and her memories of him would wear away to nothing.

'I'll try really hard not to be gone,' Theo said, just as there was the sound of a key in the lock.

Esme glanced up in time to see Allegra, then Oliver, burst into the flat, the door crashing back against the frame. They seemed frozen in motion for one split second, then they both turned to look at her.

'Oh my God . . . ' She heard Oliver mutter and she glared at them because they ruined everything. They were ruining this.

'Esme! Who have you been talking to and why on earth are you still wearing your black dress from Saturday?' she heard Allegra ask.

'Why is there paint over everything?'

Esme waved her hand at her sister and brother-in-law as if to say, not now, then she turned back to Theo before he could disappear. 'I need to tell you something before it's too late.' She placed one of his hands on her heart, which wasn't beating in the same steady rhythm as his but rather as if she was in the last stages of a triathlon. 'I didn't think I'd ever say it to anyone ever again, but I do love you.'

'I already knew that,' Theo said softly. 'And you know I love you too. But love isn't what matters right now. You *have* to have this surgery.'

'You will be here when I get back, won't you?' Esme mumbled, suddenly so tired that she could barely hold her head up. Her eyes wanted to close and she wanted to sink into sleep's soft embrace. 'Do you promise?'

Her face was buried in Theo's shoulder again, so she couldn't see it, but she could *feel* his smile. 'I hope so,' he whispered. 'I bloody hope so.'

EPILOGUE

A year and a week later

As Esme walked up one of Dartmouth Park's dreaded hills, she checked the blue dot on her phone to make sure she was still going in the right direction. No matter how hard she tried, she couldn't get left and right clear in her head, much like Summer, who had an L and an R written on the appropriate hands before her weekly ballet class.

As Esme stared at her screen, a WhatsApp message flashed up.

> **Allegra Dickenson**
> We're here. Are you all right? Do you need Oliver to come and pick you up? Xxx

> **Esme Strange**
> Nearly there! Can you order me a celebratory gin and tonic, please? Xxx

She scrolled further up the chain of messages in their Famalam group chat (Esme kept changing the name to something less naff but either Allegra or Oliver would always change it back because they knew it would wind her up) to check the address again.

Oliver Dickenson

Thought we could try this new place just round the corner from us. Same owner has another venue near Chambers, do very good veggie options and an excellent cheese plate. Shall I book lunch for this Sunday? X

Esme thought she might be lost. Then, as she turned the next corner, there was The Elwood Arms. It was almost unrecognisable from the dilapidated, then derelict, boozer it had once been. During her misspent youth, Esme had spent many evenings in there getting drunk on Jack Daniels and Coke because the bar staff never asked for ID.

Now the outside had had a smart paint job, its sandstone brickwork repointed and white render gleaming in the early spring sunshine. Hanging baskets full of brightly coloured pansies were stationed at the entrance.

Esme heaved open the door and was greeted with the noisy chatter of happy people and the enticing smell of garlic and herbs.

She looked around for their table but Allegra was already hurrying towards her, in North London Mum Sunday mufti of stripey top, wide-legged jeans and expensive white leather trainers, with a smile on her face, arms stretched wide.

'There you are!' she said, folding Esme into a brief but heartfelt hug.

'Here I am!' Esme agreed, kissing Allegra on the cheek.

'You're looking good,' Allegra said approvingly, taking in Esme's black jumpsuit and red and black polka dot top.

'So are you. Very French.' Esme let Allegra take her hand to lead her to the back of the busy pub, which was all scrubbed wooden tables and mismatched chairs, multitudes of tasselled lampshades in jewel tones hanging from the ceiling and portraits of cats and dogs painted as if they were Gainsboroughs dotted around the walls. 'This place looks fun. Oh my goodness,' she added as they reached their table, and Fergus and Oscar pointed to the clearly homemade banner that had been stuck to the wall behind them.

'Well done for not being dead!' Fergus read out for her in case Esme couldn't decipher the huge purple letters.

'I did the glitter,' Summer said, trying to launch herself at Esme, but she was thwarted by Oliver, who picked his daughter up mid-hurl.

'Why do you three insist on throwing yourselves at your poor aunt? What have we told you? We have to pretend that Esme is made of glass and we don't want to break her because she's very precious,' he reminded Summer sternly as he gathered Esme in with one arm for a hug and kissed the top of her head. 'Are you well? You look well.'

'I feel well,' Esme said, as she'd been insisting for the last eight months. She waved at Kemi and Lyndsey, who were hemmed in on the other side of the table so could only blow her kisses, then shrugged out of her puffer coat. 'Also, starving. Have you ordered yet?'

'We had to wait for you and you were ages,' Oscar said, shifting in his chair so Esme could squeeze past him to get to the seat in between Kemi and Lyndsey. There were more hugs and kisses and Esme couldn't help but glance again at the banner that hung above her head.

It was a year to the day since her second brain surgery, which she'd needed because she'd had another bleed after her first operation the week before. In his avuncular manner, Mr Choudhury had explained that there was up to a thirty-seven per cent likelihood of a subdural haematoma reoccurring. That Esme would need regular brain scans for the rest of her life, like a car needed an MOT.

'But let's get the first year out of the way and then your prognosis will be much improved,' he'd said. 'Already you've been extraordinarily lucky.'

Esme knew that she was lucky. That she'd used up every single one of her nine lives, simply by being in the fifty per cent of people who survived a brain bleed. Not just that, but she'd managed to avoid any of the more serious side effects, like seizures or permanent brain malfunction. Though as Cedric had said on Esme's first day back in the office, 'I mean, it would be quite hard to tell if your brain was scrambled. We didn't know last time.'

Esme had smacked him and he'd laughed. 'You still hit like a girl.'

Maybe that was because she now had a weakness in her left arm, which had required a lot of physio. Oscar and Fergus had been bitterly disappointed at the lack of side effects after her surgery. That their aunt only had an undercut and not a completely shaved head. That she hadn't developed some freakish new skill, like being able to speak fluent Russian or play complicated piano concertos. But Esme hadn't emerged from brain surgery unscathed.

She was pleased to be alive – so pleased and relieved and giddy that she was still breathing and could just about wiggle her fingers and toes and still remember all the words to 'Yes Sir, I Can Boogie' – but her dreams, that rich, inner life was gone.

Which meant Theo was gone.

Esme had known it as soon as she'd come round from the first anaesthetic.

Theo didn't exist, had never existed. She knew that on some profound, molecular level. Which was why, not long after opening her eyes, she'd cried for the loss of him, because it turned out that you could grieve for someone who'd never been real.

All the time that Esme had spent with Theo, being fed delicious meals, having the best sex of her life, falling in love, hadn't happened at all. As far as she could later tell, she'd more often than not been asleep and dreaming so lucidly, so intently, that it had felt like real life. No wonder that when Allegra and Oliver had coaxed her back to the hospital, it was quickly established that Esme was severely dehydrated and had lost four kilograms since she'd been weighed the week before. Oh, and she hadn't showered in three days and her hair hadn't been washed in ten days.

Even though Esme desperately wanted to believe that there was some small part of Theo that had been real, the evidence against this theory was overwhelming. Oscar and Fergus insisted that there had been no one there when they were in Esme's flat, but they hadn't wanted to say anything in case Esme took offence and stopped buying them cake and fizzy pop on their Friday afternoons. The only other person who'd talked to him was Summer, a three-year-old child, who still believed in Father Christmas and fairies. An unreliable narrator, if ever there was one.

And weeks later, when Esme was feeling up to it, Allegra showed her the video footage from the wedding reception that had circulated on the Hens' group chat. The group chat that Esme had been ejected from that very same night. There was Esme by herself. Dancing to 'Let's Stay Together'. Her arms wrapped around her torso, grinding the air and making awful smooching faces.

'Oh my God, no wonder everyone thought I was hammered,' Esme said in horror, thrusting the phone away. 'I never want to see that again.'

'Not now, but later, you will find someone who loves you the way you deserve to be loved,' Allegra said softly, because Esme had very briefly alluded to the week she'd spent with Theo, but had glossed over the details because saying them out loud made her sound completely insane. But, mostly, because she still couldn't bear to share him with anyone else.

'Like you and Oliver,' Esme said, because the two of them hadn't let her go home to her little attic flat when she was first discharged from the hospital. And after six weeks of living in their house she could see, *admit*, that Allegra and Oliver were a team. A partnership. They had each other's backs. They had their own secret language of silent looks and half smiles and whispered words.

Esme's sister and Esme's fucking divorce lawyer loved each other. And Esme genuinely, sincerely wished them all the best because a) eight years was too long to hold a grudge and b) when you found love you had to cling on to it with both hands and c) she'd loved Theo and now, without him, she was back to being that hollow girl.

So now her life was . . . not the same. It would never be the same. It was changed. Although in so many ways, it had changed for the better.

Maybe it was because they were sisters and no matter how much they might deny it, there was a bond between them forged out of blood and the neglect of their two narcissist parents. Esme and Allegra had never had a big heart to heart, a post-mortem on the grievances and betrayals of the past.

Their relationship had simply slipped into a new phase that was deeper, more *caring* than it had ever been.

It was something Esme was slowly unpacking in therapy. You couldn't come as close to death as Esme had and not need therapy afterwards. In a lot of ways, therapy was the hardest thing of all, even harder than getting her left hand to function properly again. Now she knew why people called it doing the work, because it was absolutely bloody exhausting.

Esme wasn't just processing the brain surgery with the softly spoken and never judgemental Malik, but all the other things that she'd never really unpacked: her peripatetic childhood, her disastrous marriage and the week when she'd conjured up what Malik called a totemic symbol of her most deep-rooted, subconscious desires. But Malik had also posited the theory that, on some level, Esme's subconscious had known that she was in danger and so it had created Theo. Because without Theo, she'd never have considered that she might have concussion. Would never have remembered to make that doctor's appointment. And without him making her charge up her phone and set all those extra alarms, she'd never have got out of bed that Monday morning.

Theo might never have been real but still, he'd saved her life.

That life was now more meaningful. Esme really did have an attitude of gratitude and was all about celebrating joy and seizing the day, so much so that Seren was a little cross that Esme had stolen her vibe.

She was still able to do a job she mostly loved.

She had her little flat. And though she'd never have a good relationship with either of her parents, Debbie had visited her in hospital with paint swatches so she could clear up the mess Esme had made when she'd flung the whole pot of Coal Scuttle paint at her feature wall.

'No need to apologise for the terrible things you said to me. I've forgiven you because it was obviously your wonky brain talking,' Debbie had decreed in such a breezy tone that Esme and Allegra marvelled at her sheer audacity after she'd left.

But Debbie had also repainted the whole room in a very vibrant yet richly soothing deep green, put up some floating shelves in the kitchen and installed a new, more powerful shower. Which was her way of saying she didn't *not* love Esme.

But thank God for friends who were much more straightforward than mothers. And as Esme looked around the table at her sister and brother-in-law, at Oscar reading the menu, his mouth forming the words, Fergus tugging at his sleeve, Summer sitting on Oliver's lap and fiddling with her bracelets, she was also grateful for the family that she hadn't had before. Not really.

There was just that one thing missing.

'No rush, but are you guys ready to order? Maybe I could start you off with some drinks?'

All the hairs on Esme's body stood up and waved, goosebumps breaking out along her arms as she heard a wry, deep voice with a slightly nasal Mancunian accent.

She couldn't look up. Suddenly, she was Lot's wife about to be turned into a pillar of salt as she heard Oliver say hello.

'I said I'd be in as soon as you opened. It's a bit different from your place in Clerkenwell . . .'

'I wanted more of a relaxed, family feel. Have you seen the kids' menu?'

'Can I have the burger and chips?' Fergus piped up.

'Please,' Oliver and Allegra said in unison.

'Do you know what you're having, Esme?' Kemi asked. 'Veggie roast? And shall we split a cauliflower and cheese?'

'Yeah, that's fine,' Esme muttered, and she raised her head and locked eyes with a man with a hard face but kind eyes and a soft smile.

He was staring back at her.

The whole world went silent.

It was just the two of them, unable to look away.

Her life might be better and fuller but – it was something Esme couldn't admit to anyone, not even Allegra, not even Malik – it was also a lot less. Now, Esme saw the world from behind smeared glass, the sound muffled.

Or maybe it was Esme that was a little bit less.

But as she stared at this man and he stared right back at her, all of a sudden, life was in full colour and stereophonic sound again.

'What are you having to drink?' Lyndsey nudged Esme's arm and the rest of the world came rushing back. 'Are you drinking alcohol?'

Esme had planned to have a gin and tonic but now she thought better of it. 'Could I have a fizzy water with a dash of elderflower cordial, please?' She stared down at the weathered table, watched her fingers clutch the edge like she was clinging on for dear life.

'No problem,' he said, and there was a moment's silence that seemed to affect everyone else. 'Are you ready to order food?'

It was a long five minutes before their orders were done. Lyndsey was the most indecisive person when she got handed a menu. She was always the last to order and then she'd change her mind, but eventually even she was finished and Esme could look up to watch him walk away. He was tall, lean, wearing dark jeans and a faded black T-shirt, tattoos curling around the olive skin of his arms.

'Nice chap,' Oliver said. 'He's the owner of the place in Clerkenwell too. Glad they've got some of the same things on the menu. We'll have to save some room for the sticky toffee pudding then work it all off with a long walk on the Heath afterwards.'

'I hate long walks,' Summer said as Esme put her hands to her head. Her fingertips sought the spot that she knew so well; that raised, ridged line under her hair. It felt OK. Not sore. Not tender. Not hot.

'Esme, are you all right?' Allegra asked sharply. 'You're very pale.' She was already on her feet but Esme gestured for her to sit down.

'I'm fine,' she said, but Lyndsey took her chin so she could scrutinise her friend's face.

'You don't look fine. You look like you're about to burst into tears.'

Esme tugged herself free and couldn't help another disbelieving look at the man who was now behind the bar. As if he could feel her eyes on him, he suddenly stopped in the midst of opening a bottle of wine, his gaze focused on Esme.

'Is that man really there?' she asked in a croaky voice. 'Oliver, did you just speak to that man? Did he take our orders? That was real, wasn't it?'

'Very real, I hope, because I'm more than ready for my roast beef with all the trimmings,' Oliver said lightly, but he exchanged raised eyebrows with Allegra.

'And he had stubble and tattoos? He's wearing jeans?' Esme continued, turning to Kemi, then Lyndsey.

'Yes, and he's absolutely not my type,' Kemi drawled.

'We'll let you call dibs on him,' Lyndsey said graciously, but the two of them were clearly communicating something silently over Esme's head.

'I'm not going mad,' Esme said a little desperately. 'I just . . . he just . . . reminds me of someone. Was trying to place him, that's all.'

It was a lovely Sunday lunch. One of the best Esme had ever had. Crispy potatoes, vegetables that hadn't been boiled to within an inch of their life and a nut roast that wasn't so dry that it leached all the moisture from her body. But she might just as well have been eating dust and ashes.

He didn't come over again – their meal was served and cleared away by a couple of cheerful young women – but every time Esme sneaked a glance at the man behind the bar, he was looking at her. Not in a creepy way. But in a way that made her feel alive in a way that she hadn't for a year and a week.

In the lull between main course and pudding, Esme couldn't sit there any longer. 'I need a wee,' she explained as she all but climbed over Kemi in her haste to take a moment and just breathe. But also, yes, she did need a wee.

She purposely didn't look in his direction as she hurried to the Ladies. Then she spent long moments just sitting on the loo, her head in her hands, thinking, but not really able to think at all. Until she heard her grandma's voice in her head warning of haemorrhoids if one sat on a toilet for too long.

Her face was very flushed when Esme looked in the mirror as she washed her hands. 'You're all right,' she said quietly to herself, as she'd been doing a lot over the last twelve months. 'You're going to be fine.'

Then she couldn't hide any longer and when she left the bathroom, she wasn't at all surprised to see him standing, loitering, in the little patch of space that led back into the bar.

Her body jerked once in his direction then she forced her recalcitrant limbs to still. But she couldn't control her mouth. 'Hi,' she said. 'Hello.'

'Hello,' he said gravely, taking a step closer to her. He was just as she remembered him, but also a little different: there was a hesitance, a weariness to him. His hair was threaded through with grey, but it was still him. 'Did you . . . Was everything all right?'

'It was great.' That wasn't what she wanted to say but Esme didn't know where to begin. She looked at him imploringly. Really looked at him so she could see the jagged scar that started at his hairline, bisected his left eyebrow and just grazed the outer edge of his eye. 'Your scar . . .'

'Someone once told me that women would find it rakish,' he said, worrying the spot where it disappeared into his hair with a finger. His words, the way he threaded his hands through that obstinate cowlick of dark hair, triggered a memory but Esme still couldn't tell if it was real or not.

It took two tries, two ragged intakes of breath, for Esme to get the words out. 'And do they find it rakish?'

He shrugged, the casual gesture at odds with the way he was staring at her. 'I don't know. You tell me.'

Esme nodded. 'It *is* kind of rakish.'

Even his smile was a little hesitant. 'Glad to hear it.' He let out a very shaky breath. 'I swear this isn't a line, I'm not usually this cringe, but we know each other, don't we?'

'I don't know. Maybe,' Esme said a little sadly, tears pricking at her eyes. He'd taken another step closer and she looked at his arms, his hands, his fingers, where there were no shit tattoos, just the knife nicks and burn scars you'd expect from a man who earned his living in a kitchen. 'You do seem very familiar but . . .'

'We've met before,' he insisted. 'About a year ago, in a cubicle in a hospital. Except, it's all a bit of a blur. We were both in pain and we didn't have a chance to exchange names.'

A vague vignette was playing in Esme's head. The edges hazy; nothing in focus. Could it have been real? Had some of it been real? Then she heard the words as clear as if he'd just said them.

'Gaping head wound trumps glassed in the face.'

'Are you . . . did you . . . you're Glassed in the Face?'

'And you're Gaping Head Wound.' It wasn't even a question. 'I've thought about you a lot. Though sometimes I was sure that I'd just imagined you.'

'Same. Oh my God, same.' After everything that had happened to her this past year, Esme couldn't help but be open and vulnerable. 'I thought about you too. But . . . it's a long, complicated story.'

Esme couldn't stop staring at him. How he was just as she'd pictured him, but also different, because during those fleeting moments they'd really and truly spent together, three quarters of his face had been hidden from her.

He was more careworn, his eyes creased and shadowed. Esme wanted to press her fingers into the deep grooves at the side of his mouth, but then she'd always been attracted to men who looked like they'd done some serious living.

And when he smiled the creases and the shadows melted away. Like now. His smile was grave but also hopeful. 'I'd really like to hear that story sometime.'

Esme had to keep her face still rather than give in to the urge to gurn like a gargoyle. 'Maybe I'll tell you. Many years from now.'

'Well, I look forward to that.' He held out his hand for Esme to shake but somehow they were holding hands, their fingers entwined. 'By the way, I'm Johnny.'

'Johnny,' Esme repeated, liking the way it sounded in her mouth. She could get used to it. 'I'm Esme.'

This time when he smiled, she smiled back.

'Hello, Esme,' he said in the voice which had haunted her dreams for far too long. 'It's so good to see you again.'

ACKNOWLEDGEMENTS

Thank you, thank you, thank you to my amazing agents Rebecca Ritchie who had to supply copious amounts of hand-holding on this book and to Euan Thorneycroft who still finds me on my best behaviour. Also to Harmony Leung, Alexandra McNicoll, Jack Sargeant and all at AM Heath.

I owe so much to Kimberley Atkins, publisher extra-ordinaire, who cheerfully and calmly coaxed me through a bruising rewrite on this book, which is all the better for her guidance. I have the dreamiest of dream teams at Hodder: Olivia Robertshaw, Veronique Norton, Katy Blott, Amy Batley among others.

So fortunate to have good people in my life who manage not to look bored when I'm banging on about novelling. Thank you, Lesley Lawson, for telling me that I needed a better title, you were absolutely right. Cari Rosen for yenta-ing over our early bird Côte dinners. Sarah Bailey for Saturday chat and cinnamon buns. Eileen Coulter for Eric drive-bys, pizza nights and MAFSAU chat.

To my sister writers who are always so supportive: Harriet Evans, Jane Casey, Anna Carey, Marian Keyes, Daisy Buchanan, Louise O'Neill, Cressida McLaughlin, Iona Grey, Kate Riordan, Cesca Major, Katherine Webber, Claire McGlasson, Jenny Ashcroft, and Laura Wood. And my fellow reviewers on the liveliest Group Chat: Nina Pottell, Sarah Shaffi and Fran Brown. I'm sure I've missed people out. If I have, please don't hate me.

Finally, back in May 2021, I took part in the #BooksFor-Vaccines auction organised by Phoebe Morgan to donate funds to help the Covid 19 vaccine rollout across the world. I offered one lucky winner the chance to have a character named after them and my successful bidder was Tyler Shepherd. Tyler asked me if I could name a character after their sister Lyndsey Shepherd, who very sadly died in 2012. It's been an incredible honour to commemorate Lyndsey, who was a beautiful person inside and out and always hoped to write a novel, in *The Man of Her Dreams*. Lyndsey was a passionate advocate for rescuing animals, a cause that her fictional namesake also supports. I hope in some small way that I've done Lyndsey justice.